Reviews

Blood Curse - Loved it and can't wait to read more from you. Way to go girl!!!!!!!!!!!—*Jenn Kelloway*

Blood Curse - For a new author this book is a really good read. I couldn't put it down. I really hope there is a sequel because I need to know what happens to these cool characters. – **avongirl1331**

Blood Curse - Ready for More - This is not my typical genre for reading, but it certainly had me hooked from the beginning. Once I started I found it hard to put down. It left me wanting more. I am hooked and anxiously awaiting the next book. Great job Lynn.—*Bethany Mawbey*

Blood Curse - Awsome read -- This book was a really good read. I loved the characters. Once I started I couldn't put it down and it left me wanting more. I will be watching for the next book for sure.—*Debbie Henry*

Blood Connection - I thought the book was wonderful. I enjoyed it very much and can hardly wait to keep reading the rest of the series. Keep on writing and we will keep on reading.—*Marion Henderson*

BLOOD CURSE

Jade is a member of the most feared and avoided creatures in the supernatural world, Moarté. Able to manipulate the world around them paired with the ability to shift into any shape, the Moarté are born to keep the supernatural world in line, and keep them from being discovered by the human world. While hunting a rogue *were* Jade comes in contact with the Alpha of the Lycan pack. Torn between the desires to please the only man who makes her feel truly alive, and her born duty, Jade has a big decision to make.

BLOOD CONNECTION

When her parents are murdered by a vampire, Alicia becomes the ward of the Moarté who rescued her from the same fate. Now a grown woman, Alicia discovers the truth about her own birth. With the help of the son of a God, can she survive who she was born to be to become the woman she wants to be?

BLOOD OBSESSION

Emerald is a member of one of the most powerful families of the supernatural world. Born with a powerful empathy she is drawn to strong emotions. Tortured by the pain of another she is drawn to the man who almost ended her own life; the same man who everyone presumed dead. During a daring rescue she is caught in an explosion which leaves her without a memory of whom or what she is. Can she survive in a make believe world, or will her true nature take over before it is too late?

Blood Sisters

Lynn Marie Simpson

ISBN: 978-1-926898-81-0

Pine Lake Books
Canada
www.pinelakebooks.ca

DEDICATION

I dedicate this story to Don, who is now, and who will always be, the Keeper of my Heart.

ACKNOWLEDGMENTS

I would like to thank my sisters Debbie, Susie, Jean, and June, as well as my good friend Maggie. They not only read everything I write, but their input has helped to keep me on the right track.

I want to thank my children, Christopher and Dawn Marie, for reminding me that a person can do whatever they want, all they have to do is try.

And last but not least, I thank YOU, my readers, who willingly give me their time.

Thank You!

Blood Curse

Chapter One

The silence was deafening.

No insects. No wind in the leaves. Not the whisper of wings in the night. Nothing.

An owl hooted.

His vacant eyes turned towards the sound, and searched the treetops. Black, soulless eyes clashed with bright yellow ones. "Find your own dinner. This one's mine." He dismissed the owl as of no consequence.

He was young by vampire standards. At nearly a century old, he couldn't remember much about his previous life. He did not care to remember. His life was now. Anything before didn't matter.

For years, he had survived off the blood of animals. Mostly goats. How he hated goat blood. When the rumours of The Chupacabra first began, he had been insulted. Goatsucker! How dare they? Then he had felt their shock, and fear. It was intoxicating. It fed him. It made him powerful. Invincible.

He fed their fear in order to feed his own growing strength. Shape shifting into a half-man, half-beast, he would allow them glimpses of him as he fed on their livestock. All calculated to instil fear deep into their souls.

Soon, even that was not enough.

Then, early one evening he woke to the sounds of music, and laughing. Curiosity drew him. He approached a neighbouring farm to discover a dozen or so humans having a party. He could not believe the audacity. To be outside after the sun went down. Unafraid. This was his domain. He ruled the night. He had to do something. He did not dare lose his hold on these people. He truly believed he would die without their fear to feed him. He drew on their nightmares, and began to change.

His body shrunk until he stood about four feet tall. His eyes narrowed, grew longer, and glowed red. Fur and feathers sprouted in patches out of his gray skin. At the end of his short arms burst large, powerful claws, and a row of sharp spikes ran down his back and on top of his head. His legs, short and muscular, narrowed at the bottom, ending in three, clawed toes.

Boldly he approached the partiers. A woman spotted him. Her scream filled the night. It was music to his ears. Chaos ensued. Screaming. Shoving. Pushing. Mothers and fathers reached for small children. The humans trampled each other in their haste to reach the safety of the house.

The vampire stood in the midst of the confusion, intoxicated by their panic; their fear.

An explosion rent the air. A flash of light blinded him. An unearthly scream ripped through the night when the slug slammed into his body, narrowly missing his heart. Black blood spewed from the hole. The ground sizzled and smoked where his blood landed. Plants withered and died. A woman screamed when some of his blood splattered on her face, eating away her skin. In a rage, he reached out one clawed arm, and dragged the screaming woman to him. With his other clawed hand, he twisted back her head, exposing her neck. Fangs exploded in his mouth. He sank them into her neck, and drank.

This was ambrosia.

Her warm, fear-enhanced blood swept through his body, feeding his tissues and organs. He felt himself growing stronger than ever before. His muscles worked to push the slug from his body, and the hole closed. He drained the last drop of blood, dropped the woman's lifeless body to the ground, and slowly licked every drop from his protruding fangs.

Never again would he lower himself to drink the blood of an animal.

The owl hooted again, and flew to another tree.

Two miles away, a dog's ears twitched. The dog stopped, stuck its nose in the air, and sniffed. He growled deep in his throat acknowledging the owl, and continued in the same direction. He had to move slowly, picking a path through the dense brush that his human companions could follow.

The owl settled in the tree, and watched the scene below.

The child lay on a flat rock, surrounded by trees - a sacrificial lamb. The vampire tenderly rearranged her clothing. He made her more comfortable.

He spoke one word. "Wake." His voice was velvet seduction.

The girl opened her eyes, and stared at the man. Her mind began to scream but no sound escaped her mouth. Fresh tears ran down her cheeks, and mingled with dried tears and dust. She began to sob silently. Her mind struggled to break free of the invisible chains that held it, and her body, prisoner.

The vampire ran his tongue along his teeth. His smile widened. His canines grew.

"Don't cry little one," he whispered. His voice was soft, compelling. The girl's sobs lessened, and then stopped completely. Still the child's mind screamed in terror. The vampire took a step towards her, then another. With each step closer, his canines grew longer. His tongue reached out, and touched the tip of one long tooth, licking the cloudy liquid that dripped from it. "It will only hurt for a moment. I promise." He crooned, his voice hypnotic.

The owl mentally blinked.

The child stared at the vampire in silence, unable to break free. Her eyes were two, unseeing saucers, in her small, pale face. She was staring at the vampire, but she wasn't seeing him. She could not have been more than five or six, but her mind was busy trying to find a way to break free of the vampire's thrall before it was too late.

It was too late for her father.

The memory of watching as the vampire forced her father to him, helpless as the monster fed on him until there was nothing left, had her silently screaming again. She had tried to call out to her father, to wake him from the vampire's spell, but her voice was silent. Her pleas never reached him. They were swallowed by something dark and dangerous. Something she had led to them.

Her whole world had gone black, and she awoke here. In this time and place.

The child never moved a muscle as the vampire reached out, and lovingly caressed her hair. Gently he pushed it back from her face. He tilted her neck slightly, and stared with hunger at the small pulse beating there. He could smell the blood coursing through her veins. The beating of her heart pounded in his ears. Her silent screams roared in his mind. He had been dreaming of this moment since he had first heard that quiet voice whispering across the wind searching for someone like herself. Her power had drawn him like a beacon in the night.

He leaned towards the small, pulsating vein. His mouth opened wider. His teeth dripped. Slowly his tongue traveled the length of the slender vein, savouring the taste of her fear.

The owl shrieked.

The vampire jumped back from the child. Instinctively he threw his arms up to protect his face. A razor-sharp beak tore hunks of flesh from his arm. He howled in rage. His body began to shimmer. Before he could shape-shift, the owl struck again. There was a blur of feathers and blood. His blood. The owl struck relentlessly, heedless of the foul blood that covered its feathers. It avoided the vampire's counter attacks with ease.

Suddenly, it stopped.

A snarl came from behind. The vampire spun around to face this new danger. He did not realize his mistake until it was too late.

A fully-grown wolf leapt at his exposed throat, clamping its teeth down in a vice-like grip. The two bodies hit the ground together. The vampire was frantic. Nothing had challenged him in his short life. He clawed viciously at the wolf. The wolf held tight, ignoring the blood trickling from the wounds on its side, and covering its white coat. It never loosened its grip on the vampire's throat.

The vampire's body went limp. Still the wolf kept its hold. Not until the vampire's head rolled back, nearly severed from its body, did the wolf loosen its hold. The wolf wasn't finished. It clamped its teeth in what was left of the vampire's throat, and chewed completely through.

The vampire's head rolled to the side of its body. Energy sizzled in the air. Then both head and body burst into a cloud of dust, and drifted harmlessly to the ground.

The wolf lay on the ground panting. Its body shimmered for a moment, and then changed.

Clad in a cotton shirt, blue jeans, and running shoes, Jade rose from the ground. She took a minute to listen to the familiar sounds of the jungle. The wind once again, whispered in the trees. A million insects began to buzz. A mouse scurried through the dried grass. The jungle had already begun to reclaim itself from the vile touch of the undead.

A rustle in the jungle about a half-mile away signalled the approach of the search party.

There were no silent screams. No silent pleas for help.

Jade slapped at a mosquito that thought she might provide its dinner, and limped over to the rock, one hand pressed against the wound in her side. The child lay on the stone alter, her eyes closed. If it were not for the slow, steady heartbeat, and the shallow breathing, Jade would think she had died.

Jade spoke softly, but the child didn't respond.

Tears swam in amber eyes, but Jade refused to allow them to escape.

"It's over honey," she whispered. "It's time to come back." She continued to talk soothingly to the child, as she gathered her into her arms and went to meet the search party.

It was time to go home.

Chapter Two

In another part of the jungle, a lone wolf snuffled at the body of what was once a very beautiful woman. Her translucent skin had been bitten and gnawed, having provided dinner for the very hungry jungle. Her body had been used and abused before her veins were drained completely of their life's precious fluid, and she had been discarded like yesterday's garbage.

The scent of the child was all over the woman; Strong and sweet beneath the clinging, vile scent of the vampire, the scent that had led Matthew to these grisly remains. The body of the man was two days old when they discovered it. This one was a day. If they did not find the child soon, chances were that she would be dead too.

Matthew puzzled over the strange behaviour of the vampire. It had never separated its victims before. Entire families drained and left together. Why then, had he not drained this family the same way? Never mind the fact that the vampire was traveling on foot making it easy, maybe a little too easy Matthew thought, to track him.

An owl hooted to the south. The wolf's ears twitched and his muzzle twisted into the semblance of a smile.

That one small hoot carried with it a wealth of information. The vampire was about to draw its last breath, and the child lived.

The wolf growled at a vulture that dared land too near the body, and then in a slow, fluid motion the wolf began to shift until a muscular, dark-skinned man appeared beside the body. With a casual wave of his hand, the way Jade had taught him, he clothed himself in a snug shirt that showed his rippling muscles, skin tight jeans, and non-descript runners.

Matthew preferred his wolf form, and working with Jade allowed him the freedom to be one. As part of an elite search and rescue squad, nobody questioned the presence of a wolf. If anyone wondered where the wolf went when the man was present, they didn't mention it. Right now, the man was needed. The wolf could not carry the woman's body, and the man refused to leave her behind to feed the jungle.

With several rapid movements of his hands Matthew silently chanted a few words, and fashioned a sturdy sheet. With great care, treating the woman as if she were precious cargo, he gently wrapped her broken body. Then lifting her in his powerful arms, he carried her several miles through the jungle to the town where the body of her husband waited.

Chapter Three

The door flew open with a bang, and Gemma stumbled in. Laughing, she caught the edge of the door to keep herself steady. Her heart beat frantically, in tune to the music as the noise reverberated through her mind. A dime-sized medallion, with the head of a wolf etched in it, hung from a simple chain around her neck. Her hand moved automatically to the ancient piece of metal. It was warm and familiar against her skin as she gently rubbed it between her thumb and forefinger. The mindless movement calmed her.

Dio, what was she doing here? How had Sara managed to convince her that this was a good idea? She raked the long, slender fingers of one hand through her blonde bangs, and shoved them back. Their shortness was still a shock.

"You look fine." Sara gave her a small nudge, and they continued into the room. The door slammed behind them. "Don't worry. Nobody is going to ask for I.D. Not now. With that cut and color you look five years older." Dancing blue eyes scanned the room. "Just remember, if anyone asks your name is Caitlin. Oh look, there's an empty table over there." She pointed towards the far side of the crowded dance floor. "I knew we should've come earlier. It's always packed this time of night."

Gemma peered across the room. How could Sara see anything? The room was so thick with cigarette smoke you would think they were running a fog machine. The wall lights placed strategically around the room were so dim they created more shadows than light. Overhead, lasers crisscrossed the dance floor, cutting through the fog like multi-coloured blades. It was eerie and disorienting, even with her enhanced sight.

"I'm not sure this is such a good idea." Gemma tugged her tight-fitting sweater down in an attempt to cover her bare midriff. When that didn't work, she tried to pull the waistband of her jeans higher.

Sara slapped at her hands. "Stop it. You don't want to draw attention to yourself, and besides you look great." She smiled, and waved at the bouncer who was eyeing them from the corner of the bar. The bouncer waved back then turned his attention to a couple of boys who were trying to get served.

"I told you they weren't going to bother us."

"Are you sure this top isn't too short?

"Yes. I'm sure." Sara shook her head, and let out an exaggerated sigh. Then she slipped her arm through Gemma's, and tugged her in the direction of the table. "Come on, Caitlin." She winked conspiratorially. "Quit fussing and move before someone else gets that table."

The hair on Gemma's arms bristled as a chill caressed her skin. Instantly on alert, she scanned the crowd for signs of danger. Nothing. She shrugged it off. Probably just a draft from the doorway mixed with her reluctance to be here. She gave one last, longing glance at the exit, and allowed Sara to lead her through the maze of scattered chairs and tables.

A couple of drinks on the table, and a sweater tossed casually on the back of a chair, staked a prior claim. "Damn!" Sara blurted. Quickly she covered her mouth, and glanced at Gemma. Her blue eyes were dancing with humour. "Oops. Sorry."

Gemma rolled her eyes, otherwise ignoring the slip. She had known Sara for years, and the girl was incorrigible. "Looks like someone beat us to the table." Gemma found it difficult to hide her relief, while at the same time wishing she were even half as adventurous as Sara. "I guess we should call it a night and go home."

Movement from a table near the back exit caught their attention. Sara was quick; you had to give her that. Before Gemma could do a thing, Sara approached the man sitting alone.

"Hi." She batted her eyelashes at him, flirting outrageously. "I couldn't help noticing you all alone. You don't mind if my friend *Caitlin* and I join you?"

The man shrugged, and indicated the free chairs.

Gemma couldn't shake the feeling she was being stalked. It made her nervous. Every nerve in her body screamed for her to turn, and run while she still had the chance. Again, she searched the room, but found nothing she would call threatening.

Sara sat in the chair directly opposite the man. Gemma reluctantly pulled out a chair between the two, and followed suit. She wasn't completely at ease. She had the distinct impression they weren't wanted here.

"I'm David." He tipped his beer up, and drained the bottle. "Can I buy you girls a drink?"

"No," Gemma blurted. She closed her eyes, and mentally gave herself a swift kick in the butt. "Thanks." Great. She must really come across as some kind of idiot. All the guy did was offer to buy them a drink, and she practically chewed his head off. To make things worse, at this moment she wanted a drink more than anything in the world.

Sara winked at David. "Don't mind my friend here. She doesn't get out much." Sara looked around the room. "I need to use the ladies room anyway. I'll grab the drinks on the way back."

Sara rose from the table. She waved Gemma back down when she would have followed. "Wait here, Caitlin. I can handle it."

Gemma was nervous. She knew she was out of her depth. If she were the type that cursed, she would be cursing Sara right now. What was Sara thinking anyway, leaving her at the table alone? Okay. Strictly speaking, she wasn't alone, and that, in itself, was the problem. Left to her own devices she would probably make an even bigger fool of herself than she already had.

Gemma felt eyes boring into the back of her head. She turned quickly, hoping to catch whoever it was, and found herself staring into electric pools of blue. Her breath caught in her throat. She was drowning. She couldn't tear her eyes from his. The air crackled with tension. The noise in the bar began to dim. The sound of her own breathing roared in her ears.

"Hey you two, look what I found at the bar."

The spell was shattered. Gemma turned to Sara letting her breath out in a rush.

Sara set a tray on the table, and began setting beers around. "This is Mark." Sara flashed a grin at the man standing behind her. "He was just hanging around the bar all by himself so I took pity on him and asked him to join us."

Gemma would have had to tilt her head back even if she were standing. "Hi." My god he was tall.

Mark bobbed his head in her direction. "Hi. You must be Caitlin. Sara's been telling me all about you." He winked, took a swig of beer, and turned to David. "You must be David? I hope you don't mind me crashing the party."

Gemma caught a whiff of anger, and then it disappeared. She couldn't blame David for being angry. She was surprised he was being as nice as he was considering first Gemma and Sara, and now Mark, had intruded on his evening. True, he had invited them to sit, but Sara hadn't really given him a choice.

David looked Mark squarely in the eye. "It's not my party." He seemed to take Mark's measure, and shrugged. "Pull up a chair. Take a load off."

Before Mark could sit Sara put her hand on his arm, and drew his attention back to her. "Come on, big boy. Let's see what moves you have." She began to dance her way through the tables to the dance floor. Mark placed his beer on the table, and followed her bouncy rear end.

Gemma reached for the beer in front of her. She offered David a shy smile. "Looks like you're stuck with me." Her voice nearly squeaked, she was so nervous, and that only made her more self-conscious.

David lips curved slowly into a smile. Gemma's heart did a curious little flip-flop. Damn, he was cute.

"I don't think being stuck with you will be such a hardship," he said.

His voice was husky, with the promise of things to come. Gemma suddenly found her beer bottle fascinating. This should be interesting. Her first beer. She took a small sip, and sputtered, nearly spitting it out. How could anyone drink this stuff? It was horrid!

She knew David struggled to keep from laughing out loud. "Is there a problem with your beer?" he asked.

Gemma felt the heat rise to her cheeks. "No." She ran her fingers through her bangs, and shook her head letting them fall back into place. "At least I don't think there is. It's just; I didn't expect it to be so bitter."

"Oh. That's all." David signalled to a nearby waitress. "There's a quick remedy for that." When the waitress came he asked her for a glass, and a saltshaker. He didn't say a word until the waitress returned. Gemma was grateful for the chance to pull herself back together.

David winked at the waitress. "Thanks. You may have just saved the life of a future beer drinker." He reached for Gemma's beer. "May I?"

She hesitated, and then nodded. Gemma was fascinated with the way his fingers held the glass as he slowly poured the beer. They were such long, slender fingers. She wondered what they would feel like on her body. David looked up. His grin was wicked, almost like he could read her mind. This time the heat began below her belly, and spread.

David's hand trembled as he sprinkled salt into her beer, and handed the glass back to Gemma. "Try this."

Gemma accepted the glass, and concentrated on the tiny bubbles rising through the amber liquid. Once again under control, she cautiously took a sip. She was pleasantly surprised. "I'd never have thought salt would make such a difference." She took a couple more swallows of beer, and began to relax.

"Do you live around here, David?"

"No. I'm just here on vacation. A friend told me about the Wolf Center and I thought I'd check it out."

"When are you going? I work there. Maybe I can show you around."

"Wish I'd known that before." He looked her up and down. His grin was wicked, and Gemma's cheeks burned. "I was there yesterday. I would remember seeing you."

Gemma turned her glass one-way, and then the other. Her eyes never left the tiny bubbles. "I was around," she mumbled, slightly disappointed.

They talked about the wolves at the center for a while, and Gemma accepted David's offer of another beer.

She leaned back in her chair, and smiled. David was good company. The beer was cold, and she could get to like his flirting. She danced with David. She danced with Mark. She even danced with Sara.

Gemma was laughing when she and Sara came off the dance floor. "You're outrageous," she accused her friend.

"I'm serious," Sara told her. "I'm going to marry Mark." She turned to watch him make his way back from the washrooms. She licked her lips. "Yummy."

Gemma rolled her eyes. "And what does Mark say about that?"

"Oh, I haven't told him yet." They were still laughing when Mark reached the table and sat down.

Gemma wiped the tears from her cheeks, and took a big swallow of beer. "Wow." She set the glass on the table, and licked her lips. "I put way too much salt in this one." She scrunched up her nose. Something smelled—off. "Oh well," she said, and took another swallow. "Don't want to waste it." They all laughed again.

Gemma tried to focus on Sara and Mark while they danced. It wasn't easy. The way they kept weaving in and out amongst the other dancers was making her dizzy. She blinked, and rubbed the back of her neck. She shook her head and tried to clear the cobwebs. Her mouth was dry. She reached for her beer, and took another cool drink of the amber liquid. She was drinking an awful lot of beer. The more she drank the thirstier she got. The thirstier she got, the more she drank. Funny how that worked. Gemma was finding it harder and harder to focus.

David stood beside her chair looking at her, and Gemma squinted up at him. "Is there something on my nose?"

"Come on, Caitlin," he said. "It's time to go."

"Go?" Gemma forced her eyes open wide, and looked around the room. "Go where?" And who was Caitlin?

What was wrong with her? She couldn't even string two words together to make a sentence.

"Home."

Gemma struggled a little when David took her arm. "Where's home?" She couldn't think. She looked around the room but everything was blurry. The coloured lights made her dizzier, if that was possible. Oh yeah, now she remembered. "Where's Sara?"

"Sara left with Mark." David steered her towards the back door. "She asked me to drive you home."

That couldn't be right. Sara was right there. Dancing with Mark. Or was she? Gemma couldn't see her anywhere. Maybe she did go home with Mark.

The cool night breeze slapped her face. Gemma stumbled on the steps. David put his arm around her, and pulled her closer to him. He lowered his head, and murmured softly to her. Gemma snuggled close.

"This way." He led her towards the back of the parking lot. "My van is over here." He had parked in a spot in the far corner of the parking lot. The light in that corner was broken, leaving the cars there in shadow.

"I don't feel so good." It came out 'I don' feels good' and Gemma began to giggle. What was wrong with her? She felt so strange. She tried to lift her head from where it was resting under his shoulder, but it was such a chore. Besides, he smelled so good, like a spicy muffin. Her stomach growled. She snuggled closer, and yawned.

"Here we are sleepy head." David slid the side door open easily, and half lifted Gemma into the back of the van.

Gemma struggled to focus on her surroundings. It was so dark inside the van. Normally she had excellent night vision but tonight she couldn't see her hand in front of her face. Maybe it was because the windows were painted over. Strange. Why would anyone want to paint the windows? She really didn't like how the beer was making her feel. It was doing crazy things to her thinking. She spied a mattress against the opposite wall. Perfect. She was so tired. Gemma stumbled to the mattress, and was sleeping before David turned the key in the ignition.

She was having the most erotic dream. He was a musician, and she was his violin—wound so taut she could break any second.

"Wake up, sleepyhead."

His voice was gentle, making her feel warm and safe. She struggled to open her eyes. Blinked them shut then open again. Everything had a decidedly pinkish tinge. This was different than her usual dreams. She liked it.

There was movement on her right. She quickly turned her head only to be mesmerized by the bluest eyes. Her tongue darted out, and licked her suddenly dry lips. For the first time she was seeing her dream lover's face. He was gorgeous. His lips parted in a wickedly knowing smile, and her heart flip-flopped. His chest was bare and smooth. She watched fascinated as his long slender fingers undid the button on his jeans. What would it feel like to have those fingers touching her? Caressing her bare skin?

"… most … delicious … dream." She sighed.

"That's right, baby. You're dreaming."

His eyes were hypnotic. They held hers while he gently straddled her. His warm fingers brushed feather light against her bare flesh. Funny. She didn't usually sleep in the nude.

"What are you doing?" It came out `whaya doin', and Gemma giggled.

"Hush." His voice was a gentle whisper. "I'm going to make all your dreams come true."

His fingers barely skimmed the surface of her skin. She was so hot. She was sure she would burst into flames. The muscles in her abdomen clenched. Her breath came in short rapid pants. Slowly, ever so slowly, he moved his hands in a circular motion above her nipples, barely touching. She never wanted to wake up.

"Please." She pleaded in a husky whisper. Not sure if she was begging him to stop, or continue. A voice inside her head screamed. *"Stop. This is wrong."* The voice sounded a lot like her mother's. Her body quivered with excitement. *"Shut up,"* she told the voice. *"Stay out of my dreams."*

His heated fingers barely stroked her feverish body. Her nipples grew. They stretched, lengthened, reached for the palms of his hands. They begged for his touch. Gemma gasped when his warm fingers obligingly cupped her breasts, and began to gently knead them. His thumbs, rough and warm, teased her taunt nipples, making them grow even more. She wanted to reach out and caress him, but she was afraid. Afraid that if she touched him she would wake up, and he would disappear with the dawn's early rays.

"You like that, don't you?" he crooned. "That's okay, baby." Just the sound of his voice had her quivering with desire. "You don't have to say a word. I know what you need."

Gemma stared at his mouth in fascination. The way his tongue barely touched his lips made her wonder what it would be like to feel those lips pressed against hers. She licked her own, dry lips, and tried to calm the erratic beating of her heart.

Gemma gasped breathlessly as his mouth moved ever so slowly towards hers. His teeth tugged gently on her lower lip. Then his tongue followed the path her own had recently taken, before darting between her parted lips to explore the heated cavern inside. He lifted his mouth from hers all too quickly. Gemma nearly cried in disappointment, until she felt the whisper of warm breath fluttered wing-like across her naked skin, and his lips moved to take the place of his hands. He caught her swollen nipple between his teeth gently tugging and teasing before taking the whole thing into his mouth, and suckling. Her body quivered helplessly. His heat seared her tender flesh. The bed moved slightly as he shifted position. His fingers slowly, torturously mapped a trail over the clenched muscles of her abdomen. Liquid heat pooled deep in her center.

All rational thought flew out the window.

He continued to suckle at her breast, while his fingers moved lower to tease her small nub mercilessly. Never before had her dreams been so erotic—so wanton.

Her body writhed beneath his, allowing him the freedom to do as he pleased. Her body screamed for his fiery touch. Her legs opened wider at his prodding, giving him full access to her heated core. She cried out as one long finger slid inside. Her body was on fire. Her dreams had never taken her so far before. She hovered on the edge of climax.

She wanted more of him—needed all of him.

Her dream lover positioned himself between Gemma's legs. Gently he probed her moist opening with the tip of his manhood. She spread her legs further at his urging, and he thrust into her, burying his throbbing shaft into her moist heat.

Gemma screamed as a sudden, fiery pain tore her apart.

His mouth covered hers, capturing her screams. He began to thrust faster, and harder—and deeper.

Gemma tried to wake up.

She bucked, and twisted in her attempts to throw him off. She thought she would die from the pain. Gemma tried to concentrate but the agony was unbearable. It wouldn't stop.

Gemma tried to pull him off. She raked his back with claw-like nails. He released her lips, and grabbed her arms, forcing them above her head. She snarled at him. Her swollen lips curled above her even teeth. She snapped at him. And missed.

He roared as he spilled his seed into her, a roaring river of molten lava, and slumped across her.

Gemma sunk her canines deep into his shoulder.

It was his turn to scream.

*****

If the jackhammers stopped she might get back to sleep. The scent of fresh earth washed over her. Gemma shivered. She reached for the sheet, and came back with a handful of dried leaves.

Leaves!

Her eyes shot open, and she sat up. Pain stabbed at her temples forcing her to lie back down.

Where was she?

Gemma couldn't remember leaving the bar. Actually, she didn't remember too much about the bar at all.

What was that strange metallic taste? Cautiously, Gemma opened first one eye, and when the jackhammers didn't return, the other. She was lying in a thicket, naked. *Great!* She must have shifted after leaving the bar last night. *Where were her clothes?*

Obviously they were somewhere between the bar and here...wherever here was. The other obvious question was whether they were neatly folded somewhere waiting for Gemma to return and put them on, or shredded beyond repair.

Elizabeth was teaching her to use the magic when she shifted to save her clothes, but she wasn't very good at it. More often than not she would send her clothes away, but not get them back when she became human again. Gemma sat up slowly, and looked around the thicket, not surprised that her clothes were nowhere to be found.

She tried to conjure up a shirt, but the pain in her head was so intense she couldn't concentrate. Bile rose in her throat, and she spewed the contents of her stomach all over the ground.

She had to get home before someone found her like this. It was several more minutes before she was able to stand on her own. Slowly, one agonizing step after another, she made her way out of the thicket to find herself outside the main gates to the wolf center. Her office was there, and in her office was a spare change of clothes.

Thanking her lucky stars, Gemma clamoured over the fence to drop unladylike on the other side. She would get dressed, and go home to bed.

Chapter Four

The heat was oppressive. The sun beat down, hurting his eyes behind the dark glasses. The heat wasn't the only thing making sweat trickle down his back and soak his shirt. Guilt was a big part of it.

For a moment he actually considered rejecting Manuel's offer, but something about this country spoke to him. It screamed home like nowhere else had. He shifted uncomfortably, and tried to focus on what Father Augusto Hernandez was saying as he laid to rest the tortured souls of the Martinez family.

Father Hernandez had given the last rights before the bodies were cremated, and had agreed to perform the ceremony for Alicia's benefit. Jade believed that the child needed to see her parents put to rest, and because she was paying for everything, nobody objected.

"Is there something on your mind, Matt?" Jade's voice was barely a whisper, yet Matthew had no trouble hearing.

He glanced at her. Her unique amber eyes were swirling with emotion, and her luscious lips were curled into a mysterious, knowing smile. Matthew tore his dark gaze from her brighter one to stare across the open graves to the beckoning jungle beyond. The only person who truly loved the two people being put to rest today, sat silently in a wheelchair staring at nothing at all. The doctor's hadn't wanted them to take her from the hospital, but Jade had insisted that the child needed to be here.

"Do you really think it was a good idea to bring the girl?"

Jade's sigh whispered across the space between them. "We had to bring her. She needs to see her parents are at peace."

Matthew didn't think the child could *see* anything at all, but he believed in Jade. If she said the child knew what was happening around her, then Matthew believed it was true. Sweat trickled between his shoulder blades, and Matthew once again shifted position.

Father Hernandez spoke his final words. Manuel Rodriguez tossed a shovel of dirt onto each of the coffins. Jade took the limp roses from Alicia's idle hands, and toss one onto each of the two coffins. She took the handles of the chair, and pushed Alicia back to the rented van.

While Jade was securing Alicia in the van Matthew thanked Father Hernandez, and then hurried to drive them back to the hospital. Once Alicia was safely tucked into bed Jade motioned for the others to step out into the hallway. As soon as the door clicked shut she turned her attention on him. "So, Matthew. Now do you want to tell me what's on your mind?"

Matthew reached into his pocket, and pulled out a chocolate bar. Extending his hand palm up he offered it to Jade. "Brought you a treat."

Jade snatched the bar, tore off the paper, and stuffed it into her mouth. Then she slowly licked the sticky chocolate from each and every finger, licked off the paper making sure she got every drop, before crumpling the paper into a tight ball, and then handed it back to

Matthew. She patted his front pockets. "Come on," she said as she continued to pat him down in her best imitation of a police officer. "Where do you have it stashed?"

Matthew's expression was one of quilt. "What?"

"You know better than to tease me like this."

Matthew squirmed. "I don't know what you're talking about."

Jade sat back on her heels, her hands in front of her, and her tongue hanging out. "I'm begging. Don't keep me begging."

Matthew laughed at her antics, and reached down to pull her back into a stand. "Okay." He threw his hands into the air in surrender. "I confess. I bought two, but I ate one on the way to the church."

Jade glared at him, hands on her hips. "Let me get this straight. You bought me two chocolate bars as a peace offering, because you obviously have something to say to me that you think I won't like. Then you *ate* one? You owe me Matt."

She was right. He did owe her; much more than a chocolate bar. Matthew owed Jade his life. Literally. If Jade hadn't rescued him from the lab at the Center for Psychic Research, he had no doubt that he would be dead right now.

Matthew was one of those rare *weres* to be born wolf. For the first twelve years of his life he lived in the forest with his father. Wild and free. He had known no other life than that of a wolf. Even after he received his magic, and began to shift he preferred to run around the forest on all fours. His mother had died in childbirth, and his father had no desire to live among humans. If his father was even aware of the rumours of a wild child in the forest, he ignored them.

One sunny day during his twelfth summer Matthew was chasing a rabbit when he had his first encounter with humans. He had pounced on a rabbit, missed, and landed in a trap. Snarling and snapping, he struggled to free himself. It hadn't even occurred to him to shift and remove the trap. Unable to pull his paw free, he began to gnaw on it, determined to rid himself of the large metal trap. He was so intent on freeing himself that he didn't hear the approach of the hunters.

A snapping twig was his first warning. Matthew spun around to face this new threat. Blood, fur, and bits of bone spew from his mouth, and his lips curled in a warning snarl. He eyed the humans warily as one of them raised a large metal stick to his shoulder. There was a bang, a flash of light, and a burning sensation in his shoulder. Then his whole world went black, and Matthew crumpled to the ground.

He woke up in a small white room. He was groggy, and his head felt like it was going to split into a million pieces. There was a small window too high to reach, and a bowl of strange smelling water. He drank only when the thirst was too strong to ignore. It was then, when his limps refused to obey, and he couldn't lift his head, that they would come in with their needles, and scissors to take their samples.

In his weakened state it took much longer than usual for his wounds to heal, but eventually his body ejected the bullet, and his shoulder healed. Even his half chewed off limb completely healed itself. When the change came over him, his captors were ecstatic. They came more often after that to poke and prod, and take his blood. At first they tried to communicate with him while he was in human form. Matthew hated them with their long needles, and sharp knives. He refused to stand on two feet in their presence, and would only answer in growls and snarls.

Eventually they gave up trying to communicate with him. Believing him incapable of understanding, they began to speak freely around him. He listened to everything they said, using the information to help plan his escape from this hell.

Then he'd seen her. Jade. She was with a group of researchers brought in to observe him, but she was different from the rest. She pretended interest in everything the doctors were saying, but the whole time she spoke to him with her mind. Only once did she look directly at him.

That night she came back, and freed him from his prison. She took him home with her, and taught him how to live as a human, while allowing him the freedom to live like the wolf he was. If it wasn't for Jade, Matthew would be dead because there was no way he would ever become the weapon those men had wanted him to be.

Matthew owed Jade his life, and he wouldn't desert her now.

"I do owe you," he said in his soft-spoken voice, which was in such contrast to his hard muscled body. "More than you'll ever know."

Jade smiled then. Really smiled. Her smile could fill a room with light, and bring a grown man to his knees. Her smile could make anyone, or anything, want to do her bidding. "What is it, Matthew?"

Matthew shuffled his feet, and fought the urge to confess what he so desperately wanted. "Nothing. I was just thinking about when we met, and how much I owe you."

"You don't owe me anything, Matthew." Jade paused for a second, searching Matthew's face intently. She didn't attempt to search his mind, or he would have known. "I thought you had something you wanted to tell me."

Matthew's heart twitched. Jade was his only family. After she had rescued him from his prison, they had returned to his den in the forest to find the decaying remains of his father. Unable to subdue the fully-grown werewolf as easily as they had his pup, they had decapitated him, cut out his heart, and left his remains, unaware than none of the forest creatures would dine on the flesh of a werewolf. Matthew was torn between his desire to stay, and his desire to stay with Jade.

"I have a confession." Jade gave a quick glance in his direction, and then dropped her eyes. "I need someone to stay here in Mexico, and help protect these people. I can't be everywhere at once, and you know how much I hate flying."

Matthew laughed. The only flying Jade hated was in an airplane, and they both knew it. Hope flared as he realized where she was heading. "And you want me?"

"I know it's an imposition. I know how much you hate being human."

"I don't exactly hate it." Even as Matthew spoke the words out loud, he realized they were true. Another thing he owed to Jade. She had taught him to embrace both sides of his nature. He may prefer his animal side but he no longer despised his human counterpart.

"I'm glad to hear that." Jade glanced in at the girl lying so still in the bed, and then turned her attention back to Matthew. "How would you like to head up the Mexican division of O'Connell Search and Rescue?" She held up her hand when Matthew started to speak. "Before you say anything, hear me out. All the necessary visas have been obtained. I have purchased the farm we are renting. There are hundreds of acres of jungle for you to run in. You are far enough away from town for privacy, and close enough that you can keep your eye on things. You will be working closely with Manuel. He has an open mind, and I would trust him with my life. How much you trust him with is up to you. But I would count him as a friend. So what do you say?"

It was perfect. Maybe a little too perfect. Matthew looked at Jade suspiciously, but as far as he could tell she wasn't hiding anything. Suddenly Matthew didn't want to stay. He scrambled around in his head before he hit on the perfect reason not to stay. "I can't stay. Who'd do all the driving?" Jade had never learned to drive. She had hired someone else to teach him.

Jade sucked in her bottom lip, betraying her own nervousness. "That brings me to my confession. I have an interview with that young man from Willow Bend. Daniel Dixon. He has sent me several letters, and I just felt it was time to meet him."

"Really?" Matthew glared at Jade, but she just watched him with those calm, amber eyes. "When did this happen?"

"This morning. I rang him from the farm while you were out running, and apparently eating my chocolate bar." She narrowed her eyes at him sternly, and then shrugged. "He has agreed to meet with me in two weeks. I have a good feeling about this, Matthew. I'm sure he will work out."

"In that case I accept your offer."

They both knew he would. There had never really been a question of his leaving.

Chapter Five

What had that bitch done to him?

David carefully removed the bloodied bandage from his shoulder. He used the mirror to see to clean the wound. Stupid bitch. She's lucky he hadn't killed her. He could have crushed her windpipe with just a bit more pressure. He probably would have if it weren't for that damned medallion she was wearing. He looked at the image of the wolf seared into his thumb, and cursed again. He hoped she was wondering about the bruise on her neck.

He applied antibiotic cream on the bite, as well as on his thumb. He was lucky. It wasn't nearly as bad as he'd first thought. There had been so much blood he'd thought she had ripped his shoulder right off. As it was, there wasn't much of a mark. Just a red blotch.

Damn the girl! This was all her fault. The moment she'd entered the room she had him acting out of character. The way her hand had gone to her bangs. The sexy sway of her hips as she'd crossed the room. It had all been calculated to make him want her.

It worked! He'd wanted her so badly he had broken all his own rules.

David covered the wound with a clean bandage, and popped two more painkillers into his mouth. It might not look bad but it hurt like hell. He drank a glass of orange juice, washed the glass, and set it on the drain board. God, his head was splitting. He hoped the bite wasn't infected. He had read somewhere that a human's bite could be much worse than a dog's. It hadn't looked infected, but he would check it again tonight.

He grabbed his lab coat off the hook, and made sure the door locked behind him. If he didn't hurry he was going to be late for work.

Chapter Six

Jade sat beside the hospital bed, and held the child's hand. She talked to her about the weather, the birds singing in the trees, her Da back home in the States. Alicia lay in the bed, motionless. She stared straight ahead without blinking. She might have been sleeping, except her eyes were open. The doctor and nurses went about their business, checking IV's and vital signs, adjusting this tube and that. Even they were at a loss. "She's in shock." The doctor shrugged, and gave Jade a half-hearted smile. "She'll wake when she's ready. There is nothing to do. Just keep her comfortable."

Jade sat with her, talked to her, worried about her. She looked into those black, empty eyes, and wondered where the child was. If only Althea were here. Althea would know what to do.

Talk to her, Jade. Let her know you are there, waiting for her to come back.

Jade listened to the familiar voice with her mind. She held the child's limp hand in hers, and reached out to the cosmos. She sought any trace of the voice that had screamed for help.

Mama. Where are you, mama? The mind voice was so sad, so lost, and Jade's heart melted.

It's time to come back. Jade called to the child. She reached out, and then she waited. After several, timeless moments, the child reached back.

*****

Alicia sat on the edge of the hospital bed. Her short legs swung back and forth. Her fingers were clenched in the top sheet. Her knuckles were white. *I won't talk to her.*

"It doesn't matter," Jade answered the small voice in her head. She picked up a blue denim dress with a knitted, pink bear sewn on the front.

"This is nice." She held the dress up to Alicia. Her head was tilted on a slight angle as she looked it up, and down. "Don't you think?"

Alicia's face darkened. *It's ugly.* She turned her head towards the window.

Jade was silent as Alicia's eyes blinked several times. The child could be so stubborn. Jade wanted to wrap her arms around her, and protect her from what was coming, but she couldn't. If she was going to heal, Alicia had to face what had happened to her parents. Face what had almost happened to her. All Jade could do now was surround her with the people who could help her heal, and teach her about her powers.

A grackle whistled from its perch outside the open window. Alicia took a deep breath, and turned watery eyes in Jade's direction. *You can't make me talk to her.*

"I know." Since she'd woken up Alicia hadn't spoken out loud, not even to Jade. "I also know that if you don't start talking people are going to think I'm crazy for talking to myself, and want to lock me up."

Jade folded the dress, and added it to the growing pile of discarded clothing beside the still empty suitcase.

She held up a white, frilly dress with blue flowers. "So?" She shook the dress in front of Alicia. "What about this?"

Alicia's lips twitched. "Where did you find this stuff?"

Jade smiled. Her eyes danced with amusement. She wasn't sure Alicia realized it, but the child had actually spoken. Out loud. "I thought you'd like it," she said. "I thought you were one of those girly girls."

Alicia smiled for the first time since she woke up. "You're like mama." Tears pooled in her dark eyes, and she sniffled. She let go of the sheet, and jumped off the bed. Her small hands reached for a pair of plain denim jeans, like the ones Jade was wearing.

"I like these," she said. She held them up against her small frame. About four inches of material lay on the floor in front of her. "I'll grow into them." She bobbed her head up and down. "Yeah. I can grow this much."

"Why wait. If you like them I can cut the bottoms off for you," Jade told her. "That way you can wear them now."

Alicia burst into tears. She tossed the jeans into the suitcase, and turned to clutch the front of Jade's shirt. "Where is Mama?" The shirtfront muffled her words. "Why isn't she here?" She sniffed, tipped her head back, wiped the end of her nose, and stared at Jade with black, watery eyes. *What did I do? Why did she go away? It's my fault, isn't it? She's mad 'cause I couldn't save Papa?*

"You didn't do anything, Sweetheart." Jade felt her own eyes burn with unshed tears. The poor child. She was so little. At eight she could easily pass for five. She was like a little cherub, with her mass of black, curly hair framing her face, and bunching at her shoulders. She looked so forlorn, so alone. She didn't deserve this. No child deserved this.

Jade's heart was breaking. For the first time, in a very long time, Jade wished she were normal. She'd take this precious little girl in a heartbeat. Love her, and care for her like she deserved.

But Jade wasn't normal. She had a job to do, and that didn't include caring for a child; any child. Jade's eyes burned. Whether for this child or the child she would probably never have, she wasn't entirely sure. She squatted down, and pulled Alicia into her arms. She forced a smile in her voice. "You'll like Althea," she told her. "And the Murphys will adore you."

"I like you!"

"I know honey. I like you too."

Alicia pushed herself back so she was once again looking into Jade's face. "Let me come with you."

"We've been through this." Jade sighed. She couldn't expect the child to understand why she couldn't take her. She needed special help. Eventually she was going to remember what happened, and when she did she would need all the help she could get. Help from someone who knew what the girl had been through. From someone who knew the truth. "I can't take you with me. You need to go where there is someone to look after you. I can't do that when I am working. I travel a lot, and I never know when I will be home. Althea loves children. And she will know exactly what you need. She will stay with you as long as you need her."

Unshed tears made her voice rough. "Come on. Let's finish your packing. Althea will be here any moment."

"You're just like everyone else." Alicia flung her arm out, and knocked the suitcase to the floor. "Mama doesn't want me, and you don't want me. Nobody wants me."

Jade scooped the child into her arms, holding her struggling frame gently, but firmly until she went limp. Then she sat on the edge of the bed, the sobbing child on her lap, and rocked her back and forth. How did you tell a child whose entire world had just come crashing down, that you had to send her away?

"You're wrong, Sweetheart." Jade tried to keep her own voice calm, but it cracked. "Your mother loved you very much. She would have done anything for you. I would do anything for you."

The door swung open silently. A tall, slender woman entered the room. She could have been Jade's twin. They were almost identical, but for the hair. The newcomer's fell to her waist in a dark, golden flow. She watched her niece rock the small child, and she knew what was in the other woman's heart. "Looks like I'm just in time."

Jade stopped rocking at the sound of the familiar voice.

¡Váyase!

Althea stepped back. The push to go away was strong. She drew herself up to her full height, and took two more steps into the room. She ignored the child for now. "Do you have a hello for your favourite Aunt?"

Alicia's hands clenched into small fists, and her brow furrowed. *I said, go away.*

"You're right," Althea said. She ignored the child, looking at Jade when she spoke. "She is strong." It was a full minute before she turned her attention to the child. "How long have you been able to do that?" she asked in the child's own language. She could have picked the answer out of the child's mind, but that wasn't the way to win her trust.

Alicia buried her face in Jade's shirt. She put her hands over her ears.

"I see she doesn't want to talk." Althea picked the suitcase off the floor, and set it on the bed. She picked up the jeans, making a big production of shaking them out, smoothing them down, folding them neatly, and putting them in the empty suitcase. She ignored most of the other clothes scattered on the floor, choosing a baggy sweatshirt, a pair of green shorts, and a plain white T-shirt. These she folded, and put in the suitcase. She closed the lid, and snapped the locks.

"Are the papers in order?" she asked Jade.

Jade took inventory, "passport, airplane tickets, and temporary custody papers."

"Are you sure you know what you're doing?"

Jade stared into Althea's eyes. *She has nobody else.* "You're the only one who can help her." Her strange, amber eyes pleaded for understanding.

"I know that!" Althea took a deep breath, and blew out slowly through pursed lips. "I would have come without your call."

It was the simple truth. Althea had a gift for healing both the minds, and the bodies of those touched by evil. She always knew where she was needed, and like Jade, Althea would never hesitate to use those gifts. What Jade didn't know, was that Althea was more worried about Jade's state of mind than that of the troubled child.

Althea held the eye contact. Using their special connection she asked, *Are you sure about the adoption?*

"You want to adopt me?" Alicia sat up, her small head turning from Jade to Althea, and back again.

Althea cocked an eyebrow in her direction. The child was a natural. She could see why Jade was so concerned about her. "Well, what do you know? She can talk." She didn't mention the fact that Alicia had been listening to their private conversation.

Jade on the other hand, did. "It's not nice to listen to other people's thoughts?" She narrowed her eyes, trying to look stern.

"Oops. Sorry." Alicia looked to the floor, but not before Jade saw the sparkle in her dark eyes. She swung her legs back and forth. Then her head popped up, and her face broke into a grin. "But you want to adopt me? Right?"

Jade cocked her head to one side, and studied the child. At this moment it was only an idea. One she wasn't sure would ever become a reality. Who was she kidding, anyway? There was no way she could care for a small child—at least, not yet. "I can't," she finally said. There was no sense getting the child's hopes up "Althea has been given temporary custody of you." It hadn't been hard to get custody. With no living relatives, there was nobody to pay her bills. There had been nobody willing to take the child in.

Sure, they had made a token fuss. After all, Jade was proposing to take one of their own out of the country. In the end, the judge was happy to sign the custody papers. Jade hadn't had to try very hard to persuade him. "She is taking you to the States, where you will be staying with her, and Da. Remember, I told you about my— Grandfather." Da and Althea would keep the child safe, and the Murphys would treat her like one of their own. They had been with the O'Connells for almost twenty-five years. Jade had hired Mrs. Murphy through an agency to take care of her father when she had to be away. Mr. Murphy had come along to help with the yard, and the dogs. Together, they kept things running while Jade was away. She trusted them with more than just her home. They were family.

Alicia started to protest. Jade set her on the floor and stood up. "Da raised me after my own parents were gone. You'll love him. He can hardly wait for you to get there. He's already talking about giving you your own dog."

She gathered the clothing scattered on the floor, and dumped them on the bed. "We'll leave these here. Maybe the Sisters can give them to somebody who will appreciate them."

Althea glanced pointedly at the clock on the wall. "We have to leave if we are going to catch the plane."

"I'm not going."

Alicia stood in front of the hospital bed, her dark skin pale, her eyes bigger than saucers, her legs spread out, and her hands on her hips. Jade grabbed her own pack from beside the door, and slipped her arms through the straps. She grabbed the suitcase from the bed in one hand, and held the other one out to Alicia who stared at it for several seconds. Her shoulders slumped, and she placed her small hand in Jade's. The three left the hospital room together.

While Althea showed proof of temporary custody, and signed Alicia out of the hospital, the nurses flocked around the child offering their sympathy. Alicia stared straight ahead, eyes focused on something that nobody else could see. She didn't acknowledge their presence by word or action. When they finally gave up and left her alone, she put one foot in front of the other, looking neither left nor right, and headed for the door.

"Poor thing" … "the same" … "losing her parents" … "horrible" … Snatches of conversation floated towards them, and Jade quickened the pace.

They pushed the front door open and stepped outside. Jade gasped. It was so hot. The air was sucked from her lungs. She wiped her fingers across her eyelids. The heat rolled and shimmered above the pavement. There wasn't a hint of breeze. The heat didn't seem to affect Alicia. She just put one foot in front of the other, and kept on walking. All fight gone. Althea, on the other hand, looked ready to drop.

"Taxi?"

Althea shrugged.

"I like the bus." The voice was barely a whisper on the non-existent breeze, but both women heard it, and smiled.

There were three taxis waiting in front of the hospital. The driver's were slumped in their seats, hats tilted over their brows. The first in line sat up and signalled them. Jade waved him back down. There was a bus heading in the right direction. Jade stepped onto the road and raised two fingers. The bus pulled over and stopped. Jade lifted Alicia on to the first step and gave her a small push forward. Althea had one foot on the second step when the driver shoved the bus into gear, and then pulled out in front of another bus. There wasn't time to dally if he was going to make his money.

"*Tres para el aeropuerto, por favor,*" Jade said. She had to grab the railing to keep from falling as the driver took a bend way too fast. Althea slipped past her and followed Alicia.

"*Cuarenta y cinco pesos,*" the driver said. He switched gears, and the bus went faster.

Jade held the pole in a death grip with one hand while she counted out coins with the other. She dropped fifty pesos in the container and looked for Alicia. Of course she would have to be on the very back seat. Her grin, stretching from ear to ear as the bus bounced and rattled, made it all worthwhile.

"Figures she'd pick the back," mumbled Jade.

"*Perdón?*"

Jade gave the driver one of her dazzling smiles. "*Nada,*" she told him and started for the back of the bus. The bus lurched. Jade grabbed the nearest seat to keep from being thrown down. Compared to this, hunting was a walk in the park. She finally reached the back and sat down with an exaggerated sigh.

"The back's the best," Alicia said, undaunted by the looks of the grownups on each side of her.

"Of course it is," Althea said. She winked at Jade. "You get to feel every bump from back here."

At that precise moment the bus hit a large bump and Jade grabbed the back of the nearest seat to keep from being flung to the floor. As soon as she regained her seat the bus came to an abrupt halt, throwing her forward again. The next victim was no sooner on the first step then the bus lurched forward again. Alicia laughed with glee. The locals all seemed to take it in stride, smiling and greeting each other, as the bus rolled from side to side. All the trees were clipped at the edge of the road on one side, while on the other, the side Jade was sitting on, the road dropped down a sheer cliff to the roiling ocean.

Jade held her breath on one corner when she saw a car coming towards them cut across the center of the road. The bus driver didn't slow down. He just pulled the bus further towards the edge of the cliff and stepped harder on the gas. Jade would have sworn the back wheels were airborne.

Jade wasn't afraid of much. Until now, she would have thought flying in a plane was it. It was stupid, really. She had nothing to worry about, personally. But if the bus crashed, Alicia, and the other passengers, wouldn't be so lucky. She watched Alicia. She stared out the window watching the trees fly by, like pickets on a fence, and she laughed. Alicia loved this. It was evident on her animated face. Jade preferred other methods of travel.

This just wasn't safe.

The rear exit door was swinging open and closed, the latch long since broken off. There wasn't a window on the right-hand side of the bus without a crack. Some were completely missing. The front window had a crack that ran from the top right hand corner to the bottom left. Jade was sure that it impaired the driver's vision. A nativity set was mounted just above the dash, and below that was a sign 'Vaya con Dios!' 'Go with God.' One day she hoped to—just not today.

Jade leaned back in her seat, closed her eyes, and forced herself to relax. The bus came to one of its sudden stops and Althea poked Jade in the shoulder. "Come on, sleepy head," she teased.

Apparently the airport was the end of the line for the buses; at least temporarily. The driver actually put the bus in park, opened the doors, and left the bus. The trio gathered their stuff and exited the bus with most of the others. A couple of passengers leaned back in their seats, closed their eyes, and prepared to wait for the driver's return.

The small airport was crowded. There were so many people the air conditioning had no effect at all. The beginnings of a headache scratched at Jade's temples. Emotions were running high. Tension filled the small airport. People were anxious to get home after their holidays. They were frustrated with the long line ups that moved at a snail's pace. Jade pressed the heel of her hand against her temple and tried to make her mind blank. She hated crowds. Give her wide-open, sparsely populated spaces, and she was in heaven. This was hell for her.

Jade forced herself to focus on a heavyset man in the line in front of them. He took his hat off to fan his face. He wiped the back of his hand across his forehead and plunked his hat back on top of his head. He pushed the luggage piled in front of him ahead a few inches and looked around. A couple of minutes later he repeated the process. Just as he reached the counter, his wife and daughter joined him, laden with parcels, and he sighed.

It was their turn. Jade waited while Althea handed over the tickets, the passports and the temporary custody papers, for herself and Alicia. The man at the counter lifted an eyebrow at the lack of luggage. A single suitcase for two people wasn't much. He didn't say a word.

Alicia looked at Jade, her pack still hanging from her shoulders. She didn't say a word. Jade hoped she was finally accepting the fact that she was going with Althea.

An old man with a gray beard about six inches long and wearing a ragged baseball cap kept looking at them and scribbling on a piece of paper. He cautiously approached them where they stood in line to buy a drink. "Excuse," he said. His breath smelled of cigarette smoke and his voice was raspy.

He pushed a four by six piece of paper towards them. "You like?" he asked.

Jade took the paper from the man who was shoving it at her.

It was beautiful.

The charcoal black, pencil strokes had captured their very essence. She could see the dark, golden tresses which fell past Althea's waist. Extra strokes had produced the masses of black curls tumbling from Alicia's head and bunching around her shoulders. Lighter strokes were used to represent Jade's short-cropped, pale hair, with its streaks of silver and gold.

The eyes grabbed you. In just those few minutes, the man had seen their secrets and they showed in the eyes.

Althea's eyes were ancient and kind, keeping the worlds secrets. Alicia's, huge, dark and filled with fear and loss. Jade's eyes were full of conflict. Shadows and lines depicted the battle she waged within herself. Jade could understand how the natives could believe that a picture could steal your soul.

"You like?" the man persisted.

"Oh." Jade dragged her eyes from the picture and looked at the artist. His eyes were black, like Alicia's. He tipped his head down to watch his toe as he kicked his old worn work boot at an imaginary spot on the floor. His weathered face was covered in lines and cracks. It was a face used to laughing. If Jade had to guess, she would put him at sixty, at least, maybe more. Right now his eyes kept flickering from the floor to his left, then to his right, then back to the floor.

A young man, probably in his early twenties, and wearing a brown airport security uniform, headed in their direction.

"You like?" the man persisted.

"Yes. I do," Jade told him. "Very much. It is beautiful."

"You buy," he smiled at her. He was missing a couple of teeth and those left were yellowed. "One dollar." The man held out his hand, keeping one eye on the approaching guard.

Jade glanced once more at the picture. She glanced at the approaching guard. It didn't take a genius to realize she was going to be this man's last sale for the day. She handed the picture to Alicia and reached into her pocket. She pulled out a twenty-dollar bill.

The man, once again glanced toward the guard, and then frantically waved the money away. "No. No," he insisted. "One dollar." He turned his hands up, showing his sketchpad and pencil. "No pesos."

Jade placed the bill in his empty hand, and rolled his callused fingers closed over it. Obviously he didn't rely on his art for a living. He started once again to protest. Jade smiled at him. The man's face lit up like a child in a candy shop who had just been told he can have whatever he wants.

"*Gracias. Gracias.*' The man bobbed his head several times; His smile growing wider with each nod.

"You do beautiful work," she told him. She glanced at the guard who had nearly reached them. "Go now." She gave the man a gentle push towards the nearest exit. "Thank you for the beautiful gift," she called out behind him, loud enough for the guard to hear.

Jade turned towards the guard as he was about to follow the old man, cruelty written all over his face. 'Excuse me," she said. She placed a hand on his arm as he made to pass them. "Could you please tell me where the ladies' room is?"

One smile from Jade and all thoughts flew out of the guard's head. He didn't notice the old man slip out the exit and out of his reach.

The loud speaker crackled and a tinny voice announced they were beginning to board their flight. The three walked towards the boarding gate, leaving the guard standing where he was, watching them go, with a stupid grin on his face.

"Well, kiddo," Jade bent down and pulled Alicia into her arms. "Looks like this is the end of the line for us. You be good for Althea and I'll be home as soon as I can." Alicia's eyes glistened with tears. Jade's eyes burned.

"No!" Alicia clung to Jade. Tears spilled over, dampening Jade's shirt. Her small body trembled with anguish.

Althea put her hands on the child's shoulders and gently pulled her back. "It's okay, little one," she said. "I will take good care of you." She turned her eyes towards her niece then. "We will see Jade again. I promise."

Alicia clung to Jade for a moment more, and then allowed Althea to pull her away. She wiped at her tears with rapid, jerky movements, sniffed and stared at Jade. Her large, dark eyes screamed betrayal. Jade's breath caught in her throat and her heart thudded.

"It'll be okay," Althea said. Jade wasn't sure if the words were meant for her or Alicia, but she allowed them to comfort her.

Althea took Alicia's small hand in hers, took the boarding passes from her pocket, and headed to the checkpoint. Alicia slipped her hand from Althea's and ran back to Jade. She shoved the picture at her. "You keep it," she cried. "I don't want it."

She ran back to Althea, took her hand, and tugged Althea towards the gate.

She didn't look back.

Chapter Seven

If she didn't do something to relieve the pressure soon she was going to scream. Screaming might do it. Wouldn't that be cute! She giggled at the thought; A grown woman standing in the middle of a busy street screaming for no apparent reason. Then again, she sobered at the thought, maybe nobody would notice a woman screaming in the street. That might be normal in a city like this.

It was the relentless, silent screams that had her wound so tight.

She had to get out of the city. Away from the cries of a thousand tortured souls, begging for release from their own private hells. Then she could focus on where she was supposed to be.

She was so tired. Too tired to shift, and there weren't any buses this late at night; At least not one leaving the city. It was at times like this that Jade thought about learning to drive.

There was a knock at the door. "Room service," a man's voice announced.

Jade opened the door, and stood to one side to let the young man push the cart into the room. God, he was good looking. A blond-haired, blue-eyed Adonis, like everyone else working at this hotel. She had yet to see one person with any inferior qualities whatsoever. It might make a less secure person a little uncomfortable, surrounded by all these gorgeous specimens of humanity. Jade liked beauty. She surrounded herself with it whenever possible. Even when she had to stay in the city, she could find beauty somewhere. Like at this, her favourite hotel.

"If you require anything else ..." The boy had been busy setting the table by the large picture window, while Jade had been busy watching the way his body moved.

He had managed to produce a linen tablecloth, a china plate, a crystal glass, china teacup, a silver teapot, and silver serving dishes, all from his tiny cart. There was even a vase with a single pink rose, a tall, slender candle set on an old fashion candle holder, which he was now in the process of lighting, and a real linen napkin.

There was enough food for at least two people. For Jade, that was a start. She could always grab a burger later. Part of the price she paid for her gifts. She needed a lot of fuel to keep this body of hers going. Fortunately, she wasn't one of the poor souls who needed to drink blood to survive. She loved her food way too much.

Steam escaped through the small hole at the top of the plate warmer, carrying with it the tantalizing aroma of rare meat. Her lips turned up. She ran her tongue over her suddenly moist lips. Her stomach rumbled.

"Is that an offer?" she asked. Her voice was low, husky. She almost laughed when the boy turned red and nearly tripped over his own feet when he hurried to the door. He had no way of knowing she was actually thinking of what lay beneath that silver lid.

He stopped at the door. The hotel may have hired him for his looks, but they insisted on proper training for all their staff, and his job wasn't finished. He pulled a black folder from his pocket, and opened it.

"Err ... Umm ... You need ..." He swallowed. "Sign here." He looked at her then, his young blue eyes confused and pleading. "Please," he said.

Maybe if he were a few years older, quite a few years older, she would have teased him a bit more to see where it might lead. But, alas, he was just a child. Jade took the folder, signed her name, and handed it back. She didn't release it completely until he looked up at her again. "I'll take that as a no," she said.

She waited until the door was closed before she allowed herself to laugh. That was fun. It was too bad that he was so very young though. It could have been, at least, interesting, if her tastes didn't lean more towards men than pretty boys.

Jade sat down and devoured the steak. Usually, she would have savoured every single morsel, enjoying the way the warmed blood trickled down her throat. Tonight, she barely took the time to notice the taste. She had never been able to eat while on a plane. Today was no exception. Once the steak, running with blood the way she preferred it, was gone she turned her attention to the oven baked potatoes and sautéed mushrooms. When she finished it was a struggle not to lick her plate.

The night beckoned her.

Spread out below her, in all its glitter, the city called. From her vantage point the city was beautiful. Jade knew, close up, it would be like any other city in any other county, with garbage on the streets, broken down buildings, and torn up roads. Every city had its good and its bad parts. And every city had its part where evil preyed. From where she stood tonight, all that glittered was gold. She wanted to relax, and let herself believe that it was true--just for tonight.

Jade wanted to howl at the moon. She wanted to soar through the skies.

She showered, changed into form fitting suede pants, and a pale silk blouse. The cool material caressed her skin. Her nipples peaked. She checked her appearance in the full-length mirror on the bathroom door.

Oh yeah. The clothes worked. The pants cupped the cheeks of her ass. Her nipples strained against the thin material of her blouse, begging to be released, begging to be kissed. Her short-cropped hair, so pale it was almost white with streaks of silver and gold, curled forward to caress her small, elfin face. There would be no mistaking her purpose tonight.

Jade stacked the used dishes on the cart, and rolled it out into the hall. She locked the door, and then pushed the button for the elevator. Someone, somewhere in this city of over half a million people, was going to get laid tonight.

Chapter Eight

Luke pushed his empty plate away, wiped his mouth, or rather tried to wipe his mouth, on the too thin paper napkin. It caught in his beard and tore. He scowled at the waitress. His dark, thunderous looks must have been enough because she didn't bother to ask if everything was okay. She just grabbed his plate, and hurried away as quickly as possible mumbling something about bringing his bill.

It served him right. God only knew why he picked such a dive anyway; probably because it matched his mood. The windows were dirty and cracked. The wallpaper was covered in so much grease and grime it was anyone's guess what it had originally looked like, and it was torn and peeling in places. There was dirt on the floor and counter. The waitress wore a uniform that looked like it hadn't seen the inside of a washing machine in months, if ever.

The cook was worse. She had a cigarette hanging out the corner of her mouth, and when the ashes fell off she didn't even bother pretending to try to remove them from the pot of whatever she had boiling on the stove. Her hair, greasy and limp, was in no way contained by the hair net she had half-heartedly set on the top of her head.

His first instinct had been to turn around and get as far away from this place as possible. Only he knew what his instincts had been worth lately.

Nothing. *Nada.* Zilch.

So he had sat at the cleanest table he could find. He had almost smiled - it was more like a grimace - when the young waitress had wiped a dry cloth over the tabletop, knocking several crumbs to join those on the floor. Her sunny smile was out of place. She made a few attempts at conversation, finally giving up when all she got were a few grunts for her trouble.

Luke had ordered steak, rare, and was actually surprised by how good it tasted. That would explain why there were so many people willing to risk their health by eating in a place like this.

The waitress returned with his bill. She laid it on the table in front of him, shuffled her feet a couple of times, and said, "I hope everything was to your satisfaction, sir."

Luke had to admire her dedication to her job. He wasn't sure he would have bothered if the roles were reversed. He looked at her then. This time he really looked, and he saw that the uniform had been washed so much that it was a pale shadow of its original color, and although it was stained there were no new stains. Her hair was clean and tied with a ribbon in a tight pony that hung down her back, and even his rudeness couldn't completely dampen the sparkle in her blue eyes. She glowed from the inside out.

Luke smiled, actually allowed his lips to curve into a real, heart-felt smile, showing his almost obscenely perfect teeth. "The steak was delicious," he said. He glanced at the bill, pulled out two twenties from his pocket, and handed both to the girl. "Keep the change."

She looked at the bills and her eyes widened. "You've made a mistake, sir," she said. "A twenty more than covers the bill."

Luke grinned, that devastating grin of his that usually had women falling all over themselves to please him, and replied. "Just call it an apology for my earlier rude behaviour."

"But ..."

"No buts. I haven't had such a delicious steak since I left home." It was the truth. He pushed back his chair, rose to his full height, winked, and headed for the door. Behind him he heard the girl sigh. He smiled. Things were beginning to look up.

An hour later, he was sitting at the hotel bar, brooding into his half empty glass.

"Got fifty bucks, Mister?"

Luke turned towards the voice and nearly fell off his chair. *My God! She's a baby.* "How old are you?" he blurted.

The girl shaped her garishly painted lips into a pout, and blew him a kiss. Her dress was short enough to be indecent, on anyone. Her hair was pulled into two pigtails. She looked like a schoolgirl. She probably was.

"How old do you want me to be?" she countered.

"Old enough to know you should be safely tucked in bed this time of night," he growled at her. He'd been doing that a lot lately. Maybe Erzsébet was right, and he should get himself laid.

"Are you offering to tuck me in?"

"I don't tuck in babies." Luke turned back to his drink.

"Hell, Mister. I'm twenty-five."

Luke turned back to the girl. "Yeah," he snarled at her. "And I'm old enough to be your grandfather." *Several times over.*

He waited while the girl looked him up and down. Apparently she didn't think he was worth the trouble.

"Your loss," she shot at him. She started towards the other end of the bar.

Luke put his hand on her arm. She was obviously used to dealing with men. She just looked from his hand to his face and back again, without saying a word.

"What do you charge for the whole night?" Luke couldn't believe what he was about to do.

"Three hundred," she said. "And I don't do no kinky stuff."

That makes two of us. Luke pulled out his wallet, and counted out three hundred dollars. Her eyes widened. For a minute he thought she was going to try to renegotiate. She didn't.

"There's only one catch." Luke held the money just out of her reach.

"I told you, Mister. No kinky stuff." She looked at the money. Probably more money than she had seen in a long time. Then she looked at Luke. Her eyes narrowed, and she chewed on her bottom lip. "Okay. What do I have to do?" She reached for the money.

"Go to bed."

The girl laughed. "What'd you think you were paying for Mister?" She smiled at Luke, licked her lips, and said. "It will be my pleasure."

"Alone."

"What!" The girl's eyes widened. She looked at Luke as if he were insane.

"Alone." Luke looked down at her fingers, wrapped around the money. "If you take this money, you will go home, alone. I don't want to see you again tonight."

The girl shrugged. "Whatever." She rolled her eyes. She sighed. "Figures. Someone as good looking as you had to be gay."

Luke was shocked. Gay! Him! He had a sudden urge to throw her down, and show her just how much of a man he was. He pushed his free hand through his hair. *What was he thinking? She was still a child.* He shoved the money at her, turned her around, and pushed her towards the door. "Home. Now," he ordered.

Luke turned back to the bar and downed his whiskey it one swallow. He was just about to order another when the sudden silence in the bar made him turn around.

Now she was more his style.

She was tall. Her pale hair framed her elfin features like a cloud. Her taut nipples strained at the tight fabric of her blouse. His mouth watered at the thought of those nipples in his mouth. The way her pants hugged and caressed every curve of her long legs as she moved towards him made him wish she were leaving so he could watch the way they were sure to caress her ass.

She walked with confidence. Sex poured off her in waves. It was in every step she took. Most women of her stature would try to downplay their height. Not her. She moved with poise and confidence. Even with her two-inch heels he was taller than her.

Luke caught the glitter of jewellery on her left ankle when she took a step. He looked at the symbols on the anklet, and a distant memory flickered and then was gone. He shrugged it off and slowly moved his eyes back up that luscious frame to her face.

Her eyes were a strange shade of amber. They seemed to swirl with mystery and secrets. He was instantly hard. If the child could see him now she would definitely know where his interests lie.

She stood in front of him. A dream wrapped in a woman's body. She chewed on her lower lip. On her it was sexy. Every male eye was on her, but she didn't seem to notice. She looked only at him.

He stood perfectly still as her strange eyes traveled his form from head to foot. The slow, determined movement was like a caress against his skin. Her eyes paused at his crotch.

She cocked her head. "Looks like I got here just in time." Her voice caressed him like a lover's hand. He grew harder, and almost winced. Almost.

"Depends?" He stood there, legs splayed; trying to give himself some much needed room. He pointedly looked at her straining nipples, and licked his lips. It was almost impossible to keep from leaning forward and running his tongue over the shiny fabric of her blouse.

"What did you have in mind?" He knew what she had in mind. It was written all over her. The woman was in heat. It rolled off her in waves. Her musky scent called to him. A call he intended to answer very soon. With the moon, and the scent of the woman pulling him he had no choice.

They circled each other in some bizarre mating ritual. It was a game. Nothing more. They both knew where it was going to end up.

Get out! Run! Before it's too late. A voice screamed in his head. *Shut up,* he answered. Maybe he should listen to the voice. Then, again, it hadn't been right in days.

He knew he looked good. He could see it in her amber eyes. The way they glowed when she looked at him. The way she licked her lips ever so slightly—like she couldn't wait to taste him.

"I'm pretty sure you can guess." She played her role well.

Luke grunted. "What's it going to cost me?" He liked to get rid of the business part up front.

She ran her eyes over his well-worn jeans and shirt, "A few hours of your time and the price of a room. Or would you prefer the park?" She was cocking that eyebrow at him again and he nearly lost control. Who knew such a simple gesture could be so damned sexy."

The mere thought of taking this woman in the park nearly made him cream his jeans. "Right this way," he said indicating the stairs at the back of the room with a sweep of his arm. *Oh yeah!* He was salivating as he watched her walk away. His imagination had come nowhere near the perfection as her pants caressed her cheeks with each step she took.

They didn't make it to the first landing before Luke reached out and caught one of those gently swaying cheeks in one large hand. She faltered as electricity shot between them. The scent of her need rose in the air between them, and Luke inhaled deeply letting it fuel his own need.

She smelled like heather and sunshine, and sex. Hot—creamy—sex. He growled low in his throat and gently squeezed the cheek resting in the palm of his hand. "Move," he growled. "Unless you want me to take you right here."

Jade's amber eyes sparkled with mischief and something that made his pants tighten even more. She slowly licked her top lip, and practically purred. "Where to?"

Luke swallowed, swept her up into his arms, and ran up the remaining stairs to his room. She weighed no more than a child as she nuzzled his neck. He had no problem holding her while he retrieved his key from his pocket, and unlocked the door.

Luke tossed the key on the only table, and kicked the door shut with his foot. He didn't need to check. It was the type of door that was always locked.

Jade chose that moment to lick the vein on the side of his neck. Luke was so distracted he stumbled. Jade's feet landed on the floor between them with a small thud when he reached out to balance himself against the wall, but he didn't loosen his grip. The room was filled with the scent of humour, lust, wolf, and *cat!*

Luke spun Jade around so that she was against the door, thereby putting himself between her and the unseen threat. He leaned down and nuzzled her neck, letting his own senses reach around the room. They were alone.

Definitely alone.

He sniffed, and tasted the air. Heather and sunshine, musk, wolf. The scent of the cat had already faded. Luke forced himself to relax. The scent of the cat bothered him, but he would worry about that later. *Much later.* Right now he had much more important things on his mind. *Besides, there's no immediate danger.* He nibbled the neck he was nuzzling.

Her quiet laughter reminded him of bells tinkling in the wind. *"Watch the fangs, wolf."* Luke froze, his teeth gently scraping the pretty neck. *"I don't want to kill you."* The voice was tinged with humour, but the words were very serious--and inside his head.

"Who are you?" He growled the words with his mind, but there was no answer. *Was his conscience a woman?* The little voice in his head wasn't usually female. Besides, he knew the law as well as he knew his own name. If he did bite the woman, he would be signing his own death warrant. There were only two times that were even remotely acceptable when it came to biting a human. Self-defence; and your life better be in immediate danger. He inhaled the scent of the woman in his arms. No danger there. *Unless she's planning to screw my brains out and I wouldn't fight that.*

The only other time it was acceptable to bite a human, was if the human happened to be your mate. It wasn't that rare of an occurrence either. With so few female werewolves in the world, more and more males were finding their mates in the human population; More of the females as well. As her scent surrounded him, Luke shuddered. *Now that might be a fate worse than death.* He had no intention of ever mating. Once, long ago, he had thought it an option, but her betrayal and the consequent death of his parents and most of his people had abused him of that notion.

There were times when he watched his friends with their children that he wondered what it would be like to be a father. If he were to choose a mate amongst the lycan population then their offspring would be lycan. However, if he found his mate amongst the human population their offspring would only have the lycan gene. The gene would be passed down from generation to generation, but only if it was dominant would the young actually become lycan. There were times when the gene would lay dormant for centuries in a family before one would be born with the dominant gene.

There was no worry that Luke would ever choose a human mate--again. You couldn't guarantee how a human would react. It was better just to use them for sex, and leave. All offspring had to be monitored for the gene, and those carrying it had to be watched for signs of turning. Luke had been on his way home after checking on the birth of a latent lycan when he decided to spend the night in the city. Several members of his pack had once been humans. But they had all been exceptional, and they had all been psychic. Being psychic seemed to make it easier for them to accept the lycan gene and survive the change.

Jade shifted slightly drawing Luke's attention. He welcomed the distraction from his thoughts. "Having second thoughts?" Her voice was a smoky purr.

Luke's lust rose at the tone. "Second. Third. What's it matter. They are all about you." He began opening the small round buttons on her blouse, and growled when his large hands fumbled. When she laughed, he grasped the sides of the blouse, and yanked. The frustrating buttons flew everywhere.

Jade laughed, and put her hands in his dark hair, standing on her tiptoes she reached up to capture his mouth with hers. Power sparked between them. Luke groaned. *Maybe she was going to be dangerous to his health. She was definitely dangerous to his good sense.* Cupping the cheeks of her ass in his large hands he lifted until she wrapped her legs around his waist. She didn't release his mouth. Her smaller tongue slid between his lips to explore his sharp, even teeth.

Luke moaned. "You're killing me." Jade loosened her hold on him so he could pull her blouse off her arms, to discard it by the door. Jade reached under Luke's shirt to caress the rock hard abs beneath. Luke pinned her between himself and the door as she pulled the shirt over his head, and tossed it beside her own.

Jade leaned into him, and with the tip of her tongue flicked one taut nipple. Luke's growl rumbled deep in his chest, and he grabbed her ass as he spun her away from the door. Jade laughed, and caught his shoulders to keep from falling backwards. He took a couple of long strides and they fell on the bed together.

The room was small. There was a table, two chairs, and a bed. A sliding glass door led to a small balcony, and another small door led to the bathroom. Neither of them cared about the room. The bed was the only thing they were interested in, and it was huge.

Luke stood up, not once taking his eyes from the woman on the bed as he undid the buttons on his jeans, and slowly slid them over his hips and down his muscled legs. He wasn't wearing any underwear. Jade leaned on her elbows staring, as his erection sprang free of the confines of his pants. She slowly ran her tongue over her lips, and his erection grew.

The scent of their arousal filled the room. The power sparking from her eyes should have concerned Luke; instead it turned him on more. He kicked his shoes off, and his pants followed. He reached down and tore his socks off. He hated wearing them anyway. He leaned towards Jade. "Fairs fair," he said, and caught one taut nipple between his teeth.

Jade moaned with pleasure as he laved the nipple, and then moved to worship the other. While he was busy suckling, his hands were busy with her pants. He loosened them, and slid them down over her hips. Releasing her nipples he leaned back, and slowly slid her pants down her long legs, and tossed them away.

It was Luke's turn to stare. His eyes glazed with lust, and he licked his lips in anticipation. She lay before him with her legs slightly splayed--an offering to the gods. "God you are beautiful." Her naked skin glowed with power, and her amber eyes swirled with mystery. *What are you?* he wondered. *Not lycan. I'd know if you were lycan.*

She cocked her eyebrow, and he groaned. "Do you know what you do to me when you look at me like that?" He dropped to his knees beside the bed and pulled her so she was hanging off the edge. "I can't wait to taste you." He lifted her legs exposing her most vulnerable self to his hot gaze. Then ever so slowly he leaned over, and nibbled her knee. His beard scratched her skin, and the friction nearly drove her insane. He alternated sides, taking his time. When his mouth finally reached her creamy center Jade was writhing with pleasure.

Luke inhaled deeply. "Oh, yeah."

"Oh! My! God!" Jade screamed the words as he slid his tongue deep inside her honeyed core. Luke savoured every drop of her orgasm. She was still trembling when he slid first one, and then a second finger deep inside. "You are so tight. So hot."

Luke was surprised at how tight she was. And pleased. Her fingers tangled in his dark hair. With her head thrown back against the sheets she rode his pumping fingers to another climax. Luke removed his fingers, and slowly licked them clean. Her eyes shone as she watched him. Her breath came in short, harsh bursts. God. He hadn't enjoyed a woman like this in a very long time. *Too long.*

He leaned forward and slowly licked her. She moaned and arched towards his mouth. Slowly he worked his way up her body. Nibbling and licking as he went, spending long moments to worship each nipple. When he slid his aching shaft into her hot creamy core she was already writhing in the throes of another climax. Luke covered her mouth with his, swallowing her mindless screams as he shattered with his own mind bending climax.

Mine!

The word roared in his head.

Chapter Nine

There were hands everywhere. Warm, firm hands. They stroked her breasts, bringing her nipples to firm peaks. A hand traveled down the outside of her leg, leaving a burning trail through the thin material of her jeans. It moved to the inside of her leg, and hot liquid pooled at her center.

Slowly, too slowly to her way of thinking, his hand traveled along the inside of her leg until it reached its destination. She was burning for his touch. It was both exciting and frightening. Never before had anyone touched her like this.

His hand was rough as he rubbed it against her jeans.

She opened her mouth to tell him to stop. To quit teasing her, before the flames consumed her.

No sound came.

Gemma jerked to a sitting position. Sweat trickled between her breasts. Her heart pounded. Slowly her eyes adjusted to the dark. She took a deep, cleansing breath. Relief flooded through her.

It was just a dream, brought on by the coming of the full moon, or a nightmare, depending on how you looked at it.

She was safe in her own room, in her own bed. Alone. She listened to the familiar sounds of the night, and slowly relaxed. A glance at the bedside clock told her it was four a.m. No sense trying to get back to sleep. She had to get up in an hour anyway.

She jumped out of bed and headed for the bathroom. A hot shower was the ticket. Gemma took two steps and a wave of dizziness enveloped her. She had to grab the dresser to keep herself from falling to the floor.

What was wrong with her?

Gemma was really worried now. She couldn't remember being sick a single day in her life, and now it seemed she was sick every day. Something was definitely wrong.

The dizziness passed. She clutched her stomach and ran for the toilet. Twenty minutes later she was still leaning into the bowl. The contents of her evening meal floated in the water, undigested. Dry heaves wracked her bruised body. One more, long tremor shook her, and then they stopped. Gemma waited several more minutes before carefully climbing to her feet. Maybe if she moved very, very, slowly she could make it the four steps to the shower.

The stinging spray of icy water on her skin helped her feel better. It always did.

What had she done? For days now she had wracked her brains, and still hadn't come up with an answer. The last time she could remember feeling good was the day before she went to the bar with Sara.

Stupid. Stupid. Stupid.

She knew the dangers of drinking. Not just the usual ones, either. Losing control for her kind meant the possibility of exposure. Or worse.

Why had she done it?

What had she done?

If only she could remember. She was sure that if she could remember what had happened the night she went to the bar, then everything would be okay. It would have to be. She had a vague recollection of some guy. Who was he? She tried to focus on his image. She tried to get a good look at his face. She pressed the heels of her hands to her temples, and tried to still the sudden pain.

Damn! Every time she was almost there. Every time she could just about see his face, this happened.

She looked at the clock. Great! It was five thirty. If she didn't hurry she was going to be late, and it wasn't like her to be late. If she was late today, Elizabeth would know something was wrong; if she didn't already.

Elizabeth was an alpha female, as well as being a healer, and had the gift of precognition. Gemma knew she should go to her.

She was afraid.

What if she'd done something bad? What if she'd broken one of their laws? Uncle Luke would have to punish her. He'd had to punish Gheorgès when he'd broken their laws. Gemma hadn't actually met Gheorgès. He had *died* a long time before she was born, but she knew the story. As much as Uncle Luke loved her, if she broke their laws she *would* be punished. As Alpha of the pack he would have no choice, and as a temporary member of his pack she was under his domain. Even her parents wouldn't be able to save her if she broke their laws.

When Gemma arrived at The Wolf Center, affectionately known by the pack as 'The Den', at six o'clock Elizabeth was already there. Gemma had known, deep down, that she would be. Whenever Uncle Luke was away, Elizabeth took control. On the edge of the town of Willow Bend, The Den consisted of a museum of the area wildlife and a research facility for the study of wolves. It was also a veterinary training hospital, and the reason Gemma was there. Gemma was studying to be a doctor, and because of the physical nature of Lycans she also needed training in veterinary studies. To pay for that training she worked as a guide at The Den, amongst other things, whenever she wasn't actually working with Elizabeth.

"Morning, Elizabeth." Gemma forced herself to act normal. At least as normal as possible with her head pounding and her heart racing.

Elizabeth's dark eyes searched Gemma's face carefully. Then they scanned her from head to toe, searching. On the way back up they stayed on her stomach for several seconds. Gamma wanted to squirm. She tried to force herself to stand still. Her hand had a mind of its own. It strayed to her bangs and shoved them back. They fell forward.

Elizabeth's eyes strayed to the movement. She grinned. It was a grin full of knowledge and secrets. "Good morning, child," she finally said. "I'll be glad when your hair gets back to normal."

Secretly, Gemma agreed. She had thought about coloring her hair, again, but when she'd mixed the dye, the smell had made her throw up. She was glad she hadn't let Sara convince her to use a permanent color. This should wash out completely in another week or so. Until then, she would have to put up with streaks of blonde and brown. The bangs, however, would take much longer to grow back to normal.

She chose to ignore Elizabeth's comment. "Have you been here long?" Gemma asked instead.

"Depends what you call long." Elizabeth chuckled and winked at Gemma, in a rare show of humour. "A century or two isn't all that long."

Gemma couldn't help herself. She smiled, and it felt good.

"Been here all night," Elizabeth continued. "I went running last night. Stopped in by your place but you were sleeping." Again with that searching look. "Funny thing, though," Elizabeth said. "It doesn't look like you slept much at all. Are you okay?"

"I'm fine," Gemma said quickly. Maybe a little too quickly because Elizabeth gave her the once over again. "I just didn't sleep well."

"Good to know." Elizabeth tilted her head to one side and seemed to be listening to something, or someone. Then she straightened and stared straight through Gemma. "You suppose to go out overnight"?

Gemma nodded. What was Elizabeth up to? She knew well enough that Gemma had an overnight. Elizabeth knew everything that happened, not only at The Den, but in the entire town.

"Actually..." Gemma pushed her bangs back, and then puffed at them once when they fell back in place. She glanced meaningfully at the office door. Just out of reach behind Elizabeth. "... We are heading out to Wolf Lake Falls. So if you'll excuse me, I have to check on the supplies." Wolf Lake didn't actually have a waterfall, just a series of three sets of rapids in a row. However, the sound of the rushing water, coupled with the calm waters of the lake at the bottom, made it a favourite spot to take the overnight campers. And it was the only site with a cabin for the off season.

Gemma tried to slip past Elizabeth, but her small hand caught her arm. "Don't go."

Gemma spun back to face Elizabeth. "What is it?" she asked, suddenly worried. "Are you alright?" To her, Elizabeth looked the same as she always did. Her hair was neatly plaited to her waist. Her clothes were immaculate. Her dark eyes glittered with life and laughter. They looked like they were laughing at Gemma right now.

Then they changed; became serious. "*I* am fine, child," she said.

"Then what?" Gemma knew she sounded testy. She was testy.

"*Don't* go to Wolf Lake Falls."

Gemma chewed on her bottom lip, thoughtfully, and looked at the older woman. What was going on? Don't go to Wolf Lake Falls? She and George always took the overnight to Wolf Lake Falls. Especially during a full moon, and tonight was the beginning of the cycle. "Is something wrong?"

"Sara can go." Elizabeth's tone was clipped.

"No way!" Gemma shook the hand off her arm. "Are you nuts?" Oh crap! What's gotten into her lately? Nobody. Absolutely nobody argued with Elizabeth. Except maybe Uncle Luke.

Elizabeth drew herself to her full five feet three inches and looked Gemma in the eye. Despite her smaller size she gave the impression of towering over Gemma. "Are you challenging me?"

Gemma glared down at the smaller woman. She held her eyes for about two seconds, and then dropped hers to the floor. She began worrying at an imaginary spot on the pristine floor with her right toe. "No, Ma'am," she finally mumbled.

"I didn't think so." Elizabeth turned and headed for the office. She stopped abruptly and Gemma, who had been following meekly behind, nearly bumped into her. "Call Sara. She'll need to pack."

"Yes, Elizabeth." Gemma hated the way she squirmed before the woman's watchful eyes. One day, she told herself, she would stand up to Elizabeth. One day. Just not today.

Elizabeth reached out and patted Gemma's shoulder. Gemma looked up and saw compassion in the older woman's eyes. "It'll be all right, child," she told her. "Things have a way of working out for the best."

Elizabeth turned then and entered Luke's office without saying another word.

Gemma went behind the small desk in the reception area. She dialled the familiar number, and while the phone rang she worried about Sara's reaction. This was terrible. Just yesterday Sara had threatened to claw Georges' eyes out; all because George had made her feel like a child in front of Mark. Gemma was afraid to leave the two of them alone. Sure, there would be a dozen other people with them, but Gemma knew George. He wouldn't let the presence of anyone keep him from what he wanted.

And he wanted Sara.

Gemma wasn't blind. She could see it in the way he watched her. She was surprised Sara couldn't see it. Maybe Sara did see it, and just didn't care. She treated him like a brother, which seemed to infuriate George. It really wasn't a good idea to put those two together for the night. Especially with the moon rising. Gemma prayed that without her calming presence, George would be able to control his wilder instincts.

Gemma watched with trepidation as the group climbed into the center's two Hummers and drove off. After her initial tirade, Sara had accepted the fact that she, not Gemma, would be spending the night with George.

"He better not try and tell me what to do?" Sara had stomped around, putting supplies in the packs. Occasionally she glared at George, where he lounged insolently against the doorframe. "I don't know why you can't go. You're used to handling this beast."

"Afraid you can't handle it?" George taunted. He laughed when Sara threw a can of beans at him. "Maybe it's me you're afraid of." He sauntered out the door, a self-satisfied grin on his handsome face, before Sara could reply.

Hours later, Gemma locked the office and climbed into her own jeep. Her stomach grumbled. She thought about going to the Hub for dinner. She hadn't seen Tony for a while. Tony was in his late twenties, but most of the time he acted like a teenager. His dad spoiled him rotten, probably because his mother died during childbirth, but he was always looking for a party and always a lot of fun.

Gemma decided what she really wanted was something fresh. To tell the truth, the idea of anything cooked made her stomach queasy. She honked as she drove past the diner. By the time she pulled in front of her own cabin a plan had formulated.

She would go for a hunt. Nothing big. Just a rabbit. Or maybe a beaver. Then she could run down to Wolf Lake Falls and howl at the full moon. Of course George would know it was her. She just wished she could see the look on the other's faces. If she timed it just right, Sara would be right in the middle of her story when they heard her.

This was going to be fun.

Gemma sniffed the air. She was alone. She knew she would be, but the need to be sure had been drilled into her at a very early age.

She hurried into the house and removed her clothes. Moonlight bathed her pale skin when she left the cabin, and the early spring air brought goose bumps to the surface, but she knew she would be warm enough once the change took effect. She didn't bother to lock the door. The pack owned over one thousand acres of private forest and mountain, not including what they owned in town, and her cabin was built on these acres.

Gemma walked the ten feet to the edge of the clearing. The moon beckoned. Its brilliant rays teased and enticed. She was a child again, feeling its pull for the first time. Tonight she would be free and let the moon work its magic.

She knelt. Catching her medallion between her thumb and forefinger she began to gently rub it. Gemma had always been able to control the change at will. It was one of the reasons that she and George worked the overnights. She envisioned the wolf in her head. Concentrated on the vision. A warm tingling began in her fingers. It traveled up her arms. It spread to her legs. She could feel something crawling beneath her skin. The transformation had begun. Hot, piercing pain spread through her veins. A million needles broke through her skin, as fur spread over her body. She could hear and feel her bones breaking. Gemma screamed. She let go of the medallion and wrapped her arms around herself. She rolled to the ground, murmuring a prayer as darkness stole over her.

Chapter Ten

David Woods stared at the sandwich that had just been delivered. White-hot anger slashed through his veins and throbbed at his temples. Everything around him turned red. He had an almost overwhelming urge to march down to the deli and rip someone's throat out. David tore the top layer of bread off, and ripped out the offending slice of ham. He threw it against the door. How long has he been getting his dinner from there? Five years? Moreover, not once had he *ever* bought any kind of meat.

He looked at the slimy trail down the door and the meat on the floor. Damn! Why had he done that?

David took several, deep, calming breaths. He grabbed a paper towel, and walked towards the door. He had better get this mess cleaned up. Near the door he froze, and sniffed the air. *What was that smell?* He cocked his head sideways and looked at the meat, a puzzled expression on his face. He jerked his hand down and picked up the offending slice of meat. The thought of eating it made his stomach churn. The smell made his mouth water.

He shoved the ham into his mouth and swallowed.

David Woods tore the door open. He loped down the hall and out of the building.

A rush of air hit him. David stopped. What was he doing out here? He couldn't just leave. His equipment was on the counter. There were vials of blood still waiting to be examined. His blood was in one of those vials. David had drawn it that morning. He was going to find out what was wrong with him, one way or the other. It was the perfect opportunity. The other research assistant had the week off, and Dr. Madison was at a fundraiser. He had even labelled the container 'specimen three,' just in case someone came in. It didn't happen often. Nevertheless, even Dr. Madison couldn't keep the investors from making unexpected appearances. Dr. Madison might even show up after the fundraiser to check on things. He was so paranoid about his research that even David, who had been working with him for five years, wasn't allowed in the underground labs. David wondered, not for the first time, what exactly the doctor was doing down there. There were plenty of rumours—some even hinted at the doctor's deeds being illegal. David knew it had something to do with DNA manipulation, and the government was financing the whole thing. They were merging the genes of one animal with the genes of another, in the hopes of developing a new gene therapy as a cure for cancer. So far they hadn't been successful.

David wondered, briefly, if he had closed the door. He knew he hadn't locked it.

The spicy aroma of sizzling sausages caught his attention. Hunger was a machete slicing at his insides. He forgot about the door, and everything else, as he turned towards the tantalizing aroma of sausage, and started to jog.

He bought two. He didn't bother with mustard or onions. He threw the dry buns to a flock of squawking gulls, and then wolfed down the meat.

The breeze ruffled his hair. He sniffed again. His brain took a while to sort through the myriad smells. The overpowering lavender scent of cheap perfume reminded him of the woman who had raised him. How he hated that smell. Had the stench of rotting fruit and vegetables from the dumpster behind a nearby restaurant always been this strong? Why hadn't he noticed it before? The sweet odour of freshly mowed grass; these and much, much more traveled on the breeze.

His head was splitting. David reached into the pocket of his lab coat and pulled out a bottle of pills. He shook two into his hand. He looked at them, wondering briefly where they had come from. He shrugged and popped them into his mouth. The pills began to work immediately. The tension left his body. His headache began to ease. He was floating.

Was this how the girls felt? Had they been floating on a cloud? Or had they felt like they were drowning—able to see the surface just above them, yet unable to reach it. He knew how he had felt. Powerful. Invincible. In control.

Not like in school.

In school he had been a geek. His ears had been too big. His eyes had been enormous, behind his Coke-bottle glasses. Too tall ... too skinny... too smart. He had shown them. He'd worked hard, gotten excellent grades, and continued his education. He had worked out at the gym three times a week – he still did. When he was in his first year of University he had laser surgery. It had been while he was in university that he had worked for the pharmaceutical company. That's where he had learned how to manufacture his own special party favours.

Like the one he'd slipped *her*.

He should go home to bed. That's what he should do. If he had some decent sleep he would feel better. Lack of sleep had to be responsible for his headaches.

Something crawled along his arm, just under his skin.

He thought about his blood back at the lab waiting to be tested. What if there was something wrong with him? What would he do? He couldn't worry about that until he knew for sure. He couldn't panic. When *she* bit him he'd panicked.

His fingers strayed to his shoulder and he gently massaged it. He rolled his shoulder. There was no pain. It was more like a tingling, or burning sensation, and it was in all his limbs, not just his shoulder. There wasn't a mark on his shoulder where she had bitten him. Looking at it, you couldn't tell she had even broken the skin. Thinking back, David wasn't sure it had even hurt at the time, but the blood had been everywhere, and there had been so much of it.

He had been shocked when she'd bitten him. She shouldn't have been able to move.

She hadn't been moving when he'd left her in the clearing.

David had panicked. He admitted it now. He could still feel his fingers closing around her throat. His thumbs slowly applying pressure, his arms beginning to tingle. It had been that sudden jolt, and the fire bursting through his thumb that had snapped him out of it. He'd jumped back and stared at the medallion lying against her pale skin. A wolf had stared back at him. Its eyes glowed red.

Frowning, he looked at his thumb and the image of that same wolf stared back at him. Funny it didn't hurt. A tattoo burned into the skin like that should hurt. It seemed more distinct today. Clearer. Every time he looked at it his thoughts turned to *her*.

His stomach rumbled, and David quickened his pace. He decided to stop at the grocery store on his way home. All he had in the fridge was the makings of a salad. He was pretty sure that wasn't going to be enough. What he really wanted was a nice, juicy steak.

Chapter Eleven

The park was beautiful. The full moon glistened off the tranquil surface of the fishpond. Eden in the middle of the city. Maggie couldn't see it for the tears in her eyes but she knew it was there. She knew this park as well as she knew the back of her hand. She had spent many hours here, day and night, by herself, thinking; Away from everyone and everything.

Damn them anyway. She slapped at her eyes with the back of her hand and kept walking. Who did they think they were? Brenda was supposed to be her very best friend. Just last week Jason had been trying his best to get into *her* pants.

"Come on, baby," he'd said. "If you love me you'll do it." But she hadn't and now he was '*doing it*' with Brenda. Well damn him. Damn Brenda too. She didn't need them. She didn't need anyone.

The gentle swaying of the swings in the breeze drew her and she sat down. She couldn't go home. She was supposed to be at Brenda's all night. She wasn't going back to the party. Besides, if she showed up crying her Mom would want to know what happened. She couldn't tell her Mom she'd walked in on Jason and Brenda in bed. Her Mom would call Brenda's Mom and all hell would break loose.

Maybe she *should* tell her Mom what happened. Why should she care if Brenda got in trouble? It was obvious Brenda didn't care about her.

Then again, that was the trouble. She did care what happened to Brenda. Brenda *was* her very best friend. She had been her best friend since kindergarten. They spent every weekend at each other's houses. She was the sister Maggie didn't have. Hell, their families vacationed together. You couldn't throw that away because of one stupid night.

What were they thinking anyway? They had to know she would catch them. Brenda was her best friend. What kind of a friend made out with your boy friend?

The moon slipped behind a cloud, blocking out the light. A sudden shiver passed through her and she pulled her jacket closed. The heavy scent of lilacs hung in the air. She inhaled their sweet fragrance. Lilacs were her favourite. They shouted spring better than anything else. She loved the way they smelled. She loved the solitude of the park at night. No laughing, pushy kids. No barking dogs.

No teenage boy making out with his girlfriend's best friend.

The usually calming atmosphere of the park at night did nothing for her. Not even the heady odour of her favourite flowers could calm her. She grabbed the ropes of the swing and walked back as far as she could. She jumped on the wooden slat, kicked her feet out in front of her, and soared. She pumped harder and harder, rising higher and higher. The chill air felt good against her face. Her tear stained cheeks dried and she began to relax.
*****

The wolf stepped on a twig. It snapped. The sound echoed in the quiet night. The Beast froze. Then slowly it moved forward. Its prey was straight ahead. It sniffed, catching the scent of the female, mingled with the strong scent of flowers. She was alone. The wolf could smell ... Anger. It hesitated. A voice inside its head told it to go back; to leave this place and this human.

Hunger drove it forward.

It no longer stayed in the shadows. There was no need. Clouds covered the moon. The night was dark. If the clouds moved and the human looked this way she wouldn't see it. The wolf blended into the night. She wouldn't see it until it wanted her to.

The darkness didn't impede it. It had excellent night vision. The breeze carried her scent. It was intoxicating. She was young and vulnerable. Her blood called to the wolf.

Its stomach rumbled. It growled, deep in its throat.

She looked in its direction. She jammed her feet on the ground to stop the motion of the swing and nearly fell on her face.

The taste of fear danced on the breeze. The wolf's ears leaned back. The tip of its tail began to twitch. It could smell her blood rushing through her veins. The wolf ran its tongue over its canines in a vaguely human gesture. The moon broke free from the clouds. The girl began to run.

Chapter Twelve

Gemma opened her eyes. Cautiously! Everything was dark. It was like trying to look through heavy gauze. Hunger was a living thing, gnawing at the edges of her sanity. Her body was agony and the fear was paralyzing.

Was she dead? Was this what it was like when you died? Blind, in utter agony, and terrified to move. If so, then she really didn't want to be dead. Not that she wanted to be dead if it were all fairy clouds and bliss. She had barely started living. She had the whole world to explore. No. She couldn't be dead.

If not dead, then what was wrong with her? Think. Come on, Gemma. Think.

Thinking wasn't easy with that incessant fear trying to take control. She had to calm down and think. *Take a deep breath and relax. Now, isn't that better?* A little calmer. If only her heart would quit racing. This was crazy. Now she was talking to herself. She hadn't done that since the first change. Back then she had talked to her wolf-self like it was another being, not a part of her, until she found the path between her two selves that helped to keep her sane. Without it, she might have lost herself completely to the wolf and the bloodlust. She couldn't let that happen, ever. In the meantime, she had to find out exactly where she was.

Take a deep breath. What do you smell?

Several images rushed through her mind ... grass ... pine trees ... the carcass of a decaying squirrel. This was how the wolf communicated, with pictures instead of words. These pictures didn't really help her. There were pine trees, grass and squirrels at home, and Gemma knew, deep down, that she wasn't at home.

A steady creaking noise intruded on her thoughts. A wave of dizziness swept over her at the suddenness of visions flashing before her eyes. Grass ... trees ... grass. *Stop waving your head around and let me see what's going on.*

The swaying stopped as suddenly as it began. Gemma took the opportunity to look for something familiar. She was lying on a bed of pine needles, almost completely hidden behind the long branches of a very old pine. She could see a cement wall to her left, and the grass to her right was even and tidy. A blur of movement brought a young girl on a swing into focus.

The wolf rose from its bed of needles and moved silently to the edge of the tree. Its eyes were steady on the girl. Hunger pricked its stomach. A sense of unease enveloped Gemma. The wolf should be a part of her, not a separate entity. Without her there could be no wolf.

The wolf didn't seem to realize this. It ignored Gemma and slunk forward.

What are you doing? We shouldn't be here. We need to go back to the cabin. There she would be safe in her own secure little world, not roaming around a strange park, stalking a human. *Stop!*

The wolf hesitated. A twig snapped beneath its paw. The creaking of the swing stopped. The wolf looked directly at the girl. The fear shining in her eyes was a beacon. The girl glanced somewhere to the right of them. The wolf's ears bent back and its tail began to slowly wag. The sour scent of her fear was intoxicating, urging them on. The wolf's heart pumped with excitement. The girl made her decision, turned and ran towards the far gate.

Gemma enjoyed a good chase as much as the next wolf. The adrenaline rush while hunting was incomparable, and today was no different. Gemma found herself caught in the excitement of the pounding feet, with the wind in her face, and she forgot everything else.

The wolf pounced. Its teeth closed over the girl's leg, bringing her to the ground. As realization dawned, Gemma's scream echoed across two minds. The wolf released the girl and slunk back towards the safety of the pines.

With the wolf under control, Gemma let her guard down. Once again darkness swept over Gemma, this time like a welcome blanket.

Chapter Thirteen

Amber eyes flew open.

Something was out there.

Jade was wide-awake. She snuggled against the man lying behind her, and inhaled deeply. Musky pine and campfire invaded her senses, making her tingle all the way to her toes. Jade longed to roll over and wake him with a kiss. The mere thought of his hands on her skin made her burn. Just reach up and kiss him. That's all she had to do and the pleasure would begin again. Jade allowed herself a few more seconds of fantasy before she sighed, and careful not to wake him, slid out from beneath his arm.

Their clothing was strewn around the room. Her silk blouse was crumpled with several buttons missing. Her slacks were in the same condition. A testimonial to their impatience the night before. Jade pulled on the clothes leaving the shirt to hang open.

Jade snatched a handful of grapes from the fruit bowl on the table, and shoved them in her mouth. Her mind wandered to the man in the bed. He was strong, powerful, and unnaturally quiet. Just being with him seemed to block out the city, and had done more to restore her than forty-eight hours of sleep would have. It was a good thing she didn't know how to find him again. If she did, she might be tempted to call him up and say, 'Hey, remember me? We took a tumble a few nights ago. How about a rematch?' Or, "I have an itch and was wondering if you'd like to meet me somewhere and scratch it?' No. It was just as well she didn't know his name. Less chance she would do something really stupid. *Let's not forget the fact that he is a wolf.*

Jade grabbed another handful of grapes, popped some in her mouth, opened the sliding-glass door and stepped onto the balcony. The sky was beginning to lighten. The street outside was empty, but that wouldn't last long. Lights were already coming on in the surrounding neighbourhood. Soon the street would be busy. Jade took advantage of the peacefulness and reached out with her senses. The sound of running water came from a house at the end of the block. There was fresh brewed coffee somewhere to the east. Her stomach rumbled. She bit into another grape, allowing the juice to trickle down her throat before swallowing. What she really wanted was a nice, juicy burger. The whistle of a kettle blew two blocks over. She ignored it and kept searching, sweeping the area in an ever growing circle.

Behind her the bed creaked. Once again musky pine and campfire filled her senses. Memories of the previous night brought a smile, and a warm feeling deep inside. She felt strong arms circling her and pulling her close. *He* was so close, maybe a little too close. Jade forced his image into a secret place, to be brought out and savoured later, and focused on her search.

There was something going on just to the east. Sirens and men shouting.

Jade popped the remaining grapes into her mouth, and climbed onto the railing, shifting as she went.

Seconds later a large, white owl flew towards the rising sun. Several minutes later she saw the flashing lights. The smell of blood beckoned.

Jade flew on silent wings, searching the ground. There were several police cars already on the scene. An ambulance was parked nearby. A couple of officers were busy placing police tape around the park. Others were trying to keep the inevitable reporters back. Several more officers were searching the area. Jade had the advantage of seeing the entire scene at once.

Her sharp eyesight easily found where the predator had lain in wait. The grass was matted. There were several blurred tracks in the dirt. Jade recognized the scent of wolf. It took longer to find the path the girl had taken. There was so much blood.

Jade forced her owl-self to concentrate on the scene below. Faint footprints showed the path the prey had taken. They entered the park through the main gate, and then passed the pond and the formal garden. The tracks had been taking a straight line towards the creek, and a footbridge leading to a small townhouse complex, when they had veered towards the swings.

Landing in a nearby tree, Jade scanned the prints at the base of the swing to the body laying several yards away. The scent of fresh meat called to the predator in her. Her stomach muscles twisted and clenched. A small mouse skittered through the pine needles beneath a row of trees. The owl took to the sky.

Nobody noticed the blue shimmering light between the ambulance and a news van. If anyone looked they would see an ordinary woman, wearing a beige cable knit sweater, comfortable blue jeans, and plain sneakers. A wave of dizziness washed over her and Jade caught the side of the van to steady herself. Her stomach twisted and she clenched her teeth to keep from crying out. Clothing was relatively simple but even that took energy. She had to eat. The mouse had simply been a tease.

This needed to be done. Jade pushed away from the van and walked towards the park. They were getting ready to move the body. Food would have to wait.

"Excuse me, Miss." She stopped when a hand clasped her shoulder. "No press this side of the line."

Jade turned and gave the officer one of her most dazzling smiles. She reached into her back pocket and appeared to pull out a small plastic card. She showed it to the officer. "Not press," she said. "Jade Caer. I'm with O'Connell Search and Rescue; out of New York I've been tracking a runaway."

The officer looked long and hard at the card. Then he looked at Jade. "You're a long way from home." He shook his head slightly, and looked at the card again before making his decision. "Wait here a minute, Miss." He walked over to a nearby police van and spoke to another officer. He returned carrying a small plastic tag with "Pass" printed on it. He reached forward and clipped the nametag to her sweater. His jaw dropped when the tag fell to the ground.

Jade bent down and picked up the tag before the officer moved. "That's okay." Jade smiled again. "I can do it. Sometimes the pins slip through the threads." She clipped the tag to her sweater, and pointed towards the body bag. "What happened?"

"Dog attack. Poor girl. Tore her up pretty bad."

Jade was already walking towards the body. "Mind if I take a look? Make sure she isn't mine?"

The officer hesitated, and then said. "Sure. Go ahead. Just don't touch anything."

The closer Jade got to the body, the stronger the scent of blood and raw meat. The body was still warm. The girl probably hadn't been dead more than a couple of hours. What had she been doing out here by herself, in the middle of the night? The rotting fungus stench of death was overpowering, making it difficult to pinpoint anything else. Still, there was something, teasingly familiar, that Jade couldn't quite grasp.

Jade knelt beside the body, and gathered enough strength to make herself unnoticeable. Even the officer, who had given her the nametag, forgot about her. If he remembered anything later, it would be talking to a woman, who had left without ever entering the park.

Jade took a deep, calming breath. She really hated this part. She reached under the plastic cover and touched the hand beneath.

The world shimmered and changed.

She was on the swing. Her legs pumping harder and harder as the sweet night air, filled with the heady scent of flowers, washed against her face, drying her tears. She was angry with ... Jason and Brenda.

Jade didn't know why. She didn't need to know why. That wasn't what was important.

A blur of movement near the trees caught her attention. She looked but clouds covered the moon, and the night was dark. Suddenly it was too dark. It was too quiet. Where were the crickets that had been playing their melody just minutes before?

Terror clenched her heart in its tight grip. She jammed her feet to the ground. The momentum of the moving swing threw her forward and she went down on all fours. She struggled to her feet and began to run. The footbridge was close. Her house was just on the other side.

Something was there. In the trees beside the bridge.

She couldn't see it, she couldn't hear it, but she knew it was there. She could feel it.

Her heart was thumping. Her legs burned. Her mouth was dry. Still she ran.

She could hear it now. The pounding of feet running towards her. She glanced towards the sound. She stumbled. She saw teeth, claws and fur hurtling through the air towards her. Fire tore through her right leg. Screams ripped from her throat.

She fell to the ground. The weight of the animal forced her to roll. She beat at it with her hands. It opened its mouth and released its hold on her. Her jaw dropped. Her eyes widened. Relief washed over her like a cool, summer rain easing her burning skin. She couldn't believe her luck. It was slinking back towards the trees. She was going to live.

Her right leg was mangled and useless. She looked around for a stick, or something else to use as a crutch. This part of the park, as usual, was immaculate. There wasn't a stick anywhere within reach. She started to drag herself towards the gate.

Another hundred feet, and she'd be home free. She could see the streetlights. She could hear traffic.

This time the attack came from the left. She hit, pushed and clawed. She was crying so hard now she could barely see. The dog, that's the only thing her brain recognized it as, jumped back. This time it didn't slink away. It stood about five feet away. Its dark eyes never left her face. Saliva and blood dripped from its teeth.

She pushed herself up on her elbows and tried to drag herself to the street. She was so tired. Her once burning skin was icy cold. Her legs were numb.

She was dead before its teeth closed over her throat.

Jade came to with a start. Her own heart was racing and she had to concentrate to slow it down. Her legs were numb. She was almost surprised to see them still attached when she looked down. Jade struggled to a standing position and stomped her feet to get the blood flowing. There was nothing she could do for the girl now, except find her killer.

She let her nose lead her to the tantalizing aroma of fresh brewed coffee and sizzling bacon. After a full-size breakfast, with extra ham and sausage, she hailed a cab and returned to the hotel. On the way she spotted a small butcher shop, and had the cabbie pull over. The store was just opening. There was very little meat on the counter. Jade bought two sirloin-tip steaks and a pork chop. Once again she made the clerk believe she had paid, and he gave her a receipt. She would send him his money, when she returned to her room, along with the money for her breakfast. The cabbie waited while she went up to get some cash from her room.

She ate the pork chop as soon as she got back to the room. Then, after a quick shower, she crawled into bed and fell asleep.

Chapter Fourteen

A scream rent the air. The hairs on the back of his neck stood straight. The quiet night erupted with noise. Lykos rushed out into the village square as the warning bell began to clang. His hair streaming out behind, he ran towards the screaming children. There was fighting everywhere. Men, women and children were being slaughtered. The coppery scent of blood filled his nostrils. Hot blood hit the back of his throat as he bit into an enemy. One sharp claw ripped out another's throat as he snatched his baby sister from beneath a descending blade with the other hand. The sound of sinister laughter made him jerk around just in time to see his mother fall beneath the sweep of a blade. Her head rolled in the dirt to stop at his feet. Her pleading eyes stared up at him. She still held two-year-old Gheorgès clenched tight in her arms as she slowly crumpled to the ground.

"Natasha sends her regards."

Luke jerked to wakefulness. It took a moment for the nightmare to recede, and memories of the night before to surface. He reached for the woman beside him. His hand came back empty.

He was alone. Completely alone.

He listened to the silence of the room and groaned. For one brief moment he thought he had dreamed the whole thing—but the evidence was hard to refute.

Unlike Natasha, She had been here. The scent of heather, fresh-cut grass, and sunshine clung to the room. Her scent. He remembered everything about her. The way she looked. The way she felt. The way she tasted. The way it felt when she tasted him. He inhaled deeply, tasting her again.

Her scent was a part of him.

He'd never forget it.

How had she managed to get up and leave without him waking? He stepped out onto the balcony. The breeze whispered around him, caressing him and teasing him with her presence. She couldn't have gotten far. Quickly he pulled on his clothes and set out to search for her.

He picked up her scent outside the hotel, but it was old. Several hours old.

There was a commotion to the east. Ice ran through his veins and he started running, shifting shape in mid stride. He was close enough to hear snippets of conversation, and heard the words "dog attack." Icy tendrils of fear wrapped their claws around his heart, and squeezed. Death hung heavy in the air, and blood called to the wolf in him. This was no dog attack.

Frustrated, he returned to the hotel and checked out. He got behind the wheel of his silver Jag and left the city.

Chapter Fifteen

The man, if you could still call him a man, didn't know where he was, or who he was. He wasn't even aware that the reason he was cold was that he wasn't wearing any clothes. He was running on pure instinct. His mind had completely shattered by the horror and pain of his bones breaking, and his body turning out of itself to become a wolf. His mind wasn't his own anymore. He only knew that he was cold and hungry. He had to find food and shelter because there was nobody else to do it for him.

Picking his aching body from the ground he ignored the grass and rotting leaves that stuck to his skin, and headed north.

The sudden roar of a car engine had him scrambling back into the trees. His heart beat erratically, and his breath came in short, rapid spurts. It was a long time after the car was gone before the gnawing in his stomach forced him to once again venture from the safety of the trees. Lifting his head, the man sniffed the air. Images fluttered across what was left of his mind.

Food.

Keeping the trees between the road and himself the man began to run.

He could see the house now. It was two-stories with blue siding, white trim, and a small shed to one side. One of the windows on the lower level of the house was open, and this was where the smell was coming from.

The man started to run across the clearing towards the house. A door slammed.

"Danger" flashed across his brain in large red letters. He veered to the right and hunkered down behind the shed. The pounding of his heart was deafening.

A sudden roar made him gasp. A car. It was just a car.

He rested his back against the shed, and waited. Five, ten, fifteen minutes passed. Finally, the man stood. He flexed his legs to relieve the cramped muscles and peeked around the corner of the shed.

The house was quiet. The man circled the house slowly, pausing every few seconds to sniff the air, and listen. Satisfied that the house was empty, he entered through the open window, and found himself in a small kitchen. There was a fridge, a stove, a small half-circle table, and one chair. There was a cup with the remains of cold coffee. Crinkling his nose in distaste, the man ignored the cup and sniffed the grease covered plate beside it, before licking it clean.

He opened the fridge and pulled out a carton of milk. The numbers stamped on the carton meant nothing to him. He tore open the top and lifted the carton to his lips, took a big swallow, and spit it out on the floor. He threw the container across the room. He tore open a package of cold meat that was green around the edges. He shoved it in his mouth and swallowed without chewing. He tore open several more containers of food. Some he sniffed and discarded. Others he shoved in his mouth. His mouth watered when he tore open the fresh, pink ground beef.

He devoured half the paper with it, before discarding the rest of the wrapper in the growing pile of debris on the floor.

The gnawing in his stomach appeased, the man went to explore the next room. The heat coming from the woodstove drew him. He lay down, wiggling his body between the wall and the stove, not touching either.

He slept.

Several hours later, the creaking of the door woke him. Startled, he pushed his body farther in behind the stove, making it as small as possible.

He waited for his chance to escape.

When Michael Green came home he didn't notice the naked man crouched behind his woodstove. He was having a bad day so he slammed the door shut behind him, and headed straight for the kitchen to grab a beer. One look at the mess on his kitchen floor and he went ballistic. Shouting and cursing, he stomped back into the living room intending to call the Sheriff's office. The punks that did this were going to pay. He'd make sure of it.

Michael headed for the phone on the wall beside the woodstove, and froze. He couldn't believe his eyes. Crouching there like some wild beast, and stark naked was a stranger.

With his escape route cut off, what was left of David Woods panicked. He leapt from behind the woodstove, knocking Michael to the ground. He sank his teeth into Michael's neck. Hot, spicy blood hit the back of his throat, and he was lost. Without hesitation he clamped his teeth down and tore out the other man's throat. He tore chunks of meat from the corpse, chewing and swallowing, gorging himself until completely sated. Then, leaving the ravaged remains, he climbed back through the kitchen window, and escaped to the woods.

Once again, instinct called him north, towards *her*.

Chapter Sixteen

A large white wolf with silver and gray tips wandered back and forth sniffing the ground, then pointed its nose in the air and sniffed. There was no use. The trail was definitely lost—again. In less time that it took a human to blink, Jade shifted into her human form, bent to tie a loose lace on her hiking shoe, and looked around. Lucky for her she kept not only what she was wearing when she shifted, but also anything that was in her pockets, and on her person. She had no problem conjuring clothing, but she had to carry anything else she needed.

Not many people knew that Willow Bend was the largest werewolf community in Canada. Most people believed that *weres*—men or women able to change into animals—vampires, and other supernatural entities were nothing more than superstition and fairy tales. Stories made up to amuse or frighten. Jade was *Moarté*. It was the duty of the *Moarté* to ensure any threat to their survival was dealt with quickly, and anonymously. There were laws in place to ensure the survival of all races, and when a crime was committed Jade became judge, jury, and executioner. One day, if Jade were lucky enough to become a mother, her own daughter would become *Moarté*, as her mother, and grandmother had before her.

All shape shifters were magic, and with so much magic in the area it wasn't going to be easy pinpointing the source she sought. To make matters worse she was here during the full moon cycle, when magic was at its strongest, and lust was in the air. Plus she had no way of knowing whether she was searching for a wolf or a man.

Jade wasn't a *were*. She was a shape shifter. The wolf was a wolf. The fox was a fox. Jade was everything, and nothing. She could change shape at will. She could command the energies of the universe to do her bidding. She could influence people with the power of her mind. She wasn't required to drink blood to survive. She was in full control of herself, and the things around her.

Except three days a month. For three days a month she had an uncontrollable libido. She prowled for partners like a cat in heat. She despised herself for the way she responded to a stranger's touch—any stranger. She had tried locking herself up for three days, but that was disastrous. Without the sexual release she became an irritable bear. Literally. Three hundred pounds of frustrated bear can do a lot of damage.

So three days a month Jade prowled for sexual release. *Weres* were very sexual creatures, but could become very possessive and that was not something that Jade needed in her life. Normally she would avoid *were* communities during the full moon cycle. Yet here she was—with two nights left and a virtual smorgasbord of partners—and all she could think about was a hot, sexy wolf in another city. That was so scary. She was so the love 'em and leave 'em type. Then again, nobody had made her feel the way her wolf had. Not even Larry. And she had married Larry.

Jade shifted her pack on her shoulders, and headed down Main Street. She passed several stores before spotting the Tourist Information Booth. There was nobody inside, but a huge map, dotted with numbers, covered one entire wall. Below it, the corresponding legend showed the names of businesses and other tourist attractions. She found the number for the Inner Sanctum Bed & Breakfast, and then found the corresponding spot on the map.

Ten minutes later she was climbing stone steps to massive oaken doors.

The Inner Sanctum was a six thousand square foot replica of a fourteenth century Romanian castle, built on a two-acre treed lot between a lake and the mountains. It was popular with humans and nonhumans alike. The stone structure could pass for Dracula's castle, probably why it was almost impossible to get a reservation during the month of October. Jade lifted the brass knocker, but wasn't really surprised when the door swung in on silent hinges, before she could use it. The castle was reputed to be protected by a very powerful witch. The appearance of a tiny lady with her gray hair pulled back in a bun, and a delightful twinkle in her sky blue eyes, was a surprise. So much for hunched back servants and old crones.

The woman grabbed her arm and pulled her inside. "Welcome to The Inner Sanctum, Miss Caer. Come in, come in." She pushed the heavy door and it closed with an ominous click, then turned and headed down the wide hallway. "I knew it was you. Everyone else uses the kitchen door. Or the side door. The front doors are mostly for show, except during the season that is. Tourists love using these big old doors. Makes them feel like royalty or something. We don't get many guests during this time of year though. Not enough snow left for skiing and too cold for camping. You're early. You weren't expected until next week."

The woman stopped suddenly and Jade nearly bumped into her. "Oh my," she said. "I hope you don't think I'm complaining. We love visitors any time."

Jade gave a small laugh. She had never heard anyone talk so fast, and all without a pause. "It's okay, Mrs Gray. I will be quite happy with the kitchen door." Or a convenient window from her room.

The clicking of their shoes on the marble floor echoed loudly, making Jade uncomfortable as they passed another massive door, this one with a suit of armour standing guard on either side.

Mrs Gray indicated the door with a wave of her hand, and kept on walking. "That used to be the Chapel. Folks from all around would come every week to give their thanks. And the weddings. Oh the weddings were beautiful." She sighed wistfully. "We don't have a lot of weddings here since they built the new church in town, so we turned it into a library." They continued walking until Mrs Gray indicated a door on the left, also with its attending armour. "This was the Great Hall where the knights would meet with their king and plan their strategies for war."

Mrs Gray paused for a second, a faraway look in her eye. "It acts as a conference room now. You'd be surprised how many companies actually want to book their conferences in a castle. More than once we've had to send them elsewhere. Not that I'm complaining mind you. Conferences are a real boon to the community."

They continued down the seemingly endless hall, and Mrs Gray kept up a running monologue. "This is the Hall of Knights, fitting I say, what with knights guarding all the doors. I can still hear the echo of their armour clinking as they passed down the hall. Now, the only time we get knights are during the Halloween season when we turn the whole thing into a Castle of Horrors."

The flickering glow of the electric candles lining the hall made their shadows grow and shrink, like a funhouse at an amusement park. *Maybe I can bring Alicia here for Halloween. Who am I kidding? I don't even know what she likes. I'm not even sure she will even speak to me again.*

Forcing her attention back to her surroundings, Jade noticed a slight difference in the position of one of the wallboards. Before she could say anything, Mrs Gray reached up to the wall sconce holding the electric candle for this section and twisted it slightly. The panel slid back into alignment with the rest.

"Secret passage," Mrs Gray said. "They're all over the place. We also have a dungeon in the basement, complete with torture chamber. These are off limits to guests. We wouldn't want anyone to get hurt."

At the far end of the hall was an impressive winding staircase. On either side was a door, also with their guardian knights. Jade glimpsed other doors behind the staircase. Before she had a chance to ask, Mrs Gray explained. "The door on the right leads to the dining area. Dinner will be ready in about half an hour. The one on the left leads to the kitchen. The door to the dungeon is through the kitchen. As I said it's off limits except during the guided tours. The double doors behind the staircase lead to the center courtyard. You're welcome to enjoy it whenever you want. The smaller door beside the courtyard leads to my private quarters but you'll usually find me in the kitchen."

Mrs Gray led the way up the stairs her tongue never pausing. Jade could picture her leading the way, a troop of ghosts and goblins trailing behind as she held them spellbound with tales of days gone by. Just listening to her voice, one could almost see the past come to life. "The castle was built almost three hundred years ago, each stone placed by hand. It took nearly fifty years to complete but it was well worth it. My family has been here since the sixteen hundreds."

On the next floor, Mrs Gray led the way down a narrow passageway. The windows on this side were a little larger than the tiny slits on the outer castle walls, and Jade could see the courtyard below. A sugar maple stood at least a hundred feet high in the center of the courtyard. Jade could see a fire pit and tripod.

Mrs Gray noticed the direction she was looking. "Got twelve quarts this year," she said. "Would have got more, but Peter was here with his three little ones and we made toffee in the snow. The look on their faces when they were pulling that toffee was priceless. Don't worry. We still have plenty for our pancake breakfasts."

Mrs Gray winked at Jade. "There's a sugar bush out back."

They continued to the end of the hall, where Mrs Gray opened the door and motioned for Jade to enter. "This room has a window looking out over the courtyard, as well as one that looks out over the forest. You can see the mountains from the one in your room." She flicked a switch inside the door, and several electric candles around the room flared. The lights flickered like real candles, distorting their shadows as they danced on the walls.

"If there's anything you need I'll be in the kitchen." Mrs Gray spoke while she headed back down the passageway. Suddenly she stopped and turned back. "Oh, if you want to lock the door when you go out there's a key in the drawer beside the bed. We don't usually lock the doors, but most city folk feel the need so we supply a key." With that she turned and hurried off.

Jade tossed her pack on the double bed and flopped down beside it. Kicking off her hiking shoes she leaned back and closed her eyes. She couldn't stop the sudden flow of images fluttering across her eyelids, as she remembered the events of the day. There had been so much blood. First the girl in the park. Then that poor man in the house in the woods. That was the big difference between a vampire kill and a wolf kill. The blood. Jade didn't think she would ever get used to the blood.

Jade had picked up the trail outside the park, after several false starts, and followed it through the city. Although they were generally heading north, the trail zigzagged through the streets before finally leaving the city far behind. Around six o'clock Jade found the spot where the wolf had lain down, and the man had woken. She followed the new trail to the house on the edge of the forest. It was isolated, at least a half-mile from its nearest neighbour, and set back from the highway.

As she approached the house Jade knew she was already too late. The dark cloak of Death hung over the building and the coppery scent of blood assailed her through the open window. Jade had known before she went in that he was no longer in the house. The trail clearly led back into the forest. Jade's stomach knotted. She didn't want to go in the house, but she knew she had to. What if someone were alive? She was already carrying around more than enough guilt for the death of the girl. If only she could control her libido. She could have gone out on patrol, that poor girl might still be alive. Taking a deep breath to help still the erratic beating of her heart, Jade went around to the front of the house, and forced herself to open the door. She didn't worry about leaving fingerprints, or any other evidence. Nobody would ever know she had been there.

It was worse than she feared. Blood splattered the walls, the floor, and even the low ceiling. Jade could do nothing for the man. Dead was dead, and even she couldn't change that. She was just thankful nobody else was in the house.

There hadn't been enough left of the victim to connect with, and for that Jade was thankful. She didn't have to relive this man's death to know she had to find the wolf. Tonight. Before he killed again.

Jade shuddered, gave a little bounce and snuggled into the down comforter, forcing the scene from her mind.

Her stomach grumbled, stirring Jade to action. She entered the adjoining bathroom and quickly cleaned up. Mrs Gray had said dinner was in less than half an hour, and Jade didn't want to miss it—not that she missed many meals. Besides, if she didn't take the time to eat she would be useless tonight.

She had just finished tying her shoes when there was a rap at the door.

"Will you be joining us for dinner, Miss Caer?" Mrs Gray asked through the door.

Jade flung open the door and flashed the woman one of her brightest smiles. "I wouldn't miss it for the world. And please, call me Jade." She followed her hostess down the hallway.

"I hope you like venison. It was Mr Gray's favourite. He sure did love a good roast of venison." Mrs Gray tittered like a schoolgirl. "Tell the truth Mr Gray loved a good roast of anything. He sure liked his food. Oh my! I just thought of something. You're not a vegetarian are you?"

"Me? A vegetarian?" Jade's laughter tinkled. "No way. I love meat." Venison was one of her favourites, along with moose, rabbit, bear, beaver, beef, and chicken. You name it; she liked it. Roasted, baked, or fried, it made her mouth water. It was a good thing she liked it raw too, considering she had never taken the time to learn how to cook.

Jade's step faltered when they reached the dining room and there were two other guests already seated at the table. It was strange she hadn't realized anyone else

was in the house. It made her wonder what else she had missed. There were at least a dozen other place settings. "Where are the other guests, Mrs Gray?"

"We're all here, my dear. You can never be sure who will drop in at dinner, and we wouldn't want anyone to feel unwelcome. We always set an extra plate." Or a dozen extra places by the look of it.

Mrs Gray waved her hand towards the table. "Have a seat, Miss Jade. Anywhere at all's fine."

"It's Jade," she told Mrs Gray. She tried to keep her voice stern, but her eyes twinkled. "Just Jade."

Jade chose a seat across the table from the gorgeous woman with ebony tresses and coal-black eyes. Jade felt absolutely drab in her olive-green 'Illegal Cargo' pants with their many extra pockets, and her beige fisherman-knit sweater, compared to the other woman's obviously expensive tan slacks and satin shirt. It would be better to sit across from her, than beside her where the difference would be much more obvious.

Jade felt the woman watching her and looked up into—*his eyes*. Jade pushed the idea out of her mind. This was ridiculous. The woman's eyes were as black as coal, while his had been a pale brown, except when they blazed yellow while in the throes of passion. Still, they both had that same, penetrating stare. Jade mentally gave herself a shake. She was acting like a schoolgirl with her first crush. Sure he was the sexiest, the most virile male she had been with in decades, but that was no excuse for allowing him to pop into her head whenever he chose.

The other occupant at the table rose from his chair at the end of the table, and stretched his hand towards her.

Jade reached over and shook his hand. He was tall, maybe a little too thin, with blond hair. He would never be considered handsome, but he had the most compelling cobalt eyes. Normally a male, any male, would ignite the desire. Jade felt nothing sexual for this man at all. That made her uneasy. "Hello, Just Jade," he said, and winked, breaking the spell. "I'm Randy, and this beautiful creature across from you is Helen."

He held her hand longer than was necessary, and was rubbing his thumb across her knuckles.

Jade had the sudden urge to rip her hand out of his grasp, when Helen snapped, "Give the girl back her hand and sit down, Randy."

It was hard not to laugh when Randy dropped her hand like it was on fire, and then nearly missed the chair in his haste to sit down. She covered her mouth, and pretended to cough, hiding the smile she found impossible to stop.

Helen stabbed Jade with her piercing eyes, and winked. "Men," she said and shrugged.

Jade felt the feather light probe in her mind, and quickly reinforced her barriers. She may have had the feeling Randy was reading her mind, but she knew Helen was trying to. She watched the other woman warily, but she simply shrugged. She would have liked a peak into the other woman's mind, but it was against the rules of sanctum, and she was not about to be removed from the one place she knew she would be safe.

For the briefest moment she caught the woman's scent—ginger and oranges. There was nothing threatening there, yet something niggled at the back of her brain before disappearing. Randy played with his food, while covertly peeking at Helen beneath his long lashes, who didn't seem the least aware that he was so smitten with her.

Mrs Gray glared a warning at Helen, who shrugged, her face a mask of innocence. "Help yourself, Miss Jade," Mrs Gray said, keeping her attention on Helen. "We don't like to see our guests to go hungry. Mr Gray always said, 'a full body is a happy body'."

"Thanks, Mrs G. Although you might reconsider your rates when you see how much I can eat."

Helen and Randy exchanged amused looks at the bright shade of pink crawling up the older woman's neck. Mrs Gray muttered something Jade didn't catch, and hurried back to the kitchen.

"How long have you known Charlotte?" Helen asked.

"Charlotte?"

"Mrs Gray."

"I never met her until she opened the door about half an hour ago. Why?"

Helen tipped her head towards the kitchen door. "You seem very familiar with her. I was just wondering how you met. I don't recall seeing you around here before."

Jade helped herself to a large serving of venison and potatoes, poured gravy all over, then added baby carrots to her plate, before replying. "So you're from around here?"

Helen smiled, but it didn't quite reach her eyes. "A long time ago." After several tense moments when no-one spoke, Helen laughed. It was more a nervous laugh than one of humour. "Forget me. So, how long did you say you were staying?"

"I didn't." Jade took a forkful of venison, chewed and swallowed. She wasn't about to broadcast her business to Helen, or anyone else.

They finished their meal in uneasy silence. Jade would have loved some more of that delicious venison, but there was a limit to how much a person could eat in one sitting, and Helen was already paying more attention to Jade than she liked.

Returning to her room, Jade lowered the thermostat on the electric heater and with a wave of her hand lit a fire in the fireplace. She took her time showering and changed into clean jeans and a knit sweater. The temperatures were beginning to rise during the day, but it still got pretty cool at night. She tied her hiking boots, grabbed her vest from the bottom of the bed, and headed out in search of Mrs Gray. She found her in the kitchen doing the dishes.

Jade grabbed a tea towel from the counter and started drying. "Let me help you with these, Mrs G."

Two bright red spots appeared in the woman's cheeks, and she made a grab for the tea towel. Jade pulled it out of her reach. "I can't let you do that, Miss Jade. What would Mr Gray say about me working the guests?"

Jade finished drying the plate and set it on the corner of the table. "You aren't making me do anything I wouldn't do at home." *If Mrs Murphy would let her*. Jade reached for another plate. "Besides, I'm sure Mr Gray, wherever he is, doesn't expect you to do everything yourself."

"Oh my!" The spots on Mrs Gray's cheeks grew. "Mr Gray has been dead these many long years, my dear."

"Do you talk to dead people often?" Jade teased.

"I don't talk to dead people at all!" This time, Mrs Gray caught the towel and tugged it out of Jade's hand. "He talks to me," she mumbled.

She threw the towel on the counter and grabbed the kettle from the stove. "If you must stay in my kitchen, then sit down and let me make you a nice cup of tea."

A wave of homesickness washed over Jade. Mrs Gray reminded her so much of Mrs Murphy. Apparently, neither one would tolerate her in their kitchen. Probably the reason she couldn't cook. "Don't bother yourself, Mrs G." Jade leaned against the edge of the table and watched Mrs Gray flitter around the kitchen. She was really beginning to like the old lady. "I just came down to ask if there were laundry facilities on the premises, or a Laundromat in town."

"It's no bother." Mrs Gray filled the kettle and placed it back on the stove. "Didn't I tell you? The laundry room is in the basement. If you bring your stuff down, I can wash it for you." She took a small tray from beside the fridge and started loading it up with teapot, cups, plates and an apple pie. "I'm making tea for Miss Helen and Randy. They're in the library watching the news on the television. You're welcome to join them."

"If you don't mind, I'd rather sit in here with you?" They could argue about the laundry later. In the meantime maybe Mrs Gray could tell her if any strangers had been around.

The kettle whistled and Mrs Gray added water to the teapot. "Just let me take this to the others and I'll make us a cup."

It was peaceful sitting in the kitchen, with the warmth of the woodstove and the fresh scent of the pines drifting through the open window. When Mrs Gray returned she added two scoops from a fancy jar on the counter, and boiling water to another teapot. Then she opened the fridge and started pulling out more food. Next she began cutting huge slices off a loaf of fresh bread.

"I was going to make myself a nice venison sandwich," she said, as she cut several slices. "Would you care for one?"

Jade began to salivate. It had been what, a whole twenty minutes since she had eaten? "I'd love one."

The outside door suddenly swung in. There had been no knock. From where Jade was sitting she couldn't see who entered, but from the wide smile on Mrs Gray's face they were definitely welcome.

"Luke, you're back. We weren't expecting you until tomorrow. I was just making some venison sandwiches. Sit down and I'll bring you yours."

As the door began to swing shut the man spoke. "Reading my mind again, Charlotte?"

Goosebumps traveled along Jade's skin and her heart fluttered, as the deep rumbling voice caressed her. It wasn't possible. The door closed and Jade found herself staring into the pale brown eyes of last night's stranger.

"You!" They cried in unison.

Chapter Seventeen

Luke snapped off the radio with a snarl. What the hell was going on? In over a hundred years no *wolf* has dared attack a human in his territory. And now this. If news got out there would be wide spread panic and every wolf, dog, and Lycan would be in danger. When humans were afraid they were more terrifying than the *Moarté*.

Luke grabbed his cell phone and flipped it open. The no service message slid across the screen. "Useless piece of junk." He jammed the phone back into its charger and sighed. There was no sense in trying the phone until he made it through the rock cut.

Luke had felt the magic in the park, and to be honest it had him worried. It was not the usual magic associated with a *were*. The magic he had felt was strong. Powerful. It had been cloaking the park, and Luke had been unable to pinpoint its location.

He was forced to give up his search for the mystery woman, even while every nerve in his body screamed he continued. *He had never met anyone like her before. She was powerful. There was no doubt about it. But what was she? Not lycan. He would know if she was lycan. Who and what was she? The most important thing would he see her again?*

Luke couldn't worry about any of that now. He had to get back to Willow Bend and tell Daniel and Grégoire what had happened. The Matei twins were not only the law in Willow Bend; they were also his right and left arms. He had no doubt that together they would be able to track the rogue.

Who are you? The fact that he couldn't seem to keep his thoughts from her was a little disconcerting. He hadn't felt like this about a woman since Tasha -- *and look where that had gotten them.*

For centuries their pack had been the protectors of the ruling family of Transylvania. Until Luke met Natasha. He had fallen for her like a fly zapped with Raid. Hard and fast. He wanted to spend his life with her, and had foolishly told his secret without waiting for the approval of the pack. The morning of their planned wedding she had betrayed them all. The villagers had attacked and massacred nearly their entire pack, forcing the handful of survivors, mostly children, to flee to safety. They had eventually made their way across an ocean to forge a new life for them in this remote wilderness. Luke once again pushed the unsettling thoughts to the back of his mind, and tried to concentrate on the present.

Luke tried the phone again, this time able to put his call through.

"Hey, Boss. What's up?"

He might have been gone for almost three months, but Daniel had known the second Luke had come within three hundred miles of home.

"There's been a killing."

Luke could tell by the silence on the other end that Daniel was as stunned as he had been. He filled them in with the little he knew. The minute he arrived at the police station, the three of them began searching for any sign of a stranger. This was something they had to deal with, the sooner the better.

Willow Bend was a small, closely-knit community. If a stranger came to town, someone, somewhere, would know about it.

Nothing.

Luke should have been relieved, but he wasn't. He *knew* the wolf had come here. With thousands of acres of forest and mountain there were thousands of places for a wolf to hide.

Luke was in the twins' office when the call came in about Michael Green. His wife, Debbie, was hysterical but they knew it was bad. Michael had been renting a house about ten miles from town ever since he and his wife had split up.

The hackles on the back of Luke's neck rose the moment he entered the house, and the familiar tingle of spent magic, and something more, surrounded him. It reminded him of the park.

Luke looked at Grégoire. "Do you feel it?"

"Yeah, Boss. I'm sure I can feel *Moarté*, but I wouldn't want to bet the farm on it." Grégoire looked anything but pleased with the possibility. The *Moarté* or "Death Squad" didn't leave trace scents but they did sometimes leave traces of their magic.

Daniel stayed outside with Debbie until the paramedics came and gave her something to calm her down, then he told them to take her to the hospital. "You can't do anything for Michael, but you can take care of his wife. He would have wanted that."

He squeezed Debbie's hand and helped her into the back of the ambulance. Debbie and his wife, Sondra, were co-owners of the Haberdashery in town. Deb and Michael had been guests in their house on a regular basis. "It'll be okay, Deb. We'll find whoever is responsible for this."

Daniel slammed the door on the ambulance. "Do me a favor, Mike? Give Steven a call and tell him to bring the wagon. Warn him it's messy."

"Sure thing, Chief." Daniel was technically just a deputy, but he didn't bother correcting him. Most people couldn't tell the difference between his brother and him.

Entering the house, Daniel wrinkled his nose in disgust. "What kind of animal would do this?"

Grégoire shrugged. "Use your nose, baby brother, and tell us." The older by three minutes, Grégoire never passed up an opportunity to rib Daniel. A fact Daniel took in stride, along with the crack about his olfactory powers. They both knew Grégoire's sense of smell was four times that of his brother, who couldn't smell his way out of a brown paper sack. However, what Daniel lacked in the sense of smell, he made up for with his advanced psychic abilities.

"I don't know, Bro. There's so much residual violence."

After a thorough search of the house they knew that a man had entered, and a wolf had left. A confused, scared, and very dangerous wolf. Unfortunately for them, he hadn't left any tracks they could follow, and its scent had already dissipated. And it looked like the *Moarté* was already in town.

An hour later, Luke opened the door of his private quarters to a persistent ringing. He dropped his suitcase in the middle of the hall and grabbed the phone. "Yeah?"

"You're wanted at the Sanctum." Click. Elizabeth hated using the phone even more than Luke.

Leaving the car Luke shifted and ran the short distance to The Inner Sanctum. Shifting back to man, he had just lifted the knocker when the door swung in on silent hinges, allowing him a view of Charlotte's familiar round face. Bless her soul. With Charlotte around you didn't need knockers.

"Luke, you're back. We weren't expecting you until tomorrow. I was just making venison sandwiches. Sit down and I'll bring you yours."

"Reading my mind, again Charlotte?" Luke took two steps into the room, picked Charlotte up in a big bear hug, kissed her soundly on both cheeks, and then set her back on her feet. The door swung shut and Luke blinked, not quite believing what his eyes were seeing. Sitting at Charlotte's table, and looking even more beautiful in her casual pants and form hugging knit-sweater, was his mystery woman.

"You!" They blurted simultaneously.

Umpteen questions flashed through Luke's mind. What was she doing here? Had she followed him? Did she have anything to do with what was going on? Who was she? How had she found him? Most importantly ... *How was he going to keep her here?*

His arms ached to wrap themselves around her. His lips burned for her kisses. She was a candle and he the lowly moth attracted to her smouldering flame. He took a step towards her, unable to stop himself.

Surprise, swiftly followed by wariness, and something else flickered in her wide amber eyes. The musky scent of her desire rolled off her in waves, circling and caressing him. He became instantly hard.

Luke stopped his approach, struggling to bring himself under control. He was standing there awkwardly trying to will away his hard-on, when the door to the hall opened and Helen strolled in. Spying Luke, she ran across the kitchen and threw herself at him. He staggered, and wrapped his arms around her to keep them both from falling. Her arms circled his neck, and she planted a huge, noisy kiss on his cheek.

Happy to see her, Luke swung his sister around before setting her back on her feet. "When did you get here?" Luke asked.

"If you will excuse me I'll leave you two alone." Her voice was low and husky, and pain flickered across her amber eyes. In one fluid motion she rose from her seat, grabbed the vest from the back of her chair, and headed for the door. "I'm sorry, Mrs. Gray, but I'll have to pass on that sandwich. I just remembered someplace I have to be."

Luke stared at the closed door in stunned silence. What the hell had just happened? He'd had her in his grasp and just as suddenly she was gone. He took two steps towards the door before realizing Helen was tugging on his arm. "What?" He almost growled the word.

Helen put her hands on her hips and her brows narrowed as she glared back at him. "What's with you and Jade anyway?" she demanded. "I haven't seen you in over two years and you don't even notice me."

Luke grabbed his sister by the shoulders, ignoring her startled gasp. "What did you call her?"

Helen shook his hands off and continued to glare at him. "Don't bully me, Big Brother. If you want to know something, ask."

Luke took a deep, calming breath, shoved his fingers through his unruly locks, and smiled at his sister, although it didn't quite reach his eyes. "You're right, Sis. I'm sorry, and I'm asking."

Charlotte set a plate on the table, and the tantalizing aroma of venison reached his nostrils. Luke's stomach rumbled with hunger and he was torn between the meal in front of him and the woman who had just left the sanctum. Hunger won. Besides, deep down he knew the woman would be back, and he had to find out why Helen was in town.

He chose the chair Jade just vacated. It was still warm, and her scent lingered. He inhaled the sweet fragrance, allowing it to comfort him with the knowledge she was near, and turned to his sister. "Sit with me while I eat and we can talk."

Luke took two bites and devoured half the sandwich. Licking his lips he grinned at Charlotte. "Delicious as ever, Charlie."

Charlotte turned bright pink and busied herself at the sink. "If you need another let me know. No sense wasting a good roast."

Luke finished his first sandwich before turning to his sister. He wanted to bombard her with questions about Jade, but decided against it. He didn't want his sister speculating about his interest. Instead, he took a bite of his second sandwich, chewed more slowly this time, then swallowed and asked. "What are you doing here? Thomas told me you were in Paris shopping."

Anger flashed in Helen's midnight eyes. "That Bitch wouldn't let me in to see Gemma."

By bitch, she meant Elizabeth. Fifty years ago, Helen had challenged the pack's alpha female, and lost. According to Lycan law Helen's life was forfeit, but because she was Luke's sister Elizabeth had chosen to banish her instead. Thomas Radu had declared his love for Helen on that day, and he had asked permission to leave with Helen. Unwilling to lose one of his best friends, and his only living blood relative, Luke had sent them to Italy where they had begun a new pack. According to Lycan law, once banished Helen could never return to Willow Creek. If she did, the death penalty could be invoked.

Yet here she was.

Luke counted to ten, silently. "What are you doing here, Helen? You know our laws."

Helen's dark eyes flashed. "What do I care for laws when my baby needs me?"

Luke shook his head in frustration, when what he really wanted to do was strangle his sister. When it came to Gemma, Helen was the doting, overprotective mother. The moon rose and set on that girl, and Helen had spoiled her to no end. Luke was amazed Gemma wasn't an obnoxious brat, considering the way her mother treated her. "Gemma is a big girl, Helen. She has chosen to come here to study. Both you and Thomas agreed that this was the best place for her right now. You can't keep her your baby forever."

Helen rolled her eyes. "I know all that. I came because something is wrong." She hurried on before Luke could interrupt. She may not be psychic, but she did have a very strong bond with her child. "Two weeks ago I woke up knowing something had happened to Gemma. I could taste her fear. I felt her pain. My heart nearly stopped. I caught the first plane here, and went straight to 'The Den', but *She* wouldn't let me in. She refused to even tell Gemma, my own daughter, that I was here. And she continually intercepts my phone calls."

Helen reached out and placed her hand over her brother's. "You have to find out what's wrong and fix it, Luke. You're responsible for the welfare of the pack. As much as I hate to admit it, as long as Gemma is here she is part of your pack. Protect my baby."

Luke placed his free hand over his sister's, and squeezed. "I swear on Gheorgès grave that I will protect Gemma with my life. I also need to keep you safe. You need to go back to Italy. Back to Thomas. And don't come here again." Luke gave his sister a crooked grin. "They make phones for occasions like this. Use them."

Luke stood, leaned over and gave his sister a kiss on the cheek. "I'll send a driver to take you to the airport."

Chapter Eighteen

Gemma locked the front door, and flipped the sign to 'closed'. Not that anyone would show up tonight expecting the Center to be open. They ran one overnight camping trip on the first night of the full moon over at Wolf Lake Falls, and closed the center for the next two days. It had been that way since the beginning.

This time was for the wolves. They were already gathering. Gemma could feel them all around her. They would stay out of sight until all of the uninitiated humans had left for their homes. Then they would hunt undisturbed in their territory, and afterward the unattached wolves would pair up and have sex. Hot, unadulterated, no strings attached sex. You couldn't call it anything else without feelings involved, except for instant sexual gratification. It was the same in all the packs.

Gemma had never been allowed to stay after the hunt. Her mother protected her with a fierceness that kept even the bravest wolf away. She still treated Gemma like a child, although she was almost twenty years old. She was almost suffocating at times, and her father was just as bad. Even if she had dared to disobey her parents and stay after the hunt, nobody in her pack would tempt the wrath of her parents and choose her.

Not everyone stayed after the hunt. Those with mates usually went their separate ways.

Many of the wolves capable of staying in human form, chose to party at Wulfson Mansion. Many single wolves lived at the mansion. Already virile they were nearly impossible to deny during their peak. Luke Wulfson had turned the old mansion, built at the turn of the eighteenth century in the fashion of the antebellum estates in New Orleans, into a shared home for the Lycan community. Once a month, in deference to the pull of the moon, Luke hosted the Moon Phase Dance. That way he could control, somewhat, the appetites of his wolves, making sure they didn't lose complete control.

Rules for admittance were strict, ensuring the safety of both human and wolf. Lycan children spent the night at the Hub with adult supervision. Sara and Gemma often volunteered to help with the young ones.

"Earth to Gemma. Earth to Gemma." Sara snapped her fingers in front of Gemma's face.

Gemma blinked. "I'm sorry, Sara. What did you say?"

"I asked if you were coming to the Hub tonight." With attendance restricted to twenty-five and older, Sara was too young for the dances, and if Gemma's parents had their way she would never be allowed to attend. Hell, if her parents found out she'd gone to the bar with Sara she'd be sent back to Italy … yesterday.

Gemma reached into the pocket of her spring jacket, and fingered the cold metal of handcuffs laying there. If Daniel found out that his son Greg had lent them to her, they would both be in a world of trouble. "I don't think so, Sara. There's something I have to do tonight."

"What's up with you, Gem? Are you okay? You've been distracted all day."

Gemma eyed her friend warily. "What do you mean?"

"Well. For one thing, you haven't even asked how it went with George last night."

Gemma noticed the concerned on her friend's face, and forced herself to smile. "Well. For one thing," she repeated her friend's words. "We worked in different departments all day. I haven't seen you for more than five minutes at a time."

"Yeah, and you were distracted the whole five minutes."

Gemma locked elbows with her friend and led her towards the parking lot. "Okay, Sara, out with it. I can tell you are dying to tell me what happened."

"Forget that. I want to know what's going on with you."

Gemma shrugged. She couldn't very well tell her best friend that she thought she turned into a wolf and killed someone last night. "I just haven't been sleeping very well lately," she said instead. She glanced up towards the rising moon and hurried her step towards the parking lot. "Do tell. What happened last night?"

Sara rolled her eyes and let out an exaggerated sigh. "Nothing. George was being his usual obnoxious self." Then she giggled. "'Til midnight."

It was Gemma's turn to roll her eyes. Her friend would stretch this out all night if she let her. "What happened at midnight?"

"He kissed me."

"He what?" George kissed Sara. What was the world coming to? Those two could barely stand each other. If George hurt her best friend, Gemma would kill him.

Sara dimpled. Gemma was astounded to see Sara actually blush. She hadn't known Sara could blush.

"He kissed me. And I liked it." Sara tugged on Gemma's arm. "I liked it, Gem. What am I supposed to do now?"

Gemma laughed. Almost. For as long as she'd known her, Sara had never been at a loss as to what to do with a boy. "What do you want to do?" She asked warily. She should warn Sara to turn tail and run. She knew the effect George had on women during the moon phase. The pheromones alone would have her doing flips in his bed. Although Sara was usually more than a match for any man, she had no idea the trouble she could get into with a wolf. Gemma should warn her friend, but how? She couldn't very well tell Sara that George was the epitome of the big bad wolf.

"You girls talking about me?" They both jumped at the deep, rumbling voice.

"George! What's wrong with you? Sneaking up on us like that." Sara glared at George. "And we were not talking about you." Gemma flinched when Sara pinched her arm, but she didn't dare contradict her friend.

"As a matter of fact," Sara continued her voice breezy. "I was just asking Gemma if she was coming to the Hub with Mark and me tonight."

"Mark." George growled the name "is not welcome at the Hub."

Sara removed her arm from Gemma's, and shrugged. "In that case, I guess I won't be going to the Hub after all." She winked at Gemma, then got in her car, started the engine and drove away spraying gravel at George.

Gemma had never seen George's face turn quite that shade of red. It was almost purple. She could practically see steam coming out his ears. It was a struggle not to laugh.

"One of these days I am going to give that girl exactly what she deserves."

Gemma burst out laughing. It was the first time all week, and it actually felt good. George glared at her, and she laughed even harder. Then wiping the tears from her eyes, she patted him on the arm, and teased. "It's good to see some things never change."

George laughed too. He put his arm around Gemma's shoulder and gave her a squeeze. "So? How about you? Going to the Hub tonight?"

Gemma thought about the handcuffs in her pocket, and shook her head. "Sorry, George. I have previous plans."

"Are you joining the hunt?" The shock in his voice, almost made her cringe.

Would nobody consider her an adult? "Not tonight. I have something I need to do at home."

"In that case, can you drop me off at the Hub on the way by? I was hoping to catch a ride with Sara, but it doesn't look like that's going to happening."

"You're not hunting tonight?"

George's grin was devilish. "Yeah. Later. I'm meeting Tony and we're heading over to the Strawberry-Moon Dance."

That so wasn't fair. Tony was still a child in more ways that Gemma, but nobody would refuse him admittance to the dance just because he was male. Gemma waved at George, blew a kiss at Tony who was waiting outside the Hub, and drove home. It didn't matter what she thought. Pack law was Pack law and she wasn't about to change it.

At the cabin, she heated up some tomato soup, which she ate with a ham and cheese sandwich. By the time the first moonbeam shone through her living room window, she had locked the doors and undressed. She might have been able to shift since she was eleven, but Gemma still couldn't control the magic enough not to destroy her clothes when she shifted. When the clock struck eight, she was handcuffed to the steel frame of her bed.

This wolf would not be running free tonight.

Chapter Nineteen

Stupid. Stupid. Stupid. How could she be so stupid?

A married man? Jade could just die from the shame of it. Not that it was all her fault. He had been just as eager as she had been. Maybe even more so.

No. She wasn't going to pass the blame onto him just because he was a man. She was the one who had gone out specifically to satisfy her own needs. He couldn't help himself. She knew the power pheromones had on the opposite sex. She had been the victim of them more than once herself over the years.

No, it wasn't his fault. She had chosen him the moment she had laid eyes on him.

Still the pain had been unbelievable when Helen ran across the room and threw her arms around him. Jade had wanted to claw her eyes out. She couldn't believe the effect this man had on her. It was really stupid, considering she didn't know his name, and he was married. For the first time since her disastrous marriage, she had found herself wanting more from a man than just sex.

The first time she had felt the magic of the moon on her hormones, she thought she was in love. Unfortunately for them both, the boy she chose thought so too. They were both young and naïve, and had allowed their raging hormones to lead them straight to the altar. She tried to make it work, but after three years of fighting, except during the full moon at which times they never left the bedroom, they divorced. She should have known better. Marriage wasn't in the cards for her. Not then ... Not now.

Jade wondered if her mother had felt that way before she'd met Jade's father. Jade's father was a very special man. Irish, born and raised, he'd left his homeland in his teens and moved to the States, where he became a police officer.

He met Jade's mother while on a case, and it was love at first sight. It was during the full moon, but Jade's mother was older and more mature than Jade had been, and she had learned not to let herself get carried away by the pull of the moon. Her father liked to tell Jade it only took two months of chasing her, before Caer finally turned around and caught him. Three months after they'd first laid eyes on each other they were wed. Cerridwen blessed their marriage and nine months later Jade was born. Jade still dreamed of one day meeting a man like her father.

Leaning against the closed door, Jade let her hand stray to her short locks. She could never compete with a woman like Helen.

Helen was so much like Jade's mother. Both were beautiful beyond measure and wore their hair in a long plait down their backs. As a child Jade had loved her mother's hair, and had insisted her mother plait hers in the exact same way. Then, at age five, Jade's ideal world had come crashing down around her small shoulders. A group of vampires had banded together to destroy her mother. Jade had watched from her hiding spot in the closet as monster after monster had exploded. She was not afraid because she had seen her mother fight before and her mother always won.

Soon there was only one left. Her little heart almost stopped when the monster wrapped her mother's beautiful long braid around his hand. Her mother's head was pulled back, and her slender white throat was exposed. The pulse on the side of her neck beat in time with Jade's own heart. Jade watched in frozen helplessness as the vampire reached in front of her mother with his free hand. His middle fingernail grew a lethal three inches. Slowly he slid it from one side of her mother's throat to the other. Caer's eyes widen with the realization she was dying. She stopped struggling, and threw her arm behind her, thrusting it into the vampire's chest. She brought it back with the vampire's black heart still beating in her palm. His body slowly disintegrated and when he was gone, Caer's severed head fell to the floor. Her body followed with a soft thud.

Jade had cut her own plait off the next morning, and vowed she would never let it grow again. When it came to sexy or safe, she would choose safe every time.

Still shaking from the horror of her memories, Jade pushed herself away from the door. She didn't have time for daydreams or memories. There was a killer out there and her job was to stop him. She put her vest on, leaned down to retie her hiking boot, *she really did need to get new laces,* and then took two steps into the woods before shifting into an owl.

On silent wings she lifted herself into the sky, familiarizing herself with the geography. It was so peaceful up here, away from the world and all its problems. Higher and higher she soared, as the world got smaller and smaller, until it was nothing but a road map. Jade had no problem making out the rivers, lakes, and roads crisscrossing the countryside. She called on the memory of the map at the information center to identify her surroundings. Stormy Lake, where the Inner Sanctum was situated, the next lake over was originally *Tamiita-de-cimp,* which was Romanian for ground pine, but in recent years had been officially changed to Pine Lake. The main road completely circled Stormy Lake, with different spars leading into the forest and towards the mountains. The road didn't go completely around Pine Lake. Instead it ended on the north side at the entrance to a large estate, while joining the highway on the south side. A few houses dotted the lakeshore with most of it being unpopulated.

The owl drifted silently downward until it could make out the different birch, pine and maple trees.

It followed a branch in the main road that ran from the highway across the bridge between Sycamore and Stormy Lakes, straight to the Wolf Center about five kilometres away. There were already several wolves beginning to gather there. They didn't appear threatening and Jade ignored them. Instead she flew across the lake to the west end of town. This was where she lost the trail earlier so it was as good a place as any to start the search again.

On this side of the lakes, the highway doubled as Main Street. Most of the shops were already closed for the evening, with two restaurants and one bar in town still open. In human form, Jade wandered between the buildings, searching the dumpsters and out buildings behind them. Satisfied that nobody, or nothing, was hiding there, she entered the first restaurant.

Ordering a burger and cola she found a chair in the back corner where she could see everything going on in the room. Which wasn't much. Other than herself, there were two women, one man, who surprisingly didn't interest her in the least, and a couple of teenagers. All were human. She listened to the idle conversation for a while, but nobody mentioned a stranger. Surprisingly nobody mentioned the murder, which meant that the cops were keeping it quiet for now.

Wiping her mouth, Jade left a tip under her plate and walked to the next restaurant. The burgers here were much better, but the occupants all human, were of no more help than the others. Jade finished her burger and headed for the Waterfront Bar.

Jade entered to the sounds of "Boot Scootin' Boogie" blaring from the jukebox. Ignoring the mostly empty tables scattered around, Jade crossed the dance floor easily avoided the few dancers there. Most of the crowd was in their late forties, early fifties, and the conversations ran the gamut from grandchildren to fishing. Jade returned the smiles and nods of a few, while ignoring the suspicious glares from others. She was used to small town mentalities. Unless you were born and raised in a place, you were considered a stranger--which should make it easy to find one.

Ordering a beer, she listened as Billy Ray Cyrus began to belt out "Achy Breaky Heart", and took a stool at the bar. Within seconds a tall, darkly handsome man pulled the stool beside hers closer, and sat down.

"New in town?" He moved his stool even closer so his leg pressed against hers. He leaned his elbow on the bar and flashed her a smile, she knew was meant to melt her heart, or at least her inhibitions. It did absolutely nothing for her.

Jade ignored the pressure of his leg. "What makes you think so?" She sipped her beer while studying him over the bottle. His smile was pleasant enough, but there was no mistaking the leer in his blue eyes, even in this dim light.

"I haven't seen you around before."

"What do you want, Dave?" The bartender wiped the counter, purposely knocking Dave's arm out from under him.

Dave glared at the bartender, who was a cute twenty something. "Why do care, Sue? You dumped me. Remember?"

Great! This was exactly where she wanted to be. The middle of a lover's quarrel. Was she destined to be the other woman?

"Get over yourself, Dave. I don't care what you do or who you do it with." It sure sounded to Jade like she cared. "Do you want a beer or not?"

Telltale scarlet began to creep up his neck and his voice became harsh. "Of course I want a beer. Why else would I be here?"

"Why else indeed?"

Sue returned and slammed a bottle of beer on the counter. Dave grabbed it, then turned and reached for Jade's arm. "Let's sit over there," he said, pointing to a table away from the bar.

Jade saw the hurt in the girl's eyes. "I'm quite comfortable here," she said. "I can't stay long anyway. I was just looking for a friend of mine. Have you seen any other strangers in town lately? He should have arrived earlier tonight. I'm not sure where he's staying though."

"Sorry, haven't seen anyone. If I were new in town, I'd want to stay at the Inner Sanctum. It's a real cool castle across the lake."

Unless Randy had her completely fooled, he wasn't there.

A wolf howled somewhere nearby. "Was that a wolf?"

"Sure was."

Jade turned in her chair so she could see out over the lake. The moon sparkled on the water, lighting a path almost to the other side. "Are there very many wolves around here?"

Dave shifted uncomfortably on his stool, and seemed to find his beer bottle suddenly fascinating. "There are a few," he mumbled.

Jade could sense Dave's reluctance to talk about the wolves, but she pressed on anyway. "Are they dangerous?" She leaned towards him and whispered, just the right amount of nervousness present in her voice.

"They're all dangerous as far as I'm concerned," he mumbled. "And stranger."

"What do you mean?" Jade sat back, and watched Dave over the top of her beer as she took another sip.

He glanced at the other occupants of the room, and then watched Sue pour a drink. Finally he stared at an invisible spot on the countertop. "Nothing." He finished his beer and called to Sue to bring him another.

Jade declined his offer of another beer and changed the subject. "Where's the hot spot in town?"

Dave ogled her lewdly, and raised his eyebrows in an attempt to look debonair. "My place." He said all the right things, but he couldn't keep his eyes off Sue at the other end of the bar.

Jade ignored his comment, and watched him watch Sue, like a tiger ready to pounce. It would be obvious to a blind man that his interest lay at the other end of the bar.

Jade relaxed and found her mind wondering to last night. She reminded herself he was married, put his memory away, and turned her attention back to Dave. "So why did your girlfriend break up with you?"

"It's stupid really." He took a gulp of beer, his eyes never leaving Sue as she served drinks to the other customers. "We had a big fight about the dance over at the mansion."

Jade's interest perked. "Dance?" He had to mean Wulfson Mansion. If there was a dance there tonight, she might be able to sneak in and get a peek at the leader of the pack before her meeting with him in a couple of days. "That's at the end of Tamiita-de-cimp, isn't it?"

"Yeah. But nobody calls it that anymore. That place is cool. Built like that mansion in the movie 'Gone With the Wind'. You know the one I mean. My mom has that movie on VCR and must have made us kids watch it at least a dozen times. She was always pointing out the similarities between that mansion and Wulfson Mansion. Myself, I prefer The Inner Sanctum. Now there's a real castle. Has a dungeon and everything. I took Sue there last Halloween."

Jade tried to get Dave back on the subject that interested her most. "Tell me about this dance."

"Once a month, always during the full moon, they have a Moon-Phase Dance. This month it's the Strawberry Moon."

"Is that what they call it these days? Dancing?" They both jumped as an old man slammed his empty bottle on the counter between them. "No decent citizen would be caught dead at one of those so called dances. Never let my sons go." He glared at Dave. "... I won't let my grandchild go either. Those dances should be banned."

Sue came over and picked up the empty bottle. "Goodnight, Gramps," she said. "Don't forget to tell Grams thanks for the pie."

The old man's face broke out into a wide smile, and his blue eyes twinkled. "I sure won't, Sue. And don't you forget what I said about those dances." He glared once more at Dave and left the bar.

"That," Dave watched the old man leave the bar, "Is why Sue broke up with me. Her grandfather overheard me and a friend talking about the dance. He told Sue and she assumed I wanted to go."

"Do you? Want to go, I mean."

"Hell no. That's the thing. I've never been. I've never wanted to go. I love Sue, but her grandfather has her convinced I would rather be there than with her."

"Why don't you try telling Sue the truth?"

Dave drained the last of his beer. "She won't believe me."

"It doesn't hurt to try." Jade saw the way Sue looked at Dave, whenever he wasn't looking at her. She was pretty sure Sue wanted to believe Dave. She just needed a little encouragement.

Jade finished her own beer and said her goodbyes. She would make another patrol around town, before expanding her search further.

Chapter Twenty

The moon stirred her passion. The wind whispered to her.

The owl perched on the branch of a birch, wide amber eyes taking in the activity below. Just a few candles illuminated the stone walkway from the gates to the main entrance of the house. The candles were probably more to set the mood than anything else. The sky was free from clouds, and between the stars and the brilliance of the moon, no artificial light was required.

"Sorry, sweetheart. I can't let you in tonight."

The guard, tall, dark and delicious enough to eat, was talking to a woman in her thirties who could barely stand up. Even from where she perched, Jade could tell the woman was more than a little inebriated.

"What?" Her shrill voice jarred on the ears.

"You know the rules. No drinking."

The owl listened to their conversation, pleased to learn there were at least some rules to the mating rituals.

"Oh, please," the girl continued, stretching out the please. "You know me. I've been here at least a dozen times. We've even danced together." She added the latter with, what she probably believed was a seductive wink, but looked more like someone trying to keep both eyes open.

She teetered vicariously on her high heels. The guard reached out to steady her before she landed on her face. The woman, who appeared to be in her thirties, brushed the guards hands away, and reached for the gate. In a fluid motion, the guard reclaimed her arm, turned her back towards him, and pulled a cell phone from his pocket.

"Sorry, sweetheart, but rules are rules. They're there to protect you as well as us." He pushed the recall button on his phone, and waited for someone to answer. "I'll have a cab take you home."

"I don't want to go home." The woman pouted prettily, realized she was getting nowhere, and let her body relax against the guards. "Why don't you take me home?"

"Not tonight, darling," he drawled. His voice was enough to make any woman's toes curl.

He spoke quietly into the phone and within minutes a cab pulled up. The guard helped settle the woman in the back seat, before handing several bills to the driver. "Make sure she gets home safe," he said. "Don't drop her off anywhere else."

The cab left only to be replaced by another. This one was carrying several women, all wearing low cut, and body hugging outfits, or short flowing dresses which barely concealed them.

The owl left its perch and flew to a spot just out of sight of the gates. In the blink of an eye Jade was standing in the center of the road. She had chosen a low cut, halter style dress with a short, flimsy, flyaway skirt in blood red. Not bad. She glanced down at her bare feet and frowned. One would think that after fifty years she could get the shoes right.

Jade closed her eyes and concentrated. When she opened them again, she was wearing a pair of black leather sandals with two-inch heels. Much better. She walked around the bend and approached the gate. The low, appreciative whistle coming from the bushes beside the gate sent a shiver down her spine. She turned towards the sound to watch the same guard emerge. He was even better looking up close.

He took his time as his eyes traveled from the top of her head to the tips of her bare toes. The feminine part of her thrilled at the hungry look in his eyes, but to her amazement, other than a deep appreciation of his masculine beauty, Jade felt nothing at all.

"You're new." Curiosity warred with the hunger in his eyes.

"I'm staying over at the Inner Sanctum for a few days." Would she even be granted access to the house? For all she knew, these dances could be by invitation only. If that were the case, in all probability, she wasn't going to find the killer here. Even if it wasn't the case, she didn't really think she was going to find him here. She had searched the town and the surrounding woods for any sign of a disturbance, but had found nothing. Either her prey was in human form, sleeping, or he had learned to control his hunger.

For several hours she had been trying to ignore the lure of this place, but every breeze carried it to her. The hunger inside that building called to the hunger in her until she thought she would go insane. Finally she admitted, at least to herself, that if she was going to function enough to do her job, first she would have to get a fix for her craving.

A crackling came from the guard's walkie-talkie and they both jumped. The guard pulled it from the clip on his belt and a statically metallic voice said, "What's the hold-up down there. You trying to keep the pretty lady for yourself, Mike?"

Mike glared somewhere to the right of the gate, held the button on his walkie-talkie and snarled. "Maybe. And maybe I'm just waiting for you to get your sorry ass back down here so I can escort the pretty lady to the house myself."

Jade kept one ear on the conversation, while checking out the area surrounding the gate. For the first time she noticed the camera mounted halfway up a tree near the gate and almost hidden from view by the leaves.

"No can do, buddy," the disembodied voice crackled.

Jade tuned in to the life all around her. Crickets chirped merrily, accompanied every so often by the soft, almost scratchy hoot of a barn owl. Several bats swooped over the open water dining on insects, while raccoons fished in the shallow waters for a meal of clams. A loon called to its mate somewhere in the distance. Several wolves were wandering in the gardens past the gate, and music drifted from the mansion.

The music called to something deep inside. A hunger. A need to be wild and free. It teased the animal side of her, begging for its release. Jade's foot began to tap to the beat of CCR's "Bad Moon Rising."

"Miss?"

Jade spun towards the guard. When had he quit talking on the radio? "I'm sorry. Did you say something?"

Mike held the gate open. "If you stay on the path it'll bring you to the front doors of the house.

Jade smiled her thanks, and stepped through the open gate. She heard him groan behind her, and ignored his muttered "I'm going to kill you for this, Tony." Jade followed the flagstone path, the candles more than enough to light the way, and the wolves keeping to the shadows.

"Don't worry about the wolves." Mike's voice drifted to her on the breeze. "They won't bother you." His nearly inaudible "unless you want them to," had Jade smiling to herself.

Jade was beginning to feel like Little Red Riding Hood on her way to grandma's house with the big bad wolf lurking behind every tree, just waiting to pounce. Trepidation kept her moving slow, that and walking on heels. She should be out looking for the killer. Instead she let her hormones lead her to the one place she was guaranteed he wouldn't be. She should turn around, now, before it was too late.

She kept on walking.

The door opened as Jade approached, and several drop-dead gorgeous men surrounded her and propelled her inside. Nobody actually touched her, but their hunger was so intense it felt like they were all over her. The youngest among them leaned towards her, and inhaled deeply.

"Are you sniffing me?" she asked the obvious. She didn't have to sniff anyone. Lust rolled off them in waves. The female part of her thrilled to their attention, and yet not one of these men appealed to her.

The young man jumped back, his neck and ears crimson. "No ... no," he stammered, and began to cough.

Several of the others laughed, while the one closest to him patted him on the back. "Don't mind him," he said. "This is his first dance."

Jade turned her eyes demurely to the floor, and allowed a slight smile to come to her lips. "Mine too," she said in a quiet voice.

The foyer was the size of three average living rooms, with diamond chandeliers and floors polished to a reflective shine. Music came from a live band set up on a stage at the far end. The band itself consisted of five of the hottest men. Thoughts of sex ran rampant through her mind, and yet she couldn't picture herself with any of these men. She couldn't say the same for the other women. They were practically drooling, and not just for the band. Every man in the room reeked of lust.

Jade recognized the song the band was singing as Franz Ferdinand's "Do you want to" and by the look of the dancers on the floor, and the people milling around off the dance floor, more than one person was getting lucky tonight.

Someone grabbed her hand, and dragged Jade to the dance floor. The music was a living entity that took control, and Jade moved to the beat.

"You're new around here." It was a statement.

There was something comforting about her partner. It might have been the fact that he wasn't looking at her like he was about to pounce and devour her. She found herself wanting to tell him everything. "I just got here today."

Another male sidled up to her and leaned his body into hers, whispering in her ear. "Why don't you ditch the old man and try me?" His voice was a study in smooth seduction sending shivers across her skin.

The old man, as the youth referred to him could have passed for late thirties, early forties. He held her closer, and practically growled at the youth. "Back off Tony."

Tony put both hands in the air and stepped back in surrender. "Hey, I was just trying to show the girl a good time. Not to mention trying to save your ass, old man. I wouldn't want to be in your place when Sondra finds out you were dancing with this pretty young thing."

Jade stopped dancing and stared at the two men. Great. Just what she needed tonight, another married man.

Tony smiled at the older man in triumph, only to have his smile dashed when the older man shrugged. "Since when does my sister-in-law care who I dance with?"

The music changed to "Little Red Riding Hood" which Jade found rather fitting, as she was pulled into another dance.

The outer door opened and a hush fell over the room. Jade didn't have to turn around to know who had arrived. Every nerve in her body hummed like a finely tuned violin. She was aware the instant he stood behind her, and wasn't a bit surprised that her dance partner had faded into the crowd.

"You *better* watch out." His voice was a long awaited lover's caress, a drop of cool water for a parched soul, the sun after a week's rain.

All thoughts of Helen disappeared like fine mist. "Why's that?" Her voice was an unbecoming squeak.

He grinned wickedly, and Jade felt her toes curl. "You're in my woods now."

He moved closer and Jade backed away. The music and the crowd faded until they were the only two in the room.

Jade felt the wall solid against her back, and stopped. Luke kept moving until he was pressing against her and she couldn't help notice the evidence of his interest. Her bones melted and her stomach muscles clenched. Slowly, ever so slowly, his head tipped towards hers. Jade had plenty of time to move, to avoid the connection; her lips parted slightly in anticipation of the kiss. Her breath came in short, quick spurts.

An image of ebony tresses and coal-black eyes popped unbidden into her head. Jade's blood froze in her veins and she averted her head. "What about Helen?" she whispered.

"Helen?" The stunned look on Luke's face was almost comical. "What does my sister have to do with anything?"

"Your sister!" Relief bubbled to the surface and Jade began to laugh. Several faces turned their way but Jade ignored them. She wiped at the tears on her cheeks. "I thought she was your ..." Jade's shoulders shook as her laughter escaped once again.

"My what?" Luke didn't look amused.

"Your ..." Jade wiped once more at the tears, and tried to sober. It was no use. "Wife," she blurted before once again bursting with gales of laughter.

Luke glared at their audience, then took Jade by the arm and steered her into an adjoining room, slamming the door behind them. He looked at her then, his tawny eyes smouldering. Jade found it hard to breathe normally.

"I am not now." He took a step closer to her, stretching out each word as he spoke. "Nor have I ever been."

Oh, oh. He was looking at her like he was ravenous and she was the main course. Jade backed tight against the wall, no longer laughing.

"Married."

Luke placed his large hands against the wall, one on either side of her head, and claimed her lips with his. Jade's knees turned to jelly and she had to clutch his shoulders to keep from falling.

The world around them disappeared. Jade wasn't aware of anything except his lips on hers, until she felt his fingers burning a trail along the sensitive skin on the inside of her leg.

"Mmmm," he murmured. His breath was hot against her lips. "No panties."

Jade gasped when his fingers probed her hot moistness, first with one, then two fingers. She moaned as those fingers made love to her. Her nails dug into his shoulders, and her lips burned beneath his.

She was teetering on the brink of orgasm when she heard the first scream.

Instinct took over. Jade shoved Luke with such force he landed in a very undignified heap on the floor. She stepped over him to get to the door, ignoring his blustering and the curious looks of the dancers, she raced across the room and out the door she had entered through, shifting the second she was alone.

Chapter Twenty-One

A large brown wolf crouched at the edge of the brush watching the humans through the large window. The moon shone a silvery path across the mirror surface of the lake, but the wolf was more interested in the two people still inside.

It waited.

Finally, the two people began to move across the room towards the door the others had left through. The wolf crept around the building to where it could watch the couple when they came out.

They were arguing in quiet voices. The wolf sensed the anger coming from the female and the frustration coming from the male. It wanted to skulk back into the forest and hunt elsewhere, but its hunger kept it where it was.

Finally, throwing his arms up in the air and muttering something incoherent, the male stomped over to his car, and slamming the door in anger, and sped off.

Sue watched Dave drive away and sighed. She hated it when he got so angry. Sue turned around and locked the door, jiggling the handle to make sure it locked.

Sometimes the lock didn't catch. She told the owner, more than once, that he needed to get a new lock, but the owner was male and like Dave, he didn't listen to her.

Sue was almost to the bottom of the steps when she spotted the brown wolf watching her from the bushes. Having lived here all her life, Sue had no fear of the wolves which often roamed around, especially during the full moon. The people here had learned to cohabitate with the wolves, and there had never been an attack by a wolf on a human in her lifetime. As far as she knew, there had been no attacks in her grandfather's lifetime.

At the bottom of the stairs Sue took two steps towards the wolf before crouching and reaching her hand, palm up, towards the animal.

"Hello, big boy." She kept her voice quiet so she wouldn't startle him. "What are you doing out here all by yourself? Why aren't you with your friends tonight?" Sue knew quite a few wolves by sight, but this one was a stranger. Easy enough to tell, most of the wolves around here were gray wolves.

The wolf inched out of the bushes and into the open, never once taking its eyes off the female in front of it. The blood rushing in her veins called to it, and the hunger gnawed. Slowly the tip of its tail began to wag.

The way the wolf was watching her was beginning to make Sue a little nervous. Usually the wolves around here looked at her with curiosity and went away. Sometimes they would come over, sniff her hand, and let her pet their soft fur.

The wolf growled, deep in its throat, and Sue knew real fear for the first time in her life. Her first instinct was to run to her car. Common sense told her to move slowly away from the wolf.

The sour milk smell of fear was intoxicating to the wolf. It watched the woman slowly pull her arm back and begin to rise. It leapt for her throat. Sue saw the wolf jump and instinctively threw her arms up to protect her throat. Large, sharp teeth pierced her arms.

Sue screamed. Her fear and agony rang out across the lake and echoed from the hills.

*****

Luke was stunned to say the least. What had happened? One minute he had her right where he wanted her—Okay, maybe not exactly where he wanted her, which would be a place a lot more private than the mansion during a dance—the next minute she was gone, again. Only this time he was sitting on the floor like an idiot.

He brushed his pants smooth and stalked out of the mansion. The scowl on his face was enough to keep everyone at a distance. To make matters worse, he couldn't find her. Nobody had seen her after she left the mansion, which meant she had to still be on the grounds, unless she had run into the forest in her panic. Another thing he didn't understand. What had spooked her? She wasn't a virgin. Last night attested to that. Still she had acted like some outraged puritan, and taken flight.

Whatever her problem was he had to find her. It was too easy to get lost in the woods at night, or worse.

His cell phone vibrated in his pocket. "What?" he snapped irritated with the interruption.

"Luke, Daniel. You better get over to the Waterside right away."

Fear's icy fingers clutched his chest. "Talk to me Daniel?"

"Sue has been attacked."

Five minutes later he was in the parking lot of the Waterside.

"It was a wolf." The angry words reach Luke before he reached the parking lot.

"How do you know it wasn't just a dog?"

Dave glared at the crowd around them. "I know a damned wolf when I see one."

"There's no wolf around here that would attack without a good reason."

The crowd parted to allow Luke through just as Dave took a step towards the dark-haired speaker. "Are you calling me a liar?"

Blood soaked their clothing, and Sue was extremely pale and shaking, but at least she was alive. Luke stepped between the two angry men. "I'm sure nobody is calling anybody a liar," he said. He tipped his head slightly towards the dark-haired boy, which was enough to send the young man scurrying away.

A quick look assured him the blood on Dave was mostly Sue's or the assailant's but he couldn't be sure without a closer examination. "Can you tell me what happened, Dave?"

"She was attacked by a damned wolf," Dave said, still incensed. "It attacked for no reason."

Luke spoke in low, comforting tones. "Is that what happened, Sue?"

Sue sniffed. "A ... wolf." She lifted her head to look at him, tears running down her cheeks. "Strange."

Luke tensed. *Where was that ambulance?* "How do you mean strange?"

Sue sniffed again and someone handed her a tissue. She blew her nose, and tried to smile. It came out more of a grimace. "I am so stupid." She held her arm close to her, and her body rocked back and forth as she spoke. "I was locking up and I felt something behind me. There he was ... standing in the shadows, watching me. I'd never seen him before. He was large, with brown fur, and his eyes were really strange. They were such a pale blue, and they had a milky film over them. He looked so alone ... and scared."

She took another wipe at her tears. "I was just talking to him. I didn't do anything wrong. I always talk to the wolves. Sometimes it's like they understand me. Never before has one growled at me, let alone attacked."

Sue looked so lost and forlorn, sitting on the step with blood still dripping from her wounds. "Where was Dave when this happened?" Luke asked.

"That's none of your business." Dave glared at Luke.

Sue put a hand on Dave's arm. "It's okay, Dave. It's not your fault. None of this is. I shouldn't have been foolish enough to treat a wild animal like it was a lost pet." She turned her attention back to Luke. "We were arguing and I sent Dave away."

This time when she smiled it actually reached her eyes. "Lucky for me, Dave is stubborn. If he hadn't come back when he did, I would have been wolf dinner."

Luke nodded and began to scan the road behind the crowd gathered in the parking lot. "Where the hell is that ambulance?" As if on cue, a siren blared, the crowd quickly scattered, and the ambulance pulled up in front of them.

Steven climbed out followed by a much younger version of himself. He quickly cleaned and bandaged Sue's arm then made a quick examination of Dave without touching him. He nodded almost imperceptibly towards Sue.

Luke sighed, and brushed his hand through his hair. He placed his hands on Sue's shoulders, drawing her attention to him. "The wolf that attacked you." He ignored the dawning horror in Sue's eyes and continued. "It was infected with a rare disease. There's more than a small chance you've been infected. Steven and George will take you to the Center where Dr. Hristea will examine you."

Dave jumped in between Sue and Luke, shoving Luke away from his girl. "Get away from her," he shrieked. "You aren't taking her anywhere."

Several men moved towards them, but Luke raised a hand and they stopped. "Were you bitten?" he asked Dave curtly. He had never really liked Dave, and had only tolerated him for Sue's sake.

Dave stared at the blood on his sleeve in horror, seeming to notice it for the first time. His voice suddenly small, he stammered. "I don't think so."

Luke turned to George. "Hey George glad you could help out tonight. Would you take Dave to the ambulance? He needs to be tested."

"No problem, boss."

Sue and a very subdued Dave were taken to the waiting ambulance. Luke quickly rounded up a hunting party, and sent everyone else home. The ambulance pulled onto the road, and the hunting party entered the woods on the trail of the wolf.

Chapter Twenty-Two

The woods were crawling with wolves and humans alike, all looking for signs of the wolf. Jade sat on a fallen tree and put her head in her hands. Twigs snapped under careless feet. An owl screeched and flew off. Crickets chirped merrily. The canopy of the trees blocked the moon making the woods extremely dark, except for crisscrossing beams of the searcher's flashlights.

This was useless. Jade was never going to find him like this. By now the humans, in their misguided attempt to be helpful, had destroyed any clear trail left by the wolf.

Jade closed her eyes, took several deep, anchoring breaths, and let her mind search. There was something ahead, moving furtively amongst the trees. Hunger, frustration, and fear pelted her. Her skin grew clammy and her limbs began to shake. Her breath came in painful gulps. Her eyes popped open and Jade fell to the ground on all fours, quickly leaving the other's behind.

A twig snapped on the right. The white wolf paused, and listened. When no other sound came, it lifted its head and sniffed the night air. Its prey still lay ahead, so that isn't what made the noise. The wolf stood still, barely breathing, and then heard it again.

Something was moving in the same direction as she was. Whatever it was, it stayed downwind so she caught no scent. She didn't worry about whatever it was catching her scent. While in animal form she carried none. It was a strange phenomenon. One that made it easier to hunt without being detected, but sometimes it made her feel like she didn't really exist. Like the animal part of her was a dream, or the fantasy of a broken mind.

Closing her eyes, she once again reached out to her surroundings. The forest was suddenly silent. It was like the forest knew there were hunters out and didn't want to distract them. Even the breeze stilled. There were at least four wolves hunting the same prey. They were to her right, about a quarter mile behind, so they couldn't have made the sound.

With a little more concentration she found it. A raccoon. It had been in search of its dinner when it caught a whiff of the wolves. Self-preservation overrode hunger and it had found a hiding place up a nearby tree. It had snapped a twig in its haste to get out of their path. It was comfortable in its hole and would wait until the wolves had passed by before coming down and continuing on its own journey.

The hunger and frustration was growing in the hunted. The forest animals sensed it and kept silent. Jade quickened her pace, closing in. Pain and torment tore at her mind, threatening to shatter it like the mind which screamed its agony.

Jade emerged from the forest into the open area of a public campground. A bright light stood like a beacon outside the washrooms. A few campfires still flickered, but most were no more than embers or cooling ash.

A door creaked, and Jade spotted movement in the shadows next to the building where the circle of light couldn't quite reach. A young girl stepped out of the building and the door slammed shut behind her. The shadows moved until a fully-grown wolf stood between the girl and Jade.

The girl froze. This was her first time out of the city. She had been so nervous about coming here, but her friends had wanted her to come, and her mother didn't. It was supposed to be their last hurrah before starting their jobs and their new lives as adults.

Life after high school. There had been times when Samantha hadn't believed it would ever happen. That was her name, although her friends called her Sam or Sammy. It drove her mother crazy. "Why do they insist on calling you by those awful names? You are Samantha, and don't you forget it."

Samantha gave a mental shrug. It really didn't matter anymore what her friends called her. Her mom, as always, would have the last say and there was no doubt in Sam's mind what she would have put on her tombstone. Her full name, Samantha Annabelle Wilson. God how she had hated that name. Now, because of a cruel twist of fate, she would suffer eternity lying beneath a stone which bore that dreadful name. Along with, no doubt, something like ... The girl never did listen.

Well Mom, you were right, as usual. I should never have come on this trip. Looks like I won't be coming home.

Samantha wondered if it would be quick. Would the wolf kill her instantly, or toy with her first. She really hoped it would be quick. She hated pain. Sam knew she should run, or scream for help. That's it. Maybe if she screamed loud enough she could scare the wolf off.

She stared into those pale blue eyes – eyes that looked almost human – and her throat constricted until no sound could escape. She tried to run, but her legs wouldn't move. She told them to, she begged them to, but they were a lot like the rest of her. They didn't listen.

Sam closed her eyes and prayed it would be quick.

The wolf hunched between Jade and the camper, its back to Jade. Hunger rose from it in waves. The girl was frozen by her fear, unable to move on her own. The tip of the wolf's tail began to twitch signalling its intention to attack, and it growled low in its throat. The sound didn't carry, but Jade felt it.

Jade leapt into the air, shifting into owl form in a single heartbeat. *Run!* Her mind shoved the command into the girl's.

Sam suddenly found her body responding and she rushed past the wolf without slowing down or turning to see if it had followed. Once she had reached the relative safety of her tent, she crawled into her sleeping bag, pulled it up over her head, closed her eyes, and prayed for morning.

The girl rushed past. The wolf pounced, only to howl its frustration when it caught empty air and rolled to the ground. Scrambling to its feet it began to chase its prey. The owl screeched a warning seconds before it slammed into the wolf, knocking it off its feet. Its prey forgotten, the wolf now fought to protect itself. The owl swooped repeatedly, ripping flesh and fur with each attack. The wolf howled in pain and frustration.

Jade shifted into wolf form and pounced. Shouting distracted Jade, and the brown wolf struck. Razor sharp teeth sank into fur and flesh. Crimson rivers ran over snow-white fur. Jade shook the other wolf off, knocking him to the ground. Her powerful jaws found their target, and snapped the brown wolf's neck.

There was a low growl behind her. Jade spun around to stare into the yellow eyes of a huge gray wolf. There was something heart wrenchingly familiar about those eyes. There was a slight movement to her left, and Jade realized they weren't alone. Three others were attempting to circle her. Jade had never run from a fight before, but these wolves had done nothing to warrant their deaths.

The white wolf tipped its nose in an almost imperceptible nod towards the gray wolf with the yellow eyes and leapt into the air.

The white owl circled them once before disappearing over the treetops.

Chapter Twenty-Three

Moarté. Luke had known she was here, but he didn't have to like it. Would she leave now that she had dealt with the killer? Not likely. They had interrupted her before she was finished. She wouldn't leave without satisfying herself that she had destroyed the mongrel. Luke hadn't recognized the wolf. It wasn't one of his. But it was of his blood. Of that he was positive. He could smell it.

This wasn't over yet. Not by a long shot. He offered up a silent prayer that for once in his life he was wrong.

There was a shimmer of magic and Luke, Daniel, Grégoire, and young Greg stood in a circle around the brown wolf. Daniel knelt beside the body and felt for a pulse.

"He's alive."

Luke turned towards the man approaching, his shotgun dangling from his arm at his side, and gave a curt nod. The sour milk scent of fear permeated the air, but other than the wary gray eyes, the man showed no other outward signs of his discomfort. Luke had the utmost respect for the man able to conquer his fear and face the four of them.

"Evening, Jack," he said casually.

The man inclined his own head slightly in acknowledgement of the other men. "Luke," he answered. He took a handkerchief from his pocket and swiped at the sweat now beading on his forehead. Luke noticed the shift of the shotgun, putting it into trembling fingers.

Jack cleared his throat and pointed the tip of the gun at the wolf, lying in a steadily increasing pool of blood, its head at an awkward angle. "One of yours?"

"No." Luke turned his attention to the body lying on the ground. "We'll need shovels and a couple of trucks."

Jack gave a quick nod. "No problem. I'll send the boys out to help."

Luke was staring at the body, but he was seeing a white wolf with one of a kind amber eyes, and a scent he would never forget. He shook his head to clear away the image. "We'll handle it," he said, his voice edged in anger. "Can't risk anyone else getting infected."

Jack shuddered. "Who?" was all he said.

Luke ignored the question. Jack knew enough about them as it was. "Where are the trucks," he asked instead.

"Behind the office. Keys are in them. Shovels are in the shed." Wary gray eyes glanced again at the body. "I didn't aim at them."

No, he hadn't. If he had, at least one—if not both—would be dead. Jack wasn't known for missing a target, moving or otherwise. "I know, Jack."

Jack returned to the office. Daniel and his son collected the trucks and shovels. With more care than required they placed the mongrel in one to be taken to the clinic. The other they loaded with tainted soil.

Chapter Twenty-Four

The owl flew drunkenly across the sky, coming to land in a large maple outside the window Jade had left open earlier. She took a second to make sure there was nobody lurking around, and then slipped into her room. Dropping silently to the floor, she shifted. Fire tore through her side where the other wolf had bitten her.

Undressing as she went, Jade entered the small, adjoining bathroom and stepped into the shower. Reaching for the faucet brought with it another bout of excruciating pain. It felt like a dozen sharp teeth were once again tearing into her flesh. While the water sprayed its own brand of stinging needles across her skin, Jade examined the wound. The long, red tendrils snaking out from the already healing wound had her worried.

Jade stayed in the shower until most of the soreness left her body, and the water began to cool. Reluctantly she left the shower, and wrapped herself in one of the thick, terry towels hanging on a hook. She needed sleep, but first she needed something to help with her bruises. Shifting may heal broken bones but Jade needed rest to recoup her strength. Rest denied to her at the moment.

The Lycan gene was already trying to adhere itself to her own DNA. She could feel her blood fighting it. She needed to use the connection to Sue before it was gone. The shared wolf's blood.

"Damn!" There wasn't enough goldenseal to make a poultice to cover her bruises. She would have to restock as soon as possible. Right now she needed to concentrate on Sue, and getting her through what was coming.

She pulled the covers up to her chin, and still her body shivered uncontrollably. She considered starting the fire, but was afraid she wouldn't be able to control the magic and might burn down the house. The distance across the room was much too far to reach on foot. A slight creak brought her attention to Charlotte Gray, who was standing beside her bed holding a tray. A faint, calming aroma teased the corners of her foggy brain, but was soon shoved aside by the succulent aroma of venison.

Jade struggle to sit, cringing at the sudden stabbing in her side. Mrs Gray set the tray on the bedside table and helped her, then fluffed the pillow, all the while clucking like a mother hen. "You left in such a hurry earlier you didn't get your tea," she scolded.

"Thanks, Mrs G." Jade took a sip of the offered cup and immediately her body began to relax. *How did you get in here?*

Mrs G knew she was back? Had she locked the door? Of course she had. She locked it when she left to ensure it would be empty if she had to return in a hurry. Did she unlock it? Had she started to go down to the kitchen for something and changed her mind? Jade gave her head a mental shake to rid it of the jumbled thoughts. It didn't really matter now anyway.

She bit into the sandwich, savouring the spicy meat. "This is good," she mumbled, her mouth full.

Mrs Gray smiled and busied herself straightening the blankets around Jade. Then she picked up the wet towel from the floor where Jade had let it drop.

"You don't need to do that Mrs G." Jade made a move to get out of bed when another stabbing pain laid her back.

"There, there, Miss Jade." Mrs Gray was suddenly there, gently laying Jade back against the fluffed up pillows. "You just drink your tea and let me do what I need to do." She handed Jade the cup as she spoke, and stood there waiting.

Jade was beginning to feel like a naughty child under her scrutiny, so she drank every drop of the tea. There was something familiar and comforting about the tea. Jade handed the empty cup to Mrs Gray. "Thanks," she murmured. Her eyelids were growing heavy and she let herself slip back down under the covers. *Mullen!*

She struggled to sit up, but it was like trying to swim in quick sand. "You drugged me," she accused, as she slipped into unconsciousness.

The doorbell chimed. Mrs Gray patted the covers smooth around Jade's shoulders. "Don't you worry Miss Jade. Nobody will be bothering you tonight. You just rest and let yourself heal."

Jade didn't hear the shutting of the door or the clicking of the lock.

*****

"I demand to see her. Now!" Luke pulled himself to his full height, towering over Charlotte Gray, and glared at her. She wasn't the least bit intimidated by him, and that made him even angrier than he already was. How could he have not known who, and what, she was?

"Sit down Lykos. And quit glaring at me like I'm the enemy. I'm not. And neither is that woman upstairs."

"So you admit she is here?" He was already heading for the hall when he found himself sprawled in the nearest kitchen chair.

"I said sit down." Mrs Gray's voice thundered in the silence of the house. "Do Not make me eject you from this house."

Luke's first instinct was to break the invisible restraints holding him in place. Upon reflection, he took a deep breath, brushed his hand through his hair, and forced himself to visibly relax.

"Point taken," he muttered in a much more amenable tone. The restraints were lifted, but he stayed in his seat. He may have been making a fool of himself, but he was no fool.

"Glad to see you've come to your senses." Charlotte poured a cup of tea from the ever present pot on the stove, and set it in front of Luke. "They're bringing the girl tonight. I've readied the room."

Luke cringed. Sue would go through hell in the next few hours. If she were strong enough—and lucky enough—she would make it through alive. Then, if she learned to control the wolf she would return to her family, a very different person. If not. Luke didn't even want to think about what he would have to do if that happened. The same way he didn't want to think about what he had to do once they got the DNA results from the dead wolf.

"She can't stay."

Charlotte's eyes expressed her sympathy and understanding. "She stays. And I hope I don't have to remind you that as long as she does she is under my protection."

Luke glanced up when Charlotte's small hand covered his own larger one. "It'll be okay, Lykos," she told him.

Luke's own eyes were shadowed with fear and worry. "You know, don't you?"

Charlotte smiled, a sad knowing smile, and shrugged. "They're here," she said.

The bell hadn't rung, and Luke hadn't heard a sound, but Charlotte opened the door and let Steven in, followed by two young men carrying a stretcher. Sue lay on the stretcher. Her face peaceful in sleep. Luke wished it could stay that way, but it wasn't to be. Even those born with the Lycan gene had a hard time during the first few changes. And they had family and friends to help them prepare for what was to come. Sue didn't have the luxury of preparing for what was about to happen to her.

"Steven?"

Steven's black eyes were so full of pity Luke knew what he was going to say before he opened his mouth. "We need to talk, Lykos."

No! This couldn't be happening again. What cruel trick were the Fates playing on him now? Hadn't Gheorgès been enough? Luke didn't think he would survive losing any more family.

Chapter Twenty-Five

The sun shone brightly above the Inner Sanctum. In the room below two men sat on the floor watching the girl as she slept on the mattress. There was no bed. There was no other furniture of any kind. Just the mattress. At least four inches of foam and leather padded the floor, and walls. The only light came from three fluorescent bulbs recessed in the ceiling and protected by metal grates. It was a padded cell, created to keep its occupants from hurting themselves.

The sedative Elizabeth had administered was wearing off, and Sue stirred. Luke sprang to his feet, and approached the mattress. "Hello Sue. How are you feeling?"

Sue blinked several times before finally focusing on his features. "Mr Wulfson?" Her voice was a dry rasp. She tried to grin but it disappeared almost as soon as it started, and her eyes blurred with pain. "Who's making that racket? Can't you make them stop?" she complained.

Luke placed his hand on Sue's forehead. It was on fire. *Randy, would you go get something for our patient to eat?*

"Do you need to yell?" complained Sue, tears in both her voice and her eyes. "It's bad enough they are drilling inside my head."

Luke stared at Sue in shock, and disbelief. She shouldn't have been able to hear his thoughts. It was much too soon. Her powers were developing quicker than he imagined possible. She must be a powerful psychic. That would help her through the transformation. He just hoped it would be enough.

"We will try and be quieter," he told her, his voice barely above a whisper.

Thanks. Her eyes drifted shut, and she fell back into an uneasy slumber.

Luke took his position on the floor, while Randy went in search of food. It was going to be a very long day.
*****

Upstairs the tea began to wear off, and Jade began to stir. The pain in her side was less considerable, but her mind was still far from clear.

"How are you feeling?" The voice was familiar, and comforting.

Jade's eyes flicked open and it took several seconds for her to focus on her surroundings. As she struggled to sit up, Mrs Gray put her tray on the bedside table, and reached out to help her.

Jade pushed the woman's hands away and tried to glare, but that only caused ice picks to pierce her brain. "You drugged me," she accused. She hated that her voice came out whiny instead of firm and imposing.

"Now Miss Jade. I would never do such a thing. I would never harm a soul in this house."

Jade wanted to believe her, but there was a little thing stopping her, like drugged tea.

"You needed rest to help you heal. I just gave you a nice cup of mullein tea to help you along." She held her hands out with the palms up to indicate she was harmless, then turned them down and shook them. "See. No tricks up my sleeve."

Jade really wanted to believe the woman. She *had* needed rest, and the tea *had* helped. If the truth was known, she could use another day of sleep, but she had a job to finish. First she had to find out if she had killed the wolf, and then she had to find out what had happened to it. The wolf was feral and acting on instinct alone. Had something happened to shatter its psyche or was it newly turned? If recently turned, why allowed its freedom in such a state? Perhaps it was a mongrel. If so, had he been born with the gene? Thoughts ran rampant through Jade's restless mind. Their laws were strict. No established pack would allow such a thing to happen. So what had happened? It was up to Jade to discover what had happened, and what action was warranted. She was going to need that body. Thoughts of the wolf turned to thoughts of Sue. She should have been able to connect with the girl last night. Had the tea fuddled her so much, or was something else going on. She forced herself to focus on Mrs Gray.

"What's on your tray today, Mrs G?"

Mrs Gray's lips widened in a large smile, and her blue eyes sparkled. "Today I have brought you steak and eggs, and a nice cup of mullein tea."

Drool was already forming at the corners of Jade's mouth. "Now that you mention it, I am a little hungry." Starving was more like it. Her stomach growled in response to the mouth-watering aroma when Mrs Gray lifted the lid from the tray. She gave Mrs Gray a lopsided grin, and shrugged. "Okay. I admit it. I'm starving."

She devoured the steaks and eggs, and willingly drank the mullein tea. Her senses told her there was nothing extra in it this time, and she needed the rest. The tea would help her relax. With heavy eyelids she once again slid under the covers. A faint smile touched her lips, as Mrs Gray tucked the blankets around her shoulders.

Chapter Twenty-Six

"Let your body relax. Don't try to fight it. Embrace it. You will find it much easier that way."

The voice came through the fog, distant and distorted. Like someone talking with their mouth full of cotton balls. Still she recognized the deep timber in that voice.

"What's happening to me?" The other voice quivered on the verge of tears. *Somebody help me.* There was so much pain and fear in that silent plea it tore at Jade's soul.

Where are you? Jade tried to find the source of the voice but couldn't navigate through the fog in her own brain.

Who are you? It was a timid voice. Timid, and painfully familiar.

She was close. He was close. Too close. Jade couldn't risk exposure. Not now. Not until she was sure the girl was safe. She jumped when she heard his voice again.

"Who are you talking to?" He was demanding in his quiet, forceful way.

Jade would have to be extra careful. He was too close. Why was she hearing his voice? Through the girl? It had to be. She had fully connected with the girl. She didn't dare alert him. *Don't tell him*, she warned. *Look around. Do you know where you are?*

"Nobody." Sue looked at Luke like he was crazy. "I didn't say anything." She looked around the room, at the padded walls and padded floor, up at the bright fluorescent bulbs, then back at Luke, allowing Jade to see everything she saw. "You must be hearing things," she said. "I don't see anyone here."

That's good. Don't tell him I'm listening, Jade told the girl.

Tell him? Who? Mr Wulfson? What would I tell him? That I am having a conversation in my head with a stranger. Wow! I am having a conversation in my head with a stranger, aren't I? How is that possible? Oh crap. I must be going crazy.

Jade's laughter was cut short by Sue's scream, as the pain ripped her muscles apart. Sue's brain began to shut down, and she went into convulsions. Jade quickly wrapped Sue's fragile brain in a cocoon, and drew Sue's pain into herself.

Sue's body quit twitching and she lay quietly, no longer aware of anything going on around her, or within her. She never felt Luke's gentle touch as he checked for a pulse, or heard his gentle, encouraging voice as he replaced the dry cloth on her forehead with a fresh cool one.

In the room two floors above Jade's body began to convulse with such violence her bed actually rattled against the floor. Her own body, already weakened from the poison in her veins, was almost incapable of holding on to Sue's pain. Stubbornly she clung to it, determined that Sue would survive.

The door to her room burst open, and Mrs Gray flew in. She grabbed Jade by the shoulders, and tried to hold her steady. "Open your eyes," she demanded.

Go away, Jade pushed at the voice trying to break her concentration.

"You cannot do this. Let her go," the voice insisted.

Need to help, Jade whimpered. She had no strength to converse. The strain of trying to hold on was wearing her down, and the voice wouldn't go away. Both bodies twitched, once, then twice, and then stilled. The first battle had been won.

Jade didn't open her eyes. She welcomed oblivion with open arms.

*****

Luke checked Sue's pulse. It was weak, and steady. Her breathing was shallow, but strong. That was good. She needed her rest. She was going to need all the strength she could muster before the coming night was over.

"I'm starving."

Luke jumped to his feet. Sue was sitting up, her back against the wall, and her eyes were bright with fever. She offered Luke a half-hearted grin.

"How long have I been asleep?"

Luke looked up at the ceiling. The moon was beginning to rise. He could feel the strength of his own powers rising with it. "Most of the day."

"You're joking. Right? I never sleep in." She looked around at the padded walls, and shifted uncomfortably on the mattress. "Where am I?"

"How are you feeling?" Luke asked.

"Exhausted. Hungry. Like I got in the way of the liquor delivery truck."

"Do you remember anything that happened?" Luke watched Sue closely as she struggled to remember. He gathered more from her chaotic thoughts, than from her actual words.

"I was closing the bar. Dave and I were arguing, and I sent him home." She tipped her head back to gaze at the bulbs in the ceiling, and chewed on her lower lip. "There was a wolf."

Her eyes widened in shock. "Oh my god. It attacked me." She shuddered. "If Dave hadn't come back. If he hadn't rammed it with his truck. I'd be dead right now." She stared at the arm which showed only faint scars where open wounds should be. She rubbed at the skin, and looked at Luke, the question clear in her eyes. "How is that possible? There was so much blood."

Her eyes widened in fear and she frantically searched the room. "Why am I here? Where is Dave? He's alive, isn't he? He didn't get hurt did he? Why can't I remember?"

"Dave is fine. You on the other hand, were infected when the wolf bit you."

"Infected? With what? Did it have rabies or something?"

Luke brushed his hand through his hair and faked interest in the ceiling while he tried to figure out how to explain this.

"Am I going to die, Mr Wulfson?"

Her voice was so fearful and childlike. Luke fell to his knees beside the mattress and caught both her hands in his. He looked her straight in the eyes. "Not if I can help it," he promised. He knew it didn't go a long way towards making her feel any better, but it was all he could do.

There was a rap at the door and Randy entered with a tray. The tantalizing aroma of bear reached Luke and his mouth began to water. His stomach growled, and he realized he hadn't eaten since Mrs Gray's sandwiches the night before.

"Ew. What is that horrible smell?" Sue wrinkled her nose is disgust.

When both Randy and Luke gaped at her, she turned bright pink. "Oh. I'm sorry. That was awfully rude of me. I hope I didn't offend you. Randy, isn't it?"

Randy nodded but kept his eyes on the floor in front of him.

"I am sorry, Randy. I hope you didn't think I meant you." She sniffed the air, and grinned. "Actually, you smell rather good. I meant the food. I can't stand the smell of meat. I'm a vegetarian."

Things keep getting better and better, thought Luke. "Maybe we can dig up a salad for you," he suggested.

Randy thrust the tray at Luke and hurried out the door, eager to please their guest. *Looks like Randy won't be making puppy dog eyes at my sister anymore.* He turned his attention back to Sue who was busy examining the wall where Randy had just disappeared.

"Something bothering you?" he asked.

"I was just wondering how Randy opened the door," Sue said. "I don't see any doorknob, or any lever."

Luke winked at Sue, and smiled. "Don't worry. We'll open the door in the case of an emergency."

The aroma from the tray in his hands was torture. His stomach growled again, and Sue actually laughed at him.

"Sounds to me, like you're a little hungry yourself."

Luke felt foolish holding a tray of food with his mouth watering in anticipation, and his stomach growling in frustration. If he was alone he would have already devoured every morsel. Instead he sat it in the farthest corner, and sat down beside the mattress to wait for Sue's salad to arrive.

*****

Upstairs, Jade woke to find a tray on the bedside table. She used the bathroom, and had a quick shower.

The wound in her side was almost healed, but her ribs were bruised, and painful. She returned to the bed, ate the two sandwiches made with thick slabs of homemade bread, and even thicker slabs of bear roast.

Returning to the bathroom she dumped the tea down the drain and filled the cup with cool water from the tap. Ten minutes later she was sleeping peacefully.

Chapter Twenty Seven

"Why am I here and not in a hospital?"

Sue had enjoyed her meal of fresh fruits and vegetables, but the aroma from Luke's plate of bear roast and gravy had actually started to smell good. She wiped her mouth on the napkin provided, and set it on the tray with the empty dishes. On cue, the door swung open and Randy entered to collect the trays and dishes. He had changed into a clean pair of jeans, and a white button-up shirt.

"You must be psychic," Sue teased. She faked a cough to hide the bubbly laughter when he turned bright pink. He moved gracefully, for a man of his size, and spinning around he left the room without saying a word.

Sue shivered, and began rubbing her arms vigorously. "It feels like ants crawling under my skin," she complained.

"How's the head?"

Sue put her hands up, and gently patted her head in several places. "Wow!" she said. "I can't believe it's still in one piece."

Luke's laughter rumbled in the small room. Sue relaxed against the wall. "Okay, Mr Wulfson. I think it's time you levelled with me. Just how serious is this, and what are my odds?"

"You were infected by a rare … virus … when you were bitten so you have been quarantined."

"Quarantine I understand, but a padded cell? Do you expect me to go mad and try to hurt myself?" Her eyes widened. "I am going to go mad, aren't I? In fact it has already started."

"I won't lie to you. It happens. But I have a feeling that it isn't going to happen to you."

Sue pulled her legs up to her chest, wrapped her arms around them, and began rocking. "Then why?" Sue began, and then decided not to mention the conversation in her head. After all, she wasn't even sure it had actually happened. If it did happen, that was strange she would admit, but if it didn't happen, then that meant she was going crazy. Crazy wasn't something she was planning to do well.

"Why what?"

The way Mr Wulfson was looking at her, like he was trying to read her mind, scared her. She could almost feel something moving around inside there, searching. For what, she didn't know. "Nothing," she mumbled. "I must have been dreaming."

"Not everyone goes mad."

He wasn't very convincing. "If I don't go crazy, what does happen to me?"

"If you don't go mad, you learn to live with it."

"And what is it, exactly?"

Luke seemed very uncomfortable. He tried to loosen the collar on his t-shirt while feigning interest in the ceiling, again. He began to speak just as Sue was beginning to think that he wouldn't answer her.

"You have been infected with the Lycan gene. It is passed through saliva, and blood."

"Like aids?"

"Somewhat, yes."

"Dave was covered with blood."

"True. He has already been tested and sent home. He doesn't have it."

"I do."

"Yes, Sue. You do."

"Is it fatal?" She may as well get rid of the big worries first. After all, if she were going to die, the rest didn't really matter anyway.

"Rarely."

So far so good. "Will my hair fall out?"

"If it does, I can personally guarantee that it will grow back," he teased.

Sue quit rocking and offered Luke a weak smile. "I'm ready to listen. Tell me exactly what to expect. Forewarned is forearmed, my Grandpa always says."

Luke took a deep breath and expelled it very slowly. "The Lycan gene is carried in the saliva and blood. When a human is bitten, the gene travels through their blood bonding with their own DNA and changing it. The person becomes two joint, but separate beings. A human that can shape-shift into a wolf."

Sue laughed, but she wasn't exactly sure that the man telling the story didn't believe it himself. He couldn't be serious. Werewolves? That was ridiculous. Wasn't it? *That is ridiculous, isn't it?* She asked the voice in her head, but it was silent. She asked the man in the room instead.

"A werewolf?" She shook her head. This was unbelievable. "You don't actually believe in werewolves, do you?"

"We are Lycan, not werewolf."

His serious expression scared her. He couldn't actually believe what he was telling her. "You're nuts."

Sue started to rise from her place on the mattress but Luke's steady gaze held her in place. "You are serious. You do actually believe what you are saying." She looked towards the wall where she knew the door should be. If only Randy were to walk through that door right now.

"I am serious, Sue. And no matter how hard you look, nobody is going to come in here and save you from me."

Oh! What was he doing now, reading her mind? "Okay." Maybe she could trick him into opening the door. He did say he could from in here. She would ask to see a werewolf. Then when he opened the door to go find one, she would escape. "If werewolves exist, prove it. Go find me one."

The words were no sooner spoken when Luke shimmered, and a large gray wolf squatted in his place. Sue's screams bounced off the walls, and just as quickly the wolf became Luke.

"How? How did you do that?" Sue stammered.

"I was born Lycan. I have had centuries to perfect the change."

Sue eyed him a little more warily than before. She had been born in Willow Bend, and thought she knew everyone. Apparently, she didn't know Mr Wulfson all that well. Then again, maybe she did? Maybe he was exactly who she had believed him to be her whole life. Maybe she was already crazy. That was it. She was already crazy. If so, what did she have to lose? She'd just play along.

"How old are you?"

"Let's just say I'm a bit older than you." *Quite a bit older.*

You could say that again. He had to be at least forty. "If I'm a werewolf, can I do that?"

Luke grinned, baring his teeth, which suddenly looked a whole lot larger than before. "As leader of the pack it is my duty to teach you."

"There's a pack? Cool. How many?" Sue gave herself a mental shake. Way to go, stupid. Like that is the most important thing he said.

"Let's just say, this is my town."

Sue cried out, and doubled over clutching her stomach. It felt like something was trying to tear its way out. "What's happening?"

"The moon is rising. With the rising of the moon, your powers will increase tenfold. With the rising of the full moon comes the change. Later, when you are stronger, you may be able to control when you change. I can change at will. I am able to stop the change at will. Many never get strong enough to stop the change during the full moon."

She watched as he reached behind his neck and removed a chain with a small medallion, placing it around her own neck. Then he put his arms around her, and gently rocked her. His voice was hypnotic, lulling Sue into a false sense of security, and she began to relax. As she relaxed, the pain subsided.

He lifted her hand to the medallion. "Take it," he told her. "Rub it between your fingers. Envision the wolf. Become one with the beast."

Sue's limbs began to shake, bend, and twist. She tried to stop them, but it only made the pain worse. The first bone snapped. She screamed. A million tiny needles pricked her skin as hair thrust through. Her clothes began to tear as her body warped and grew.

Through it all she could hear his voice. "Don't fight it Sue. Embrace your inner beast. Become one with the wolf."

Her screams became vicious growls as a hundred and twenty pound brown wolf, with gray around its collar and forepaws, rose to its feet and faced Luke. The wolf snarled and snapped at the human in front of it. Instead of cringing in fear, or fleeing, the human stood and faced the young wolf, stretching itself to an impressive height.

The young wolf was wary of this human who showed no fear. Its eyes darted from side to side, frantically searching for a means of escape. With no escape in sight, the wolf's instinct was to attack. Growling low in its throat it advanced slowly, the tip of its tail twitching in warning.

There was a shimmer and a two-hundred-pound gray wolf stood in the man's place. It stood perfectly still, not a hair moving, and stared at the younger, smaller wolf.

The younger wolf's growls turned to whimpers, and it cowered with its back to the wall.

Chapter Twenty Eight

Moonbeams streamed through the open window, teasing Jade to wakefulness. The soreness in her ribs was almost completely gone, and there was no trace of a bite. Jade jumped out of bed and stretched, letting the moon's magic caress her, chasing away the last of her small aches and pains.

She put on clean, olive cargo pants and a tan sweater. She pulled a pair of clean socks out of her pack, and a small paper fluttered to the floor. Jade picked it up, and found herself staring into two of the blackest, saddest eyes she had ever seen. She couldn't believe it had only been a couple of days since she left Alicia at the airport. She hoped she was settling in okay. If anyone could pull the child out of her shell, Da could.

Jade carefully refolded the picture and returned it to her pack, put on her socks and hiking shoes, and went downstairs in search of food. When she entered the kitchen, Mrs Gray was busy piling food onto a plate. "Hello dear. Sleep well?"

Jade smiled brightly. "Like a log," she replied. "Thanks for everything, Mrs G."

Mrs Gray's head bobbed and she clucked her tongue. "Just doing what anyone else would. I'm sorry the chamomile tea wasn't to your liking."

Confused, Jade looked at her curiously.

"The tea dear. You didn't drink it with your sandwiches. I had thought that you would find the flavour soothing, but not everyone likes chamomile."

Jade vaguely remembered pouring the tea down the drain, but how on earth did Mrs Gray know about that? "It's not I don't like chamomile," Jade hedged. "I just felt like water."

Mrs Gray patted her hand in a motherly fashion, and set a plate piled high with steak, home fried potatoes, and three eggs in front of Jade. "That's okay, dear. I understand perfectly."

Jade was sure she did. Nothing seemed to get by the lady in charge of the Inner Sanctum.

Jade ate her meal in silence, savouring each bite as if she hadn't eaten for days, instead of a few hours. After sucking the marrow from the bone, she licked her fingers slowly, not wanting to waste a single drop of the spicy goodness. If only she could cook like that.

She wiped her face and fingers on a napkin, placed it on her plate, and slid the whole thing forward; afraid she might be tempted to lick the plate clean. Patting her stomach she said, "Delicious."

Mrs Gray grinned, her round cheeks ruddy, and quickly cleaned the dishes.

"Did you hear what happened to Sue over at the Waterfront Bar?"

"Yes I did. The poor child."

"Do you know where they took her? I'd like to go see how she is doing. I met her and Dave last night. They seem like a very nice couple."

"Nobody can go see her. She's in quarantine."

"For a wolf bite?" Jade knew it wasn't going to be easy. Luke had her hidden somewhere and she had to find her. It wasn't that she didn't think that Sue would be safe with Luke; she just wanted to see for herself. Jade had tried to reach out to Sue when she woke up, but the connection was lost.

"They think the wolf might have been carrying some kind of disease."

"Like rabies?"

Mrs Gray gave Jade a strange look. "Something like that," she said. She suddenly remembered she had forgotten to clean one of the guest rooms, and excused herself, leaving Jade alone in the kitchen.

Jade went out but the town was unusually quiet. It was almost like they were in mourning. The humans had locked themselves in for the duration of the full moon. One of their own had been hurt, and they were not taking any more chances.

She went by the mansion, but the wolves there were subdued, eyeing her with as much suspicion as lust. She hung around for a while, but when Luke didn't show she left. Jade hadn't really expected him to show. He would be holed up somewhere with Sue. Unwanted jealousy clawed at Jade's insides, and she berated herself. What was wrong with her? She was feeling, and acting out of character and she didn't like it one little bit. For the second night in a row the males around her held no interest, even though their pheromone levels were high.

Jade went back to the sanctum of her room, and allowed her dreams of Luke to carry her into the night.

The sun was just beginning to rise. The air was still crisp this time of day, but the coming heat was evident in the first rays of the sun. It wouldn't take long before the sun rose above the surrounding trees, and then even here she wouldn't be safe from the heat.

Jade stopped near the small creek, and listened as the water trickled over stones as it race to join the lake. A babbling brook. The thought brought a slight smile to her lips. This would be the perfect spot. There were no houses nearby. Sanctuary stood tall and formidable between herself and the road. Charlotte was busy in the kitchen. Helen had left suddenly, and Randy was still in bed as far as Jade could tell.

Perfect.

Jade lifted her arms slowly, drawing air deeply into her lungs, and expelling it just as slowly as she lowered them. She did that a couple of times before swaying back and forth with them extended to stretch the muscles in her sides, before bending forward to touch her toes, and work the kinks out of her back.

Aw. She needed that. As each vertebra gently stretched before falling back into place the tension began to leave her body, and her mind began to focus. She placed her hands flat on the ground before her, and began to walk them forward until she was in a downward facing dog position. She held the position until she could feel the strain in her muscles, and then held it for a couple of minutes longer. Jumping her feet together, Jade slowly stood upright, once again raising her arms to reach for the sun. After a few more basic stretches she bent over backwards until her outstretched fingers touched the earth behind her.

The earth was cool beneath her fingers. She was at one with the earth around her. Then there were two. Jade sensed his presence. He stood down wind so she didn't catch his scent but her body knew instinctively who was there. Heat began at her core, and quickly spread.

Jade held perfectly still, focused on her breathing, and waited. Every sense reached out to him. He moved closer, and her skin tingled with electricity. She hated him for the way he made her feel. Her bones began to melt and she had to concentrate to hold her pose. He was far too distracting.

Distractions could get her killed.

With her eyes closed, Jade scanned the immediate area. Charlotte was still busy in the kitchen. Randy was in his room on the third floor just beginning to stir. She could detect no other movement in the house. That didn't mean they weren't there. She was actually surprised that she knew where Randy and Charlotte were at this moment. The enchantment on the building was there to keep the occupants safe, and prying minds out.

A squirrel eyed her warily from a tree a couple of yards away, and a small bird burst from a nearby bush.

He was mere inches from her feet.

In one continuous, fluid movement Jade swung her foot out, caught Luke by the ankle, and dropped him to the ground. She flipped her body up and over, and balanced on her toes ready to move. Luke started to stand, and Jade swung her foot out to perform a near perfect round house kick, and knocked him on his backside again. This time she pounced on him, her arm across his neck.

Jade knew he wouldn't take this lying down. She waited, tensed, readying herself for his next move, her skin humming in response to his close proximity. She was entirely unprepared for what happened next.

Luke ignored her arm against his throat. He moved his hands to her waist, and tickled. Jade burst into laughter, and attempted to push his hands away. Luke took advantage of her unsteadiness, flipped her over onto her back, and covered her body with his.

Heat flared between them.

This was so not good. Jade had never reacted to a man like this. Not even during the moon cycle. Her first instinct was to buck him off, and run. She reached up, and placing her hands on the sides of his face she pulled him closer until their lips met.

Musk filled the air around them. The scent of his arousal nurtured hers, and she groaned beneath the onslaught of his kisses. When his teeth scraped against her lower lip, she opened to the invasion of his tongue. Desire roared to life like an angry beast. With a thought, neither was sure whose; their clothes vanished leaving them skin to skin. With hungry hands they explored each other's bodies.

Luke was possessed with the need to mark her, to claim her as his own, so that the entire world would know. It didn't make any sense. Unable to control the rising need Luke spread Jade's legs and impaled her, at the same moment he sank his canines into her shoulder, and held her writhing body still as he released his seed into her.

His scent, musky campfire and spices surrounded her; entered her; marked her.

Chapter Twenty Nine

The taxi turned down another dirt road, bouncing over the rutted path. Jade's knuckles were white, but she didn't loosen her grip on the bar in front of her. *What is this the Indy 500?*

It was on the tip of her tongue to ask him to slow down yet again, when the cab came to a screeching stop. The seatbelt was the only thing keeping Jade from the front seat beside the driver.

"I should have walked," she grumbled under her breath. *Or flown.* But she would need her strength when she found the wolf so she had opted for the local taxi service. *I really need to learn to drive. I couldn't do any worse than this.*

She paid the driver, and told him not to wait. "I'm meeting a friend," she lied. "I'll get a ride back." There was no way she was getting back in a taxi with that maniac.

The driver beamed when she gave him enough to cover what would have been her return fair, and left with a squeal of tires that left her covered in dust. *Oh this is just great. I would have been cleaner walking.* Jade brushed the dust from her favourite pair of "Illegal Cargo" pants. She would have just changed into something else but suddenly the parking lot was overflowing with people.

While patting the dust from her clothes, Jade felt something in her side pocket. Distracted, she reached in and pulled out a half eaten chocolate bar. Things were definitely looking up. She peeled the paper away from the squished, melted chocolate, and popped it in her mouth. Now this was heaven. Music may soothe the savage beast, but give her chocolate anytime. She slowly licked the gooey mess from the paper, crumpled and returned it to her pocket, and turned to enter the Wolf Center.

She froze.

It was beautiful. The building was built from a combination of field stone and logs. It appeared to grow right out of the ground. A part of nature rather than a man made abode. The thatched roof blended with the trees that towered over it. Jade wasn't sure she would have been able to distinguish it from the forest from the air. If she hadn't already been impressed with the way Mr Wulfson ran his holdings, this building would have sealed the deal. Jade could look at this building all day, except she still had a job to do.

Last night the Willow Bend pack had stopped her from destroying the rogue wolf. An innocent woman was infected, and a child was threatened. Not to mention that poor girl in the park, and the man in the cabin. By every law known to *were* that beast needed to be destroyed. She knew the healing abilities of Lycans and she was not leaving until she was sure the killings had stopped; even if it meant turning Luke against her. She was still having a hard time with the fact that Luke was related to the pack Alpha.

Lykos Wulfson was a legend. He had led a handful of survivors from their homeland, across the vast ocean to start their lives in a strange new land. He was well-known for dealing with his pack fairly and firmly, meting out justice when the need arose. He had personally destroyed his own brother when Gheorgès had gone on a killing spree, negating the need for the *Moarté* to intercede. Jade had to speak with the male. Normally she wouldn't bother. She should just go in, do her job, and leave. There was no reason to inform anyone that she was even there. If they didn't uphold the law, she would. Anonymity was important in her line of work. If they didn't know who you were they couldn't come after you. How many times had her aunts drilled that into her head?

Jade braced herself, and entered the front doors. The inside was even more impressive than the outside. There were stuffed wolves of every species scattered around the room. Potted trees, along with very realistic fake trees helped to create an ambiance of being in the wild. Wolves skulked among the trees making Jade feel like they were actually watching her. On closer inspection Jade realized that they were actually stuffed wolves, not artificial like she had first assumed. She couldn't stop the shiver that crawled along her spine.

Near each wolf was a plague telling a little about it. These wolves had all been a part of someone's family. They had names, and history, and came from around the world. There were a couple of Iberian wolves from Spain, Alejandro and Amada, and wolves from Romania named Bogdana and Ciprian. There were Lobo, or Mexican wolves, the list went on and on. Jade pulled her attention away from the exhibit to take in her surroundings. The fourth wall was glass, and overlooked the compound where Jade could see a pair of wolves indulgently looking on while their pups romped.

Above her head Jade could hear the murmur of voices, and the shuffling of feet. That would be the main offices, and where she would find Lykos Wulfson. She glanced at the clock above the receptionist's desk, and hurried over.

"Hi." She smiled at the girl behind the desk. Although she was human, Jade could detect the lycan gene lying dormant. Jade wondered if Wulfson knew. Probably. Why else would he keep a human on here? All the other employee's wandering around were definitely lycan. "I have an appointment with Mr Wulfson."

The girl glanced at the book in front of her, and smiled. "Of course, Miss Caer. Mr Wulfson is expecting you. If you go up the stairs it's the first door on the right."

Jade thanked her, and hurried up the stairs. It was two minutes to twelve, and she really didn't want to be late. She was just about to knock on the door when she heard voices. Her hand froze.

"I need to talk to you Uncle." The voice was young, female, and very timid.

"Can't it wait, Gemma? I have an appointment." The voice was brisk, distracted, and then there was an uncomfortable silence. Jade could hear the shuffling of feet through the door. "What's wrong, Gemma?" This time the voice was much more compassionate, and held the same seductive timber she was so familiar with.

"It's." The female's voice cracked with nervousness. "Never mind. It can wait until after your appointment. Are you coming to Elizabeth's for supper tonight?"

"I was planning on it. Are you sure you don't want to tell me what's wrong. I can cancel my appointment."

Good for you, thought Jade. It gladdened her heart that the man was willing to cancel an appointment for the sake of a member of his pack.

"No. It can wait." The girl forced a brighter tone to her voice. "I'll see you tonight."

Jade rapped on the door. It swung open revealing a very young, very beautiful female. She reminded Jade of Helen. Jade extended her hand. "Hello. I'm Jade Caer. I didn't mean to interrupt, but I have an appointment with Mr Wulfson. The receptionist said to come right up."

Gemma hesitated, and then took Jade's offered hand. "I'm Gemma Radu," she said, her voice much more confident that it had been through the door.

Their hands touched and Jade felt the younger woman's pulse. She smelt the blood rushing through her veins. She tasted fear, and confusion. Jade listened to the rapid beat of Gemma's heart, and the quicker, gentler tapping of the second heartbeat. *She's pregnant.* Relief swept through Jade a mere heartbeat before the vision nearly knocked her to the floor.

She felt her sharp white teeth sink into the man's flesh. The salty tang of his warm blood hit the back of her throat in a rush.

Gemma blanched and tugged her hand free. "I was just leaving." She slurred the words like a drunk. "Uncle Luke is all yours." She slipped past Jade and pulled the door shut with a loud click.

An impatient sound came from the man behind the desk, and Jade snapped back to the present. The taste of blood lingered on her tongue. She forced her attention to the only other person in the room. *Could this day get any worse?* She wondered. "You have got to be kidding me. You are Lykos Wulfson?" Dark eyes sparkled, and Jade nearly groaned again. *Oh this cannot be happening.*

"Lykos was my great grandfather." His voice was gruff with emotion as he waved her towards an empty chair across from his desk. "I'm Luke Wulfson." He didn't offer his hand, and Jade didn't offer hers. They both knew full well what would happen should they touch. This morning had proved that.

Luke leaned back in his seat; his hands in front of him on the desk formed a tepee. He tapped his index fingers together. He appeared outwardly calm, but his insides snarled in a knot. "How can I help you Miss Caer?"

This so wasn't going to be easy. She may as well just jump right in. "Last night a woman was bitten by a wolf." Luke's eyes narrowed. Jade took a deep breath. What was it about this man that made her lose all her ability to think clearly? "I want to know what happened to the wolf." Well at least she wasn't stuttering.

"And what makes you think I'd know anything about that."

This was getting them nowhere. Jade rose and offered her hand to Luke. "Let's start over, shall we? I am Jade Caer O'Connor of O'Connor Search and Rescue."

Luke looked at her offered hand as if it were a viper about to strike. He cautiously took it in his much larger one. *Moarté!*

Jade cringed as the hated word leapt between them, and he dropped her hand like he would drop a hot poker.

"What brings you here, Miss Caer?" His voice was curt.

Jade sat back in her own chair but kept her eyes on the man in front of her. His mind had snapped shut against her the minute he realized what she was. It was inevitable the moment she sent him the knowledge. Still it hurt, which was another reason Jade usually kept the knowledge to herself. She was the dreaded *Moarté*. Born of death and destruction she killed without remorse. If only they knew the truth. She bled with every life she was required to destroy. Hers was a thankless job, that of policing the magical creatures thought to be extinct, or myth. The human police were ill equipped to deal with them, and it was Jade's job to protect all their species.

She swallowed her hurt. "A wolf killed a teenage girl in Toronto the night we met."

Those black eyes didn't flicker. *He knows,* she thought. *I wonder just how much he knows.* "I followed him here." She could hear the guilt she felt in her own voice, and took a deep breath before continuing. *I should have been out patrolling. Not having mind blowing sex with the hottest male to ever walk the planet.*

"Of course you know that," she snapped, her voice harsh. "I would have put an end to the killing last night if your wolves hadn't interfered."

Luke moved then. He slammed his hands on the desk in front of him. Rising off his chair he leaned forward, eyes snapping yellow fire, power sparking around the room. "My wolves," he snarled in barely controlled fury. "Had every right to interfere. You are on my land. I am the law here."

Wow! He is magnificent when he is angry. Jade forced her mind back to business. "You may be the law here under normal circumstances." It was funny. Now that Luke was angry Jade felt much calmer; more in control of the situation. "But the minute any *were*--Lycan, fox, eagle, it doesn't matter--Once a human is bitten it becomes our jurisdiction. I only came here today to warn you to stop interfering. That wolf is feral. Feral and blood thirsty. He will be stopped."

Luke sat back in his chair. Relief warred with some other emotion in his dark eyes. Lust? Regret? "Then you are free to go back to where ever you came from Miss Caer. The wolf died last night. Our doctor wasn't able to save him."

Jade stood. "Of course you will be able to provide proof of that."

"Of course. The body is still over at the Veterinary Hospital. Elizabeth hasn't disposed of it yet. I'll call and let her know you are on your way." Luke picked up the telephone and punched in some numbers. He spoke briefly, and hung up. "Elizabeth is busy but she will be able to see you in about an hour. That will give you time to collect your things. You can see her on your way out of town," he said hopefully.

I know you are not that stupid. Jade didn't bother to offer her hand. She knew he wasn't about to touch her again. Not now that he knew who she was and why she was here. And definitely not after he discovered she was going after his niece.

She opened the door, and left without a word or a backwards glance.

Chapter Thirty

Luke stared at the door long after Jade had left. She wasn't going to leave town. Not until after she had finished her business, and as much as he wished it wasn't true that business involved his family.

He should be angry, worried, or both. Instead he felt relief. He would be seeing her again. That scared him more than anything else.

Damn! He had to protect his family. There was no denying that the mongrel had Wulfson blood running through its veins. He had sensed it at the park, and again at the Green's house. It had been elusive, mingled with the strong residue of power, but he had suspected it. And when he faced the mongrel as he lay dying, he knew. Blood called to blood. Erzébet had run the tests three times before confirming it. If Luke hadn't turned him, and Gheorgès was long dead, that left Gemma. Luke didn't have any offspring. That boat had sailed a long time ago—with Natasha's betrayal.

Gheorgès had hated the humans, blaming them all for what a few had done to their parents, and their entire pack. Only by the grace of God, and Erzébet's help, had

Luke managed to save as many of them as he had. His baby brother had only been two summers when his parents were murdered, but he had remembered every single detail of that night. It had haunted his dreams for years until he had finally snapped. He had set out to avenge his parents' deaths by destroying as many humans as possible. Unable to turn Gheorgès from his destructive path, Luke had destroyed his only brother.

Natasha's betrayal had cost him so much Luke hadn't allowed himself to feel anything for a female since. Not until a pale haired woman with glowing amber eyes.

Luke may not have been able to save his brother, but he was determined to save Gemma. Even if it meant destroying the one woman who had managed to chip the ice from his heart. Gemma was innocent. She didn't have a mean bone in her body. If she had bitten this human, then she had a very good reason, and he was determined to find out exactly what that reason was.

Tonight.

The phone rang, and Luke jumped. *Hell.* He grabbed the receiver. "This better be good," he growled into the mouth piece. He listened for a few moments. "No. Nobody talks to her. And for God's sake, keep her away from the body."

Luke replaced the phone, and smiled to himself. It wouldn't stop her but it should slow her down. At least until he had a chance to talk to Gemma. He hit another button, and waited.

"Yes, Mr. Wulfson."

"Take messages for me, Sara. I'll be out for the rest of the day."

"Yes sir. Where can you be reached in case of an emergency?"

"Call my cell if it is an emergency. But only if it is an emergency."

"Okay. Have a great day."

Luke shook his head, a half smile on his lips. "You too. And thanks Sara."

He made a mental note to give Sara a raise. She was always happy, and always willing to fit in whenever they needed her. In fact Elizabeth had told him that Sara had gone on the overnight with George this month. He'd have to remember to ask her how she liked that. Luke made it a point to try to keep up with everyone he was responsible for.

That got him thinking. Usually Gemma went out on the overnight. He was going to have to ask Elizabeth why she made the change. He should have thought of that before, but he had other things on his mind. Like a pale haired, amber eyed goddess.

Luke almost forgot to shove his cell phone in his pocket before he left the office. If he hurried he could be at the hospital before Jade. He was sure she would use conventional modes of travel, especially during the day. He, on the other hand, had no intention of using conventional methods.

He should have known better. He arrived to find an absolutely livid Elizabeth pacing outside her examining room. "What's going on?" he demanded.

"Her." Elizabeth spit out the word. "She marched in here like she owned the place. She told Ellie that she had your permission to see the body, and then ordered her out of the room." Elizabeth's dark eyes spit fire. "The stupid girl actually left her in there alone with the body. Now the door is locked and we are out here."

"Where were you when she arrived?"

"I had taken the results of the blood tests to the incinerator. I didn't know she would get here so quickly. I should have known she would not wait in case we tried to destroy the evidence. Not that it matters now."

Luke nearly laughed aloud. Not even Elizabeth could possibly know everything, and it drove her crazy. Besides, he had a feeling that nobody, not him, not Elizabeth, not anyone would have been able to keep Jade from that room.

He looked through the window. Jade was sitting cross-legged at the end of the gurney, both hands on the dead wolf's head, and her eyes closed. "What's she doing?"

Elizabeth shrugged. "Who is to know? Maybe she is asking him who he is." Luke thought she had meant it as a joke, but Elizabeth seldom joked, and she had never looked more serious. Then he felt it.

The power.

He felt compelled to look back into the room where he saw the dead wolf. Where had Jade gone? Then he noticed the shimmer of light and realized that she was still there. He watched that shimmering light for what seemed like hours, and then Jade slumped forward. He felt a lump of fear in his throat just before he heard the lock click. Luke shoved the door open and rushed to gather Jade into his arms.

She was ashen. Her skin was clammy. Her pulse was beating faster than a hummingbird's wings. *She's dying.* The thought came unbidden to his mind and he felt panic rise. "Do something, Elizabeth," he growled.

She did.

She threw a glass of ice water in Jade's face.

Jade sputtered and coughed. She struggled to sit up, but the arms holding her were warm, and safe. She settled back. *Arms!* He eyes flew open, and she found herself staring into two dark pits of worry.

"What did you do?" she snapped as she pushed away from Luke.

"He did nothing." The voice was beautiful, and commanding like the woman who possessed it.

"You must be Erzébet." Jade offered her hand but Elizabeth put her own hands behind her back. *Things were so much easier when they didn't know who she was.*

"Did you find what you need?" Elizabeth's eyes were piercing, and Jade had the feeling that she was trying to see right into her soul. Maybe she was. The woman relaxed visibly, and smiled. "Luke let the woman sit up. She is not dying this day."

Luke seemed reluctant to let her go, but he finally moved his arm from around her shoulder. Jade slid off the table, and onto the floor—in a heap. *Oh what she wouldn't give for a chocolate bar right now.* As if he had read her mind Luke reached into his shirt pocket and pulled out a granola bar.

"I don't have any candy, but this might help."

Jade took the offered energy bar, and ate it while sitting on the floor where she had landed. It was only after she had swallowed the last crumb that she realized what a vulnerable position she was in. Whether she liked it or not these people were her enemies. *Why wasn't the door locked?*

"You are safe here," Elizabeth said.

That clinches it. The woman is reaching my mind. Jade tried to throw up a mental shield, only to grab her head as two burning spears seemed to impale her. *Okay. No shields. At least not until I've gotten my strength back.*

Jade stood up with the help of the gurney, and waved off Luke's attempt to help as she staggered towards the door. "You can dispose of the body," she said. "I've seen all I need to here." In truth Jade hadn't seen what she had hoped to see, and to top it all off she had to get in another taxi.

From the instant she had touched Gemma she had known something was wrong. That girl wasn't tainted. Jade would bet her life that the child would never bite a human—except when mated. A Love Bite—that's what they called it.

Jade's heart slammed against her ribs at a flash of memory. Had Luke bitten her? No. It wasn't possible. She would know if she mated to a wolf wouldn't she? There was no battle for control going on inside of her. Of that she was positive. Could she be channelling someone else's memories?

What had happened?

Are you all right? Do you need me to come? The familiar voice brought a smile to her lips, and a glow to her face. The taxi driver looked in his rear view mirror, and nearly drove off the road. Jade clutched at the back of the front seat and glared at the driver.

Jade? The single word brought the smile back to her lips. *Do you need me to come? Are you hurt?* There was worry now in the sing-song voice.

No. I'm not hurt. Just confused. She could feel her probe. *Stop that Althea. I'm fine. I'm just trying to figure out something. How is Alicia? And Da?*

They are good. Your father dotes on the child, and she is an absolute angel. She is learning to control her powers very well for someone so young. And I have discovered that she has even more hidden talent than we first thought. Sometimes these things are buried so deep only the subconscious is aware.

Of course! Thank you. As always Althea you are a genius.

Of course! Jade heard the laughter in her voice. *How is your young man?*

Jade nearly fell off her seat, and this time it had nothing to do with the driving. *Young man?* She enquired cautiously.

The one you have gone to recruit. Her aunt's laughter spoke volumes. *I see. You will have to tell me all about this other young man when you return home. I can't wait to meet him.*

Not likely happening. Jade sighed. *Not after I'm finished here.*

The taxi came to a screeching halt at the front of Sanctuary. Jade paid the driver, and walked slowly around to the kitchen door. She couldn't ever remember when she had felt so completely exhausted. At least her aunt's short visit had reminded her that she wasn't alone. It also reminded her of her original reason for coming to Willow Bend. She had an appointment in less than an hour with Daniel Dixon at the Waterfront.

The kitchen door opened. Mrs G pulled Jade inside, and led her to a chair. "Come in child," she said. "I have a nice bowl of bear stew all ready for you."

A bell dinged, and Mrs G turned to the oven. When she opened the door the aroma of fresh bread wafted over to Jade. Her mouth began to water.

"Perfect timing," Mrs G said.

Jade couldn't have agreed more.

Chapter Thirty One

Luke studied his niece from behind his glass. Her face was too pale, and her eyes usually so full of life were haunted. It couldn't hurt worse if someone actually kicked him in the guts.

"Uncle Luke," she began. Her voice quivered.

"Not now, Gemma." Luke glanced at Elizabeth who shrugged, and gave him a probing look. She wasn't going to be any help. "Elizabeth has cooked us a wonderful meal. Let's just enjoy it. We can have our discussion later."

Gemma forced a smile that didn't quite reach her eyes. Luke couldn't tell if she was grateful for the respite or not. "I hear Sara went out on the overnight. How did she like that?" Luke sought to change the subject and was rewarded with a genuine grin from Gemma.

"She found it very interesting." Gemma pushed her food from one side of her plate to the other. The smell of it nauseated her. If she didn't tell her secret soon the guilt alone was going to eat her alive. But if Uncle Luke wanted to postpone the telling then she would have to abide by his decision. "George kissed her."

"What!"

Both Luke and Elizabeth spoke at once, and Gemma couldn't help but laugh. "George kissed her. They were arguing, again, and he just kissed her."

Luke covered his mouth and coughed to hide his laughter. What was it about Gemma that always made him laugh? He resolved to do everything in his power to save her -- even if it meant giving up his own life.

Gemma was once again pushing her food from one side of the plate to the other. She had still to take even one bite. "Is something wrong with your food?" he asked.

"Gemma ate earlier," Elizabeth volunteered, surprising them both. "She's probably not hungry."

Luke studied Elizabeth's clear eyes. *Why are you lying?* He wondered. *What do you know that I don't know?*

"Charlotte tells me that Randy is taking exceptional care of Sue," Elizabeth ventured.

Two sets of eyes turned when Gemma slammed her fork down, and shoved her plate across the table so hard that it slid off the edge, dumping her food all over the pristine floor. "It's my fault." The words burst out. "I think I turned the wolf that bit Sue. I need to be put down."

"No!" Once again Luke and Elizabeth spoke at the same time.

A small sob escaped before Gemma took a deep breath, and brought herself under control. "I was drinking. I don't remember what happened." She took another deep breath, and the words poured out." I don't know what is real anymore. I think I'm losing my mind."

Elizabeth was sitting in her chair one moment, and standing beside Gemma patting the girl's shoulder the next. "There, there child," she murmured soothingly. "Take a deep breath, let it out very slowly, and then tell us what is going on."

Once started, Gemma couldn't seem to stem the flow of words. "I have the bloodlust. I must be put down."

"Tell us why you think you have the bloodlust." Luke encouraged his niece, his gentle tone only succeeded in making her cry harder. He watched Gemma's tears flow, and his heart broke. He didn't think for one single moment that Gemma had the bloodlust. If she did, she wouldn't be sitting here so calmly telling them about it. Well, not exactly calmly. She was clearly agitated, and her eyes mirrored his confusion, but at least she was talking to them.

Ghèorges, his own brother, had lied right to the end. Even after Luke had caught him in the act, a half devoured corpse in front of him and Ghèorges covered in blood, he had denied his guilt. But Luke had seen the guilt in his eyes. For a long time he had tried to ignore what he knew to be true, but in the end he had done his duty. It had been Ghèorges or them. Luke didn't care about his own life, but his small group was all that was left of his father's pack.

Luke could detect no guilty knowledge in Gemma's eyes. There was only fear and confusion.

"It began right after I snuck out to a bar and I drank too much. I'm pretty sure there was a man there, although I don't seem to be able to remember much about that night at all. When I try to recall that night it feels like someone using a power drill on my brain." Gemma pushed her short bangs back, sighing when they fell back into place. Neither Luke nor Elizabeth spoke, waiting for the girl to continue.

"I woke up with the coppery taste of blood in my mouth." Gemma grimaced at the memory, and then continued. "I don't feel well. I can only eat fresh meat. If it is cooked I can't keep it down. The nightmares started the first night of the full moon." She looked at Elizabeth then, her eyes wide with horror. "You knew," she whispered.

Elizabeth shook her head, her eyes on Luke. "No."

"Then why did you send Sara in my place. It was so I wouldn't kill our guests, wasn't it?" Gemma's limbs began to shake, and her face grew even paler. "It didn't stop me," she cried. "I killed a girl. An innocent child. She was just a child. I tried to stop myself but I couldn't control the beast."

My god! It's not true. "You did not kill that girl, Gemma," Luke told her.

"I did, Uncle Luke." Gemma's voice broke, and Luke thought his heart would break. "I killed her as surely as if I had sunk my own teeth into her young flesh.

"No you didn't. And you didn't kill Green. And you didn't attack Sue."

"Sue. Oh my god! Is Sue all right? I don't remember attacking Sue."

Luke slammed his fist on the table so hard the dishes rattled, and both women jumped. "That's because you didn't attack Sue. I told you that. A man named David Woods killed those people."

Gemma licked her lips, and wiped her hands on her pants. Her eyes were wide with shock. "David?" That's the name of the man I met at the bar." She looked both relieved and determined. "Thank god I didn't actually kill anyone. But that doesn't change the fact that I am responsible for their deaths. I must have bit David that night. By our laws that means I must be put down."

Chapter Thirty Two

Jade ate three bowls of stew and almost an entire loaf of bread herself. As usual everything was cooked to perfection. She stopped herself just short of licking the bowl; after all it was almost spotless from the bread anyway. She patted her stomach. "Delicious as usual, Mrs G."

Mrs Grey beamed, and then she set about preparing a tray with two bowls and another loaf of bread. "Randy has a guest," she offered at Jade's questioning look.

Jade was pretty sure she knew who the guest was, and felt better knowing that Mrs G had a hand in taking care of her. She rose from the table."Thanks again, Mrs G," she said. "I have an appointment in town so I'll just get out of your way."

"Would you like me to call you a cab," Mrs G offered.

Jade barely concealed a shudder at the mere thought of getting into another one of those death traps. If she ever set foot in a cab in this town again it would be too soon for her. "Not this time, thanks."

After a quick shower, and changing into a clean shirt, and faded but comfortable jeans, Jade pulled on her hiking boots and took probably her last look around the room. She was really beginning to like this place. Too bad she probably wouldn't be coming back. She stuffed everything she owned into her pack, and left the room. In never paid to get too comfortable.

Ten minutes later a snowy white owl hopped between two dumpsters, and Jade stepped out. She fluffed her hair with her fingers, and then shook her head. *Get hold of yourself girl. It's only an interview. It's not like anyone cares what you look like.*

Jade stepped into the dimly lit bar, and all eyes turned to her. It was a lot busier than the first time she'd been here. She spied an empty stool at the bar, and headed directly for it. She nodded at a few people, not surprised when they turned their heads away without acknowledging her presence, only to follow her with their eyes when she was past them. A few went so far as to move their chairs back when she drew near. By the time she reached the bar stool she felt like a pariah.

Moarté! The hated name echoed in her mind. *I'm only doing my job,* she thought mutinously. *Someone has to protect your sorry asses.* She didn't know why it bothered her so much this time, but it did. She should be used to being ostracized. She was the equivalent of judge, jury, and executioner. Death! *Moarté!*

She sat on the empty stool, now a good two feet away from the patrons on either side. She turned her attention to the bartender. "I'll have a beer, please."

The bartender wiped the counter in front of her. Then he stopped at the stool beside her. "Can I get you anything else," he asked ignoring Jade's presence.

So now I am invisible. Why am I so surprised? She wasn't sure why, but deep down she knew that Sue wouldn't have treated her so, even if she had known who she really was.

"Sure, Mike." The man's voice rattled with barely controlled fury, but the gorgeous smile never once faltered. "You can get me another beer, and grab one for the lady while you're at it." He turned to Jade then, and offered his hand. "Hi. I'm Daniel. Daniel Dixon. You must be Miss Caer O'Connor from O'Connor Search and Rescue. I've been waiting for you."

At least he is friendly. And gorgeous. He wore an aura of power that was very becoming. *It has to be the wolf in him.* Jade glanced at the clock above the bar. She was five minutes early. "Have you been waiting long?"

"All my life." His voice was soft, sensual, and didn't do a thing for Jade, although she definitely enjoyed the eye candy. A couple of patrons guffawed. They may not want anything to do with Jade, but they were all very much interested in what Daniel might say to her. Daniel glared at them, and they quickly silenced. "Okay. You caught me. It has only been since I sent my first letter, nearly four years ago."

Jade winced. Had it really been four years since she had received the first letter from this man?

"Hey, don't sweat it. I understand people must apply for positions with your company all the time. I can't blame them. You have the best reputation around. That's why I was so persistent."

Jade visibly relaxed, and her natural smile made her face glow. "Shall we get right to business, or do you want to finish our drinks first."

Daniel looked around the room at all the wary, but too interested faces. "To tell the truth I'd rather do this somewhere else."

Jade didn't blame him. It couldn't be easy for him to be talking to the dreaded *Moarté* in front of his friends. Not to mention she was almost positive that he, and everyone else, had been ordered not to speak to her.

Jade took a swallow of the beer the bartender had finally placed before her. "Thanks, Mike," she called to his retreating back, as if he hadn't completely ignored her. She pulled a ten out of her pocket, and stuck it under her bottle. "This one's on me." She indicated both hers and Daniel's beers, and slid gracefully off the tall stool. Waving her hand towards the door, she said, "Lead on McDuff."

They grabbed a corner booth at the greasy spoon at the corner. Jade didn't even glance at the menu when it came. "I'll have a hamburger, very rare, with the works, and a beer," she said.

"I'll have the same," Daniel said. "And could you add some fries to that?"

"No problem, Danny." When the waitress smiled at Jade it held real warmth. "Would you like fries as well Miss? We make them from fresh potatoes."

Her eyes are the color of a stormy sky, Jade thought. "No thank you."

She was rewarded with another sunny smile, and the waitress flounced off to place their orders.

"Danny?"

Daniel groaned. "I've known Missy since grade school. For some reason she refuses to acknowledge we aren't kids anymore."

"Well I for one like it. Makes you seem more approachable."

Daniel let out a low, rumbling laugh. "Is being approachable a prerequisite to the job?"

"It does help, sometimes. But a good nose and compassion are far more important."

The waitress returned with their food, and Daniel insisted on paying. He took a swig of beer, and Jade sensed more than saw, him eyeing her warily over the bottle. "A good nose?"

"That and a driver's license." She narrowed her eyes at him. "You do drive don't you?"

Once again, low rumbling laughter erupted. "Driver's. Pilot's. Do I get extra points for the pilot's license?"

Jade regarded him seriously. "Helicopter or plane?"

"Both. Helicopter and small plane. I don't have a commercial license. Mr Wulfson thought it would be a good idea if some of us could fly. He paid so we went."

A wave of desire washed over Jade at the mere mention of his name. Jade groaned inwardly. This was so not going to work.

Daniel took a bite of his hamburger. "You should eat your burger while it's hot. They're really good here."

They finished their meal in silence. The waitress cleared their plates, and brought them each another beer before Daniel finally broke the silence. "Listen, Miss Caer, I have to be honest with you."

"Honesty is good."

"I really want this job. If you give me a chance I know that I am the right person for this. I have been working for the Willow Bend Search and Rescue Team for eight years, and my recovery record is very good."

"That was in your letters -- All six of them." She smiled at him. He was so earnest. Her instincts had been right. He would be perfect for the job. It was too bad if his relationship with Wulfson was going to be a problem. "The company is based out of New York. We have a ranch at the bottom of the Catskills. We are often called to other countries so your passport needs to be current. Is that going to be a problem?"

Daniel shook his head, and Jade continued. "When we are not out in the field we live at the Ranch and help train the dogs. My Da ... Grandfather makes his living raising and training search and rescue dogs. He is getting along in years, but refuses to retire. You will get eight weeks vacation a year to start. We try to accommodate you for time, but that is not always possible." She mentioned a salary that was several times higher than Daniel had expected.

"When can I start?"

Jade smiled at his enthusiasm. *There are still a few things you need to know.*

Daniel sat back in his seat, positive he would pass the rest of the interview. "So inform me."

Daniel wasn't even aware that he had responded to an unspoken question. With a little work he would be able to communicate with her silently. "I came to town because your letter intrigued me. I'm offering the job because I like what I see."

"Thank you."

I take my privacy very seriously.

That is understandable.

Jade smiled. Their connection was strong, which was a very good thing. There were times when that connection could be the only thing to save their lives.

"There is one other question I need to ask before we settle this. Is there going to be a problem with Luke Wulfson if you work with me?"

Chapter Thirty Three

Jade knocked on the door, but didn't wait for an answer. She turned the handle and walked in, followed by Daniel Dixon. Luke didn't look surprised to see her there, or even to see Daniel with her. He just seemed broken.

"Hello Jade, Daniel." Luke inclined his head slightly. "Come in and have a seat."

"Are you here for me?" There was quiet acceptance in Gemma's voice.

"That depends on the answers I get here today." Jade replied.

They were standing in a large open room. There was a table set for three, with several extra chairs, at the end of the room that was obviously the kitchen area. There was a window over the sink, with the fridge and stove flanking the long counter. The other end of the room held a sofa, two chairs, a radio, no television that Jade could see, and one entire wall was a bookshelf. There were three windows at that end of the house. There were two closed doors which she presumed led to a bedroom, and a bathroom.

"I did it."

"Did what?" Jade watched the girl carefully for any signs of deceit.

"I need to be put down but Uncle Luke refuses to do it, and I'm not strong enough to do it myself."

Jade's heart melted at the sadness in the younger girl's eyes, but she stayed firm. "Why do you believe that you should be 'put down'?"

Gemma took a deep breath, her dark eyes tormented. "I am responsible for destroying the lives of at least four innocent people that I know of."

"Four?"

Gemma's voice broke. "I'm pretty sure I bit the man at the bar."

Oh you bit him alright. But he wasn't innocent. Not by a long shot. "Tell me why you bit him, Gemma? Did he do anything to you?"

"No. I don't know."

Jade's expression didn't change. She held Gemma's dark eyes with her own, glowing slightly with power. "You don't know. Or you won't say?"

Gemma struggled to break eye contact. Jade's own eyes flared slightly, and she held the girl steady.

"I can't," she whispered. "I don't remember."

Is she telling the truth, Daniel?

I have known Gemma for many years. I can't recall a time when she was ever dishonest.

I understand that she is a friend, and a pack member. I want you to disregard all that, and tell me whether you think she is lying at this moment.

Daniel saw the haunted expression in his friend's eyes, the trembling of her lip as she tried to hold back her sobs. She wasn't fidgeting. Her skin was not clammy. She didn't look anywhere except at Jade. She didn't look like anything other than a brave child, trying to own up to her mistakes. *No. Gemma is not lying.*

"Okay then." Jade glanced towards the two closed doors. "Elizabeth, is there a room we can use for privacy?"

"What are you..?" Luke stepped between Gemma and Jade.

Gemma placed her hand on her Uncle's arm, and gently moved him aside. "Please, Uncle Luke. Let us end this with some dignity."

That Luke wanted nothing more than to send Jade away, was evident in the way he glared at her. He shoved his hand through his hair, looked from Gemma to Jade, over to Elizabeth, and back to Jade, then he stepped aside.

Jade wanted to go. She wanted to go home, and hug Alicia, and Da, and Althea. She wanted to leave this child here, amongst the people who loved her, and let them sort this mess out. *She wanted to grab Luke and drag him somewhere they could be alone, and screw his brains out.* Jade shook her head to clear away the rampant thoughts. None of that was about to happen. She had a job to do.

Elizabeth indicated the closed door on the right. Gemma led the way into the bedroom. It was a comfortable room. A large skylight allowed the night stars to twinkle above them, and a cool breeze drifted in through an open window. A large bed was positioned directly under the skylight. Other than the bed, the only other furniture was a chair in front of a small vanity. The door to the closet was open.

Jade could see Luke through Daniel's eyes when she closed the door behind her. His face was thunderous. His eyes were so hopeless she wanted to cry when Daniel took up his position outside the door.

"Daniel." Jade couldn't help but hear the silent plea in Luke's voice.

"I am sorry, Alpha, but I cannot allow you to interfere."

Jade snapped the connection. She pushed the bed from the center of the room, and sat cross legged on the floor. She indicated the spot before her.

"Is this going to hurt," Gemma asked in a small voice.

"I hope not," Jade replied.

Gemma hesitated slightly before sitting on the floor facing Jade. Now that she was actually face to face with her judge and jury, Gemma was scared. Terror flared in her dark eyes. The only other indication of her fear was the nervous way she chewed on her bottom lip.

Jade reached across and took both of Gemma's ice cold hands in her own. "Close your eyes, Gemma. Take a deep breath. Now let it out very slowly, and think of the first time you saw David Woods."

The room was dark, and smoky. It was so crowded you could barely move. Gemma was with Luke's pretty secretary, Sara. She pointed across the room, and then dragged Gemma with her.

Gemma was sitting at the table with David Woods. Gemma was dancing with Sara. Gemma was at the table with David Woods again. She was drinking beer. She was happy. She had her wolf firmly under control.

Gemma rose, and left the table. She was almost across the room when she suddenly turned around, and looked at David across the room. He pulled a small package from his pocket, and dropped something into Gemma's glass.

The son of a bitch drugged her. No wonder Gemma lost control.

Gemma finished her business in the bathroom. She didn't realize that David had put something in her drink. She returned to the table and drank her beer. It tasted funny, and she wrinkled her nose, but she swallowed it. She watched Sara dancing with a man.

Gemma staggered out to the parking lot. She inhaled David's scent. He smelled like spicy muffins.

Gemma was on fire. Her body burned. The pain was unbearable. She was screaming. She bit down on the scream. Her canines sank into flesh. Everything was black.

How dare he? Not only did he drug the child, he raped her. The rage built until sparks flew from Jade's eyes. Gemma's eyes popped open, and she screamed. The chair flew across the room, and slammed into the wall, landing in pieces on the floor. There was a scuffle outside the door. Energy flew from Jade, and the door lock slammed into place. *Stay out.* As quickly as it began, the scuffle ended.

What was wrong with her? If David Woods was alive, and standing in front of her at this moment, she had no doubt that she would rip him apart--again. Jade had to struggle to get herself under control. "It's okay, Gemma." She was hoping to sound calm, but the words came out in a growl. "I'm not going to hurt you."

"But?"

"It isn't your fault. None of it was your fault. You were drugged. David Woods drugged you. You were not under control of your actions when you sank your teeth into him."

"What about the bloodlust?"

Jade shook her head.

"I can only eat raw meat." Gemma was genuinely confused.

"That's because you are pregnant."

Gemma stared at Jade as if she had two heads. "What?"

"That bastard drugged you. And then he raped you. You are pregnant."

"Is that why you won't carry out my sentence? Because I am pregnant?

Jade sighed. "Gemma, listen to me very closely. You are not responsible for David Woods. His destruction was brought about by his own actions. He drugged you. Not the other way around. David Woods is responsible for his own death, and the deaths of the child in Toronto, and the man outside of town. David Woods is responsible for Sue. Not you."

Tears ran unchecked down Gemma's face. "I don't understand. I was there."

Jade wiped the tears from Gemma's face. "You saw what was happening through David's eyes, because you were connected to his wolf." Jade placed her hand on Gemma's abdomen, and closed her eyes for a moment. "You are carrying a life inside of you that you will be solely responsible for. It won't be easy for either one of you. Just be good to yourself and your son. Teach him to live by our laws, as well as those of man. I don't want to have to come back for either one of you."

Gemma sat in the middle of the floor, tears streaming down her face. Energy shimmered in the room, and the lock snapped open. *We will expect you in two weeks Daniel.* She had already planted the true location of the ranch deep in his subconscious where only he would ever find it, along with safeguards so he would never be able to pass on the information.

Jade flew out the open window.

Chapter Thirty Four

Two months.

It felt like a lifetime. A lifetime spent with half of her heart missing.

Jade folded the letter she had just read, and shoved it into the pocket of her jeans. Gemma was in Italy. Her parents were happily spoiling her. Everyone was counting the moments until the baby was born. *They're not the only ones.* Jade place her hand protectively over her own abdomen. *Only seven more months kids.* Seven months to go, and already her pants were growing snug.

Alicia ran past laughing, several pups nipping at her heels. *Come play with us.*

Jade smiled. "I have to feed the dogs first," she told her.

Alicia ran back, and grabbed the bag of food out of Jade's hands. Several nuggets fell out only to be snatched up by the tumbling pups. "Let me do that." Alicia narrowed her eyes at Jade, and tried to look stern. She failed miserably.

Jade laughed. Alicia shook her head, black curls flying, and dark eyes laughing. "You have to take it easy mommy. The babies."

Jade took the bag back from the child, dropped it on the ground, and pulled Alicia into her arms. "Are you happy, sweetheart?" Jade was. She could hardly believe how much life Alicia had brought to the ranch. Everybody adored her. She was growing stronger with each passing day, and the nightmares had almost stopped.

"Oh yes. I love you, and grandpapa, and Auntie Althea. When is Auntie Althea coming back anyway? We were going to make brownies today. Oh yea. I love Uncle Daniel, and I will love our babies." Alicia started giggling. "I think Uncle Daniel loves Auntie Althea too. I caught him making gaga eyes at her when she wasn't looking."

Jade laughed. Life was certainly good. If only Luke could be here it would be perfect. She forced the wayward thought from her mind, and made a point of looking around to see if they were alone. Then she leaned into her daughter and whispered. "Don't say anything, but I caught her making gaga at him last night."

The two of them laughed, the chores temporarily forgotten.

Later that night after tucking Alicia in and reading her a story, Jade took a cup of tea, and went out to sit on the porch swing. This was one of Jade's favourite times of day. Alicia was sleeping, Da was in bed, Daniel and Althea had gone for a run in the woods, and she was totally alone with her fantasies. The night was dark. Only a dim light showed through the window of the house, making the shadows dance along the porch rail. Jade relaxed, and her mind began to wander.

The smell of smoky pine tickled her nose, and her pulse quickened. It was amazing how a simple smell could make her body react. Luke appeared through the steam from her tea cup. His eyes were haunted, his face more gaunt than she remembered, and there was a small amount of gray in his hair. He looked so real. She could almost reach out and touch him.

"Mind if I sit?"

Jade sputtered, and the tea spilled. A hand snaked out, and snatched the cup from her shaking fingers. "Whoa. You don't want to burn yourself."

"What are you doing here?" Jade was stammering. She couldn't help it, and it made her angry. She couldn't believe he was really here.

"I couldn't stay away any longer." He stood on the edge of the deck looking across at her. "You left before I could thank you for Gemma."

"That's why you came? To thank me? I was only doing my job. You could have sent a letter." He was so the hottest male to ever walk the planet.

"If I sent a letter I couldn't do this." Luke crossed the deck, and gathered Jade into his arms. His lips, hot and strong, covered hers before she could blink.

She moaned as his tongue sought the moist heat of her mouth. It was a good thing he held her because her knees were jelly, and every bone in her body was melting.

"God I have missed you."

"What took you so long?" Jade slid her tongue between his lips for a little exploration of its own, while her hands slid under his shirt and caressed his bare skin.

"I had some business to tend to. Then I had to wait until the full moon had passed." He sat on the porch swing, and pulled Jade on his knee, sliding his hand beneath her sweater to caress her midriff. His hand slowly rose.

Her breath was coming in short quick pants. Why was he taking so long? She started unbuttoning his shirt. "Why wait until after the full moon. I like the full moon." Visions of them during their last full moon jumped into her head. She panted harder.

"I wanted you to realize this is us," he said. "It has nothing to do with the moon."

"Oh yes," she moaned as he gently thumbed one nipple. "This is definitely not the moon."

"I'm glad you see it my way."

Luke withdrew his hand from beneath her sweater, and Jade almost whimpered. When he lifted her, and set her on the porch swing she eyed him warily. When he knelt before her, and reached for her hand she laughed.

Luke growled at her. "Don't laugh. I'm serious."

Jade sputtered. "Sorry. Please continue."

Luke jumped up, and sat beside her on the swing. "Forget it. You ruined the mood."

Jade snuggled closer to him, snaking her arm around his waist and tucking herself beneath his arm. She looked up into his face, attempting to look contrite. "I'm sorry," she said. "Maybe I can restore the mood."

Luke leaned down, and captured her pouty lips, kissing her until her toes curled. When he finished, she looked up at him with passion glazed eyes.

"Forget it. I'm not asking. I'm taking charge. We are going to be wed as soon as possible. I can't live without you. You are my mate. Wolves do not let their mates go."

Jade sighed contentedly. She did so love a take charge kind of guy. Not that she had any intention of letting him have his way in everything, but it would be interesting watching him try. "That's good," she told him meekly. "The children will need a strong daddy to handle their mommy."

"Children?" Luke's expression was a mixture of horror and hope.

Blood Connection

Prelude

She awoke with a jerk. Fear thrummed through her veins, as her eyes furtively searched the room for the reason she was awake.

Nothing.

She relaxed slightly, and listened to the sound of a train barrelling down the tracks. *Wait a minute.* Was that a tornado? Yesterday she watched a news program where a tornado swept through a small town leaving behind a trail of destruction. Everyone the reporters talked to said it sounded like a train screaming through the sky over their heads. Besides, there were no trains anywhere near the ranch. There wasn't a whole lot of anything near the ranch.

The ranch lay in a densely wooded area in the foothills of the Catskill Mountains, about five miles from the nearest public road. South of the ranch lay the Ashokan Reservoir, and west of them was the town of Phoenicia. There was a train station in Phoenicia, but the tracks didn't come anywhere near the ranch. Not many strangers came visiting, partially due to the fact that the exact position of the ranch was a well guarded secret and accessible only by all terrain vehicles, horseback, or air. She supposed that one could hike out to the ranch, but for some reason the hikers avoided this area. She remembered the first time she came to the ranch with Aunt Althea. The closer they drew to her new home, the more intense the desire to turn and run; to go anywhere as long as it was far away from where they were going. Then Althea had wrapped her warm, soft fingers around Alicia's smaller ones, and squeezed.

"You belong here child," she whispered, and the oppressive feeling vanished, allowing Alicia to see the beauty of what was to be her home for the time being.

There were several Jeeps, a Hummer, and a couple of smaller ATV's in the large barn, but they seldom used the vehicles. Alicia's favourite mode of transportation was by horse because riding on a horse reminded her of her other life. Before her parents were murdered, and before Jade adopted her, Alicia lived on a small farm in Mexico where their only modes of transportation were by foot, and by mule.

Alicia lifted a corner of the Disney princess curtains, and peeked out the window beside her bed, careful not to wake her German-shepherd pup that slept peacefully on the foot of her bed. What she saw made her gasp, and she started to whimper.

Do Not Move. It was a command, one that she followed instinctively. *If you don't move they won't see you.* The harsh voice soothed and quieted her, even as she watched the two giant black bears, their heads turning first to the right, and then to the left. She could hear them snuffling as they tasted the air, searching for her scent. She knew that the voice was right, and that if she moved they would discover her. She stopped breathing. She became a statute, not moving, even her heartbeat slowed as she watched in mixed fear, and wonder.

The two black bears pawed the air before them like two great steeds dancing anxiously, blowing smoke out their nostrils with each exhale. The bears pulled a giant, black coach, its only color the grotesque gold inlay around the doors and windows depicting thousands of souls screaming in agony.

Where are you girl? Show yourself to me. The spirit voice crawled through her mind, like ants crawling through a picnic, even as it thundered around her making the house shake. She wanted to look, to see if anyone else heard it, but fear held her immobilized.

She would not betray her presence this time. This time she would stay quiet, and protect her new family.

Suddenly both bears turned as one, and stared straight at her. They could see her through the wall. She knew they could. She could feel their eyes burning into her soul.

I see you. The voice dripped with smug satisfaction.

Alicia screamed.

One

Alicia sat up with a jerk, and pulled the covers to her neck. Her breath came in short, quick gasps, and her body felt chilled even in the eighty-degree heat.

It was here.

She could not stop the trembling in her limbs. She had to go. For a heartbeat, white-hot anger coursed through her veins. *Why me?* The questions raced through her mind in a matter of seconds. *What did I do to deserve this nightmare? Why can't you just go away and leave me alone?*

Just as quickly as the anger flared, it vanished. She knew what it wanted—what they all wanted.

Her death.

Well it would not be long now, and they would have their wish. Only it would not be on their terms. She had always been small for her age, and pale, but at least she had been healthy. Then three months ago she started getting horrendous headaches accompanied by flashes of light, and hallucinations. At first she had been afraid that she was going blind, but after numerous tests the only thing the doctors could agree on was *she was dying*. It wasn't cancer, at least not any cancer they had come across before. With all their modern equipment they couldn't detect any tumour. Still her headaches persisted, and she grew weaker with each passing day. She was hungry all the time, but food upset her stomach. There was a very good chance she wasn't going to see her twenty fifth birthday, and her biggest regret was that she wouldn't see her family again. Never tease her brothers, or sneak out of the house with her sister. Although she was nearly a decade older, the two girls were closer than most sets of twins.

What did it matter now? She had been nothing but trouble since she was born.

Alicia? The familiar and beloved spirit voice of her little sister broke through her reverie. *Are you all right? I feel pain. Has someone hurt you?* She should have realized that Emerald would sense her pain, even at such a distance. Emmy was such a strong empath that she had trouble tuning out the emotions of strangers. When it came to her family she had only to think of them, and she could pick up what they were feeling, and thinking, although she tried very hard to tune out the latter. Not an easy task as Alicia remembered from her own youth.

I'm fine, Emmy. Alicia forced a calm she did not feel into her own spirit voice. She spoke freely with her sister, on a path shared only by her family. A path developed over many years.

At seventeen, Emerald still looked up to, and adored her older sister, and it wasn't just because Alicia always sided with her against her domineering brothers. Two against the world was their motto. Long after Emerald was more than capable of looking after herself, she still looked to Alicia for aid when it came to her brothers. Sometimes it was hard to believe that they were triplets. Quinn and Gheorgès were both tall, dark, and even though they were going through their awkward age, already extremely handsome. Emerald was slightly taller than Alicia which wasn't hard considering Alicia's own small stature, she was slender, moved with the grace of a swan, and had white blonde hair with streaks of gold and silver; the mark of the *Moarté*. She was already very powerful, and by the time she came of age she would be one of the most powerful creatures on earth.

You're not coming. Emerald said petulantly. She did not wait for Alicia to answer. *That is so not fair. I have been looking forward to this for months. Quinn and Gheorgès are so beastly to me when you aren't here. They treat me like a child.*

Alicia was supposed to meet with her family in Willow Bend to celebrate her birthday. A quarter of a century was a big deal, and her family did not know that she would probably never see it. She had said nothing about the headaches, or the doctor appointments, not wanting them to drop their lives and run to her. God she missed them. For a fleeting moment she actually considered going. What better way to spend her final days than with family and friends. The Inner Sanctum and Charlotte were in Willow Bend.

Charlotte was the woman who ran the Inner Sanctum. The Inner Sanctum was a six thousand square foot replica of a fourteenth century Romanian castle, built on a two-acre treed lot between a lake and the mountains. The stone structure could pass for Dracula's castle, and was a place of sanctuary for mortals, and most importantly immortals. Charlotte liked to tell the story of how the first settlers from Romania had built the castle stone by stone—although she never made mention of the fact that the first settlers were Lycans. Funny thing was that if you asked any of the original settlers, they would tell you that the castle just appeared there one morning, and has been there ever since.

Alicia spent a lot of time at *The Inner Sanctum* when she was a child. Her adoptive father Luke Wulfson was once the Alpha of the Willow Bend Pack of Lycans, and the family still returned there for yearly retreats. Luke had given his mansion to the Pack for the use of the single pack members, and so they stayed at the *Sanctum*. It was a comfort zone.

A safe zone.

You will not be safe there, her inner voice whispered, and she knew the truth. Nobody could stop the inevitable, not even her mother. And if the evil that stalked her while she slept and was vulnerable found her it would find her family. No, she could not go to Willow Bend, and risk their safety.

She had to disappear.

Alicia was not immune to heartbreak, but it was better the heartbreak of not seeing her family, than the heartbreak of seeing her family slaughtered—again. The memory of helplessly watching while another monster had drained the life from her precious Papa still haunted her. She had survived her first encounter with evil thanks to the *Moarté* who had rescued, and then adopted her, but neither of her parents had survived, and no matter how many times they told her it was not her fault, she knew they were wrong. It was her fault. She was the one who had reached out to a stranger. She was the one who had led that monster straight to her family.

Well this time it would be different. This time when the monster found her, for there was no doubt in her mind that it would, she would be alone. There was no way Alicia Martinez Wulfson would be responsible for the death of another person, especially when it was inevitable that she die anyway.

I am sorry, Emmy, but something has come up. Besides, you are smarter than your brothers. You only need to out think them. If she didn't leave soon she was going to change her mind and fly straight to Willow Bend, and the ones she loved. *I have to go, Em. I have a plane to catch.*

Alicia snapped her mind shut, slipped from her bed, showered, and dressed. Fifteen minutes later she was packed and on her way. She did not stop to say goodbye to anyone. She already said her goodbyes last night at her going away party. As far as everyone here knew, she was going home for a short vacation before heading for a dig in Egypt. That had been the plan before her diagnosis. Nobody knew that she had turned down the coveted position so she could spend the last few weeks of her life with her family.

You are not alone. Alicia smiled at the gruff voice, the only voice she had never been able to block from her thoughts. This was her guardian angel, her life line to sanity.

No, she was not alone, even though she dared not answer.

At the airport, she purchased a ticket for Romania. There was a dig at the foot of the Făgărus Mountains she wanted to check out. Even if there weren't a dig, she would have chosen to go there. It was the birthplace of her adoptive father, Lykos Wulfson. If she could not be with him, she could at least feel closer by touching the soil he had touched.

Alicia wiped the sweat from her brow, and looked out the window as the plane took off. She marvelled at the scenery below, and was thankful to have seen the wonders she had seen. At twenty-four, Alicia was already a respected archaeologist. She had been on numerous digs since the age of sixteen. For as long as she could remember, she had been fascinated with other countries, and cultures. When others her age were reading teen mysteries and romances, she was reading mysteries of another kind.

Mysteries of the dead.

She had an affinity for it. The dead spoke to her. They didn't exactly come up to her and say, "Good day,

Alicia. How are you today?" It was more like watching a video playing in her head, in fast forward. When she stood on or near a grave she saw the life, and death, of the person buried there. They called to her, often leading her to the exact spot she needed to be. It was this uncanny ability of hers to find those long dead and buried that helped to build her reputation, opening doors which otherwise might be left closed to her.

If any of her colleagues felt she was too young for the job, they changed their opinion after working with her. With her sixth sense, and her meticulously thorough attitude, she soon won them over.

She had been lucky enough to have seen and done more than an average person would in an entire lifetime. Her only regret was not seeing her family again.

You will see them again, little one. This I promise you. He was wrong. She would not see them again in this lifetime, but at least they were alive.

With her forehead pressed against the cool glass, Alicia let her eyelids drop, shutting out the vanishing earth. She felt more alone on this plane full of strangers, than she had as a child living with her parents in the wilds of Mexico. Thinking about her childhood opened the floodgates of memory.

"Stop, Papa," she screamed at him with her mind. Her body and voice held immobile by the monster with the face of an angel that beckoned her father to it with a crooked finger. Her father's movements were jerky and awkward, like a puppet's, as he inched closer to the monster. His eyes were glazed over, and he was unaware of anything around him.

Alicia wanted to turn away from that hideously handsome face, the face of a demon, as her beloved papa stood in front of the beast, and docilely tilted his head to one side baring the rapidly beating pulse at his neck. The beast's smile widened, and its fangs grew until they were too large for its mouth, distorting its features grotesquely.

Those fangs glistened obscenely in the night, dripping a vile liquid that seared all that it touched. The monster leaned forward, and sank those horrid fangs into the vein offered so meekly by Papa. Alicia continued to stare unable to turn away or even close her eyes, as the beast drank Papa's life from his veins. The monster withdrew its fang's from Papa's neck, and as Papa's lifeless body fell noiselessly to the ground it held Alicia's gaze, and slowly licked the crimson drops from its fangs.

Alicia's head jerked and she blinked rapidly several times to clear the image from her mind. *I'm so sorry, Papa*, she whispered against the cold pane of glass. She was responsible for his death, and the death of her beloved Mama. She was the one the monster had come for. Her entire life she had heard the thoughts of those around her. Sometimes their thoughts were clearer than their actual voices, making it difficult to know when a person had spoken aloud, or merely had a passing thought.

Her abilities had terrified her parents, who took her to the more remote parts of Mexico where it was less likely anyone would find out about her. Alicia had tried to be a good girl, and not listen to the voices in her head, but she did not know how to shut them out. At first, she thought she was just like everyone else, until she discovered that nobody around her knew what she was thinking.

Until the fateful day when her entire world turned upside down; the day her thoughts led a monster straight to their door. He had been toying with her when he destroyed her parents, and he made sure she knew it. They were simply appetizers, while she was the main course. If the *Moarté* had not come when she did, Alicia would have died on her eighth birthday. Instead, the

Moarté destroyed the vampire, rescued Alicia, and gave her a new home and family.

God she missed them already, but there was no way she was going to risk their lives because she did not want to be alone. She owed them that, and so much more.

Alicia was fascinated with ancient history. When she was nine she began reading everything she could get her hands on to do with ancient civilizations, and their languages. She had an exceptionally high IQ, and discovered that she had a photographic memory. To help feed her thirst for knowledge, Jade arranged for her to have private tutors. By the time she was eleven, she had read nearly every book on the subject, and was completely captivated with the idea of being an archaeologist.

When Alicia was twelve, Jade took her to attend a seminar on archaeology at the University of Leicester, in England. That was the day she knew for certain that she would be an archaeologist. At home, Alicia immersed herself even more in her schoolwork, and research. She graduated high school with honours at the age of fourteen, and enrolled at the University of Leicester at the age of fifteen, signing up for as many ancient history and archaeology courses possible. Languages came easily to her, and by the time she was sixteen she was fluent in English, French, German, Romanian, and Latin. By eighteen, her fluency included Polish, Egyptian, and Ancient Greek. She was expert in hieroglyphics, which was the reason they chose her over some of her more established colleagues for the Egyptian dig. What she wouldn't give to find out what the ancient Egyptians had to tell her, literally.

When Alicia was sixteen, she was the youngest intern on a summer dig in Belize. That was when the dead first spoke to her. It was also when her nightmare stalker returned. She did not need her guardian angel to tell her to be still. Fear held her in its icy grip, and she could barely breathe. She did not dare tell anyone about the nightmares. Jade would have insisted she come home. That was something she was not about to do. Nothing short of a death in the family could have dragged her from her dream.

She did leave Leicester. With the help of several tutors, and the internet, Alicia graduated with her BA in Ancient History and Archaeology, while managing to attend several digs around the world. Whenever the *Seeker*, as she grew to think of her stalker, got too close she simply moved on. Perhaps, deep down, Alicia thought she would discover something to help her fight the evil thing that stalked her. Her inner voice insisted she go to Egypt. The answers were there amongst the pyramids.

What did it matter now? She was dying. She could not change that simple fact. All she could do now was stay one step ahead of the *Seeker*, and keep that evil from her loved ones. The *Seeker* had been hunting her for years, seeking the miniscule powers she possessed—the ability to hear thoughts, move small objects with her mind, and communicate with the dead. She could not imagine what it would do if it got scent of the *Moarté*.

You do not have to die. Come to me, her angel said.

Tears filled Alicia's dark eyes, and escaped down her cheeks. She did not bother to brush them away. She could not go to him. She did not dare.

Two

Alicia quickly found a taxi willing to take her to a small village nestled in the foothills of the Făgăras Mountains which are the highest mountains in the Southern Carpathians. The taxi refused to travel any farther than that, citing the road conditions, or lack thereof, as the reason. The village lay in the shadow of a giant Citadel that loomed above them like some sinister guardian. The ruling families had once lived in the Citadel; way up high where they could look upon their people, and somewhere below, closer to the actual base of the mountain was the remains of the small village of the guardians.

Hiring a donkey cart to take her to the Inn was not an easy task. The roads were long and winding, and nobody wanted to be out on them after dark. The people were a superstitious lot, and their fear of the dark was tantamount to a terror Alicia understood completely. Alicia loved the night, the scent of night blooming roses, the chirping of the crickets, the peeping of the tree frogs as they called for a mate, even the buzz of the hungry mosquito was music to her ears. She loved the night.

What she hated was the long dark hours when she slept, and was vulnerable to the *Seeker*.

Finally she found a farmer willing to take her along with him. He had a small farm just a few miles past the Inn, he told her, and would be happy for the company.

The journey was pleasant enough with the farmer regaling her with tales of the past in the mountains, while the cart bounced over the pothole-ridden dirt road that wound its way along the mountain pass. They travelled for miles along the winding road, sometimes with the mountains so close she could reach out and touch them; other stretches ran through valleys, and forests. The farmer made several stops at farms along the way dropping off supplies he had picked up in the village. Alicia got used to the farmers looking at her curiously, although not one questioned her presence.

The road wound its way through a forest with the trees so dense they blocked the sun. Alicia had the feeling that someone was watching them as they wound their way along the trail. The farmer clicked his tongue to encourage the donkey to move faster, and as if the donkey didn't want to be in the woods any more than they did, the cart bounced along the road. There were only a couple of hours before sunset when they finally reached the Inn, but the farmer ensured Alicia that he would make it to his own home in plenty of time before dark.

Alicia was entranced with her first view of the inn. An old cedar rail fence surrounded it and the immaculate gardens. A gate stood open to a crushed stone walkway leading to the two-story building. The back of the inn faced the mountain, but Alicia could see that the lower deck, as well as the upper balcony, both ran the full length of the outer wall, plus wrapped around both ends. There were several potted plants hanging from the upper balcony, their blossoms a riot of color against the darkened wood.

Across from the wooden gate, on the other side of the road was a flat area with the grass cut short. There was a large "Parking" sign with an arrow pointing to the grassy spot on the side of the road, not that it looked like there had ever been a car parked there. Alicia could not imagine too many drivers either brave enough, or stupid enough, to attempt to drive their vehicles down the so-called road.

The Inn was quiet when Alicia arrived; the only sound that of a child's laughter. She smiled at a young American mother and her two-year-old daughter, as the child chased the bubbles her mother blew for her. The mother was in her early thirties, with long straight black hair, and wide green eyes. The little girl had short curly hair, a shade lighter than her mother's, but the same wide green eyes. Their laughter drifted over to her, and Alicia sighed. She would never have a child of her own. There would be no curly-haired little girl chasing bubbles, or dark-haired little boy catching frogs.

Alicia climbed down from the cart, thanked the farmer when he handed her bag to her, and watched as he disappeared around a bend in the road. *Let's hope there's room at the Inn,* she thought, and walked up the path. The farmer did say that several of the archaeologists were camping at the site. She smiled at the mother and child.

"Hi," the mother said. "I'm Molly, and this is my daughter Megan." She indicated the little girl who had taken up shelter behind her mother's leg.

"Alicia." Alicia smiled at the little girl, and held her hand out to her. "How are you, Megan," she said.

"Hi," Megan said from her safe spot behind her mother.

Molly glanced at the duffle bag Alicia was carrying. "Have you come to join the dig?" she asked. "Mike, that's my husband, didn't tell me they were expecting anyone else."

"That's because they aren't expecting me. Until this morning, I wasn't sure I was coming here."

The front door of the Inn opened, and a short, plump woman on the far side of sixty stepped out, wiping her hands on the apron she wore. "Welcome," she said, her accent making her W sound like a V. "I am Magda, welcome to our Inn. Pietro come out here. We have a guest."

An elderly man wearing baggy brown trousers, a white shirt, and a woollen vest rushed out the door, and grabbed Alicia's duffel bag. When he smiled there was a gap between his two front teeth.

"Show our guest to her room, Pietro," Magda said. She reached into the pocket of her apron, and pulled out a cookie which she gave to Megan. "Take her bags to number fourteen."

"You're right beside us," Molly said. "We have thirteen."

Alicia checked into the Inn, had a quick wash, and within the hour arrived at the dig. Professor Raven was thrilled to have Alicia on the site, although he regretfully informed her that they had no funds to hire her.

"Don't worry about it," she assured him. "I am actually on vacation, and was hoping that you would allow me to join you as a volunteer for a while."

"That we can manage," the professor told her happily. A student shouted excitedly, and the professor all but forgot Alicia in his haste to witness the new discovery.

Alicia was wandering around the dig when the buzzing started in her head. The further from the actual site she got, the louder the buzzing, until she was about a half mile away from where they were digging. Suddenly the buzzing stopped, and her vision blurred before it became very clear.

Screams rent the air. The ground below her feet ran crimson. Headless bodies littered the ground. A young

couple, barely out of their teens, led a small group of
children from the carnage. Even the smallest of the
children was helping to carry the babies, as they
disappeared into the surrounding forest. In the unearthly
silence that followed the massacre, the village burned to
the ground, and the remaining bones scattered in the
wind.

These were her father's people. Alicia understood
why it was so important to keep their presence a secret.
People hadn't changed much over the years, they were
still afraid of what they did not understand. She took
several, calming breaths. Although they were not digging
anywhere near this area right now, she vowed to do
whatever was necessary to ensure that they never did.
She would not allow those bones to be dug up, and proof
that Lycans existed be found.

What could she do? She would be dead in a couple of
months.

You do not need to die. Come to me.

The words were harsh with emotion, the guttural
Egyptian accent evident. Even if she knew how to go to
him, would she dare? Could she dare? Or, would going to
him lead her right into another nightmare of her own
making?

It must be your decision, little one. I will not force you.
There was overwhelming sadness, and resignation in the
voice. *I will stay with you to the end. You will not be alone.*

Alicia spent every day at the dig. Sometimes she
would grab a brush and work alongside the other interns,
slowly, painstakingly uncovering old relics. So far, they
had only uncovered a few trinkets, and the tools of
humans, but Professor Raven was optimistic that they
had found the ancient village of the protectors. The
supernatural race of beings rumoured to have protected
the ruling families by turning into wolves to fight their
opponents. A trail led from the spot they were digging, up

the side of the mountain to the Citadel which towered above them, convincing Professor Raven that he was digging in the right spot. Alicia was not about to tell him any differently. It was his lifelong dream to find proof of their existence, and Alicia meant to do everything in her power to ensure that his dream did not come true.

~~~

Alicia was bone weary, and her face smudged with dirt where she continuously wiped away the sweat that ran steadily from her brow. The rubber band that held her hair had loosened, and several curly strands tickled her nose. She brushed them away, smearing another streak of dirt across her cheek. She didn't care. There was no room for a prima donna on an archaeological dig. It was hard, meticulous work, and even the cooler, wet temperatures did nothing to ease her discomfort. Alicia looked around her at the other smudged grinning faces, and could not stop her own returning grin. They had uncovered their first bones today, and spirits were definitely high.

Professor Raven had personally supervised the careful extraction and packaging of the bones. They would send the bones to the University of Leicester for identification and carbon dating, and then Professor Raven would find out what Alicia already knew. They were simple canine bones. The bones were those of a wild dog that had starved to death. Nothing more—nothing less.

It was dusk when Alicia trudged the four miles to the Inn with a male intern who spent the entire time flirting outrageously with her. He was taller than Alicia by several inches, which didn't necessarily make him a tall man, and even with his dirty blond hair plastered to his face he was good looking, in a frat boy kind of way. For the past week he had found every excuse possible to be near Alicia, and she was beginning to find it rather annoying.

"At least have a drink with me before dinner," he pleaded.

There was a sudden lightshow in front of Alicia's eyes, and her head began to throb. Hunger clawed at her insides like a wild beast trying to claw itself from its prison. Her teeth exploded in her mouth. Stepping closer to her companion, she leaned into his throat. The naked fear in his blue eyes made her wet at her core, as she sank her fangs into his common carotid that carried the hot, fresh blood from his heart.

Swallowing the rising horror, Alicia shook the image from her mind, brushed a wayward lock from in front of her eyes, and forced a laugh she did not feel. "Before dinner I am going to have a warm bath." The water at the Inn was never warm, but it would help erase the horrid image of her drinking from his vein from her mind. "Then I am going to do something with this mop of mine, and change into something more comfortable."

Her companion did nothing to disguise the blatant desire that flared in his eyes. "You look fine to me," he drawled. "More than fine."

Of course I do. I'm absolutely gorgeous covered in dirt, and wearing an old filthy rain slicker.

A sudden crash of thunder made them both jump. Alicia looked up into the clear blue sky, very different from the dark clouds that threatened rain in the early morning, and this time she did laugh. Her guardian angel was at it again. Too bad he couldn't protect her from her own horrifying thoughts. "Nonetheless, I think I will stick to my original plans and pass on that drink."

When her companion pouted, she could not help but tease. "Don't look so sad. We can still sit together at dinner." Sit was about all she could manage these days. It was getting more difficult each day to hide the fact that she was barely eating, and everything she did force herself to eat just came back up once she was in the privacy of her room. Liquids were about all she could stomach, and even those were beginning to cause her problems. Just the thought of forcing herself to eat something in front of these people had her stomach churning. *Or was it hunger that churned?*

"Right. You, me, and an Inn full of people." The more people the easier it would be to hide the fact she was barely eating. Besides, the last thing she wanted was to encourage a relationship with this, or any man. It would not be fair, not only did she not have the time for a long-term relationship, but the man held no more appeal to her than her brothers did.

A fleeting memory of one of her more disastrous dates flickered through her thoughts, and she sighed. A week, a month, a lifetime. It didn't matter how long she had. She had long since resigned herself to the truth that she would never find a flesh and blood man who could even remotely compare to the man of her dreams.

They rounded a bend in the road, and the Inn came into view. The young American mother, Molly, was again blowing bubbles for little Megan to chase while they waited for her husband to return from the site. Megan saw Alicia and forgot about the bubble she was chasing. "Lisa, Lisa," she called in her baby voice. The baby ran towards her as fast as her chubby little legs would carry her, with her arms stretched out in front.

Alicia smiled at the chubby girl, and waved. "Hello Molly," she called to the mother. "Mike asked me to tell you that he will be about an hour or so still. They are bagging bones."

"Eew. You make it sound so gruesome." Molly laughed. "Come here, Megan," she called to her daughter, who continued on her way ignoring her mother. "Alicia will see us at supper."

"Right supper," Alicia's companion muttered, and stalked towards the Inn without even trying to disguise his rancour.

Megan was about half the way between her mother and Alicia, when Alicia heard the rumbling.

Do not move. They can't see you if you don't move.

The wind roared like a freight train barrelling down the tracks, straight for them. Alicia stared in horror as the massive ebony coach pulled by its two mammoth black bears burst through the clouds. *They can't see you if you do not move.* She prayed for divine intervention as she watched death coming for her.

The bears stopped, and snuffled the air. They couldn't find her. She was safe.

There was movement to her left. Terror gripped her throat, as little Megan ran straight for her. The bears turned as one, and sped straight toward the little girl.

Do not move. Do not move. Do not move. Even as the words ran through her mind, Alicia leapt toward the child.

She snatched the startled child into her arms, and stumbled, rolling as she fell to protect the child with her own body. Coming to a sudden stop, she sat up with the whimpering child tucked safely against her chest.

Thunder roared in her ears, as the bears' hot breath brushed her cheek. Megan whimpered. Alicia knew if they stayed where they were Megan would die. She couldn't live with the death of another innocent on her conscience.

There was a flicker of movement in her peripheral vision.

He stood there; Tall, Egyptian, and wearing only a loincloth that did nothing to disguise his manhood. His tanned body rippled with muscles, and flames flickered from the golden sun tattooed on his broad chest. His eyes locked with hers, and she stopped breathing. Heat pooled at her center, and her blood ran hot. Alicia melted beneath the radiating heat of those golden orbs. He silently offered his hand.

Alicia's eyes flickered to the fluttering nostrils of the giant bear, and back to the nearly naked god.

Three

There was a complete absence of light. She was standing in a fog so thick she couldn't see her hand in front of her face. The thick fog distorted the sound of their beating hearts, and their rapid breathing. Alicia drew in a deep breath, and slowly exhaled in an attempt to still the rapidly growing panic. Megan squirmed in her arms, and Alicia lifted her up so she was resting against her shoulder. "It's okay, sweetheart. Alicia can't see either." She gently rocked the child, murmuring sweet platitudes that helped to calm both her and the child, while she considered what to do.

The child does not belong here.

Shivers trailed down her spine at the deep timber of the familiar voice. She prayed her legs would hold her and Megan upright. "Who are you?" she whispered, even now afraid to open her mind completely to him.

You know who I am little one.

She did know him. At least, she knew his voice. This was her guardian angel. She swallowed the lump in her throat, and whispered. "Where are we?" She had to know if the sound would penetrate the deep fog.

This is simply a passage between two places. The child does not belong here.

Alicia clutched Megan closer. *I will not allow you to harm this child. I will not be responsible for any more death.*

You misunderstand, little one. No harm will come to the child.

Alicia wanted to believe him. Every fiber of her being screamed the truth of his words. Megan did not belong here. She was a child with her entire life before her.

There was a sudden bright light, and the mist cleared slightly. He was so close she could smell his musky male scent. His blood called to hers, making her own blood burn, and her teeth ached for a taste. Alicia stared. She couldn't stop herself. He was without a doubt the most magnificent male specimen she had ever laid eyes on. When he moved, the muscles on his arms rippled, sending heat straight to her core.

See for yourself. He made a wiping motion, and the fabric of the universe opened giving her a window to the Inn. The usually immaculate garden was a disaster, the plants torn and tossed. Mike and Molly stood in the center of the chaos. Alicia was surprised to see the stubble of a beard on Mike's usually clean-shaven chin. There hadn't even been a hint of five o'clock shadow when she left him at the site barely an hour ago. Mike had his arm around his wife's shoulder, and he seemed to be helping her stand.

"Why aren't they looking?" Molly's voice was thick with tears.

"They have been looking for three days, Molly. They are not here."

Molly put her face in her hands muffling her voice, but Alicia heard every word as easily as if she were inside the other woman's head. "I know what I saw, Mike. I can't believe it, but I saw it. How can I convince anyone else when I cannot believe my own eyes?"

They walked to the exact spot where Alicia had stumbled with Megan. "Megan was running to meet Alicia." Molly sniffed, and swiped at her nose. "She loved Alicia because she always treated her kindly, even when she was so tired I thought she would drop where she stood." Molly sniffed again. "All of a sudden the sky darkened, and the wind began to howl. Megan suddenly stopped running. She just stared at the sky like she was seeing something that couldn't really be there. Alicia was staring at the sky too. You should have seen the look of terror on her face. Before I knew what was happening Alicia ran over and grabbed Megan. She stumbled, and they both fell."

Molly's wide eyes pleaded with her husband. "It all happened so fast. One second they were sitting on the ground staring into the sky. The next, they were gone. Alicia reached toward the sky, and they simply vanished."

"It was a tornado, Molly. Alicia must have realized Megan was right in its path. She was trying to protect Megan."

A tornado? What is going on? Exactly how long have we been here, and where exactly is here? Are we dead? Am I dead? Is that why you said Megan doesn't belong here, because I am already dead, and she is still alive?

Deep, rumbling laughter sent delicious shivers down her spine, at the same time it sent anger coursing through her veins. Before Alicia could vent, the nearly naked man started to speak, and Alicia relaxed as the deep timbers of his voice soothed her anger. *You are not dead. You have been here three earth days, and it is time to send the child home.*

Megan chose that moment to squirm around, and she spotted her parents through the window. "Mommy! Daddy!" She squealed, and tried to wiggle free.

At five foot four, Alicia did not normally feel small but her guardian angel towered over them. He had to be six foot six at the very least. She watched warily when he knelt on one knee, bringing his face level with Megan. "Are you ready to go home, little one," he asked. Megan's head bobbed and wide green eyes so much like her mother's stared at the strange man. She reached one small hand towards his chiselled features, and touched his cheek. A small gasp escaped Alicia when his face began to glow, and then he passed his hand in front of Megan's small face, and her eyes glazed over. "It is best if you do not remember anything of this," he said gently.

He took the child from Alicia's suddenly limp arms. "Wait here," he said to Alicia, and stepped through the window. *Sure, why not? She didn't have anywhere to go anyway.*

Alicia watched as the tall Egyptian set Megan carefully on the ground, and once again wiped his hand over her face. His body shimmered, and disappeared. Megan ran towards her parents. "Mommy, Daddy," she called in her little girl voice.

Alicia watched the couple bend as a single unit, and clutch their child close. They were laughing and crying as they took turns hugging Megan, all the time running their hands over her arms and legs checking for injuries.

"Are you okay baby? Are you hurt? Where were you? Where is Alicia?"

Megan squirmed uncomfortably in her parents arms. "You hurt me," she whimpered, and they immediately loosened their hold. They did not relinquish her. They were afraid that if they let go she would disappear again.

Mike and Molly searched every inch of their daughter without finding a scratch on her. Not so much as a smudge of dirt marred the child. If they had not lived through the agony of the past three days, they would think she had just been out playing.

Finally convinced there was no serious injury to their daughter, they reluctantly gave in to her persistent wriggling, and set her on the ground, although Molly still refused to release her grip on the child's hand. Mike made a quick search of the area Megan had come from, but although the ground was soft, the only thing he could find were about ten feet of Megan's prints. She had appeared as suddenly and as mysteriously as she had vanished.

Mike knelt so he was eye level with his daughter. "Megan." Megan's innocent gaze met her father's serious one. "Do you know where Alicia is?"

Megan's curly locks bobbed and she turned so she was staring straight at Alicia. Mike followed the direction of his baby daughter's gaze, and saw only a few clouds in a very blue sky. With a puzzled look on his face he repeated, "Do you know where Alicia is?"

"Yes daddy. With the glowing man."

Four

"Forfeit," Jade purred, grinding against Luke's obvious erection.

"Oh yeah," Luke growled lifting his lower body, and Jade with it off the floor. "I agree to do anything you want." He lowered his lids, and wiggled suggestively. "What doth my lady desire?"

Jade sighed, and relaxed against her husband's hard chest. She reached up and ran her fingers through the straggly ends of his normally thick beard, and then she gave it a little tug, grinning triumphantly.

Shit. She wouldn't, Luke thought suddenly wary. He should have realized what she was up to. Jade had been after him to trim his beard for months now. He didn't particularly like his beard as long and straggly as it was, but he refused to trim it to prove a point; that he could grow it if he wanted to.

"Oh yeah," she laughed. Her warm breath kissed Luke's already heated skin, and he groaned. "Cut it off."

"What?" *That is so not what he was expecting.* With a growl, Luke flipped them over so he was looming above his wife. God he loved her. Had from the first time he saw her, walking toward him across the crowded room at that seedy bar almost eighteen years ago, all sex and woman. It just took his brain a little longer to realize what his body knew instinctively, and with every moment they spent together their bond only grew stronger.

He would kill for her. He would die for her. And yes, he would shave his beard for her. Right after he did something else for her.

Jade's lips twisted into the crooked grin he adored, and her amber eyes shone with love. "Are you trying to weasel out of our bet, husband." Her voice was husky with need.

"No way." He was so close he could taste her breath as it came out in small pants of anticipation. "A deal's a deal. I just have one thing I need to do first," he said, and captured those soft lips.

The door opened, and Gheorgès strode into the room. At seventeen he was tall, and already showing signs of the man he would soon become. His features were dark, with a hard quality about them that some people found extremely intimidating.

"Get a room," he said, and then laughed. "Man, anyone saw you two would think you were newlyweds."

Luke kissed his wife again, stood up, and offered his wife a hand, almost surprised when she actually accepted the offered hand, and rose to stand by his side. He adjusted his sweats, which did nothing to hide his massive erection, before turning to his son. "I see you finally made it. Wasn't our workout for two?" Luke glanced pointedly at the clock on the far wall. "It's now three."

Gheorgès shrugged. "Something came up," he said. "Besides, it looks like Mom was a better workout partner anyway."

Luke ran his fingers through his straggly beard, and frowned. Then he smiled at his wife. "More interesting that's for sure."

Jade laughed, and reached up to give her husband a kiss. She was a tall woman, but Luke still towered over her, making her feel small and feminine. She playfully tugged at his beard. "Don't forget our bargain," she said.

"Luke's eyes darkened, and he waggled his eyebrows in a *Snidely Whiplash* sort of way. "How about a rematch," he said. "All or nothing."

Jade gave her son a kiss on the cheek. "Don't worry," she said in a stage whisper. "I wore him out for you."

Gheorgès pointedly looked at the bulge in the front of his father's sweats. "Doesn't look like he's worn out to me." He didn't need to see the physical proof of his father's desire for his mother; he smelled it the moment his walked into the room.

Jade laughed again, and crossed the room. When she reached the door, she half turned back. "Completely off," she threw at her husband. "And a rematch would have the same result."

As the door closed behind her she heard her son's voice. "You're not really, right?"

"A deal is a deal," Luke said as the door clicked shut.

The moment Jade left the bottom level of the ranch house where their training area was, she felt that shift in the universe again. It was nothing she could pinpoint, but it was there just the same. Something big was coming. She only wished she knew what it was. Jade didn't like this not knowing, especially with Alicia out there somewhere on her own. Not for the first time, Jade cursed the restrictions on her own powers. As *Moarté* she knew when one of their laws had been broken, where the crime had been committed, and often found herself in the right place on a feeling that she was going to be needed. She sometimes wished she got the feeling before the crime was committed. The trouble was, until a crime was committed she had no authority. That didn't mean that when a crime was committed she automatically knew who the guilty party was. She didn't just swoop down, and exact justice, but she did have excellent tracking and investigative skills which she used to her advantage. In most cases the best witnesses to a crime were the victims themselves. All Jade had to do was find the body in time.

Right now the urge to go to Mexico was nearly overwhelming, so overwhelming in fact that she found her feet taking her to the telephone instead of the shower. She picked up the phone and dialled a number by rote. After a half dozen rings the other end picked up.

"O'Connor Search and Rescue, how may we help you?" The pretty voice belonged to Theresa, Matthew's mate.

"Hi, Theresa, is he around?" The *he* Jade referred to was Matthew. Matthew was *Lobo*, born a wolf with the ability to take on human form. His mother had died during childbirth, and his father had raised him in the forest far from human contact. Matthew had very little experience with humans until he was caught in one of their traps and his father had been killed trying to rescue him. When Jade found him, he was in a cage at the Center for Physic Research, where they were doing secret experiments on him. Jade rescued him, and taught him how to embrace his human half, and how to control the magic he possessed as *Lobo*. Matthew soon became a trusted member of O'Connor Search and Rescue, the company founded by Jade's human father, Sean O'Connor.

Matthew had stayed at the Ranch, working with her father, training the search and rescue dogs when he wasn't on assignment with Jade, until Jade opened a division of O'Connor S&R in Mexico, and asked Matthew to stay there, and run it.

"Jade. How are you? Matthew is out on patrol. He's been edgy for about a week, but there hasn't even been one missing person's report let alone anything strange." There was a pause, and then, "Matthew wants to know what's happening."

Jade sent an image of herself rolling her eyes at Theresa. They were too far apart for her to have a private conversation with Matthew, but the open phone line helped her connection with Theresa. "Not one for small talk is he?"

Theresa's soft laughter tinkled over the open line. "I wouldn't exactly call you a master at chit chat. It's 'hi Theresa is he around?' No, how are you? How's life? Any news you'd like to share?"

Jade cringed. That's exactly what she did. Luke would have asked all the usual questions before asking for Matthew, but Jade still had trouble getting too close to people. In her business it wasn't always a good idea, but that was no excuse for rudeness. Besides, she actually liked and trusted Theresa. She had from the moment she met her, and she was thankful that Matthew had found her when he did. "I'm sorry, Theresa. How are you, and Matthew?"

"We're good, Jade." Jade couldn't help but catch the hint of excitement in Theresa's voice, and wondered why she hadn't noted it before. "How are you, and the family?"

"Luke is shaving his beard off."

"No!"

"Today."

"I thought you liked his beard?"

"I do, but he decided to grow it long, and refused to trim it so I challenged him. Of course I won. I think he was looking for a way to save face. He doesn't like his beard long and straggly any more than I do, but it became one of those he couldn't cut it off without looking like he was giving in to me."

"But he is just trimming it, right?"

"No. I told him to shave it *all* off."

Theresa laughed. "You are so evil."

Jade snickered. "You should have seen the look on his face. It was worth all the whisker burns I'm going to get in retaliation when it starts to grow back in." "So are you going to tell me, or are you waiting for Matthew to say something?"

With a rush of excitement Theresa burst out. "We're pregnant."

Wow! Jade really was not expecting that bit of news. "That is great," she said. "When?"

"Six months. And don't worry, Jade. Matthew and I aren't quitting you."

"But..."

"No. We discussed it. We love this job. And it's not really that dangerous."

"Fighting vampires, and rogue werewolves isn't dangerous?"

Theresa sighed. "You know what I mean. I did agree to phone duty for the duration of the pregnancy, but not a moment more."

There was the sound of a door opening and closing, and then Matthew's voice. Jade could picture him giving his mate a kiss, and patting her belly, just from the muffled sounds that carried over the wire. "How you feeling?" "Tired?" "Hey Junior you being good for Mommy?" "We are so not calling him Junior." "We'll see," and then his voice got louder. "Jade. What's happening? I've been edgy all week, but I can't pinpoint the cause."

Before Jade could get a word in he continued. "Aren't you supposed to be in Willow Bend with the family?"

"What makes you think I'm not?"

"Telephone I.D. Call came in from the ranch. Ain't technology a hoot? What gives?"

"Alicia cancelled. Told Em something came up, and ever since I have been edgy myself. Can't seem to track her down."

"What can I do?"

It was a long shot, but Jade couldn't shake the feeling that she should be on her way to Mexico. "Can you check out the farm?"

The *farm* was the property of Alicia. She inherited it when her parents were murdered. The locals considered it cursed, although the official story of the Martinez family deaths was attack by a wild animal. Stories of the *Chupacabra* have been around for years, and the locals would believe what they chose to believe.

"Nobody's been around. I just came from there."

Jade was disappointed although she hadn't really expected anything different. It was just this feeling she had that would not go away. "Thanks, Matthew. Could you check again in a few days? I can't shake this feeling."

"Will do, Boss."

"Thanks. Oh, and Matthew."

"Yeah, Boss."

"You're going to make a great dad." Jade hung up before Matthew could respond.

Five

He was generating so much heat Alicia was sure she would burst into flames, and he wasn't touching her—yet. She wanted to lean back and let those flames devour her. She was tired of running. She was tired of the constant pain that made her head feel like it would explode. She was tired of the horrid hallucinations where she became the creature she dreaded the most.

Most of all she was tired of being alone. Just once she wanted to feel a man's arms around her, and actually *feel* something. Well something besides hunger which is all she ever seemed to feel these days.

The mist gathered, closing the window on Megan and her family. It was so quiet she could hear the beat of their hearts, and their irregular breathing. She nearly jumped when he broke the silence.

"So much for forgetting," he whispered the words close to her ear, the deep sombre tones sending waves of desire coursing through her body, and need clenching at her womb.

What was wrong with her? She had never reacted to any man this way. In fact, she had never had any reaction to a man at all. What was it about his voice that made her want to rip her clothes off, and his? Not that he was wearing much. "I can't imagine it would be easy to forget being whisked away to...," Alicia indicated the surrounding mist with a flick of her wrist. "Where did you say we are? And while you're at it, who did you say you were?"

"This is merely a passageway."

"Hmm." Alicia chewed on her lower lip, and her eyes narrowed thoughtfully. She absently rubbed her forehead against the growing pain. "Where, exactly, does this passage lead?"

"Nowhere." His muscles rippled when he shrugged. "Everywhere."

Well, didn't that narrow things down a lot? Alicia felt his body stiffen, at the same time a tickle of unease began in her stomach. *Oh god, it was back. How had it found her here?* Alicia turned to warn the Egyptian, and had to shield her eyes. The tattoo on his chest was glowing blood red.

This time there was no hesitation on her part. Alicia placed her smaller hand in his much larger one, and closed her eyes against the wave of dizziness that enveloped her. When she opened her eyes she was standing in a large courtyard, completely surrounded by pyramids.

She blinked. They were still there.

Her right hand tingled, and she realized that *He* was still holding it. She gave it a small, reluctant tug, not really wanting him to relinquish his hold. He held on tighter.

The large stone door to one of the pyramids opened silently, and a man who was taller and broader, yet could be twin to the man holding her hand—right down to the sun glowing on his bare chest—strode toward them. The two men clasped forearms, before the taller man pulled the smaller one closer and clapped him on the back, ignoring the fact that he still held Alicia's hand firmly in his.

"Kamenwati," the new stranger boomed. *So that was her guardian angel's name.* "It is good to have you home." He stepped away from Kamenwati, and bowed low. "Welcome to our humble home, daughter of Alaric."

Home! Alicia gaped at the opulence of her surroundings, and the God who stood before her. This had to be another hallucination, although she had to admit it was a lot more pleasant than her usual ones.

She blinked, and the bronzed God remained before her—definitely the Egyptian Sun God Ra Horakhty. She would recognize his image anywhere. She should have seen the similarities in the man who held her hand. She probably would have if she weren't so distracted by the attraction she felt. Ra Horakhty was the reason she had worked so hard to be accepted on the Egyptian dig. She had to admit his pictures didn't do him justice. He was absolutely magnificent. It took Alicia several moments to process everything that was happening, and then it hit her. *Daughter.* "Hold on a minute. You must have me mistaken for someone else. I am Alicia Martinez Wulfson, adopted daughter of Luke Wulfson and Jade Caer. My real parents were killed when I was eight, and I have never heard of the Alaric."

"Alaric is Prince of the Magi." Kamenwati's deep, seductive tones threatened her sanity, and turned her knees to jelly. She was grateful her knees didn't buckle right then, and make a fool of her.

Me the daughter of a Prince, that's a laugh. "You definitely have the wrong girl."

Kamenwati heard her silent laughter, and his feelings for the slip of a woman whose hand he held made his tattoo settle into a steady golden glow. He had been watching over her for what at times felt like eternity, waiting for her to acknowledge his presence, understanding why she was terrified to do so.

Ra raised an eyebrow at his son. "So that's how it is." Ra's voice boomed in the stillness of the courtyard.

"Yes," Kamenwati answered. There was no sense in trying to hide anything from his father, and he was not ashamed of how he felt.

Alicia looked from one stoic face to the other, unable to read anything in either. "How what is?" she finally asked, but neither offered her any explanation.

The all too familiar tickle began in her stomach, and she was suddenly terrified as that glowing tattoo shifted from a soft golden glow to a blood red blaze. How had the *Seeker* followed her here? She tried harder to tug her hand from Kamenwati's, but he held it tight. "I have to go," she pleaded quietly. "Please, Kamenwati let me go."

Both men stared at her silently. Kamenwati held her hand a tiny bit tighter. *Do not fret, little one.* His deep voice enveloped her, giving her what she knew was a false sense of security.

It couldn't be real. She was not safe. Not as long as the evil hunted her. *Please, Kamenwati,* she begged silently. *Do not make me responsible for any more death.*

Kamenwati gave her hand what he hoped was a reassuring squeeze. *You were never responsible.*

The warning tickle in her stomach grew stronger, and Alicia grew frantic. She tugged her hand free, and stared at the two men with her hands on her hips. "What is wrong with you? *He* is close. Can't you feel it?"

Two pairs of golden globes stared at her as if she had suddenly grown two heads.

Fear and anger made her limbs tremble. "What is wrong with you," she demanded. "I need to leave here immediately. If *He* finds me I won't be able to save you."

Kamenwati reached out to take her shaking form in his arms, but she slapped at his hands and stepped aside, resisting the urge to just give in and allow him to protect her. She would not give in to her own desires, and delay leaving here any longer.

Go inside. The push was strong, and Kamenwati's step faltered.

You are safe, little one. His spirit voice surrounded her, caressed her, and made her want to believe.

Almost.

"I am not safe," she said loud enough for both men to hear. "I am not safe, and you are not safe. Not as long as I am here. I need to go—Now! Before *He* finds me again." Although she had never seen the creature inside the black coach, she instinctively knew it was male. She looked into Kamenwati's golden orbs, and her voice broke. "I can't let him hurt you." *Please,* she begged silently. *Don't let me hurt you.*

The taller Egyptian roared with laughter at the thought of a mere slip of a girl protecting his powerful son, and Alicia's blood began to boil. She turned to Ra then, her dark eyes blazing with fury as all rational thought fled. "This is not funny you Pompous Ass. This *thing* has been chasing me for years. I have lost everything once because of these creatures. I will not stand here and let that thing take anyone else from me."

His golden orbs sparking, the bronzed god held her in thrall. "Pompous ass? Me?" His voice was barely above a whisper, and yet it reverberated like thunder.

Alicia refused to let him to see how much his anger terrified her. So maybe she shouldn't have called him a pompous ass, but he was acting like one, even if he was a god.

I see you.

Sheer terror clutched her heart in its icy grip. It was too late. She had to get out of here—now! Before anyone else got hurt because of her. Her head began to throb, and her vision blurred. Power coursed through her body.

When Kamenwati reached for her, instinct took over just as it had when she was two and chased by a very large dog. She threw her hands out to ward him off, and shock waves threw him off his feet. Out of the corner of her eye she saw Ra swing his arm towards her. She heard Kamenwati's "No!" at the same time the sparks flew from Ra's hand, and her whole world disappeared.

Six

The wheels of the custom built Cessna gently touched the tarmac, and the large plane rolled silently to a halt. Luke's voice came over the speaker as clearly as if he was standing in front of Jade. "You can let go of the armrests now," he said. "We have landed."

After nearly twenty-four hours of flying time, Jade was a wreck. It was no secret that she was terrified of flying in an airplane. "If Cerridwen wanted me to fly in a plane she would not have given me wings," she would say. Unfortunately great distances made it necessary to sometimes take to the skies by other than her own steam. Besides, Luke and the boys couldn't take to the skies like her and Emerald. They were Lycan, and able to shift only to wolf form.

The Cessna had been custom built with over seven foot ceilings to accommodate the Lycans larger size, and each of the twelve seats not only had vast amounts of head and shoulder, and foot room, every one reclined for comfort on long flights. Along with the larger headroom, the plane had a full service galley, while the larger washroom had hot and cold running water for showers, and flushing toilets.

Emerald unsnapped her seatbelt just as Gheorgès and Luke stepped out of the cockpit. Luke insisted that they all knew how to pilot all their personal aircraft in case of an emergency, and that included this much larger plane. This trip Gheorgès was getting his first lesson on piloting the larger Cessna, which didn't bother Emerald in the least. She preferred to pilot the helicopters because she liked the view better.

Luke glanced over at Jade's bloodless fingers, her nails digging into the leather upholstery on the armrests, and sighed. "I guess you won't want a flying lesson anytime soon."

Jade laughed, and loosened her grip. "I fly quite well thank you," she replied. "I don't think I need any lessons." The family laughed at the familiar exchange, and Jade announced. "I'm starved." She never could eat on a plane.

There was another burst of laughter. Quinn reached into his jacket pocket, and pulled out a chocolate bar which Jade grabbed, and had unwrapped in the blink of an eye. Her love for chocolate was as legendary as her fear of flying.

Daniel Dixon came out of the cockpit, the flight book and a pen in hand. "Hey Boss," he said, scribbling something on the paper. "I will get this bird fuelled up, and ready to go at your command. I'll bring on supplies if I can get any here. We need fruit and veggies, gas, water, the usual." Daniel Dixon was not only a trusted employee and friend, he was also family, the official pilot, and chauffeur, etc. Daniel glanced up from his paper and winked at Jade. "There's roast beef sandwiches in the fridge. I wouldn't let this hungry mob eat it all on you."

Ten minutes later they were through customs, and Daniel had already started to refuel and restock. The airport was small but Luke had called ahead to ensure they would be able to get what was needed to continue their journey.

The moment they stepped out of the airport they were aware of the curious looks from the few locals who were out and about at this time of day. Not many tourists came to this part of the Carpathians, and those who did flew in on the regular weekly flight. Five strangers arriving in the middle of the week by private plane were bound to generate a lot of curiosity.

Jade smiled at an old woman wearing an ankle length black skirt, and a colourful top. "Hello," she said. "We were ..."

Before she could ask directions to the archaeological dig they had traced Alicia to, the woman made the sign of the cross in front of her chest, and hurried across the road muttering to herself. Jade glanced over her should to see Gheorgès and Luke glaring after the woman, while Quinn seemed as surprised as she was.

"What do you suppose that was about?" asked Quinn.

"Gheorgès scared her," Emerald said, a hint of laughter in her voice. Emerald narrowed her amber eyes at her brother. At seventeen he was already six foot tall, and where at fifteen he had been all skin and bones, now he was packing on some well developed muscle. With his straight dark coffee hair, and ebony eyes he should have been gorgeous but his penetrating looks, and almost permanent scowl made him appear too intimidating to be handsome. Top that off with his black T-shirt, and black leather pants, both tight enough to show off every one of those well-developed muscles when he moved, and the knee-high black motorcycle boots he preferred, and he was downright scary. Emerald asked him once why he dressed to intimidate, and his answer was "If they are scared they won't pick a fight." It made sense, but Emerald still liked her brother better when he wasn't trying to be intimidating.

Gheorgès scowled at his sister who laughed aloud, and Quinn rolled his eyes at the pair of them. "I'm serious," Emerald finally said. "She thinks he is the *vârcolac*, and I don't blame her. When he scowls like that he scares me, and I love him."

"You made that up," Gheorgès growled. "And what is this *vârcolac* supposed to be anyway?"

"Werewolf." Luke's voice was barely above a whisper, but they all heard it loud and clear with their super hearing.

Emerald's amber eyes widened with shock. "You're kidding, right Dad?"

"No." Luke adjusted the pack he had to both shoulders, and strode down the street his own dark features twisted into a scowl. He ignored the few people that actually turned to watch his progress. "Let's go," he growled. "We're burning daylight."

Jade shrugged her own pack into a more comfortable position, and fell into step beside her husband. She was used to being shunned, or feared, but it rankled that a stranger's passing thought had the power to hurt her mate.

I know where she would have gone. Luke sent his wife a mental grimace. *It was superstitious villagers like her that destroyed my family and home not far from here. There is an archaeologist up the road that is trying to find evidence that my race exists. That's all we need, irrefutable proof that Lycans exist.*

Luke was born in these mountains, in a small village nestled in the foothills beside the Olt River. His race were the protectors of the ruling family until a group of villagers afraid of the *vârcolac* banded together and tried to massacre every last one of them. Luke watched while they murdered his mother, his baby brother in her arms, before he managed to escape with a small band of children. They made their way to the new world where they settled in what was now Willow Bend, Canada.

Luke shoved the painful memories from his childhood back where they belonged, in the past, and the moment he rounded a bend in the road hiding them from prying eyes he shifted into a large grey wolf. Within a heartbeat there were two white wolves, two grey wolves, and a large black wolf standing in the middle of the dirt path that passed for a road.

With a growl, the leader took off into the woods knowing that the others would follow. An hour later the pack stopped at the edge of a clearing. Voices drifted toward them on the breeze, and they lifted their noses to taste the air. In a blink of an eye the wolves were gone, leaving the Wulfson family unit standing in their stead.

She's not here. Jade sent the thought to her husband.

We will find her. Luke's voice was husky over the private link he shared with his mate. The group waited for instructions, not wanting to bring attention to their selves. *It will be better if we don't all show up,* he said on the common path he shared with the rest of the family.

Quinn eyed his brother's dark countenance, and strode towards the clearing before anyone could object. *I'll go.* "Hi." He smiled at the two teenage girls nearest to him. They were carefully dusting off some old piece of pottery while chatting about someone named Steve. His voice must have startled them because they jumped, almost knocking over the fragile piece, and turned to face him. They were both dressed in dusty denims and t-shirts, but that is where the similarity ended. The girl closest to him was tall, about five foot six with long blonde hair that was trying its best to escape the rubber band she had it gathered in, to frame her round face. She stared at Quinn with pale blue eyes, and her mouth slightly open, but no words came out. The other girl was shorter, no more than five foot one with short curly red hair, a pale heart shaped face speckled with freckles, and flashing green eyes.

Those green eyes took in every aspect of his appearance; the dark coffee coloured hair that covered his ears and curled at the nape of his neck, the ebony eyes that stared without blinking, and the knowing smirk on his handsome face. His white button up shirt was open at the top revealing a small medallion with a wolf etched on it nestled at the vee against his bronzed skin. The white shirt tucked into the waist of comfortably worn blue jeans, and he wore brown hiking boots. There was paint under his fingertips. When she looked back at his face, his smirk grew as if he were laughing at her.

Her green eyes flashed. "Who are you?" she demanded, eyeing his backpack suspiciously.

I would love to paint you, Quinn thought. *Those flashing green eyes full of fire and subtle strength. That fiery hair and those freckles. God I could kiss those freckles.*

Concentrate baby brother. Gheorgès voice growled through his mind, and Quinn mentally rolled his eyes throwing the image at his brother. "Well I haven't come to steal your relics," he said, adoring the way the female blushed. "I am supposed to meet with my sister. Perhaps you know her, Alicia Wulf, uh, Martinez." For a moment Quinn forgot to use Alicia's professional name.

The redhead still eyed him warily while the blonde suddenly came alive. "Oh. You are Miss Martinez's brother? She didn't tell us she had any brothers. Then again, Miss Martinez doesn't talk about a whole lot unless it has to do with the dig. She is a very quiet person."

Unlike you once you get going. Quinn's lips parted showing a row of straight white teeth. "Do you know where I can find Alicia?"

"Miss Martinez isn't here today. She was staying at the Inn down the road, but nobody has seen her or Mike for...," she glanced at the redhead but didn't wait for an answer. "What has it been, three days?" She paused when she realized the redhead was glaring at her. "Uh, anyway, she was staying at the Inn down the road. It's about two miles down the road."

Quinn pointed toward the only road. "Which way?"

The redhead eyed him with even more suspicion, as if that were possible. "You must have passed it on your way. It's the only place between here and town."

"Oh, *that* Inn." Quinn flashed his brilliant smile at the girls again, grateful to see the redhead blush. "I probably should have asked there on the way by, but my sister usually stays on site," he lied.

He could feel those green eyes burning into his back until he rounded a bend. He wasn't surprised to find his family there waiting for him.

Seven

She was tumbling head over heels as silent gray mists swirled around her. She should have been trembling with fear, instead her heart rejoiced. "Find me now you bastard," she screamed, and began to laugh hysterically. She was free. Ra had killed her, and by doing so had saved his son.

Her guardian angel.

Her soul.

As suddenly as it appeared the mist disappeared, and Alicia landed with a thump on the hard ground. Dust flew up and tickled her nose. She sneezed. Her butt hurt where it connected with the hard surface.

"So maybe I'm not dead." The sound of her own voice echoed eerily in the silence making her wince worse than the pain in her backside. Alicia stood up and checked herself for broken limbs before brushing the dust from her clothes. Not that it helped much. She was still wearing the same dusty clothes she had been wearing at the dig. She shielded her eyes from the bright sunshine, and peered around cautiously. The churning in her stomach had ceased, confirming that she was alone—for now.

Alicia took a few moments to get her bearings, wished she had thought to bring her sunglasses when she had left the Inn this morning, and then she began to laugh hysterically. During the short time she and Megan had been in the twilight zone three days had passed on earth. She had no way of knowing how many days had passed in the time since then. A sense of loss so strong it nearly brought her to her knees enveloped Alicia at the mere thought of Kamenwati. She wiped the tears from her eyes, snuffled, hiccupped, and forced herself to calm down. She thought longingly of her sunglasses sitting on her dresser back at the Inn, and suddenly they were covering her eyes. Alicia grabbed the glasses, and stared at them. They were definitely her glasses. There was a small scratch on the left lens from when she dropped them on the ground last week.

Then it struck her. Her head didn't feel like it was going to explode at any moment. She had better take advantage of the reprieve, and find shelter quick. Alicia placed her glasses over her eyes, and studied her surroundings.

The air was hot and dry. The vegetation was scarce, some cacti and shrub brush which reminded her of Mexico. Her heart started to pound with excitement, and she took a closer look at the surrounding yucca and mesquite. Her head began to buzz, low at first and then louder, and stronger as the murmur of voices urged her toward the low ridge of mountains to her left.

Four hours later, hot, thirsty, and exhausted Alicia stared at the little stone cabin where she had spent most of her childhood. Some of the boards that covered the windows were cracked, and others had rotted away completely. The building was in obvious need of repair, and felt deserted. Still she hesitated before approaching to reach out with her senses, and listen. The house was empty. The barn, what was left of it, was also empty.

There were a few wild chickens strutting around in the yard, but other than them, the farm was completely deserted.

Still, Alicia approached the house cautiously and peered through a broken board on one of the windows before going back and pushing open the front door. She staggered under the onslaught of emotions that assailed her. There were no living residents in her old home, but that did not mean it was completely empty.

The door to her bedroom was hanging on its hinges, and she thought she saw a shadow glide past the opening. She moved silently, drawn by an unseen force to the bedroom. Across the room under the boarded up window sat the hand carved bed she had slept in as a child. Her favourite toy, a monkey her mom had made for her from a pair of her Papa's old woollen socks sat on the floor at the foot of the bed. She loved that sock monkey when she was a baby, and it slept on her pillow every night as a little girl.

She sat on the bed and clutched the monkey tightly, ignoring the bugs that made their home in its stuffing. Her vision blurred, and she was no longer in her bedroom, instead she was in the room she shared with her parents in their old house.

Alicia sat with her chubby legs crossed, one hand holding the bar of the handmade crib. Her other arm was stretched out through the bars, reaching for the half-emptied bottle of milk setting on the cupboard top. "Bottle," her baby voice said in her native tongue. The bottle wobbled, and then straightened itself. "Bottle," she said more forcefully. This time the bottle wobbled, but instead of steadying itself it rose from the cupboard top, and drifted toward the crib. Alicia's small fingers wrapped themselves around the bottle as soon as it was near enough, and with a satisfied grin on her face she popped the bottle into her mouth.

Her mother came into the room, and rushed over to the crib. She took the bottle from her daughter, and scolded. "You cannot just take whatever you want, Alicia. It is not safe. You must wait to get things like a normal person."

Alicia's baby self did not understand the words her mother said, but she had no trouble understanding the tone. She began to sob. Her mother lifted her out of the crib, and held her close rocking her.

"I'm sorry, little one," she crooned. "I did not mean to upset you. I just want you to be safe."

Her Mama's voice soothed her, and she closed her eyes. When she fell asleep, her mother laid her in her crib, carefully tucked the blankets around her, and tucked her sock monkey in beside her. "You must learn to hide what you are, and what you can do," she whispered to the sleeping child.

"What am I, Mama," she whispered into the silence of the empty room. "When do I quit hiding?"

Alicia walked on leaden feet to her parents' bedroom. She loved this bed as much as her own. She often came into her parent's room in the middle of the night after a bad dream, and crawled between them. She would go back to sleep then, knowing she was safe with her parents to protect her.

The howl of a coyote broke the silence, and a shiver ran down her spine. She sat on the edge of her parents' bed, closed her eyes, and let the images of the past wash over her.

She was barely two when it really hit him. She was not his daughter. She held his heart and soul in the palm of her tiny hand. He would give his life for her without hesitation. She called him Papa, but he did not father her. His genes did not make her different—make her special. When she scrunched up her tiny, round face so much like her mother's, and reached for a toy just out of reach it would float through the air until she could wrap her chubby little fingers around it. She did not get that from him—and her mother did not do those things. That was the legacy from her true father.

He could not love her any more if she had been of his seed. The moment he laid eyes on his Maria, the most beautiful woman he had ever laid eyes on, bravely facing the world around her while pregnant and alone, he was lost. Her beauty drew him to her; her courage and determination captured his heart. She could have a dozen children, and he would love them all because they were a part of her.

It was hard to hide Alicia's difference from others. He would never forget the day they had fled to this place. The neighbour's dog chased her. She was running with her tears streaming down her cheeks when she suddenly stopped. Everything happened in slow motion, yet not slow enough that he could stop it. She turned, threw her arms out in a protective fashion, and the dog went flying through the air. Accusations of witchcraft travelled quickly amongst the superstitious people of their small village. That night they barely escaped with their lives when their neighbours burned their home to the ground in an attempt to rid themselves of the witch.

Gilardo Martinez took his young wife, and baby daughter, and brought them here to his family's farm.

She was five when she first realized she was different from other children, and that she was the reason they didn't venture into town very often. Not that they needed to. Almost everything they had was here on this farm. They raised goats for milk, and chickens for meat and eggs. Her Mama's garden was small, but she managed to charm the soil into providing them with enough to support their needs, with a little left over to take to market. Papa was an excellent woodcarver and he not only made the furniture in their home, he made furniture for others as well. They kept to themselves most of the time, only going to town about once a month to the local market where they sold eggs, milk, and homemade cheese. Maria had a reputation for making the best cheese in the area, and sometimes people would come out to the farm looking to buy some. They also sold fruit from the small orchard her mother coaxed from the dry earth.

Alicia was happy on the farm. It was her job to feed the chickens and collect the eggs. She would pretend it was a game, distracting the hens while she made their eggs float into her basket. Alicia was happy, but she was a little girl, and sometimes she felt lonely. Sometimes at night, she sat on her bed and wished for someone just like her. A girl who could hear people's thoughts, move objects with her mind, and would be her friend.

What she got was a monster.

Alicia gasped, and her eyes flew open. Her heart was thumping, and her breath came in rapid gulps. Poor Papa. Poor Mama. They had died because she was lonely.

Alicia swiped a tear from her eye, adjusted her sunglasses, and walked out into the yard. A couple of chickens scratched and pecked at the dry earth. They were either offspring of their own chickens, or had escaped from a nearby farm. Although there were no flowers in view, the sweet scent of morning glory filled the air. A grackle whistled from its perch on top of the barn. The cicadas droned merrily in the background, all completely unaware of the ghosts that lived on this small farm.

Her stomach growled, and Alicia tore a leaf from an Aloe plant. She broke the skin, peeled it, and bit into the slimy fruit. Someone had boarded up the windows in an attempt to keep the animals from encroaching on the house, probably Matthew, Jade's man, or rather wolf, in Mexico. Alicia appreciated his thoughtfulness. She would have to look him up and thank him, but the boards gave the farm a deserted feeling that saddened her.

She was not going to leave the farm like this. Her mother had loved this farm. She had coaxed tiny saplings into mature fruit trees despite the dry soil, and even now Alicia could see those trees struggling to survive in the orchard beside the house. She had made this simple dwelling into a home anyone would be proud of, a haven of sunshine, laughter, and love. Alicia was not going to let her mother's life have no meaning. Just because her own children would never play on the old wooden swing in the yard, climb the trees in the orchard, feed the chickens, or collect the eggs didn't mean that no child would. She would turn this farm back into a place anyone would be happy to call home, and then she would put it up for sale, if she had the time. Oh well, if she did not get it done it wouldn't be for lack of trying.

With more determination than strength, Alicia tackled the boards on the windows. Lucky for her, most of them were already loose, and some had actually fallen off. Still, by the time she had finished her nails were torn and bloody. Now that there was more light in the small house, Alicia went in search of something to use to clean.

She found the broom, or rather what was left of it, in the cupboard behind the wood stove in the kitchen. The handle was still in one piece, but the bristles had either fallen out, or been pulled out, perhaps to make a bed for some rodent. Determined to finish what she had started, Alicia headed for the old barn.

She lifted the bar that held the doors shut, and set it against the wall. The doors opened a lot easier than she anticipated. Their sudden movement startled a flock of bats from their roosting place under the rafters. They darted at her a couple of times before settling back down. The interior of the barn was dark and damp. Over the smell of stale hay and mould Alicia detected dried animal feces, and the scent of blood making her wonder what else had made its home in the old barn.

Ignoring the bats, she grabbed a handful of straw from one of the lofts. Alicia bent the straw over, and then used some wire she found in her Papa's old workroom to fasten it to the broom handle, surprised that nobody had ransacked the barn before now. Satisfied with her makeshift broom she returned to the house, and swept all of the rooms.

Now that the thick layer of dust was, if not actually gone, moved around a lot she realized that the house definitely needed soap and water. Alicia leaned over the deep well in the front yard. It was too dark to see the bottom, but she could definitely *smell* water. She dropped a pebble from the yard, and listened for the kerr-plunk as the pebble hit the surface of the water. Satisfied she would get water, she grabbed the long handle to wind up the water bucket, frowning at the sound of falling water with every turn. *This can't be good.* The wooden bucket that hung from the old rope was missing some slats, and by the time it reached the top it was empty.

This required another trip to the barn where Alicia found an old tin bucket. The handle was missing, but she used some more wire from the workroom, and made her own handle. Armed with water from the well, and an old hunk of lye soap she was lucky enough to find in a cupboard in the kitchen, Alicia set out to remove every trace of dirt from her family's home.

Alicia pulled out the bottom drawer of her mother's dresser, and an old yellowed envelope fell to the floor. She set the drawer to the side, and picked up the envelope. The moment she touched the paper she felt her mother's arms wrapped around her, making her safe. Her mother's voice whispered in her ear, words of love and encouragement, as she had in life. Alicia sat on the bed, and turned the envelope to read the writing on the front that was in her mother's handwriting. *Why had Mama felt the need to write this letter so long ago?*

Alicia Martinez

To be opened on your 21st birthday.

Alicia turned the envelope over several times, squeezing it with her fingers. It felt several papers thick, and there was a hard bulge in one corner. With shaking fingers she carefully opened the envelope, and pulled out the carefully folded papers. She ignored the small gold chain that fell out, her eyes glued to the familiar slant of her mother's handwriting.

My darling Alicia

This is the hardest letter I have ever written, because if you are reading this I have not survived to your twenty first birthday.

I have started this letter a hundred times, and even now I am not sure how to say it, so I am going to just come right out with it.

You are Bruja.

You come from a long line of Bruja. *You were born with psychic abilities, as were all the females in our line, although none have displayed these abilities at such an early age. I fear that has something to do with who your father is.*

Let me tell you a bit about our line so you might understand some of your powers. I received the Gift of Earth. I encourage things to grow in the most barren of places. The proof of this is my beloved orchard. My mother, your grandmother received the Gift of Voice. She could hear thoughts, and speak to others with her mind. I have never seen proof of you speaking in this way. You have never reached out to Papa or me but I know you can hear our thoughts. Your great grandmother had the Gift of Movement, the ability to move things with her mind. This also I have witnessed in you. We can all cast minor spells, although I very seldom call on this ability as there is always a price to pay. It is rare for any Bruja *to receive more than one gift, but you have always been special and I have seen the signs even while you were very young. Before your second birthday you were already displaying a rare amount of power, and I know that one day you will grow into a very powerful* Bruja.

Do not be afraid.

Embrace your Gifts. To try to deny them can be quite painful. One day you shall pass them to your own daughter, as they have passed to you.

Your papa, Gilardo Martinez, is a fine, proud man. He loves us very much, as we love him. He has been a wonderful papa for you. I met him at a time when I was once again alone and scared, and this time very pregnant. He never asked about the man who fathered you. Not even after you began to demonstrate your amazing abilities. He never asked, and I never volunteered the information. It was not that I wished to keep this information secret but every time I start to tell him about your father my memories grow fuzzy, and I am unable to utter a word.

I would not say anything now except I made a promise to your birth father, and I am afraid that if I do not put this in a letter I might not be able to fulfill my promise. His name was Rick, and he came to me in the night. I was sixteen when I met him. I was alone. I had just buried my mother, and he was strong, kind, and oh so handsome.

I do not remember much about my own father. I remember his coming home from the fields, dirty and tired, and always with a smile and a kiss for Mama and me. He died of the fever when I was five. Poor Mama was heartbroken, but she struggled to make a life for the two of us. It was not until I was thirteen that I received my Gift. We were beginning to think I had been passed over, it sometimes happens in a generation although rarely.

How I wish it had come sooner. I could have helped poor Mama coax a living for us from the earth, and maybe she would not have given so soon. Maybe she missed my papa so much that she could not wait to join him again. I prefer to think that this is true. I hate to think she gave up on life, and me.

If you are reading this letter, I have already gone to join with Mama and Papa. I know there is no proof, but I believe that when we leave this life we move on to another with those that have gone before us. Please tell your Papa, my beloved Gilardo, that I am anxiously awaiting his arrival. Not too anxiously. I wish him a long and happy life. I will wait forever if that is how long it takes him to join me. Alicia hoped they had finally found each other again in the afterlife.

You are probably wondering about the pendant. Alicia barely glanced at the pendant before continuing the letter. *It belonged to your birth father. His name is Rick, and he came to me in the night when I needed him the most. Poor Mama caught the fever the winter I was fifteen. It was a long, hard winter and she joined Papa the day after my sixteenth birthday. It was almost as if she was afraid to go before then. The day I buried her I was heartbroken.*

Rick came to me that night. He was so handsome I could not resist him. He stayed for nearly a month, making those long nights bearable. He taught me I could survive without Mama. He helped make me strong again. And he made me happy. I thought I loved him, until I found my wonderful Gilardo.

I do not know what to tell you about your father. He was wild and handsome, and very powerful. He could do the most amazing things. This I remember now, which is very strange because whenever I think about Rick, those nights, or the things he could do my memories become very hazy. My only clear memory is the night he left me—left us. It was early, barely dusk when he came that night. It was the first night of the three moons, and I was thinking how lovely it was going to be walking in the path of the full moon with the man I loved at my side. Rick was very anxious that night and it made me afraid.

Rick took this pendant from around his neck where he always wore it and he slipped it over my head. I remember how my chest burned when the pendant touched my bare skin.

"Give this to our daughter," he said. I thought he was going to cry, and I felt tears in my own eyes. I knew then that he would not be coming back.

"I will," I told him. My own voice was shaky with the tears that I was trying so hard not to shed. I didn't know how he knew about you. I was planning to tell him the night he left.

"Promise me," Rick repeated. He grabbed my arms then. I remember that he was holding me so tight that it hurt. His eyes went black and I felt like I was falling into an abyss. "On our daughter's twenty first birthday you will give her this pendant."

All I could do was nod. I had no voice. Even now while I write this letter I can feel his words burning into my mind. "Give it to our daughter. Tell her to put it on, and call my name. Alaric."

No, that cannot be right because your father's name is Rick. My beautiful Rick. Still the name he said to say was Alaric. I can hear his voice as clearly today as the day he spoke those words. "Tell her to put it on, and call my name. Alaric." He definitely said, Alaric.

The pendant has power. Too much power for me, but I know you will be able to handle it. Your own power grows each day. I can see it. Embrace your destiny, Alicia. Do not be afraid of who you are.

Do not be afraid of the pendant.

I love you

Be happy
Mama

Alicia picked up the pendant from where it lay on the bed. It was a miniature golden sun, set inside a cage of the thinnest golden strands, and hung from a fine golden chain. It looked so delicate Alicia was surprised that it had not crumbled with time.

Her palm began to itch, and her vision blurred. The room disappeared, and she saw herself in a graveyard kneeling beside a freshly dug grave. Alicia knew instinctively this was her mother as a young girl. Her face streaked with dried tears, and her eyes were puffy and swollen. Alicia drifted towards her mother where she floated above her for a moment before she pulled into her mother's body with a snap. For the first time in her life, Alicia was not seeing a vision, she was living one. She was her mother, seeing through her mother's eyes, thinking her mother's thoughts, and experiencing her mother's feelings.

Night rolled in like a steamroller blanketing her and everything else in darkness. Her knees were beginning to ache from kneeling so long on the cold, hard ground, but Maria didn't notice. She didn't notice much of anything these days.

For months she looked after Mama while she lay abed burning up with the fever, and now she did not know what to do. She had tried so hard to keep happy thoughts while she bathed her mother's weakening body, but Mama knew how scared she was. Maria could see the knowledge in her dark eyes, as Mama fought so gallantly not to succumb to the fever, not once complaining. Now there was no reason to hide her fear, no reason to pretend.

She didn't hear his approach, but she felt his presence, and she turned towards him. His dark eyes rimmed in gold, and his full lips parted to show straight white teeth. Her heart skipped a beat, and Maria wasn't sure if it was fear, or the man himself that caused the reaction. When he offered his hand she willingly placed herself into his care.

The vision changed, and Alicia was no longer looking at the stranger, but she was the stranger, see her mother through his eyes the way she was at sixteen, young, alone, and vulnerable.

The way she was looking at him with those dark, troubled eyes, her every emotion flickering to the surface, fear, curiosity, and above all the pain. Her pain cut him like a knife inflicting a wound so deep he thought it would suck the very life from his soul. What was it about this slip of a female that drew him, made him feel her pain? The way her eyes dipped down in the corners with the weight of her emotions gave her an exotic look that he found very sexy. He wondered what she would look like with a smile on those full lips, and happiness sparkling in her eyes. Even tired, with dirt on her knees, and her hair sticking out awkwardly from the severe roll she had pinned it into she was so beautiful she astounded him. He couldn't wait to sink himself deep inside her while he tasted her divine nectar. The spicy power rushing through her veins teased him. His fangs began to elongate even as he felt the first stirrings in his groin. He licked his lips in anticipation, the need to taste her urging him forward.

Alicia gasped, and dropped the pendant onto the bed as if it were on fire. "You bastard," she hissed into the approaching night. "She was my mother."

Eight

Alaric paced the black marble floor of his throne room without seeing the beauty of the candles reflected on the polished stone surface. The sounds of cascading water from the waterfall in the center of the vast room did nothing to soothe his anxiety.

Where was she? The nearest he could pinpoint was somewhere in the north of Mexico. That made sense. He had met her mother in Mexico, his sweet Maria. It had broke his heart to leave her on earth when he returned to his duties as Prince of the Magi, but although she was not completely human, she was not Mage and she could not have survived for long in his world, as he could not have survived in hers. As Prince of his people he had a powerful enemy, one that would gladly destroy his sweet Maria to get to him. No, it had been better to leave her behind.

At least that is what he kept telling himself.

Where was she? Why had she not come to him? Where was Conall?

With a thought, the huge cast iron bell at the end of the room began to clang, the two massive oak doors silently opened, and a tall lanky redhead strode into his chambers. He wore straight legged blue jeans tucked into cowboy boots, a buttoned shirt, opened at the neck and rolled to the elbows, a cowboy hat, and the gun belt and holster he wore slung low over his hips wasn't just for show. The man had been a Texas Ranger in the 1800s before his transformation, and was an excellent shot. The guns sitting in the holsters had special bullets, and he was quite capable of throwing the knife he wore tucked into his boot.

"You wanted me, Sire?"

Alaric cringed. He hated it when the man called him Sire. He was not this man's father, but he refused to rise to the bait today. "Where is Conall? I *requested* his presence in my chambers." Every mage knew that a request from the Prince was tantamount to an order.

Tex loved to rile his Prince, but he also knew the signs well enough to know when not to push. "Conall has been cooling his heels in the anti-chamber for the past six chimes," the redhead said. Time in their realm did not pass the same as on earth. Their days were long, measured in chimes rather than hours, and equivalent to roughly thirty earth days. Their nights were much shorter, coinciding with the three nights of the earth's full moon.

"Why was he not brought in immediately he arrived?" Alaric almost spit the words, and forced himself to take a deep breath to help him calm down.

Tex mentally rolled his eyes. Something was definitely up with his Prince. The man simply did not get distracted this close to nightfall. "You said to have him wait until you called for him. I'll bring him in now."

Tex strode through the massive doors, returning before they had time to close completely accompanied by a bear of a man. At six foot six, Conall was a good four inches taller than Tex; he was built like a warrior, with eyes as flat as frying pans.

Conall knelt on one knee before his Prince, his long black coat billowing out behind him, and laid his sword at Alaric's feet. "My Liege," he said. "My will is yours. My life is yours."

"Rise Conall." Alaric had no time for formalities today. "Leave us," he ordered Tex.

Conall rose, sheathed his sword, and cocked his head at his old friend. He was dressed in black leather pants tucked into motorcycle boots, a black t-shirt, and his favourite black duster. With his black hair tied behind his head with a leather bind, and his obsidian eyes boring into him, Alaric found it easy to see why his fellow Magi referred to him as the Fighting Irish, or the Black Irish. The second the massive oak doors clicked shut behind Tex, Conall said, "You look like hell."

Alaric shrugged. "I feel like hell." He hesitated for only a heartbeat, and then blurted. "I need you to go to earth."

"Now? Are you insane?"

"Don't be impudent, my old friend," snapped Alaric. "And yes, now. If I wanted you to go tomorrow I would have sent you tomorrow."

Conall was not the least bit intimated by his Prince. "Who am I going for this time?" was all he said. One of the things that Alaric trusted him to do was find human descendants of the Magi who were about to make their transition. Depending on the outcome he would bring them into the *Chimera*.

"My daughter."

"Daughter?" Conall squeaked.

Nine

Kamenwati picked himself up off the ground, and glared at his father. "Why7"

Ra's golden orbs glittered dangerously, but Kamenwati ignored the warning. "What have you done?" he growled.

Ra flicked his wrist, throwing his son back onto the dusty ground, and strode into his home. How dare that little chit come between his son and him; his own flesh and blood? Kamenwati had never spoken such to him. Perhaps he should not have sent the girl away, but she had threatened his son, and that he would *not* tolerate from anyone. Besides, she would be a lot safer on earth than she would be here when night fell in a couple of hours. At least that was what he tried to convince himself, knowing she would not be safe on earth during the early days of her transition. The Betrayer had reached her once, and he would reach her again.

His footsteps were silent as he strode across the vast marble chamber, and approached the throne room. Throne room what a joke. He had not felt like King of anything in more centuries than he cared to remember.

There was a time when he was King of all he surveyed, a God, worshipped by man. Now the only bright spot in his sterile existence was his son, and it looked like he was about to lose him to a mere chit of a girl.

Ra Horakhty sat upon the high backed chair made of solid rock, and took a moment to survey the vast chamber. The onyx walls reflected the emptiness of his existence. This room was quiet. Too quiet. What it needed was the patter of little feet, and the laughter of children; his grandchildren.

Ra felt a slight stirring of the air around him, and Kamenwati stood before him. His golden eyes still blazed with barely contained rage, but he never said a word. Ra sighed. "This isn't a home. It's a tomb."

Kamenwati lifted one brow slightly.

"I sometimes wonder if I was a little hasty when I left earth."

"You think?" Kamenwati's voice dripped with sarcasm.

Ra snapped his fingers, and a large wooden chair fitted with comfortable cushions appeared behind Kamenwati. "Quit your posturing and sit down Kamenwati. We need to come up with a plan."

"I need to go to Earth." Kamenwati sat stiffly in the chair. It was a small rebellion, but he was satisfied with the slight frown on his father's face.

"You know that is impossible. You will break the seal."

"The seal is broken." Kamenwati ran his hands through his golden tresses, and tried to still the sense of urgency he felt. *Where are you, little one?* She was blocking him from her mind, and it hurt so much he could hardly breathe. She thought she was protecting him from the evil that hunted her, but she was not. He faced that evil every setting of their sun, along with his father and the Magi.

"The girl?"

"She has a name." Fear, and a need like he had never experienced before made his voice sharp.

Ra glanced up at the ceiling, which was a colourful depiction of his last days on earth. A reminder of what he left behind, and what they fought at the end of every rising. He had it done so he would never forget that even his most trusted friend could betray him.

His enemies had stormed his temple intent on destroying it, and him. These were his Magi. Mortal men he had bestowed with the powers of the Gods. The Mage who led his enemies was once a High Priest, a man he should have been able to trust like a brother, the second mortal to ever drink from the *Ankh*. Not satisfied with the powers he already had, the Mage lusted for more. After several days of battle, and many deaths, Ra managed to ensnare his betrayer with magic. He cast him out into the void between the Heavens and the Earth, and then in a fit of rage Ra Horakhty cursed those who worshiped *The Betrayer* and their descendents to walk forever in darkness. He gathered his loyal Magi, and gave them the option of staying on earth or joining him beyond the Heavens.

Ra returned to the *Chimera*, and sealed it from the earth. Only those who possessed a key could traverse across the seal, and visit both worlds.

When he left, Ra took the *Ankh*, the Well of Eternal Life, with him into the Chimera forcing the Magi who chose to remain on earth and continue the battle against the vampire to drink blood to survive. Some tried to survive on the blood of animals, but human blood was more powerful, and the blood of a human possessed of magic was very powerful. Blood born of magic was a beacon in the night, calling to both predator and prey, and those who possessed it were always a target.

Vampires were those who forsake the sun to follow Theron in his evil quest to rule the world, and those who remained faithful to Ra remained able to walk in the day. These are the Children of Ra–Magi. The offspring of the union between a Mage and a human were born with unique and sometimes very powerful gifts. By the time they reached their early twenties food alone could not sustain their bodies, and they were forced to seek blood to survive. *The Betrayer* searched for these newly transitioned Magi in an attempt to turn them to the dark side. When they drained their victims, it released magic into the universe that the Betrayer could use to enhance his own. If the newly transitioned Magi chose not to listen to the urgings of the Betrayer, he simply sent those who did to destroy the Magi, thereby releasing their magic back into the universe for him to claim. As far as the Betrayer was concerned, it was a win-win situation.

Still, there were those who were strong enough to resist the *Betrayer*, and avoid the attempts on their lives, instead becoming part of the army that hunted the vampire. The Magi were not alone in their fight against the vampire, but still their numbers increased, and *The Betrayer* grew stronger.

Although the girl, Alicia, was not responsible for the seal being broken, she was in danger from *The Betrayer*. Until she accepted who she was, she was a threat to them all. Her power was strong, stronger even than that of her father. Ra knew why the *Betrayer* had chosen her. With her power, he would be able to remain on the human realm.

Darkness was falling in the *Chimera*, and they had to prepare for the worst. The seal was broken, and that meant the Betrayer would probably take this battle to Earth where his followers would be at their strongest, during the full moon. If he did, it could mean disaster for them all.

"You might want to prepare," Ra told his son. "You are going to Earth."

Ten

Two white owls silently landed in the branches of a great pine. Their wide amber eyes took in the mess of the yard and garden, in stark contrast to the well kept Inn with its wrap-around porch, and top deck. A small female child accepted the fussing of her parents with barely any squirming. Emotions ran wild in this small group of humans. Relief. Love. Fear. Grief.

The smaller owl on the limb beside her shuddered and Jade wrapped her in a feeling of warmth, and protection. As if they were reading each other's thoughts they drifted to the ground below, and shifted to human form.

Mike turned at the sound of cart wheels and hoofs, and watched the two strangers walk through the open gate. They both wore t-shirts, one blue the other grass green, well worn snug fitting denim jeans and they carried identical back packs. One woman was tall and lithe with short cropped white blonde hair streaked with strands of silver and gold. The other was about five foot tall with the same white blonde streaked with silver and gold, only her hair hung to her waist. It was their identical amber eyes that captivated him. He had never seen anything like them.

"Hello." Jade smiled at the man, and turned her attention to the woman and child. "Hi. I'm Jade," she said. "And this is my daughter Emerald."

My God, thought Molly. *They look more like sisters. I hope I look that good when Megan is that old.* Molly realized she was staring at the pair with a dopey expression on her face. "Uh, hi," she finally stammered. "I'm Molly." She lifted the squirming child into her arms, and held her close. "This is my daughter, Megan." Molly glanced furtively toward her husband who was still staring at the newcomers with a strange dazed look. "That's my husband, Mike. Mike. Say hello," she prompted.

"Hello," he said.

Molly narrowed her eyes until her forehead puckered, looking first at her husband, and then at Jade and Emerald. She squeezed Megan tight enough that Megan yelped, and tried to wiggle out of her mother's arms. "What brings you to this part of Romania?"

"We are looking for my other daughter. We were told she was staying at this Inn."

Molly ran through the guests at the Inn. It didn't take her long. Besides her family there was the newlywed couple from Brisbane, Antonio, Marcus, and Steve who left right after Alicia disappeared. *Poor Alicia. God she hoped she was alright.* Molly could think of nobody who looked remotely like these two. Molly neared dropped Megan when Jade said. "Her name is Alicia."

"Lisa," Megan squeaked, and wriggled harder. "I want to see Lisa."

"Shh baby," Molly crooned. "We all want to see Alicia."

A wolf howled in the distance, and Mike stepped closer to his wife and daughter, his eyes clearer. "Take

Megan inside," he ordered Molly. He offered his hand in greeting to Jade, who shook it, but she couldn't read him at all. "I'm Mike. I was working with Alicia at the dig before she disappeared. Maybe you better come inside where we can talk."

"Disappeared." Emerald's voice was a whisper of pain.

Another wolf howled sending shivers through Mike. "Let's go inside. Magda will be happy for the company."

The door to the Inn opened to the main dining room. There were two long picnic tables on the left built out of logs, and were sturdy enough to hold twenty large men easily. There was a bar on the right made of pine, with four tall stools, and a mirrored back board that made the entire place appear doubled in size. An ancient woman came rushing through the swinging door at the end of the bar, wiping her hands on the apron that protected her black skirt. Her long sleeve white shirt was somewhat covered by the slightly embroidered leather vest she wore. Hot on her heels was a shorter man wearing baggy brown trousers, a white shirt, and a woollen vest. His grin revealed a missing tooth.

"Welcome back, Miss Megan." The woman spoke with a thick accent. Her sparkling eyes smiled at Molly. "I told you Miss Megan would be returned safely."

"Yes you did Magda. I am so glad you were right." She squeezed Megan who yelped. Laughing, Molly set her on the floor, comfortable now they were safely indoors. "You stay right where I can see you," she warned her daughter, who was already heading toward Pietro. "I don't want you to get lost again."

"I wasn't lost." Megan pouted at her mother. "I was with Lisa."

Emerald dropped her pack to the floor, and knelt in front of Megan locking her amber eyes with the child's wide brown ones. "Did you and Alicia get lost?" she asked in a quiet, compelling voice.

Megan shook her head until her curls bobbed crazily. Emerald lifted one eye brow slightly. Molly and Mike felt the urge to pick up their child, but neither could move. It was as if they were frozen in place.

"We weren't lost," insisted Megan, her small voice growing thrill. "We were with the glowing man. He saved us."

For a heartbeat the room was so silent you could hear a pin drop. The door exploded in and three very large men stroke in. The two wearing jeans and button down shirts were scary enough, but the large one wearing black leathers and motorcycle boots was absolutely terrifying. Molly moved then, with a frightened gasp she snatched up Megan, and ran for the stairs beside the kitchen door.

Quinn calmly picked up his sister's pack, and helped her to her feet. Luke walked over, put his arm around his wife, and kissed her on the cheek, nodding to the Inn keepers in silent acknowledgement. Gheorgès scowled, and strode toward the staircase, stopping suddenly when Mike jumped in front of him.

Gheorgès glared at the human who was half his weight, and a good eight inches shorter, but the man held his ground. The smell of his fear was acid in Gheorgès' nose, and Gheorgès was surprised to find he was impressed with the human who dared stand between him and his prey.

They are not prey, admonished Jade. *They are humans who have just been through a very traumatic experience.*

Gheorgès nodded to the human barrier. "Forgive me," he said his voice a soft growl.

Mike sagged against the railing in relief when he realized the huge male was not going to pursue his family. Meanwhile, Magda seemed completely oblivious to what was happening around her. Her full attention was on Luke. Suddenly her dark eyes widened, and she whispered in Romani Carpathian. "Lykos."

Luke's head whipped around, and his gaze locked with the woman's. "You are mistaken," he growled in the same language.

Magda hurried over to the wall on the other side of the picnic tables, and removed a picture from the wall. When she returned she shoved it into Luke's hand. Luke's hand trembled when he looked down at the photograph. It was a very old black and white photograph, and it was a photo of his family. His father was smiling, and he had his arm around Luke's mother. Even in the ancient, grainy photo you could see the love in her eyes as she gazed upon the face of the infant she held in her arms. Luke was standing beside his sister Helen. He remembered when they took this photograph. He was sixteen, his sister Helen was five, and Gheorgès was only a couple months old. His father warned them about the dangers of capturing their images on film, but his mother had wanted the picture.

Luke's eyes burned, and his throat ached with unshed tears. This was his family two years before the massacre that took the lives of his beloved parents, and nearly his entire pack. The massacre he was responsible for. He sent Jade a mental smile when she squeezed his fingers. Her love poured over him like a security blanket. *I love you.* They sent the thought at the same time.

Luke swallowed painfully, and looked up to see everyone in the room staring at him. The room hummed with power. The human male looked confused. There were tears in Emerald's eyes, and Quinn was holding her while her body trembled. Emerald was already a strong empath, and she was experiencing Luke's feelings. She was still learning how to control her ability but was having difficulty being in such close proximity. It was slightly easier with strangers and only then if her mother was near enough to be her buffer.

Dad? Her spirit voice was wet with tears. His tears.

My family. He made an effort to get his emotions under control, and was relieved when Emerald's body quit shaking.

Magda's dark eyes flickered from father to daughter, and she sighed with satisfaction. It was true then. Everything that passed from generation to generation was true. The Protectors did exist. They were still out there. She stepped closer to Luke, and tapped his image on the painting. "This is you," she continued to speak in the old Romani Carpathian dialect so the human would not understand.

I nearly killed him to deny them, but Luke handed the grainy photograph back to her. "I don't know these people." He didn't realize he had answered in the old language, until Magda grinned, and nodded her head.

The Innkeeper looked at him as if she was looking straight into his soul, and she pursed her lips. "The young." She tipped her head toward the three siblings now standing together. The two males flanking their sister. "The young might like to see their elders." She tapped the image of Luke's father. "Your father left his photograph with my people with instructions to give it to you when you returned." She locked eyes with Luke, but he managed not to show her how much she unnerved him. "That photo has been on that wall for centuries waiting for you. Are you going to deny your own family?"

She is telling the truth. Your father gave the photo to the original Innkeepers. He knew you would come here one day, and he wanted you to have something to remember the good times. Did your father have the gift of prescience?

I remember when he had this taken. He forbade everyone to let the photographer capture their images. When mother said she wished she could have something to *look at when we were not together anymore, Father got this strange look on his face, and suddenly gave in. He said `it will give him something to remember us by.' God. Did he know then that they were going to die?*

Your father wanted you to have that picture, Lykos. Take it.

Luke thanked Magda, and carefully put the picture in his pack, before turning toward the human male. "We are going to need to speak with your daughter."

Mike's spine stiffened, and he grew taller. "I'm not going to allow you to scare my daughter."

Jade patted Luke on the arm, and stepped between the men. Her amber eyes locked with Mike's, and she smiled. "We are not going to scare Megan," she said in a soft, hypnotic tone. "We need to ask her about Alicia. She will not be frightened, I promise you."

Mike's head nodded slowly, and he didn't even try to stop his wife and daughter from coming down the stairs.

Jade knelt in front of Megan so she was level with the girls wide green eyes. "Orange eyes," Megan said.

"Yes I do. And you have beautiful green eyes. Like your mother's."

"Lisa eyes brown." *I like Lisa. I want to see Lisa.*

Jade reached out and took the child's hands in hers. There was an almost audible hum in the room, as Jade's power focused, and she saw what happened.

Eleven

The room grew dark as the sun faded behind the mountains. Still Alicia could see the room as if it were noon. The sounds of the night sang to her. The buzzing of a mosquito as it searched for its dinner, the scuttling of small rodents in the dry grasses, the huu-huuu of an owl. The walls of the small room seemed to be closing in on her. Alicia wanted to leave the pendant where it lay but her hand snaked out and picked it up. Although she fought the urge to do so Alicia slipped the pendant over her head, and walked out into the night.

A million stars twinkled against the black velvet backdrop of the night sky. A bat flew past her head, and a wolf howled in the distance. Hunger beat at her. She needed to go to the nearest village to get something to eat.

There was a rush of air around her, and Alicia found herself standing on the edge of town. A wave of dizziness hit her, and she fell to her knees gasping for air until it passed.

You need to feed.

Hunger brought her to her feet, and carried her forward. Her legs moved on their own without her knowing where she was going or what she was going to do when she got there. She moved through the night like a shadow, silent and dangerous. Alicia wanted to stop, to turn around and go back to the safety of the farm, but something forced her to keep moving forward. She felt like a puppet on a string, and it terrified her.

The night breeze carried the scent of jasmine and moon vine, the overpowering stench of dead fish, and human sweat. She was in a fishing village she had visited as a child.

Alicia crinkled her nose in distaste, and stepped from the shadows. Hunger was a wild beast clawing at her insides, urging her forward.

She needed to feed. *No. I need to eat.*

She rounded a corner, and the scent of male and blood assailed her. Her womb coiled in anticipation, and her fangs lengthened until they pressed against her lower lip. She followed the scent silently, a predator of the night. Desire and hunger at war within her, all thoughts of retreat gone.

He was alone on the pier. His muscles rippled as he loaded the heavy boxes into the cart. His heart beat steadily, pushing warm, delicious blood through his veins. The coppery scent made her mouth water.

Call to him.

The need was too strong to ignore. *Come to me,* she called out to the human with her mind, and the spicy scent of desire filled the air. The male tilted his head as if listening, and he sniffed the air. He dropped the heavy box he was holding, and it broke on the surface of the pier spilling its contents. His hazel eyes searched the shadows until he spotted the dark alley. He shuffled toward her, one foot in front of the other like a zombie. He struggled to halt his progress, afraid of whatever hid in the shadows. Compulsion carried him forward.

Fangs exploded inside her mouth, and her tongue slipped over the tips tasting the yellow liquid that dripped from them. The male was near enough she could see the stark terror in his eyes, and still his legs carried him forward. He was less than a foot in front of her when he stopped. His eyes glazed over but his thoughts screamed for him to stop, to escape while he could. It was already too late. Terror raced through his veins making his blood more potent.

The male tilted his head to one side offering her his throat, his blood, his life. Her fangs grew longer, and hunger clawed at her urging her to feed. She leaned into his neck. The call of his blood a compulsion she could no longer ignore. The tips of her fangs touched his skin and his fear was pungent. The tips of her fangs pierced his skin.

An image of her Papa standing before the beautiful monster made her stomach clench in distaste, and horror. *No,* her mind screamed.

Alicia shoved the male away. *Run.* The compulsion was strong, and the man stumbled in his haste to flee. Alicia fell to her knees as exhaustion overwhelmed her.

You need to feed.

I will not feed. I will not become the monster that killed my family. I will die first.

Then you will die.

Twelve

The girl was strong, the *Seeker* would give her that, but she was no match for him. Already the hunger ate at her soul, and her refusal to embrace her fate made her weak.

It made no difference to him if she lived or died. Either way he would control her power.

Thirteen

Kamenwati reached out to the fleeing man's mind, filling it with false memory.

A noise startled him, and he dropped the box he was holding spilling coconuts everywhere. Ignoring them he listened to the night. There was something at the end of the alley. Cautiously he peered into the darkened alley, but he could see nothing except the outline of a dumpster. He was about to turn back when there was a loud screech, and something jumped out of the shadows. He ducked, but he was not fast enough. Its outstretched claws caught the side of his neck. Shaken, but relieved it was nothing more than a cat, he returned to the pier to clean up the scattered coconuts.

Satisfied that the man would remember nothing more than a run-in with a stray cat Kamenwati gently lifted Alicia's trembling body as if she were a mere child. Compared to him, she was. An infant in a world she could barely fathom, who possessed more courage in her soul than the most courageous warriors he knew.

With a mere thought he opened a doorway, and stepped through to the small stone cabin she once called home. Kamenwati laid her on the single bed, instinctively knowing she would be unable to rest in the bed where her parents had once slept. He held her in his strong arms until her trembling ceased. Kamenwati's hand moved of its own accord, gently sweeping the hair from her face; his eyes feasting on her beauty. His heart constricted in his chest. He wanted nothing more than to lean into her and taste those blood red lips. As if she could read his mind her eyelids fluttered, and the look he saw in those dark eyes made his pulse race.

Kamenwati swallowed. "Go to sleep, little one," he whispered, his voice husky with desire.

"Stay with me." Her own voice was thick with desire, and her eyes were huge in her pale face.

"I'm not going anywhere," Kamenwati promised.

Alicia shifted to the far side of the bed, even that small amount of effort nearly proved too much for her. She laid her hand on the empty space beside her. *Please. I don't want to be alone. I'm afraid.* She was tired. Too tired to talk anymore, too tired to fight anymore, and she did not want to die alone.

You are not going to die, little one. Kamenwati lay on the small bed beside her, and gathered her tightly against him. She seemed very tiny against his much larger form. Alicia sighed, and her breath caressed his bare chest. *I have waited too long for you. I refuse to let you go.*

Safe in his arms, Alicia closed her eyes.

Fourteen

Jade sat in a small clearing surrounded by tall pines, and majestic firs. She felt so small, so helpless. It wasn't a feeling she had often, and she damned well didn't like it. Her daughter, her first child, was out there alone somewhere, and Jade didn't know how to find her.

Of all her children Alicia was the one she worried about the most. Alicia was strong and powerful with her own special gifts, but Jade could never completely forget the first time she saw her. She was laying on that flat rock surrounded by trees, a sacrificial lamb with a vampire leaning over her. Her power shimmered in the air above her, a calling card for the monsters who craved her. Her silent sobs were daggers in Jade's chest. Jade wanted to protect her then—as she wanted to protect her today.

Where are you Alicia? She cried out to the surrounding night.

When no answer was forthcoming, she turned to the heavens. *Blessed Cerridwen. Goddess of Inspiration. Goddess of Knowledge. Bestower of thine gifts upon my unworthy soul. I need your inspiration and guidance now more than ever. Please show me the way.*

The compulsion to go to Mexico intensified. She was not going to be able to ignore it much longer. There was a power base building there. A shift in the universe that was unlike anything Jade had ever experienced. She tried to ignore it.

Sometimes our paths take us where we most need to be.

Quick on the heels of that thought was an image, flickering like an old black and white movie on a cracked screen. There was a tear in the universe, and a man stepped through. He was well over six feet tall, with the build and stance of a warrior. He reminded her of Gheorgès in black leathers, and black motorcycle boots, only this man wore a leather duster that flared out behind him giving her a glimpse of the weapons he carried. Jade tore her vision from the man, and studied the surrounding terrain. The sparse vegetation consisted mostly of cactus and scrub brush.

It looks like I'm going to Mexico.

~~

Conall stepped through the portal, and froze. There were eyes on him. His eyes tracked his surroundings without uncovering their hiding place. His nostrils flared. He was alone, but that didn't lull him into thinking he had not been seen. Someone had watched his entrance to earth, and that meant he had to work fast to find the prince's daughter before someone else did. The air around him vibrated with power, and the portal closed.

Damn you Alaric. What in hell had his prince been thinking? Slumming on earth—procreating. He knew better than most the dangers of a mating between a Mage and a human. He knew the risks involved. But he was Conall's prince, and as such it was not Conall's place to question him.

Conall's nostrils flared once more as he sensed the air around him. The air was rife with power fighting for release. A faint glow on the horizon beckoned him. Conall prayed he was not too late, and strode toward the source of power.

Fifteen

Death was coming for her. She could smell its rotting breath on the night breeze. Alicia did not fear death. It would be a welcome release to step into death's embrace and escape the hounding of the *Seeker* with his glistening black coach, and those ferocious black beasts that hauled it.

Death wasn't supposed to be like this. She thought she would simply go to sleep and not wake up.

The fire started deep inside her belly, and quickly became an inferno burning her from the inside out. Her blood was already beginning to bubble in her veins, and it felt like they would burst to let the steaming fluid escape. Pain stabbed at her belly. Her body went rigid, and then doubled over onto itself as the scream escaped her lips.

Flames engulfed her, burned into her brain. She held her breath to keep from searing the delicate tissue of her lungs.

Breathe little one. Kamenwati's voice washed over her like a spray of cold water and her skin began to sizzle.

She gasped, and began to pant, trying to work through the pain. Her clothing was melting against her skin. She had to get it off. Alicia started to tear at her clothes with nails that had grown into claws not even noticing that she tore her own skin. The coppery scent of blood wafted in the air. Her nostrils flared and her fangs elongated. Another wave of pain ripped through her veins tearing another scream from her already torn throat. Her body stiffened.

Breathe baby. You keep forgetting to breathe.

It was hard to keep the panic from his voice. Kamenwati had never witnessed a human's transition to Mage. It was terrifying to watch. He knew the risks. Not every Mage was strong enough to walk through the fires of the universe, and not all those who did survived with their minds intact, never mind their bodies. Kamenwati could understand why so many went insane, forgetting they were ever human, and embracing the dark. He felt the fire burning through her, attempting to burn her memories away one by one so she could be reborn. He was trying desperately to hold the link with her, to help her through this, but he was afraid it might not be enough. What was the good in being a God if you couldn't help the one you loved?

Loved? Hell, when had that happened. Kamenwati had been watching over Alicia since she was a child, impressed by her bravery in the face of so much pain and heartbreak. He had heard her silent cries, felt her power, and it drew him to her, as it had drawn others, and Kamenwati had not been able to stop the vampire from destroying her family. She had been through so much already, and now she had to suffer this.

"Kam?"

Kamenwati usually cringed at the shortening of his name, but her quiet voice was a welcome relief from the screams that tore from her throat, and her mind. "Is this what dying is like?"

"You are not dying little one. I refuse to allow it." His voice was stern, aristocratic, the voice of a man who demanded obedience, but Alicia could hear the fear he was trying desperately to hide.

She reached out to pat his arm but a wave of pain chose that moment to rip through her, and instead of patting his arm she dug her claws in until the blood began to bubble around her fingernails. Lightning flashed in her eyes, the fire burning away his image until she was blind to anything but the flames inside.

"Alicia." His voice came from far away, floating, edged with panic.

Flames licked at her mind trying to burn away the memories of her life, trying to burn away her humanity.

"NO." She was not going to allow them to take anymore from her. She was not afraid to die, but she would not simply disappear into oblivion.

You cannot stop this, child. Soon you will be one of us.

Revulsion made her want to vomit as the voice of the *Seeker* crawled through her mind. *I will never become one of you,* she screamed back. *I will die first.*

Evil laughter danced in her mind, and the image of a hateful smirk floated in front of her. *Oh you* will *die, child. And when you do I shall claim your power.*

Someone moved towards her in the flames. Alicia squinted trying to focus on the image.

Was that Mama walking toward her? It was so hard to see her face. The flames were making it fuzzy. Alicia began to panic when she realized she was having a hard time remembering what her Mama looked like.

Mama. "Don't leave me," she whispered frantically.

Kamenwati's voice sounded as if it were encased in cotton. A fragile lifeline in a vast ocean of fear that she clung to with both hands. *It's going to be all right, little one. I will never leave you.* His words were comforting, and she let herself drift through her memories, no longer alone.

Kamenwati ignored the claws drawing blood from his arm, and struggled to keep his mind linked with Alicia's in a feeble attempt to dampen her pain. Although she seemed unaware of his presence he was sure that on some level she was aware of his presence. He wanted to share this battle to keep her memories alive, to keep the part of herself that was human alive.

She was two. She was running across the front yard, chasing a butterfly as it flitted through the air, landing just out of reach before flitting off again when she got too close. Alicia laughed, and ran after it on short stubby legs. She heard a low growl and stopped. Terror wrapped its icy fingers around her tiny little heart, and squeezed until she didn't think she would ever be able to breathe again. She did not see the dog. All she saw were its huge white fangs, and the saliva dripping from the monster's jowls.

She turned, her short legs pumping as quickly as possible, but she knew she would not escape the beast. She was too slow. It was too fast. She could feel its hot breath on the back of her neck. Fear made her stumble. Instinct made her turn. The beast leaped at her throat and Alicia instinctively threw her hands up to protect herself. Her eyes widened in shocked disbelief when the dog stopped in midair, and then flew backwards to land on the ground several feet away.

She was shivering with fear. Papa ran and snatched her into his arms. He lifted her high above the ground away from where the vicious dog lay snarling. She could hear voices around her, the screams, and the accusations. She didn't know how her papa had stopped the dog chasing her, but she was glad he had.

It was you, little one. See the truth.

What did Kamenwati mean it was her? Papa had saved her. She couldn't save herself. She was too little.

Alicia drifted through her memories of Papa, forcing herself to remember when his face began to blur with wave after wave of pain that tore through her, leaving her weak and confused.

The sound of her mother's screams woke Alicia from a deep sleep. She sat up in bed, and clutched the blankets to her, afraid to move. *What is happening? Why are there flames outside my bedroom window? Why are the neighbours yelling?*

Mama and Papa ran into her room. Mama pulled the blanket from her numb fingers, and lifted her nightgown over her head. "Hurry," Papa whispered in a voice laced with fear. Alicia could hear her Papa dragging the drawers open. She tried to see what he was doing, but Mama chose that moment to drop the sundress over her head. Alicia automatically lifted her arms to help dress herself and Mama lifted her into her arms. While she watched in shocked silence Papa tossed a sack out her window, and climbed out. *Why didn't he use the door*, she wondered. The moment Papa's feet touched the ground he lifted his arms toward the window and Mama dropped her down to Papa. He set her on the ground beside the pack while he helped Mama out the window. Alicia stared, mesmerized by the flames that devoured her bedroom.

You caused this child. Alicia shuddered at the dark words spoken in that evil voice.

Alicia clutched her lifeline as the flames lick over, and through her body. *Did I do it? Did I bring this on my family?* Once the doubts began they grew rapidly. If she was the one who stopped the dog, then she was the one who brought the angry mob to their home, just like she was the one who brought that *monster* to their door when she was eight. She was evil. She deserved to die. Mama and Papa would be alive if it were not for her.

Yes. The velvety voice oozed, driving despair deeper into her soul. *You are Evil. Embrace your destiny, child. Come to me now.*

"No." Kamenwati would not allow her to go to *him.* He placed a hand on each side of Alicia's face, a face so hot it would have seared the skin off a human, and forced her to look at him. "Listen to me, Alicia. You are not evil. You did not do this." She moaned, and her eyes closed. "Look at me," he snapped. "Open your eyes, and see me. See yourself through my eyes."

Alicia's eyelids fluttered, but stayed closed. She wanted to open her eyes, but she was afraid of what would happen. The flames were too bright. If she opened her eyes they would burn out her pupils, and she would be blind. Or worse, they would escape and burn Kamenwati, and she would be alone again. *I can't,* she moaned.

You can.

Come to me.

Stay with me.

Evil.

Not evil.

The voices warred inside her head making her head ache, and Alicia wanted to scream at them to stop. She let go of her lifeline, and sank beneath the waves of flame. As her head disappeared beneath the flames she thought she heard Kamenwati's voice demanding that she fight, but it was far away, and hard to hear over the evil, sinister laughter that had chased her relentlessly her entire life. She was so tired of it all. Maybe she could just take a little rest.

Beneath the sea of flames she risked a peak, and was surprised at how calm and clear everything was. Mama's face, Papa's voice, they were perfect.

~~

Conall stood in the darkened alley, and cursed. *Where in hell did she go?* He knew a female had been in this alley recently. Her scent was strong in both the alley, and on the human cleaning coconuts off the dock. Cloaking himself in a chimera mist, he moved closer to the human male. There were fresh bite marks on his neck. That they were easily visible to anyone who looked was not good, but the fact he was still alive was promising.

Conall took a peak into the man's memories and caught a glimpse of a cat. The man believed a stray cat bit him in the alley. It would have been comical if it the implications were not so serious.

She should not be able to weave memories like these so soon after her transition, if indeed she had survived the transition intact. This meant someone was either with her, or following her. That someone had to be very powerful to be able to disguise their presence, and that worried Conall.

A lot.

Sixteen

Kamenwati felt Alicia let go, and icy fingers clutched his heart making it difficult to breath, and nearly impossible to focus. What was wrong with him? He had never felt like this before. He was a God. He was one of the most powerful beings in the universe. He was not afraid of anything.

Until now. He watched Alicia's head dip beneath a sea of flames that existed only in her mind, and he was terrified. He just found her. He refused to lose her now.

Her auburn hair spread out on the surface fanning the flames in the growing inferno. Kamenwati mentally reached out and grabbed it, yanking her head above the surface, ignoring her spluttering.

Alicia's head broke through the surface of flames, and she gasped as the fire burned her throat and lungs. She shoved at the hand tangled in her hair. *Let go.* She shoved the command with the full force of her mind, the flames making it impossible to speak without inhaling them. Anger quickly replaced the fear that coursed through her veins. *Are you trying to drown me?* She spat.

Right. As if she could drown in a sea of flames. She was more likely to become a shish-ka-bob, or a lump of charcoal. Her fury grew until her vision blurred. What was wrong with her? All she had to do was extinguish the flames. She could do it. How hard could it be? She could do things that other's could not do. She could talk to people with her mind, move small objects, and see the past. Putting out a fire should be a piece of cake.

Alicia let the flames roll over her, in her, through her. She felt herself rising above the surface of the fiery sea. She sucked the flames inside of her until her lungs were full, and then she pushed—hard. Flames shot from her eyes, her fingertips, the very ends of her hair, from every pore of her body.

Kamenwati barely had time to throw up a shield to keep the flames from devouring him. This had never happened before. The flames were not real. They were a product of Alicia's mind. They were a part of the transition from human to Mage, a way of cleansing her soul. But Alicia's mind made the fire real and dangerous. Kamenwati had never witnessed such power in a newly born Mage before, and he was truly impressed. No wonder the *Seeker* as she referred to the Betrayer had been stalking her for so long. Even as a child her power had been great. That untapped potential had been a beacon for every power-crazed creature on earth. It was about time she used it to her own advantage.

Kamenwati watched helplessly, unable to use his own powers while hers were so out of control, afraid that he would cause more damage than good. Alicia's body continued to hover above the bed, firing pouring from every pore of her skin, igniting the bed, the walls, and even the ceiling.

Alicia kept the flames streaming through her for several moments before finally collapsing on the mattress. Now that her own power had diminished, Kamenwati

doused the flames with a mere thought, and wiped all
traces of fire from the room. A moment later, a bowl of
clear water and a clean cloth appeared beside him. He
could have cleaned her body with only a thought, but he
preferred to do this job himself. Gently, almost reverently,
he washed the soot from her still glowing skin; skin that
was warm to touch, but no longer feverish. He hoped the
worst was over. With gentle fingers, he brushed the hair
from her temple, and her eyelids fluttered, and then
opened. The hunger he saw in those dark orbs called forth
an answering hunger that made his groin ache, and his
fangs lengthen.

Alicia wet her lips with the tip of her tongue. A wave
of lust rolled over Kamenwati, and filled the air with hot
spices. She could hardly believe how incredibly sexy the
man was. He was absolutely drop-dead gorgeous, and he
was in her bedroom nearly naked. In her mind that made
him fair game.

Her eyes roved over his granite features, stopping
when they came to the small cuts where her fingernails
had dug into his arms. Hunger and lust beat against her,
tightening her womb, and lengthening her own fangs.
Every breath she took filled her with the scent of blood,
musk, and mouth watering spices until she was quivering
with hunger and need. Alicia leaned in and nuzzled his
chest letting his scent wash over her. Her fangs exploded,
their tips piercing her lower lip. Alicia gasped at the pain,
and then licked the tiny droplets of blood from her lip. She
nearly had an orgasm just from the taste. It was like
nothing she had ever tasted, and she wanted more.

Alicia slid her leg over Kamenwati's rubbing herself
against his heated skin. With a little nudge she flipped
him onto his back, and straddled his enormous erection,
but not quite touching the tip. She leaned over him,
inhaling his unique aroma, filling her lungs. Her fangs
ached, and grew longer, until they were scraping against

the skin stretched taut over the muscles on Kamenwati's chest. Her womb clenched, and she trembled helplessly as his hands came up and his hot palms trailed over her hips. Alicia snuck a peek from beneath her heavy lashes, and a different fire raced in her veins as his golden orbs flared with desire. Her own pupils widened in response, and fire pooled at her center. She melted beneath that look.

His skin looked as hard and cold as marble, but the heat radiating from him was enough to sear human skin. Her fingers splayed across his chest to rest on either side of his sun tattoo, and she listened to the erratic beat of his heart. Alicia traced the outline of that fiery tattoo, and then trailed her fingers along his ribcage, and lower, slipping her hand beneath his loincloth she gently cupped his balls in the palm of her hand.

Kamenwati's golden orbs flared brighter, and he groaned. She could feel the heat from his tip against her core, and she bit down on her lip to keep from groaning aloud.

It was the wrong thing to do.

Blood, even her blood, was an aphrodisiac sending lust coursing through her. The flames of desire spread until she was sure they would devour her, and this time she wouldn't be able to stop them.

Not a bad way to die.

I will not hurt you, little one.

Alicia knew Kamenwati would not hurt her. He would never get the chance. She was going to spontaneously combust, and it would be over. Already the fire in her core was growing stronger. *God he smelled delicious.* Alicia nuzzled his neck.

Just one little sip, that's all I need. Just a tiny drop to keep me going. Alicia let her teeth scrape the throbbing vein in Kamenwati's neck.

This is what Kamenwati was waiting for. *Drink, little one,* his velvet smooth voice sent quivers racing through her body, cooling the flames only to have them flare up again. *I offer myself so you may live.*

Alicia's lips parted, closing over that throbbing vein. She felt his skin pushing against her fangs. She could already taste the rich coppery liquid that lived there; the power that coursed through those veins.

That's right. Drink. Drink it all. The dark sinister voice of her nightmares ran through her mind, urging her on, encouraging the hunger that clawed at her belly.

Just one little sip. I can stop after one little sip.

Alicia sank her teeth into pure heaven. Light exploded behind her eyes. Power surged through her with each swallow. Kamenwati groaned from pain or ecstasy, Alicia couldn't be sure.

Drain him. The dark voice urged gleefully.

Shock halted her actions. *No! I am not a monster.*

There was a flash of light, and Alicia disappeared.

Seventeen

A flash of lightning over the horizon wouldn't normally be a cause for concern, but tonight was different. There was power running rampant through the night air, uncontrolled, unleashed, and that was dangerous for them all. Not to mention the tight feeling he had in his gut. The one that told him the Betrayer was near. But how was that even possible? The Betrayer had locked in the Shadows between the Earth and the Chimera for centuries. His presence should not be so strong here on earth. Not unless something, or someone, was acting as a conduit for him. Was this then, why his prince had sent him to earth so near to the coming nightfall?

Conall's eyes flickered to the night sky, and his heart nearly stopped. Not something that happened to him often. He didn't have much time. He had less than twenty-four earth hours to find Alaric's daughter, and drag her home.

That's if she survived the transition, did not turn vampire, and wanted to meet her father. At least he knew he was looking for a female, which made him wonder why Alaric had not sent for her sooner. Female magi were coveted for their very uniqueness. Not many of them survived the transition at all.

The time limit posed another problem. Travel. He was going to have to travel as a human. Once he stepped into the Gloaming, those doorways through time and space the Magi preferred to travel, time would stand still while it kept on moving here on earth. Not a problem if he knew exactly where he was going. He could be there in a heartbeat. On the other hand, searching could take several earth days—days he did not have. He needed to find Alaric's daughter, and get back into the Chimera before nightfall. His place was beside his Prince in the coming battle, not gallivanting around earth looking for someone who might not want to be found.

Conall manipulated the energy around him, and a Honda two stroke appeared in front of him, black of course, with a matching black helmet. *Where are you girl?* He started the bike, appreciating the way it purred quietly, and the vibration between his strong legs. His black duster twisted and warped forming itself into a black motorcycle jacket that wouldn't interfere with his ride. Conall twisted the right handle and revved the engine. Satisfied with the way it sounded he donned the helmet, and took off in a cloud of dust.

Using the fingerprint of magic he felt in the alley as a beacon he left the small fishing village behind, and aimed his bike toward the mountains. Conall liked it here, the quiet of the night, and the warmth of the breeze against his cheeks. By morning it would be hot as hell but that didn't concern Conall. As a Mage he could control his environment if the need arose, but he wouldn't waste the energy it took to do so. He liked the feel of the wind on his face, and come morning if he was still here he would savour the feel of the hot sun. The Chimera was beautiful, but there were no such changes. The sun shone without ever getting too hot. The rain fell when needed without feeling warm or cool against your skin. The Chimera went through the seasons without any real change at all and Conall treasured his times on Earth, if only for its inconsistent weather.

~~~

The wheels of the Cessna rolled to a stop and Jade stood up, or rather tried to. Luke unsnapped his seatbelt, and quickly reached over to unsnap his wife's. He was worried about Jade. She had been an automaton since bursting from the clearing to tell them she was going to Mexico. When he called Daniel on his cell, he was already preparing the Cessna for takeoff having received his orders directly from Jade.

They would fly to Mexico to drop Jade off, and then Daniel was to fly the rest of them home.

Yeah right. Like he had any intention of leaving his mate alone in Mexico. Daniel could take the children back, but he was staying with Jade. Luke looked up to see three pairs of eyes glaring at him. *Maybe sending them home wasn't going to be all that easy.*

The moment Jade's seatbelt was free she stood up, and strode toward the door of the plane. Her body was here functioning on some level, but her mind was on the back of a motorbike flying along a dirt road somewhere in Mexico. The glimpses Luke was getting from Jade's mind were confusing and disorienting. They were rushing past trees and hills, and small lonely farms heading toward something.

Crap. Was this how it was when they summoned Jade? This confusing chaos of the mind, being in two places at once. How did she function at all?

When the door slid silently open Jade breathed in the cool Mexican air. Dawn was a mere glimmer over the horizon, and already she could taste the heat it would bring. Jade turned to Luke who was crowding her at the door, followed closely by all three of their children. She placed her hands on the scratchy surface of his cheeks, and rubbed her palms on the stubble.

Had it only been two days since Luke shaved, and they traced Alicia to Romania? God she was tired. Maybe she should take something before she got on a plane. Something that would help her sleep. Not that she would have taken anything this trip. She could not afford to lose her connection with the man on the dirt bike. He was her only lead.

Jade stood on her tiptoes, and tugged Luke's face lower until their lips met. *I love you.*

Luke closed his eyes and tasted the sweetness of his wife's lips, and tried to shut out what was coming next.

Take care of the children.

Always. Luke had every intention of taking care of his young. They would be safe with Daniel.

Daniel. Luke narrowed his eyes, and watched his wife. He could feel the power flowing from her. *Take this plane out of here.*

Yes Boss. Boss?

Daniel?

Bring Alicia home, and stay safe. Althea would never forgive me if anything happened to you.

I will.

Jade's amber eyes were swirling with power; power that made the inside of the plane shimmer. "I love you," she said. "Now go home." Jade shifted as she stepped through the doorway, and flew away.

Luke jumped back when the door slid shut. "What in hell?" He tried to open the door but it wouldn't budge.

Damn you, Jade. Open this door.

Jade's voice was a mere whisper inside his head, as if she were preoccupied, or couldn't afford the energy a conversation with him took while flying. *Go home, Lykos. Keep our children safe.*

My god. She hasn't' eaten. Jade never ate while on a plane, and her body needed fuel—lot's of fuel. Luke growled, and smashed his fist against the door. It didn't budge. *Eat.* He ordered her. *That is an order, Jade. You get something to eat. Now!*

Jade's laughter echoed in the corners of his mind, but it did nothing to soothe his temper. *I so love a man who thinks he can order me around.*

Daniel came out of the cockpit. "It's no use Boss man. This isn't the first time she has done this. That seal will not break until we leave."

Luke growled at Daniel who just shrugged. Luke's eyes flashed. "Then take this bird up. Now."

Daniel was from the Lycan Pack in Willow Bend. At one time Luke was his Alpha. But that was before Daniel left the pack to become a member of the O'Connor Search and Rescue team. A move Luke sanctioned at the time, not yet realizing he too would leave the pack to be with Jade. A move he did not regret, although sometimes he could throttle that female.

Luke moved toward his seat, the triplets were already buckled in.

"How far does this bird need to get before the seal is broken?" Gheorgès asked. "Once around the airport?"

It actually took five.

Eighteen

Alicia crouched on the cool black marble floor, her hair dancing wildly around her head, her dark eyes blazing, her fangs elongated and dripping red. She was totally focused on the male dressed all in white standing before her with his arm raised as if to throw a weapon. The splendour of the room meant nothing to her as she glared straight ahead trying to figure out how she got here. The last thing she remembered was the *Seeker* urging her to drain the life from Kamenwati and thinking, *God, if I were with my father right now I would kill him.* Guess she had better be careful what she wished for, or even thought for that matter.

The raised hand before her was empty but that didn't mean anything. The air in the room crackled with power, and tiny lightning sparks bounced off the walls; whether from him or her Alicia wasn't sure. A door burst open with surprising speed considering how monstrous it was, and a lanky red head rushed in with a gun in each hand.

Get out!

The male flew backward out the door, his white fangs flashing in his astonished face. The massive doors slammed shut. *Wow. Did I do that?* Alicia didn't have time to worry about what just happened. She tracked the male with her eyes and senses as he slowly lowered his hand to a less threatening position.

So this was her father; the monster whose blood ran in her veins. Funny, he didn't look like a monster. He had the face of an angel—a dark angel. Then again, so had the monster that killed her beloved Mama and Papa; the face of an angel, and the dark soul of a demon. It was easy to see how her mother fell for his lies when he came to her wearing that face.

Alicia was not going to be that stupid. She would never believe anything that came out of that mouth. Her gaze narrowed to the tips of his fangs, and her blood began a slow boil. He sank those fangs into her mother's smooth throat, and drank her essence.

Like I drank Kamenwati's, came the unbidden thought. *Oh my God. I am a monster just like my father.* She looked around the room, frantically searching for an escape route. "I hate you," she spat just before she vanished.

The massive door to the throne room burst open so suddenly that Tex and two other Magi nearly landed face down on the black marble floor. Tex's eyes tracked the large chamber but the Prince was alone. The only evidence that the nearly naked female was real was the remnants of power still sparking throughout the chamber.

Alaric was staring at the empty spot where his daughter had stood, crouched actually. She never did get out of her defensive position, and for a heartbeat he had thought she was going to actually attack him.

His daughter. My God she was beautiful, like his sweet Maria. The power emanating from her was mind boggling. He wasn't sure that if it came down to a battle between them that she would not beat him; at least once she learned to control it. He did know that if she was crazed he would not be the one to bring her down.

He wouldn't be able to do it.

His daughter.

She hadn't looked crazed. She was definitely pissed, and just before she vanished he thought she looked horrified.

But not crazed.

Who had she fed from? Not Conall. Conall was a very powerful Mage, and his best friend, but Alaric did not detect any of Conall in her.

"Where did she go?" Tex asked, still tracking the four corners of the large chamber for signs of movement in the shadows.

Alaric shrugged. *Where did she go?* "The better question is 'how did she get in here?'"

"Could she have got hold of a crystal?" Ramka asked while rubbing his forehead as was his habit when thinking.

"No crystal was used." Alaric was distracted, and didn't notice the look of bafflement on the Magi's faces. His daughter had not used the crystal, although he had glimpsed it nestled in the hollow of her throat. He was remembering the day he gave the crystal to his sweet Maria.

"Give this to our daughter on her twenty-first birthday. Tell her to put it on and say my name, Alaric." Granted he did not always keep track of the passage of time on earth but he had a reason to watch now, and she should have called to him at least three cycles ago. When she did not he had accepted the fact that his daughter had not survived. Then the crystal woke, and he sent Conall to find her.

She should have called to him. *Why hadn't she called to him?*

His daughter should have put on the crystal, and said his name, and he would have gone to her. Under no circumstances should she have been able to come to him, to throw his man out, and slam those massive doors. Alaric's chest filled with pride for the child he had sired. *You are magnificent.*

To the Magi he said, "Get the candles."

If the three of them were confused before, the look of astonishment on their faces showed they had not realized how serious the situation was. Alaric could not remember the last time he had summoned Ra.

Less than a chime later seven Magi in white robes stood in a circle of stone, seven golden candles flickered in the absolute blackness of the underground chamber. Their melodic chanting had barely begun began when there was a flash brighter than an exploding sun, and a male figure appeared.

The Magi bowed before their God.

"My Lord," Alaric's tone was unassuming as was expected in the presence of a God.

Ra had no such inclination. "Cut the crap, Alaric." His deep voice reverberated in the chamber. "Why have you summoned me? You should be preparing for the coming battle."

Alaric cleared his throat, but his voice still cracked. Ra would kill him for allowing this breach to happen. It was his fault the seal was broken. He was the one who had left a crystal on earth. "The seal, My Lord, it's been broken."

Ra's lips turned up slightly in the corners. "Tell me something I don't already know." Ra seemed to notice the presence of the Magi priests in their white robes for the first time. "Leave us," he barked the command and the room emptied, all but Alaric.

Wasn't this a day for surprises the priests thought as they found themselves outside the chamber doors.

"Is there something you wish to say to me?" Ra's voice was an echo in the silent chamber.

Alaric thought of those flashing eyes in the perfection of that alabaster skin. "Forgive me, My Lord." Ra cocked his head, and lifted one eyebrow waiting, and Alaric continued. "It is my fault the seal has been broken. I left a crystal on earth a quarter century ago."

Ra's laughter rolled like thunder until the walls themselves shook. "Hardly. If it is anyone's fault it is mine. When I created the seal centuries ago I was so full of myself I did not even consider the possibility of it weakening. Regardless, it was not the crystal that allowed the seal to be broken."

Alaric bowed his head until his eyes were in line with his toes. "I went to Earth." Alaric paused. Ra said nothing to interrupt as his friend continued. "I found an angel there ... Maria. When I left she was with child. A girl. I could taste her in her mother's blood. I couldn't stand the thought of losing her. I left behind a key to the portal in the form of a small crystal pendant. When it didn't wake I believed my daughter was dead." Alaric raised his eyes to his God, and braced his back. "I just saw her. She was in the throne room. She sent my guards flying through the doors, and locked them out, all without raising a finger." Alaric's voice rang with pride.

Ra nodded his head. "Indeed you have a lot to be proud my old friend."

Alaric shrugged. "Wouldn't you be proud if Kamenwati surpassed all your expectations?"

"Indeed I am, as you have a right to be." Ra held his palm flat and an image played in the air above it, like a three dimensional movie showing Alicia before her transformation facing the wrath of Ra with no fear whatsoever. "She is a true warrior. That may be the only thing that saves her."

Nineteen

Oh God. This is incredible. Never before had anyone drank from Kamenwati's vein. It was the most erotic feeling, her hot breath on his neck, the gentle tug at his throat as she drew his rich blood into herself. The initial sharp stab as her fangs pierced his skin quickly turned to streams of pleasure. Wave after wave of unimaginable pleasure coursed through his body. If he was any harder he would explode.

Kamenwati rolled his hips aiming himself for her core, wanting all of him in her; his flesh as well as his blood. He willed away his loin cloth. Alicia stiffened. There was a flash of light.

Alicia vanished.

Kamenwati lay on the small bed staring at the cracks in the ceiling. *No!* His mind screamed, lightning flashed, and thunder rumbled, even while he tried to figure out what in hell had happened.

The rumbling grew louder until it was a roar. Kamenwati forced his mind still while he felt the air around the small farmhouse. Someone was coming.

Black fighting leathers, motor cycle boots, and a long black leather duster materialized on his lean body. Kamenwati checked his weapons although he knew exactly what he had summoned; a knife, a sword, and his weapon of choice—a morning star. A morning star was a spiked metal ball on a length of thick chain. The chain wrapped itself around his thick forearm, and he gently swung the ball back and forth checking its weight.

Severing the head was the quickest way to ensure the death of their enemies. A bullet through the head and heart almost simultaneously would put them down, but incineration was the only way to ensure they didn't rise again. Death was such a fickle thing. Beheading worked. Once the head left the body it simultaneously combusted, becoming nothing more than ash, but you still had to bring then down first.

Kamenwati strode through the door in full fighting mode just as a black figure on an even blacker motorbike turned into the yard from the dirt road that ran past the farm.

The motorbike skidded to a halt, and the driver casually reached up and removed his helmet shaking out his long black hair. He eyed Kamenwati's clothing and weapons. "You expecting someone else?"

Kamenwati swung the morning star with deliberate menace. "You call that a motor cycle?"

"Hey, don't be dissin' my ride, Kam. She may not be pretty but she's great on the hills."

Kamenwati cringed at the shortening of his name. Only two people in the universe dared call him Kam. Sounded like a car part when Conall said it, but he rather liked the way it came out when Alicia said it in. When she said it in that soft whispery voice of hers it was an intimate caress.

Conall threw his leg off his ride at the same time Kamenwati stepped forward. Hey met like warriors with their hands clasping forearms, and then they embraced, slapping each other on the back.

"Con you old bastard how you been? Still chasing after the skirts?"

Conall survived his change more than two centuries before, and was brought into the *Chimera* by his father, but not before he had gotten a reputation for loving and leaving. When the townsfolk saw him coming, the mothers locked up their daughters while the fathers headed for their guns. After the change the need for blood accompanied his worsened sexual appetite.

Conall was a rogue when it came to women, but he had a code of honour that he lived by even after the change came. He never went after the truly innocent or married women, and he never allowed himself to drink enough to weaken them. The blood enhanced the sex, but it did nothing to sustain him and by the time his father found him he was dying, determined not to take a life in order to save his own. Refusing to listen to the compelling voices in his head and turn vampire.

Kamenwati had fought by Conall's side during the long nights against Ra's betrayer, and they fast became friends. Conall fought with the same single minded determination he did everything else, and he soon drew the attention of the Prince of the Magi, Alaric. When Alaric realized Conall's potential he immediately brought him to the palace as part of his personal guard. Alaric like everyone else that met Conall was drawn to his boyish charm, and enthusiasm for everything he did, and they began a friendship that continued to this day.

It didn't take long for Alaric to realize Conall was not cut out for the mundane life the palace offered. It wasn't uncommon for the Magi to spend time on earth. There were not many females in the *Chimera*, and the Magi were males with the same needs as all males. Conall was the perfect Mage to send to earth to seek out the offspring of the Magi and help them embrace their new lives. He was unattached, loyal, and the craved women.

Kamenwati's eyes narrowed. "Who brings you here?" He already knew. No coincidence would bring Conall to this remote part of the world at this exact time.

"Alaric's daughter."

A blast of heat so powerful Conall staggered beneath it radiated from Kamenwati's chest, and Conall laughed. "Oh shit," he sputtered. "This day just keeps on getting better." Kamenwati glared and Conall continued. "First Alaric finally owns up to being as much as a male as the rest of us, and admits he has a daughter, and then you go and fall for her."

As realization dawned Conall quit sputtering. "Crap. She's the one isn't she? The one you've been monitoring all this time."

Kamenwati knew the instant Alicia returned. He felt her materialize beside him, and saw her crouched ready to attack Conall. Her hair stood on end as power crackled in the air around her, and her fangs were elongated. Her naked body radiated with the power of the sun.

A low whistle escaped Conall's pursed lips. *My God she's magnificent. I can see why everyone wants her.*

Alicia caught Conall's passing thought, and she stole a glance at Kamenwati. He was staring at her with such heat in his eyes, and he didn't appear in the least concerned about the stranger's presence. Alicia took her cue from Kamenwati, and forced herself to relax. Her hair settled into its usual curly mass, and the air around her began to calm. She realized she was naked, and wished she had her clothes. There was a gentle shift in the air as a pair of pale blue jeans, and a long white button-up shirt settled over her skin.

Well done, little one. Kamenwati's deep voice caressed her, and she could feel his warm fingers on the back of her neck. She snuck a peek from beneath her long lashes while keeping an eye on the stranger. Kamenwati had not moved, but she could still feel that gentle pressure on her neck. *Where have you been?*

I've been to London to visit the King. Kamenwati's deep laughter reverberated through her body making her *hot*. She swallowed. The man didn't even have to touch her and he could make her tremble.

The stranger cleared his throat, and both sets of eyes flipped to him. *Damn. How could I forget we are not alone?* "Who are you?" Alicia demanded.

"Conall. I am ..."

"He's a friend of mine," Kamenwati interjected before Conall could spill that Alaric sent him. Instinct alone warned him Alicia wasn't going to be very welcoming of anyone sent by her father.

"So my father sent you." She spat the word father with such venom even Kamenwati cringed. *No sense trying to hide shit from me Kam. Seems I can see what's on your mind. Don't worry. I promise not to disintegrate him because he knows the monster that fathered me.*

There was an inaudible hum in the air, and Conall found himself looking for a place to escape to. Funny, he never felt like a third wheel around any of the mated males in the *Chimera*, and yet he definitely felt like an extra spoke here. The sun's fingers crept over the horizon, and Conall cleared his throat. "Time is running Kamenwati."

"Well I am not." Alicia watched the rays of the already hot sun crawl across the land turning the dried brown grasses a deep rich golden as they stirred in its first rays. A grackle whistled from somewhere nearby, a rooster crowed hello to the morning, and the chickens stirred from their resting places to begin scratching at the dirt in search of substance. Everywhere she looked life went on, and it was about time she took a stand, and took her own life back.

"Ma'am," Conall spoke with quiet urgency, as if he knew she would argue if he tried to tell her what to do. Besides, with the possessive way Kamenwati was standing, so close to her side he was practically a part of her, he knew he wouldn't get anywhere.

"You can leave." Alicia's dark eyes flashed with barely controlled power, and her right hand was rubbing small circles over her stomach like she eaten something that didn't agree with her.

Kamenwati stepped even closer, his eyes anxious. He could feel the glitch in the universe. Something was coming; something powerful. "What do you feel?"

Dark eyes swirling with power and emotion pegged him. "Something is coming ... evil ... the *Seeker* ... many others ... we don't have much time." Alicia gave her head a small shake like she was clearing cobwebs and her swirling eyes settled back to their normal dark coffee. "We don't have much time." She turned her attention to the tall man dressed all in black, with long black hair that hung past his shoulders, only he wasn't a man. He was like her, a victim of his father's lust. "Conall. Emissary of Alaric, Prince of the Magi." She had picked the knowledge from his mind. Conall betrayed his surprise with a mere flicker of his dark eyes, but he did not interrupt. "I know who you are. I read it in your mind. I make no apology. You are a stranger, and you have sought me out. I have a right to know who is enemy, and who is not."

"And I am?"

Alicia kept her eyes locked with Conall's. "You don't want to be my enemy, but you will if the need arises. You are Kamenwati's friend. You are loyal, and you would give your life for what you believe is right." Her stomach was a pot of boiling acid, the bile beginning to rise in her throat until she thought it would spew out of her mouth. "Stay or go. It is no concern of mine. I already know Kamenwati will not leave, but I refuse to run anymore."

The presence was so strong Conall wouldn't be surprised if something suddenly reached out and touched him. "Something's coming." He knew it as well as he knew his own name, he just didn't know what. He could feel the Betrayer, the *Seeker* as Alicia referred to him. An apt name he thought, as the Betrayer sought out newly matured Magi and tried to convert them to vampirism, or just have them killed so he could take their power when it released back into the universe. He knew the fingerprint of the *Seeker's* power, but this other was unknown to him.

There was a brief flicker of surprised recognition, and then relief in Alicia's dark eyes. If Conall had not been looking at her at that moment he would have missed it, but it was there. She recognized the power signature. Of course Kamenwati would have sensed it. It was even conceivable that Kamenwati would know what was coming, but that didn't necessarily mean he would tell them.

The vibration in the air was so tiny a human would not have noticed the difference in the atmosphere. He was Mage. He noticed, and frowned.

Kamenwati's body shifted into a fighting stance, and Alicia reached over and placed her small hand on the soft leather of his duster. Kamenwati relaxed, slightly. "We have about two hours."

Alicia's voice was soft, and the eyes she turned on Kamenwati were a blatant invitation. His blood thickened in his veins, and his cock thickened beneath the leathers. His morning star vanished, and ignoring the smirk on Conall's face he scooped Alicia in his strong arms, and strode toward the small farmhouse. "You can bunk in the barn," he said over his shoulder.

Twenty

Kamenwati gently lowered Alicia onto the small bed, and dropped his duster and the rest of his weapons to the floor. He couldn't wait to crush up against Alicia on that small bed, skin to skin, mouth to mouth. He wanted inside her with a vengeance still needy from their earlier encounter. He needed his blood inside her, his body inside hers. He had glimpsed what it would be like when she drank from him earlier, and he was so ready to finish what they started.

Kamenwati tugged his shirt over his head, and froze, staring at Alicia. *You are beautiful.* His voice was a husky whisper. He loved the heat that crawled up her neck and infused her cheeks with color. Her fingers were busy working on the buttons of her shirt.

"No," Kamenwati growled low in his throat. He knelt over her, captured both her hands in one of his much larger ones, and stretched her arms above her head, lifting her breasts and pulling her shirt tight across those taut nipples. "Let me."

With exquisite slowness he unbuttoned her shirt with his free hand, his lips and tongue discovering every inch of her silken skin revealed.

Alicia gasped when his rough tongue flicked over her taut nipple. Kamenwati called in the *Chimera* to blanket the small house from prying eyes and ear, conscious of Conall moving around in the barn.

Kamenwati flicked the taut pink nipple a couple more times before changing the rhythm to long slow licks like he was savouring an ice cream cone, swirling his tongue around the tip, and then sucking in while Alicia moaned and squirmed beneath him. His own body pounded with the urgent need to claim her, and he pulled the rest of her shirt open ignoring the buttons that popped off, and rolled on the floor.

Kamenwati kept his mouth on her breast suckling like a newborn while one hand slid down her taut stomach to the slip beneath the waistband of her jeans, and stroke her sex, quickly bringing her to a lust filled stupor. Alicia couldn't get enough. She had a voracious appetite for sex—and blood. As the inferno in her grew so did her fangs. It didn't help when Kamenwati's hot lips released her breast to follow the blistering trail left by his magic fingers.

Moaning and twisting she tried to get closer. She wanted his lips where his fingers were. She wanted them everywhere. The denim of her jeans was too constricting. No sooner had the thought crossed her mind and the problem was solved.

No jeans.

In a blink of an eye Kamenwati's lips were on her sex, his tongue flickering in and out tasting her spicy honey. Alicia's body jerked and shuddered as the inferno grew until she erupted like a volcano.

Kamenwati crawled up Alicia's quaking body licking his tongue along her heated skin, twirling it in her belly button, flicking the taut nipples, and finally capturing her moans as he caught her lips. His tongue traced the tips of her fangs, and he could taste her hunger, her need. His body grew harder at the thought of those fangs piercing his skin as he fed both her appetites at once.

With merely a thought his leathers went the way of his duster and weapons freeing his painful erection. Kamenwati was no saint but he had never wanted, never needed, a woman like he needed Alicia. She looked so fragile, so dainty, but her appearance hid an inner strength he found erotic. He was going to feed that strength, only this time he was going to be in her when he did it.

God was he hot. She was burning, consumed by flames, her bones were melting in their heat fusing the two of them together until she couldn't tell where she ended and he began. They were one body, one soul, one heartbeat forcing liquid strength through their veins. As their flesh pounded together, and their hearts beat louder Alicia's fangs exploded. That hot fiery liquid called to her, begged her to be taken, and Alicia didn't have the strength to deny her hunger.

Fangs pierced the vein running to Kamenwati's heart, and he exploded. As his life's essence flooded her mouth, his life giving seed filled her womb.

Twenty-One

On silent wings the white owl lit on a branch high in an apple tree that had long given up bearing fruit, where it should have a clear vision of the farmyard, the small stone farmhouse, and the larger barn. The feathers on the scruff of its neck ruffled.

Where was the farm?

There was a strange mist that gave the area a hazy, unreal look, and where the farm should be was fog. Bright yellow eyes concentrated on the mist in front of them and the farmyard appeared, and then the barn shimmered into view. If she relaxed the concentrated effort to see what was right in front of her, she would not even know it existed.

Chimera. Jade was familiar with the concept of blanketing yourself in illusion to appear invisible to the naked eye but it would take something very powerful to hide an entire house, let alone the barn and the yard.

The owl concentrated on the yard until it could see the chickens pecking in the dirt. It looked away, and back again, and the chickens were still there. The silence suddenly filled with the sounds of their clucking and scratching. The yellow eyes swirled as the owl concentrated on the house that continued to fade the moment her concentration left it. The power was emanating from there. She could sense it, but she could not identify its fingerprint.

All magical beings left a unique fingerprint, and each fingerprint was identifiable by species, and then in a more personal sense by individual. For example, the fingerprint left by a vampire was different than the fingerprint left by a Lycan, and each Lycan or vampire left their own individual fingerprint. It worked the same as fingerprints left by humans at crime scenes. Jade could not identify this particular signature.

One thing she was certain of, Alicia was in that house.

The owl tilted its head slightly focusing its stare where the barn should be. With an audible pop the mist burst, and the barn stood solid. The large doors flew open and the stranger she watched step through the breach in the universe strode into the yard. His leather coat was once again long and flowing, as was his black hair. He halted just outside the door, a sword in his right hand, and let his eyes track the yard. His aura shimmered with power, and Jade tossed up a little illusion of her own. She wasn't really surprised when his eyes passed the branch she was perched on, only to quickly return.

The owl's yellow stare locked with the dark stare of the stranger. The pull of those eyes was strong, mesmerizing. The owl tilted its head a little more to better focus, and its yellow eyes flared. The owl lifted from its perch as a fireball hit the branch it vacated.

Conall stepped back, another fireball at the ready when the owl shifted into a tall slender woman with strange amber eyes, and settled to the ground a couple feet in front of him. Her white blonde hair was streaked with gold and silver, and cropped very short.

"So you want to play ball." Her voice was soft, melodic, and he almost dropped the ball of fire he was readying.

Conall was fascinated with the way those amber eyes sparkled, and almost lost track of what her hands were doing. The top of his head felt the heat from a ball of fire that passed by way too close.

The two combatants circled each other warily, eyes locked together, as they sized each other up. Most of the battles Jade fought were on a physical level and she was a little rusty, but that didn't mean she wasn't going to play the game. The sky above rumbled, and a streak of lightning struck the ground inches from Conall's feet. He jumped back, his eyes flashing with fury.

This was so not going to happen. He readied a blast, fully aware of the similar blast readied in the female's palm. It was like looking in a mirror. Eyes locked. Arms lifted. Palms opened.

The two fireballs hurtled toward each other like trains on a collision course.

Alicia felt the explosion of power as the fireball hit the apple tree. She tore her fangs from Kamenwati's vein, and looked up at him dizzy with power. "What was that? It sounded like a gas tank exploded."

Kamenwati was the first to pull his self together. Keeping between Alicia and the door he instantly donned his leathers, duster, and weapons. Another explosion rocked the small farmhouse, and lightning flashed outside the window. He turned to make sure Alicia was all right. She stood beside the bed dressed in jeans and a t-shirt, her dark hair a mass of uncontrolled curls, her cheeks slightly blushed. He wanted to kiss her, and drag her back to bed. He wanted to send her far away where she would be safe.

Neither one was an option. She had to fight her own battles; the best he could offer was to fight by her side.

Alicia's eyes widened with recognition, and she vanished. Kamenwati snarled. *I wish you would quit doing that.* He strode through the door and froze, his eyes taking in the scene before him. Conall was standing in front of the barn a *Moarté* across from him. Two fireballs were on a collision course between them, and Alicia materialized right in the middle of it all.

He couldn't move. He couldn't breathe. He couldn't just stand there and watch her die. He threw a shield around her just as the two fireballs sizzled and fell harmlessly to the ground.

Kamenwati wanted to blast both the *Moarté* and the Magi for putting Alicia in danger. What was the *Moarté* doing here anyway? Hers must be the power he felt earlier. A loud thumping drew his attention to Alicia trapped in a bubble of his making, and the thunderous look on her face made him wish he were brave enough to leave her in there for a while, at least until she cooled down. She did not look too pleased with his interference.

Kamenwati Horakhty you remove this barrier immediately or I will.

Shit. Alicia did not have enough control yet to pull off such a feat without consequences. Maybe it was time to show her what could happen if you could not control the magic.

The air inside the barrier started to glow as both Alicia's power and anger grew. The barrier began to vibrate as it tried to hold against her will. The air in the protective bubble was stagnant, and it was getting hard to breathe. Alicia gasped for air, and started to panic, losing the hold on her magic. There was a blast of white light and the magic splintered, like shards of glass, pieces flying everywhere. Shards struck both the *Moarté* and the Magi, and they fell to the ground writhing in agony. Their magic haphazardly filling the atmosphere until chaos reigned. Chickens squawked in the yard, and ran for cover as feathers flew and the scent of cooked meat filled the air. Flames caught the dried grass quickly spreading across the yard to lick up the wooden boards of the barn until that too was an inferno, and the flames started toward the farmhouse.

It took less than ten seconds for the entire scene to play out in Alicia's mind. With a horrified gasp she quickly reigned in both her temper and her power, and waited meekly for Kamenwati to lower the barrier he had created.

The *Moarté* was staring at Alicia with all the protectiveness of a she-bear with her cub. So this is the one who saved Alicia from the vampire all those years ago, and she looked like she thought Alicia needed saving right now, from him and Conall.

The instant the shield dissolved the two females flew into each other's arms. They hugged, and the *Moarté* held Alicia back so she could check her for injury, and then they hugged again. There was both love and anxiety in her voice when the *Moarté* finally spoke. "If you ever pull a fool stunt like that again I'll ground you until you're eighty."

Kamenwati could get behind that. In the short time he'd been with Alicia she had managed to shear years off his life.

Alicia laughed, and finally released her hold on the *Moarté* conscious of the males watching them. She knew Jade was tracking them even though she wasn't looking at them. Jade would know exactly where they were, and what they were doing. "Grounded? Are you kidding me? I haven't been grounded since I was ten."

"Doesn't mean it can't be done young lady." The entire time she was lecturing Alicia, she was checking her for damage she might have missed. "Seriously, Alicia," she scolded. "Whatever possessed you to jump into the middle of a firefight? What were you thinking?"

Alicia shrugged, and smirked at Conall. "I couldn't very well let you kill him now could I?"

Jade shook her head, and then turned her amber eyes on Conall. "He started it." She sounded like a recalcitrant child, and the pout on her lips had Alicia laughing again.

Alicia threw her hands up in the air like she had seen Jade do a thousand times when the triplets were fighting. "Fine," she mimicked. "Go at it then. See if I care." She stepped back, bowed at the waist, and swept her arm toward Conall. "Have at him, Mom. He's all yours."

"Mom," said Conall, his eyes wide.

"Mom," said Kamenwati at the same time. That he didn't know. He knew the *Moarté* had rescued Alicia when she was eight, but not once had Alicia let slip who her new family was, and Kamenwati would never have guessed the *Moarté* had adopted her.

Conall threw his own hands up in surrender. "If I apologize can we call a truce and start over?"

Jade's amber eyes sparkled with mischief as she narrowed her gaze on him. "Hmm. Apologize for trying to knock me out of that tree, and I will consider it."

Whoa, Kamenwati shot at Conall. *You didn't. Tell me you did not attack a Moarté. What were you thinking?*

Apparently I wasn't, answered Conall in a droll voice. Conall had heard the stories of the *Moarté*, and was well aware of the power they possessed. Not only were they powerful and deadly, once they caught your scent there was no escaping their justice. It was hard to picture any of the *Moarté* he had heard about having a sense of humour. Lucky for him this one seemed to.

Jade shook her head sadly. *I wouldn't believe everything you hear Magi.*

Startled by her voice in his head, although he didn't know why he should be, Conall quickly recovered his equilibrium and bowed at the waist. "I offer my apologies for trying to knock you out of the tree," he said seriously, no hint of sarcasm or humour in his voice.

Jade's own lips twitched and then lifted into a crooked smile. "Glad you said tried. Apology accepted."

Jade. Are you all right? Answer me dammit. Luke sounded worried, and out of breath.

Jade's amber eyes took on a dreamy look. *I thought I sent you home husband. Where are you?*

We are still several miles away.

We? Jade's laughter tickled his mind. *I should have known. There's not one in the lot of you that ever listens.*

"Hey. I listen."

Jade raised her brows at her daughter. "And how many times have I told you that it is not polite to listen in on other's conversations?"

Alicia shrugged, and grimaced, and rubbed at her temples. "What can I say? You are so loud right now that a human couldn't shut you out."

The color drained from her face, and her eyes rolled back in her head. Kamenwati stepped closer and she staggered against him.

Luke. I need you to go get Matthew and bring him to the farmhouse. Tell him to bring the med kit. And be careful. Something big is coming.

Ra paced across the black marble floor of Alaric's chamber, the flare of the candles barely noticeable compared to the incandescence of his male form. Alaric stood with his hip leaning against a large stone table covered with weapons. Up until a couple of chimes ago he too had been pacing until he thought he might wear a pattern in the floor. The sun was setting and they were running out of time.

"He will go for the girl." Ra continued his pacing. "She is his connection to earth."

I am such a fool thought Alaric. "When this night is over I will step down and surrender myself for judgment."

That caught Ra's attention. He stopped pacing and spun around to face his high priest. "What are you talking about?" he demanded.

Alaric reached over the table and chose a long sword with a black blade. He took a few practice swings with it. He liked the weight of it, and the feel of it in his hand. "Stepping down. I cannot rule if I cannot see what is best for our people. And going to earth to sire a child definitely was not in the best interests of our people."

"You cannot."

"Beg your pardon?"

"You cannot. I do not allow it."

Alaric shook his head, his dark eyes serious as a heart attack as they met the glowing golden eyes of Ra. "It is my fault the seal was broken. You said it yourself. She is the connection. Her blood opens the door to his return."

Ra shrugged. "We all do things we regret. So we fix it."

"And how do we do that?" Alaric slid the sword into a scabbard at his hip. "I will not allow her to die. She is my daughter."

Twenty-Two

"Kamenwati." Alicia's voice was a husky whisper until she cleared her throat. "Kamenwati, I'd like you to meet my mother Jade Caer Wulfson." "Mom, Kamenwati Horakhty."

"As in...?"

Meeting the parents is not something that Kamenwati, as the son of the Sun God Ra ever expected to have to worry about. But here he was hoping the *Moarté* approved of him as a mate for her adopted daughter. Not that it would keep him away if she didn't, it just made things easier. Alicia loved her family. They were the reason she stayed away and faced her nightmares on her own, in an attempt to protect them, like she pushed him away in an attempt to protect him. "My father is Ra Horakhty."

Now that put a different spin on things, as well as help explain why the males wore fighting leathers, and were fully loaded with weapons. The Magi took the offensive the moment he sensed her presence. Was he protecting Alicia or Kamenwati? She would have guessed Kamenwati but couldn't forget that his fireball was smothered the instant she appeared, and not because it came in contact with that shield the god had thrown up around her.

It took Jade exactly two seconds from the moment Alicia poofed herself between Jade and the Magi to know what her daughter was. Had the Magi been sent to protect her? And if so who gave the order? And she hadn't missed the way Kamenwati was looking at her daughter. She had to get Alicia alone, but she couldn't forget protocol. One didn't ignore a god.

"I am pleased to make your acquaintance." Jade inclined her head only slightly.

Alicia turned to Conall, as if only now realizing he was standing there. "This is Conall. He is," she hesitated only a moment, "a friend of Kamenwati's."

Friend or bodyguard?

Conall dipped his head in acknowledgement of the introduction, and wondered why Alicia hadn't told her mother that Alaric had sent him. He still couldn't believe it. Alaric and the *Moarté*. That explained keeping it secret. It explained a lot.

Conall started when he felt as much as heard the incredulous laughter licking at his brain, and the *Moarté's* musical voice. *Not in this or any other lifetime Magi.*

Before he had a chance to react Alicia continued. "Jade saved me from the *vampire* ..." The word vampire had a guilty ring to it, after all that is what she was—vampire. She ignored the resounding *No* along with the other voice, the one that kept insisting, *yes. Call to me child. You are one of us.* She had thought it was her father's voice, but now she wasn't so sure.

Been there done that when I was young and too stupid to know better. Not happening again.

She wasn't really surprised when the voice took on the evil resonance of the Seeker. *You belong to me,* it screeched. *You will be mine.*

Something besides the voices warring in her head nibbled at her brain even while her hand went to her stomach to try to ease the butterflies that flocked there whenever the Seeker drew near. Something was off, but she couldn't figure it out. While she worried the problem with one part of her mind she continued the conversation.

"...That murdered my parents. She adopted me when I was eight." He soft look she gave Jade and the glow in her eyes said it all. Theirs was a connection just as strong, if not stronger than any blood connection.

A shadowed passed over the sun and four pairs of eyes looked up. The air was stifling with nary a breeze to offer relief, and there was not a single cloud in the sky. The chickens had ceased scratching and decided it was time for a siesta, roosting in clumps of dried grasses at the base of trees and along the old rail fence along one side of the yard. Alicia shivered at the evil that crawled along the trail the sun left in its passage across the bright sky as if it were trying to hurry it along on its journey, as it paved the way for its master.

Jade felt like there was a blanket rubbing over her skin, its rough texture catching in the short hairs on her arms. Soon it would cover her head making it difficult to breathe. *Bring it on,* she thought. She had waited a long time for a shot at the unseen monster that chased her daughter from her home, and kept her away for far too long. Jade knew about the nightmares. In the beginning when the dark haired child screamed in the night Jade had held and comforted her long after she had fallen back to sleep muttering "Don't move. He can't see you if you don't move." After several months the nightmares ended.

Then the child had grown into a beautiful young woman, and the nightmares returned. Jade knew exactly when that happened. Alicia might not scream in the night anymore, but the dark circles beneath her eyes, and the haunted look in their depth told the story. The hardest thing Jade was forced to do was to allow her daughter the freedom to leave, study, and become the successful adult she was today.

Jade couldn't help her daughter then, but tonight she would not face her nightmare alone.

Magi. Jade knew there was something special about Alicia when she first saw her sprawled out like a sacrificial lamb, and heard her lost and alone searching for a mother who was no longer within her reach, while morning a father she already knew was gone. She knew Alicia was a witch, which was what she thought had brought the vampire to her in the first place. Her psychic ability would have been a beacon shining in the night to any of the undead within hearing. Althea had helped Alicia come to terms with her brush with the undead, and taught her how to control her abilities so she did not unwittingly call out to them anymore. She learned so quickly, and was so brave in the face of danger, Jade couldn't be prouder if she had given birth to her.

Magi. The children of Ra. The chosen few who were given the powers of the Sun God, and then followed him beyond the heavens into the *Chimera* when he left the earth so many lifetimes ago. Unlike the vampire the magi were strongest during the daylight hours while they harnessed the power of the sun.

Jade's stomach growled.

"You are hungry," Kamenwati said. He stared into the passing sun as if they were communing, which they probably were. "We must eat."

Jade had to agree as another wave of hunger washed over her. She wondered if there was any chocolate in her back pack. Her owl had caught a couple of mice, and an iguana while it followed the trail Conall left, but that energy was pretty much gone. Too bad there wasn't a *MacDonald's* or a *Wendy's* handy. She could use a couple burgers and fries. "Sounds like a plan to me," she said. "Food. Lots of it. First I need a word with my daughter in private."

"Come inside, Mom." Alicia headed toward the small farmhouse, Jade followed, Kamenwati disappeared without stirring as much as a dust ball, and Conall eyed a couple of the fatter chickens that squawked as if they knew exactly what he was thinking.

Four wolves ran full out across the Mexican landscape not bothering to follow any road. Their beacon called to them across the vast land. They headed for one of their own, and each one would be able to find her no matter where she was. The smaller white female staggered, and two grey furred males immediately flanked her. She was exhausted and needed to feed before she collapsed, but she refused to show any sign of weakness.

They needed to reach their destination before it was too late. Suddenly the largest male veered from their path and headed northwest instead of due north. It wasn't their place to question their Alpha, and so they turned as a well trained unit and followed.

The wolves came up against a stone fence that surrounded a farmer's field, and stopped short. The wall was too tall for them to jump, and stretched as far as they could see. *Shit.* This was going to cause a delay they couldn't afford. It was bad enough his mate had sent them on this side trip. He would have denied her, except that he found it difficult to deny her anything she requested, except when he was positive it was not in her best interests. He hadn't wanted to make this side trip but she had insisted he find Matthew.

Over there. His bright yellow eyes spotted a break in the wall about a hundred yards to their right; the stone was crumbled enough they could easily make it over. They jumped the rubble, and resumed their full out run through the field, veering slightly to the left to make up for the detour. Ahead of them a farmer dressed in a white shirt and baggy brown trousers was holding the handles of a plow pulled by a mule. The mule caught the scent of the wolves and panicked.

The farmer fell back when the mule bolted, although it didn't make it very far with the heavy plow still attached. It stopped several feet ahead shivering and whimpering in terror. The farmer's own eyes grew like saucers when he spied the wolf pack heading for him at a dead run.

"Shit." He frantically looked around for some sort of weapon but all he saw was the acres of freshly tilled soil. He'd left his shotgun back at the house as usual. Wasn't his wife going to love this? She was always yapping at him to take his damn gun when he went to work in the fields but he never did. Why would he? In the fifty-one-years he'd been working the fields there had been no need for a gun. There had never been so much as a coyote come to raid the hen house, and now there were four fully grown wolves heading right for him.

Oh yes. Patricia was going to love being right. He could hear her now. "I told you to carry your gun. Why do you even have it? It's not like you ever use it. Do you even know if it works?" But wait. He wasn't going to get shit for leaving his gun behind. Hell, he wasn't going to get shit for anything anymore. He didn't have a chance against one full frown wolf while unarmed, never mind a whole damn pack He wondered what he would miss the most. Her harpy voice when she nagged him, which was most of the time, or the way her eyes softened when she didn't think he was looking.

The wolves were only ten feet away now. He should get up, make himself look larger, face them like a man. He sat where he was with freshly tilled soil stuck to the seat of his pants, hands and feet covered, too terrified to move. "I love you Patricia," he whispered. "I'm sorry I left you."

Hot tears splashed down his cheeks. Terror clamped its icy fingers around the heart that tried frantically to keep beating, and squeezed. The wolves were so close he could see their yellow eyes, and the bright orange eyes of the female. At the last possible second they veered to pass through the space between man and beast.

Relief didn't last a moment before the man grabbed his chest, and buckled over. Fifteen minutes later he woke to his wife's harpy voice; it was the most beautiful thing he'd ever heard. "Wake up you lazy lout. What's the idea of taking a nap in the middle of the day? The mule could have run off." Not that it would have got far with that plow dragging behind.

The farmer stared into the sky as a shadow passed over the sun, and shivered. He sat up, wrapped his arms around his wife who was kneeling beside him, and bawled his eyes out.

A few miles northwest of the farmer's field the wolf pack came to a skidding halt. A huge shaggy black wolf blocked their path, its paws the size of basketballs, and its teeth bared. Its shaggy fur gave it an unkempt, feral appearance, and its dark eyes glittered viciously. The white female staggered, shimmered, and shifted into its human form. As if by mutual agreement the males followed suit.

Twenty-Three

Come to me my children. The Seeker called to every vampire within migrating distance. The ground roiled as if there was a great earth quake as the vampires strained to escape their daytime prisons. As soon as the sun set they would rise and continue the journey many had begun the night before. En masse they followed an instinct to obey they could resist no more than they could resist their need for blood. *Bring her to me.*

Twenty-Four

Luke glared at the lobo that worked for Jade. Okay with Jade if you wanted to get technical, considering he headed up the Mexican division of O'Connor Search and Rescue, but Luke wasn't in the mood to be technical. The mere thought of this lobo and his Jade doing anything with this lobo made him crazy. Jade was his. He was Lycan, and Lycans did not share—especially with a lobo. Lycans and lobos didn't mix well. Lycan were humans that shifted to wolves while lobos were wolves born with the ability to shift into human form. One could probably argue they were the same—wolf and human—but Luke wasn't about to argue that point either.

"What do you mean you won't take us?" Luke's voice was a low threatening growl in the back of his throat. He was Alpha and did not take kindly to refusal of any kind, and especially not from a lobo.

"You heard me lycan. I am *not* taking you to that farmhouse."

They were facing off outside the house that was both the office of O'Connor S&R and Matthew's home. Although he was no longer in wolf form the hair on the back of his neck still bristled. He'd been feeling antsy for days, and it wasn't getting any better. Something big was going down. He could feel it in the air. Matthew trusted his instincts; instincts that were well honed after years of hunting with Jade. When he stepped off the porch to start his rounds and saw the Lycans running across the yard he thought they were the cause of his unease, only now he wasn't so sure. That didn't mean he wanted those two unmated males anywhere near his female. He might be lobo but that didn't mean he was stupid, regardless of what the Lycans thought.

The door behind him opened and Theresa stepped onto the porch, her hand hovering protectively over the slight swell in her abdomen. Matthew sucked his breath in sharply, tasting the unique scent of wildflowers that was hers, and the lust that rolled off the larger of the unmated males. He growled a warning, baring his teeth. Theresa stepped closer and placed a hand on his forearm, her smile secretive and meant for him alone. *Relax wolf. He is only a boy. You have nothing to worry about.*

Matthew's body relaxed beneath her soothing touch, but he did not relax his posture.

Jade's daughter, there was no mistaking for any other, except for the length of her hair and her diminutive size they could be twins, pushed aside her two burly brothers who were trying their best to block her from view, and snarled at them when they tried to restrain her. "Shove the testosterone boys before this becomes a useless free for all." She staggered slightly as if her own slight weight was too much for her legs to carry, and faced him.

Matthew bit back a smirk, no sense inciting the males when he was out numbered, besides Theresa was present and he wasn't about to risk her or their young.

"You too Matthew." She was so sick of their stupid petty prejudices and distrust. She got enough of that when they visited Willow Bend. Don't get her wrong, she loved the place, especially Mrs Gray and the Inner Sanctum, but the Lycans didn't trust her or her mother any more than her father and brothers trusted Matthew, just because they were a little different. She was surprised they accepted Quinn and Gheorgès considering who their mother was, but Dad had been their Alpha, had led them to safety all those years ago, and they accepted the boys for that—and they looked like him. Still, she had listened to enough garbage today, and Mom needed them whether she would admit it or not.

Ignoring the males Emerald smiled at Theresa, her face lighting up, and her eyes swirling with power. "Hi," she said in a gentle tone that held no detectable compulsion, and Matthew relaxed more. "You must be Theresa. We spoke on the phone several times."

"And there is no mistaking you. You look like your mother." Theresa stepped forward after first giving Matthew's forearm another gentle squeeze, and put her arm around Emerald's shoulders in a motherly fashion. "What is wrong with you men," she reprimanded. "Can't you see this poor girl is falling down on her feet?" Her voice was gentle but firm and Emerald liked her immediately. "I am pleased to finally meet you. Jade has spoken of all of you so often I feel like I know you already."

As Theresa steered Emerald toward the steps she glanced over at Luke. "By the way you look good without the beard Luke. Makes me wonder what you usually look like."

Matthew growled, and Luke looked distinctly uncomfortable. There was only one reason this female would mention his beard, Jade had talked to her. He rubbed the short dark stubble that shadowed his chin and hoped it would grow in soon. Gheorgès guffawed in the background, and Quinn looked anywhere than at their father. Luke bared his teeth at Gheorgès which only made him grin, and look unrepentant.

Maybe it's time to knock Gheorgès up the side of the head, Luke thought, *teach him who's Alpha around here.* He settled for a low warning growl, and this time Gheorgès had the good sense to look, if not completely remorseful, at least a little discomfited, and his grin disappeared.

Emerald and Theresa exchanged glances. "Males," they said in unison.

A shadow passed over the sun, and Emerald had to force herself to stay where she was. Never before had she felt such a compulsion to take wing and fly. She needed to travel north, and she could only assume it was because her mother needed her. It wouldn't do to take flight and go, if she left the males alone she couldn't be sure they wouldn't come to blows. "Matthew." She wanted to compel the male to take them to the farmhouse but he was her mother's trusted friend, and she couldn't do that to him. She had to trust that he would do what he needed to do of his own free will. "What my father meant to say." She flicked her eyes at her father when she sensed him move behind her, and he stilled, but his voice rang in her head.

Do not apologize to this lobo.

Not once in her seventeen years had Emerald spoken back to or disobeyed her father but something was controlling her that she couldn't fight, and so she said. "Would you *please* take us to the old farmhouse? We were on our way when my mother requested we come here first."

Luke growled, but didn't say a word. He wasn't angry at his daughter for apologizing for him as much as he was angry at himself for letting his personal prejudice dictate his behaviour. He was used to dealing with people, and the lobo should be no different than anyone else. What kind of leader couldn't deal?

Gheorgès was staring daggers in the back of her head, and Quinn was picturing Theresa sitting on a stool, her expression wistful, her hands covering her abdomen, sheltering the child nestled there. She wasn't surprised, Gheorgès was a warrior, and Quinn was an artist at heart. He could turn a bloody battlefield into a piece of art.

Matthew's thunderous expression softened, but he looked uncomfortable. "I cannot go to the farmhouse." His eyes shifted to Theresa's abdomen and back to Emerald. "I cannot leave my mate alone. You don't understand."

He was worried for Jade, but he was terrified to leave his wife alone. For the past few nights he could sense the restlessness in the vampires, and last night he felt them getting closer. There was no violation of the law, no attacks on humans, nothing to betray their presence, but that didn't mean they were not here. Besides, Theresa was pregnant. He could not leave her alone.

Emerald fought the need to leave. Her form wanted to shift, needed to shift, she could feel feathers poking beneath her skin. "I do understand. You are worried for Theresa and you young, as it should be. But we need to get to Jade. At least tell us why she would send us here."

Theresa locked eyes with Matthew. "You must go Matthew," she said. "You owe it to Jade."

"Fine." Matthew didn't sound like it was fine. If anything he sounded like he wanted to mangle something.

Theresa smiled at her husband, and patted his arm as she led Emerald across the porch. "That's better. Now everyone come inside. I have lunch all ready and Emerald is not the only one who needs to eat."

Twenty-Five

Jade and Alicia sat at the small round wooden table that Alicia had so lovingly polished by hand. Alicia filled two tin cups with well water from the bucket on the counter, set them on the table, and then sat across from Jade. "I'd make tea but all I have is water. I haven't been to town to get anything yet."

Scattered images of a dark alley, head bent over a stranger man, fangs elongated as hunger clawed at her insides haunted her. Did she really sink her fangs...even now she had trouble believing she had fangs...vampire. She had become the vilest of creatures. A monster, destined to survive from the innocence blood of others, their life's essence. But she didn't do it. She did not drink. She was stronger than that. She had sent the man away. She was not a monster. But she was a monster, wasn't she? She had fed from Kamenwati, drank from the vein that ran from his heart. When the power of his blood hit the back of her throat she'd felt more alive than she had in years. Strong...powerful...alive! She wanted to take every drop while she rode him like a bronco.

"Alicia, are you alright?" Jade reached across the table and placed her steady hand over Alicia's which was shaking so badly the water in her cup was splashing over the rim.

Alicia jumped and blinked at Jade as if only just realizing she wasn't alone. "Yeah...um..." She swallowed, and cleared her throat. 'I'm fine."

"You sure?" Jade tilted her head and watched her daughter with a critical eye.

Alicia patted her head. "What's the matter? Is my hair sticking straight up? Or maybe my fangs are showing just a tad too much," she added sardonically. She put her hand to her mouth and checked the tips of her teeth. "I know they're here," she mumbled with her finger in her mouth, moving her finger back and forth frantically, and hysteria making her voice rise. "They are right here." She caught her finger on the tip of one, and pulled back to stare at the tiny bubble of blood. Hunger was the demon that controlled her as fangs exploded. She stuck the finger in her mouth and sucked.

Minutes passed, or hours, or maybe it was only a moment. Alicia pulled her finger from her mouth and stared at it horrified by what had just happened. God, even her own blood was a trigger. The eyes she flickered toward Jade reflected her panic. Alicia swallowed once, twice, three times before she could force the dreaded question past the lump in her throat. "Will you destroy me like you destroyed the monster that killed my mama and papa?"

Jade lifted the tin cup to her lips and took a sip, not once losing eye contact. The water was warm, which wasn't surprising, but it was clear and refreshing. Chickens squawked in the yard, and Jade couldn't miss the odour of burning feathers. She hoped the mage knew what he was doing because she would rather eat raw meat than meat that was overcooked. Maybe she was spoiled. Okay, she had to admit that she *was* spoiled. There were people in her life that enjoyed cooking for her, and because she loved to eat and couldn't cook boiling water, she was more than willing to let them do so.

Across the table from her Alicia looked like a lost soul, but she had a determined look in those dark eyes, a resolve to do whatever was necessary. "Do you remember the story the Children of Ra?" Jade asked.

Alicia blinked. Of course she remembered that story. She had been obsessed with the Sun God and his followers her entire life. She lived to prove the stories were true, that there really was a group of men that had become gods and followed Ra to live beyond the heavens. One of the reasons she wanted on that Egyptian dig, was so she could find evidence of their existence. "That was my favourite story. The reason I became an archaeologist, so I could dig up truth of ancient civilizations, and prove the existence of the Children of Ra. Why do you ask?"

"Priests chosen by Ra to gain immortality, and the powers of a god." Jade reached across the table and clasped Alicia's hands. Their eyes locked, and Jade's swirled with power. "It will take too long to tell the story. It is easier to show you."

The room grew hazy and a movie began to play in Alicia's head. Her brows furrowed when she realized the men looked like her father—without fangs.

Two men of identical dark looks and build entered the sacred chambers draped in white robes, and nothing else. Theron watched his brother beneath hooded eyes like a hawk watching his prey; his expression gave nothing away of his thoughts. Alaric was Ra's favourite and it made his blood boil. *Why did everyone favor Alaric?* Alaric had been their mother's favourite as well. Theron had only joined the priests of the sun god's temple because their mother had made such a fuss when Alaric had become a priest. But what did it get him? "It pleases me you are following your brother into the light," she had said in a tone that spoke volumes for her indifference to whether he became a priest or a stable boy. *Following his brother.* Theron nearly sneered at the memory, but caught himself just in time.

"Is something on your mind, brother?"

Alaric's solicitous voice grated on Theron, but he forced a small smile on his handsome face, and held his brother's eyes. "I was wondering why we have been summoned?"

"It is not our place to question our God."

Theron allowed his eyes to dip, more so Alaric would not be witness to the hatred that burned in his soul than in repentance. "Forgive me brother." Theron forced a hint of shame into his voice, and mentally rolled his eyes at his brother's gullibility. *Does the fool really think I care what he or anyone else expects of me?*

"There is no shame in curiosity." Alaric quickly said. He hated making his brother feel bad. His mother did enough of that. Since they were small boys Alaric made it his mission to try to make up for the hurts inflicted on his twin by their mother's cruel neglect. He could not fathom the reason for her indifference towards Theron. They were twins, of the same build, of the same features, of the same voice. There were no differences, and yet their mother was cruelly callous in her treatment of Theron.

There was an explosion of light and Ra appeared before them, a shimmering image of a man. They watched silently as the image solidified, and became corporal. Ra stepped forward holding a golden chalice with the fiery sun emblazoned on the side. The twins bowed before their God and kept their eyes respectfully lowered.

"Raise thy eyes." Ra's voice boomed in the large chamber; echoing off the stone walls like thunder over a mountain.

Four identical black eyes lifted to land on Ra's glimmering form. "I offer a gift."

Theron fumed inwardly when Ra offered the chalice first to his brother, although it did not surprise him, only confirmed what he already knew—Alaric was his favourite. With no outward signs of emotion he accepted the chalice gracefully when offered.

"You are the chosen." Ra's voice thundered around them, over them, through them. "My children. With this offering I bestow strength, wisdom, the power of the universe, and eternal life to you and all that come after you."

Agony struck with the viciousness of a she-bear defending her cubs. The twins doubled over clutching their abdomens. They walked through an eternity of flames as their human bodies were burned away, leaving behind a vessel capable of containing the powers of the universe.

Hours, days, or maybe only moments passed, there was no way to be sure. Time stood still while the brothers fought for survival. When it was finally over, they were no longer the young men who stepped into the sacred chamber. They stood taller, more powerful, the hunger in their bellies reflected in the dark orbs of their eyes.

Alaric and Theron stood and faced Ra, their lips parting to reveal long, sharp fangs. And so the Magi were born.

Alicia gasped, and pulled her hands away to end the vision. Her tongue toyed with the tips of her own fangs, and the hunger eating at her insides reflected that she felt in the vision. She swallowed convulsively several times, and took a deep breath. *How could this be? How could Ra create a race of monsters?* "What happened?" she finally whispered.

Jade reached out to scan their surroundings. Some of the chickens had settled back in their roosts, while others were once again scratching at the barren earth. The mage was in the orchard searching for edible fruit, and the godson had not yet returned. She reached further and found Luke and her triplets with Matthew. They weren't more than a couple hours away.

I love you. She sent the message across the miles, and quickly closed her mind. She could feel Luke there, he was always there, hovering, a part of her as she was a part of him, but she could not allow their connection at this time. It was not safe, not when the enemy hovered so near. Jade sighed inaudibly. If she had her way she would lock her entire family up where they would be safe, but she was *Moarté* and they were Lycan, and neither species were ever truly safe. And now there were Magi to contend with, and their dark sides. The only way for Alicia to face her nature, and her future, was to first know the past. She had been heading in that direction from early in life, and now it was up to Jade to help her get there.

"Theron was not satisfied with what he had been given. He was weak, and unable to control his impulses."

Lies. Do not listen to the Moarté. She spouts lies. Alicia ignored the voice in her head that was growing stronger, and concentrated on what her mother was saying.

"...he wanted more power. He wanted to be a god. Like many cultures he believed you gained the strength of your enemy by consuming a part of them. He was obsessed with the need for power. He kept his desires well hidden, a priest by day...a beast by night." Jade reached her palms out and waited until Alicia placed her own palms on top.

Theron watched the girl down by the river while she beat the clothing against a flat rock with another in an attempt to clean them. Her slim body bent over made an inviting offer. He wanted her. He had for months, even before the change, and now the need to take her, all of

362

her, was excruciating. He wanted to be in her while he took her blood into himself. His cock stirred, stiffened, pushed at its restrictions as it sought the source of its distress.

Theron approached the girl on silent steps. When he was almost upon her something gave away his presence away, and she jumped covering her rapidly beating heart with one delicate hand. When she realized it was only a priest, her pink lips turned up in a relieved smile. "You near gave me a heart attack," she said in a soft voice. "You should not sneak up on a person like that."

Theron took another step closer to the trusting girl. He loved being a priest. Everyone went out of their way to do a priests' bidding, after all he was their voice to the gods.

When Theron was close enough to smell the hot spice of her blood, he smiled, revealing his fangs for the first time. Fear flashed in the girls blue eyes, and her heart began to pump that delicious blood faster. "Offer yourself to me, child." Theron's voice was both evil and seduction at the same time. The girl wanted to scream. She wanted to run. Theron read her thoughts as easily as if they were his own, but he held her in his steady gaze.

"Offer yourself," he demanded. A wicked smile played over his lips as the female slipped her shift from her shoulders.

"The rush of human blood was incredible, intoxicating, addicting, and like any drug the rush soon wore off leaving Theron needing more." Jade's voice was a whisper in her mind even while Alicia watched Theron with the female he had chosen, unable to tear her hands away to end the vision.

"Theron drained the female and hid the body, but he was a smart man and realized it wouldn't be long before she was missed. He went back to the village and planted a false memory in her father's mind of an argument between them involving a village boy. When his daughter did not return from the river he went to search for her. Finding nothing but the abandoned wash he assumed she ran off with her lover. Theron was more careful after that. He moved to a nearby village to start a new Temple of the Sun to worship Ra, always careful to shield his thoughts lest Ra or another of his chosen read his mind and discovered his secret."

"Theron used his newly developed powers to convince the villagers to send their young daughters to be sequestered at the Temple where they would devote their lives to Ra. It was a perfect arrangement. The villagers willingly turned over their females, and Theron had an unending supply of victims to feed both his carnal appetite, and that for blood, but he soon realized that human blood was not powerful enough to sustain him for long, and he wanted more."

Jade paused to take a sip of the tepid water. "In the meantime Ra's magi grew in number as he offered his *gift* to those he deemed worthy. His only mistake had been to offer the *gift* to Alaric's brother. He could sense the evil laying dormant and festering in that human's soul, but he knew his favourite would not accept the gift otherwise. When it came to the dark one 'out of sight out of mind' was how Ra looked at it. As long as he didn't have to see the man he didn't care what he did. Ra should have been more careful. While his priests were sleeping peacefully one night Theron snuck into the Temple and stole the chalice from under their noses. The chalice held the essence of life, not only the way of converting more of his kind but also the way to destroy Ra's children. By withholding the contents of the chalice he would force them to become like him and drink human blood. Theron knew he had to work quickly before the priests woke with the dawn and discovered their loss. Theron hurried back to his temple intending to force his novices to drink thinking that the power enhanced blood would be more fulfilling."

Theron unlocked the massive wooden door and entered his temple. *His temple.* The entrance was a barren six by six square where he could control who was allowed to enter his domain. As in the other Temples of the Sun only the priests and the chosen females ever set foot past the small induction chamber. The villagers didn't have to know that he was the only priest and that once the novices entered the temple they left their lives behind—literally. If anyone made it past the first chamber they would enter a huge empty chamber with symbols of the God Ra embellishing the walls, ceilings, and floor. What they couldn't see was the secret door beneath the sun that led to the real place of worship.

Theron stepped near the image of the sun that adorned the center of the floor, and shuddered at the revulsion that raced through him. The symbols of Ra, although abhorrent to him were a necessary evil should anyone make it past the first room. The sun began to rise and Theron stepped onto the dark stain covered platform that rose beneath it. The platform descended to the darkness below and he listened for the frightened whimpers of his chosen. It was music to his ears, and an adrenaline rush to his soul. The platform stopped. It was dark, but Theron did not need any artificial light to see. He surveyed his place of worship, and his dark eyes glittered with anticipation.

He stood in a large circular chamber surrounded by several small doors with small slits that he opened to reveal the occupants. Behind each heavy door was a small four by four chamber with cold, damp stone walls. These were where his chosen rested while they waited their turn.

The center of the room, the spot directly beneath the painting of the sun on the main floor, was stained dark with blood and other bodily fluids. This was his domain where he had discovered a new high—fear. The scent of their fear strengthened him and fear-enhanced blood was a powerful aphrodisiac. It was to this exact spot he brought the novices of the temple and taught them what their devotion meant to him. This was where he took their strength for his own.

There were four metal rods hammered into the stone floor with a length of chain fastened to each hook. These he used to immobilize the novices. Theron had discovered that if he controlled them it held their fear at bay, and he thrived on the fear he could instil in them.

The vision flashed from the center of the chamber to the interior of one of the darkened cells, and the image of Theron turned into a young female.

Sangria shoved at the heavy wooden door but it didn't budge. Her fingers were torn and bloody by the time she finished systematically searching every inch of the walls that she could reach. Nothing. The cell was empty, and silent now except for her own shallow breathing, the whisper of her footsteps, and the scratching of her nails along the stone surface. She couldn't hear his sisters breathing or their fearful whimpers, which was both terrifying and a relief.

Had it only been two days since her father brought her to the temple? It seemed like a thousand years since she had begged him to take her back home with him, and he had refused her pleas. Her mother was dead, and her father did not like the way the village boys watched her since she began to fill out like a woman should. She understood his reasoning, he believed he was doing what was best for her, but the moment she set foot on the stone steps leading to the temple door she could feel bugs crawling over her skin, and a shadow passed over her soul.

Her father told her she was being childish, kissed her goodbye, and turned her over to the priest Theron. Her father loved her, but he did not understand the feelings she sometimes got, and he believed the priests were the only ones who would be able to help her.

Sangria wasn't so sure, but she loved her father and did not want to cause him any more concern than she already had. She had trembled as she preceded the priest into the larger chamber, but she refused to give in to the impulse to turn and run. *The next time she would obey her impulses.* The inner chamber while decorated as other sun temples, *felt* wrong.

The heavy door to the outer chamber closed behind them with an audible click, and Sangria felt as if someone had cut off her air supply. The priest placed his hand on her back and pushed her forward. She stumbled, and nearly fell, but caught herself just as the center of the floor where the sun was blazing began to move. Sangria stumbled backward but Theron grabbed her roughly by the arms and dragged her onto a platform covered with dark stains that stopped in front of them.

The moment she touched the platform with her bare feet she gasped and nearly doubled over. The image that came to her was so strong there was no escaping it. It was a girl from their village who had been Sangria's friend up until she entered the temple a couple of months ago. She was laying spread eagle on the platform, held immobilized by heavy chains while a male ravaged her. Sangria watched helpless as he sank his fangs into her neck. It seemed like hours had passed before her body quit struggling, and her screams grew silent, then the man lifted his head and looked right at Sangria.

Theron.

Theron had dragged Sangria from the platform and thrown her into this barren cell. How long ago was that? It must have been hours ago. Although there was no light in this hellhole she could sense the rising of the sun on the surface. Sangria clawed frantically at the wooden door desperate to be gone before that monster came back for her.

Help me, she pleaded silently. *If anyone is out there please help me.*

Almost as if someone had heard her anxious pleas the cell door was flung open, and Sangria staggered into the main chamber, stopping short when she saw the priest standing in the center of that cursed platform, surrounded by images of the dead, and holding a shimmering golden chalice.

"My child." Theron spoke in a quiet, soothing voice that belied the monster she knew him to be. "You look distressed. Are your accommodations not to your liking?"

The priest was acting as if he were truly a disciple of Ra, and she were a true novice to the temple. Sangria blinked against the light coming from the golden chalice, so bright in the dark chamber that it nearly hurt her eyes, and watched the priest warily. "Where are my sisters?" she demanded.

Theron's eyes narrowed, and he frowned at her. "Do you dare to question me?"

Sangria's head shook rapidly, and she lowered her gaze submissively while keeping a wary eye on her captor. She had to figure a way out of here before she ended up like her friend. "Forgive me," she whispered. "I have no wish to offend. I was merely curious as to the whereabouts of my sister novices."

Theron waved his hand and several cell doors flew open. Sangria watched as the occupants of the cells walked with jerky movements to the open doorways to stand and stare at Theron with lifeless eyes.

"As you can see your sisters are all accounted for."

Not exactly you monster. Her childhood friend was not present among the living, rather she was hovering on the edge of the sacrificial platform a mere spectre of her former self.

As Sangria watched with narrowed eyes, Theron beckoned each of the females to him. They approached on jerky, unstable gaits like puppets with no will of their own.

Stop! The word sprang to mind but Sangria could not push it past a throat blocked by some unseen hand. One by one her sisters accepted the golden chalice from the priest, and drank. When it was Sangria's turn she found the will to turn her head, but Theron's hand snaked out and wrenched it back so he could pour the golden liquid down her throat. Sangria was surprised by the coolness of the liquid that came from the glowing chalice. It was cool and sweet as it trickled down her throat but the moment it hit her stomach it started to burn. Sangria clutched her abdomen and keeled over in agony as the screams of her sisters rent the air.

Even as the agony that ripped through Sangria and her sisters ripped through Alicia the vision changed and they were once again in Ra's temple, and the priests were rising with the dawn.

The priests entered the sacred chamber to offer their morning devotions to Ra, and froze in shocked disbelief. The stone altar was empty. The golden chalice was gone. The chamber was completely empty except for the altar so it was easy to see that the chalice had not simply fallen.

Their first thought was they had somehow offended Ra and the god had taken their source of life away. Hunger gnawed at their bellies making it hard to think, and images of fangs sinking deep into human throats as they drank their fill haunted their thoughts. They had no way of knowing that Theron had figured out how to send his own desires into their minds, making them think things they wouldn't normally consider. The images coupled with their desire to survive proved too powerful for some of the magi who attempted to leave the temple in search of prey.

Alaric stepped between the magi and door to the temple, and tried to reason with them. "Ra did not do this," he insisted. "This is the work of another." He did not tell them that he could smell his twin all over the room, and that Theron had not set foot in the temple for months. "I can return the chalice to its rightful place," he reasoned.

The group nearest to him pushed him aside, and the starvation that rolled off them, and glittered in their eyes giving them an inhuman appearance took Alaric aback. *How was it possible they were so hungry? He also felt the need to feed but it did not dominate him.*

"You can get nothing back," they threw at him. "Ra has abandoned us. We will not just sit here and die."

Alaric pulled himself to his greatest height, and puffed out his chest much like a bird trying to show he was bigger and stronger than he really was. "You will not leave this temple." He could read their thoughts, and knew they were intent on feeding off the humans. He would not allow this. He could not allow this. They were not animals without thought or reason. Ra had given them a gift, and they would have to learn to live with it.

Alaric willed the door to shut. The magi turned on him and snarled. Alaric faced the row of fangs in front of him and wondered if he had the strength to keep them in check. *Where is Ra? I could use his help right about now.*

"Open this door and move out of our way," they demanded.

"Give me a chance to prove that Ra did not take the chalice," he almost pleaded. "I know you are hungry. I am hungry too, but we cannot give in to our baser needs and simple feed on the villages. Think about it. They will hunt us down and destroy us like the animals we have become."

Several magi had taken position at his back, and Alaric hoped they were there to back him, not attack him. He was relieved when one of them took position beside him.

"Alaric is right," he said. "If we go out into the village and feed they will destroy us. I know you want to. I want to. I can picture it in my head as clearly as if I had done it a hundred times, but that does not make it right."

"Ha," spat a mage. "We are much more powerful than the humans. They cannot harm us."

"You are being foolish my brother," another mage said. "Give Alaric the chance to bring the chalice back."

There was a blast of light and the mage thrown back as the door to the temple blew open.

The visions were jumping around so much now that Alicia had the beginnings of a headache, but still she clasped Jade's hands, afraid she would miss something important.

Poison! Sangria could not believe the priest had poisoned them all, even as she clutched her stomach in a futile attempt to squelch the inferno growing there as the poison ate away her insides. It seemed like hours had passed in agony before the screams of her sisters died away to whimpers, and then silence as they exhaled their last breaths. Sangria was dying too. She knew it as well as she knew her own name. She could sense the priest moving amongst the bodies of her sisters but did not have the strength to open her eyes to track his whereabouts. It didn't really matter anyway. She was dying and he could do nothing more to her.

Theron could not believe it. *Dead. They were all dead.* Angry he grabbed the female nearest him and threw her limp body against the cold stone of the wall. It hit with a satisfying 'splat' and he threw another, and another, but soon that was not satisfying enough. *This was all Ra's fault. Ra had tricked him into destroying his children and he in return would destroy Ra's children. Every breathing one of them.* He was so angry when he stepped onto the platform and willed it to rise that he did not realize that one female still breathed. Already he could feel the magi's hunger and he played on that.

Sangria winced each time a sister's body hit a wall. She tried to judge where in the chamber the priest was, and when it would be her turn. Suddenly he stopped his rampage. Sangria listened to his steps as he grew nearer to her. She bit her tongue to keep from making a sound, and willed herself to stop breathing when his foot came out and kicked her in the ribs, before stepping on the platform and rising to the surface. She sighed with relief when the platform returned empty. Sangria waited for several long minutes after she sensed the priest leaving the temple completely before she dragged her weakened and bruised body across the floor and onto the platform.

"Rise," she whispered but the platform did not move. Sangria could not help herself. She began to sob in desperation, and willed the platform to rise and take her from this hellhole. *Please do not make me die down here.*

The platform began to rise.

The godson was back from wherever he ventured. Jade could feel his power boost her own, and the visions became more intense. Alicia had a death grip on her hands, and although her own shook uncontrollably, Alicia did not release the vision.

The door to the temple blew inward knocking those closest back into the room. Theron stood outlined in the doorway, the morning son surrounding him like a halo. While the mage stared in startled surprise at the intruder, he dragged forward two struggling humans that were bleeding from wounds on their necks. "I brought breakfast," he taunted and tossed the frightened humans into the mob of hungry magi.

The scent of fresh blood was too powerful to ignore. Chaos erupted. Magi fell upon the screaming humans like a pack of wild dogs on a deer carcass ruled by blood lust. Fangs pierced the veins on their necks, arms, and legs. They tore the humans apart in the frenzy before they ever bled out.

Alaric knew there was no way to control the blood-crazed mob, and still he fought to save the humans. At least not all the magi had succumbed to Theron's temptation, and those that remained in control fought alongside Alaric. There were too many now crazed, and those in control were too few.

The battle raged on for hours, soon turning to one of magic. Lightning struck at the temple as the magi attempted to blast each other. The battle escaped the confines of the temple and continued out in the woods. The humans came to see what was causing all the commotion, and those controlled by the blood lust fell upon them.

Ra realized what was happening with his children. He crossed over from his home in the Chimera and took on Theron who had grown very powerful, but not yet as powerful as the god. With a blast of power that nearly destroyed the entire village, Ra threw Theron into the shadows between the Chimera and Earth where he could not take on corporal form. Those magi who had fought to protect the sanctity of his temple and his followers he offered to take with him into the Chimera were he resided. While many of the magi decided to follow Ra into the Chimera there were those who chose to stay on earth and continue the fight against the followers of Theron. Alaric wanted to stay on earth and hunt those who betrayed Ra, to protect the humans from what his brother unleashed. Ra refused him. Alaric and Theron were of the same blood, and the connection could open the portal between the two worlds. Blood called to blood. Although

Theron cannot take corporal form here on earth without the aid of his blood to call him home, he can reach out to those of mage blood and try to manipulate them to his ways. Ra was angry when he took his children and left earth, so angry he cursed those who listened to the betrayer to a life of eternal darkness. His power comes from the sun, and so he cursed them to burn with the burning rays of the sun.

Vampires.

The visions dried up, and the two of them sat in the tiny kitchen. A grackle whistled in a tree outside, and a rooster crowed in reply. The aroma of cooking chicken reached their noses. Alicia looked at Jade. "What am I?" she asked.

Jade's lips curved into a cooked grin, and she winked. "You are who you have always been. Alicia Martinez Wulfson. My daughter."

Twenty-Six

Across an ocean, Megan watched the dark shadow drift across the sky, and started to sob. Her heart feeling like it was suddenly caught in a vice grip, Molly scooped her sobbing daughter, and didn't stop running until they were safe inside the inn with her back leaning against the closed door. It was several long minutes before her heart settled into its regular routine.

Twenty-Seven

The jeep bumped along the dirt road sending dust and rocks flying in its wake. Emerald's knuckles were white on the roll bar, and it had nothing to do with the drive. Caught in a vision shared by her mother and sister, she was not aware of the way her oversized brothers crowded her on the seat, but she was fully aware of the pain and suffering of each of the victims in the vision. She felt their pain as if it were her own. She shared their pain with her sister, and still it was overwhelming.

The vision ended with a snap, much like the film on an old fashion movie reel broke, and Emerald collapsed against her brothers who had shifted her nearly off the seat.

"Hey," Gheorgès complained. "Get off me." He tried to push her forward but she shifted so she was leaning almost completely on him, and barely on Quinn.

"Welcome back baby sister." Quinn ducked when her small fist shot out at his head. "Hey," he pretended to whine. "Dad. She tried to hit me."

Emerald rolled her eyes, and smacked her back heard against Gheorgès, settling against his chest with a satisfied smirk when he gave in and wrapped his arms around her.

"Look who's being a baby," she teased Quinn. "Crying to his daddy cause a girl hit him."

In the front seat, Luke growled low in his throat, and the back seat rumbled with laughter. "See what you have to look forward to," he said with a wink at Matthew. "With kids you get no respect."

Everyone was feeling a whole lot more relaxed after sharing the excellent meal Theresa prepared, and Luke had to admit that he liked the lobo in spite of himself. He should have known he would, Jade was an excellent judge of character and she loved the lobo, acted as if he was a member of her family, and in a way he was.

Luke listened to the banter of his children in the backseat and wondered how they had grown up so fast. One moment he was holding all three in his powerful arms, the next they were fully grown Lycans.

Quinn eyed his sister now settled against their brother's broad chest. Outwardly, she appeared calm and relaxed, but every male in the jeep felt the turmoil inside her. "Seriously sis," he said watching closely for a sign she might try to weasel her way out of an answer. "What did you see?"

Emerald shrugged, and pulled Gheorgès arms tighter around her, uncaring if Gheorgès felt her shaking. She needed the comfort. *What did she see? What exactly were they heading toward?* For the first time since their father had ordered Daniel to return them to Mexican soil, she almost wished they had obeyed their mother and returned home.

The sudden need to reach her mother had her leaning into the front seat. "Can you make this thing go any faster, Matthew."

Matthew gave the jeep a shot of gas and it leapt forward spraying dust and stone in its wake. The jeep bounced over a rise and stopped. Below them lay the farm. The small house and barn was in need of repair, the orchard beside the barn looked like it had once been tended by loving hands, even now the branches were hanging with undersized fruit, but it was easy to see it had long been neglected. There were several chickens. Some were scratching at the bare earth digging up insects for their dinner, while others roosted lazily along an old rail fence.

The yard was otherwise deserted but every one of them in the jeep knew Jade was in that small house. They could feel her presence as easily as they felt the presence of Alicia and the other two men. As easily as they felt their presence, they could also tell there was no immediate danger. The air was hot with a hint of sulfur. Emerald stiffened, and Luke growled a warning low in his throat. Matthew lifted one brow, and Emerald leaned forward to place her small hand on her father's powerful shoulder.

"Be calm father," she counselled.

Luke's head whipped around and his dark eyes locked with his daughter's amber ones. The moment their eyes met, he felt the connection he was missing in his mind.

Do not come rushing in here all macho and stupid my love. The teasing lit of his mate's voice whispering in his mind both calmed him and brought a tightening to his groin. He wanted to reach out to her, demand to know what was going on, but he knew it would be useless to try when Jade locked him out. He had learned to live with it, but that did not mean he liked it. That she could not keep him completely from her, or vice versa, was his only consolation. That tiny connection was the only thing that kept him sane when he thought she might be in danger.

Luke sighed, and while he didn't exactly relax, he did calm down. His gaze searched the lay of the land. There was a buzzing by his ear and he gave the obnoxious mosquito a satisfying swat. The small farmhouse looked vulnerable sitting in the open, but on the other hand, they would be able to see any approach, at least by road. He needed to check the back of the house for windows.

He made to get out of the jeep when his daughter once again stilled him merely by placing her much smaller hand on his shoulder. "Let me dad," she said.

Before he could answer, a small grackle took shape and flew from the back seat toward the farmhouse.

"Damn. I hate it when they do that."

Twenty-Eight

Jade felt the presence of the rest of her family on the road above the farmhouse, and her lips curved into a secretive smile. Her eyes met Alicia's, and she nodded. She watched the way Alicia placed her hand on Kamenwati's arm, and the godson smiled indulgently at her. There was not hiding the way he felt for her daughter, and Jade relaxed. He would not be a problem. It was the mage she was concerned with.

Conall suddenly felt as if every fiber of his being was on high alert. Someone was approaching. He knew the moment the jeep stopped at the top of the hill leading to the farmhouse. He let his senses roam. It was easy to identify the four wolves that occupied the vehicle, but the fifth occupant was more of a challenge. She was hidden to him.

Until she spoke.

The moment his mind heard the female speak his entire body tensed. *Speak,* he urged with his mind. He needed to hear that voice again. Just the sound, as soft as velvet and as strong as steel caused a stir in his blood he had not felt in a very long time. Maybe never. *Say something. Anything*, he pleaded.

Let me dad.

Those three simple words had his pulse racing. His mind's eye searched for the source of the voice, but the jeep sitting atop the hill only held the four wolves.

Where was she?

A grackle whistled from the orchard. There was an answering whistle from behind the house. Conall's head whipped around. *There you are.* His lips curled into a smug grin.

Emerald landed in the sagebrush behind the house and reached out with her senses the way her mother taught her. The power emanating from the farmhouse was both awe inspiring, and a little bit terrifying. It was easy to locate her mother. Her essence was as familiar to her as her own. Emerald could have located her mother anywhere on the planet. The family had an unbreakable connection. Luke's was the strongest because he was her mate. He would follow her into the afterlife and fight to bring her back, such was the connection. One day Emerald hoped to have a love like that; someone who would keep her heart safe.

One day far away. Right now she was young and having way too much fun flirting with the boys back home, and driving her brothers crazy. They were probably the main reason she enjoyed flirting so much because the boys back home were definitely not exciting enough to bother with on their own, but the way Gheorgès, and even Quinn, puffed up like blow fish in an attempt to frighten them off was absolutely hilarious. One day she might get annoyed with their over protectiveness but right now she was young enough to enjoy it.

Emerald could feel her mother's comforting presence like strong arms wrapped around her. Jade knew she was here, and was letting her know it. She could feel the presence others in the room. Alicia was one, although there was something different about her, and two males. The small grackle quaked under the heavy weight of the malevolent air that seemed to be closing in on it. Emerald tried to pinpoint the source of the evil but it was too elusive. The only thing she could tell for sure was that it was not coming from inside the farmhouse.

She was focusing on the farmhouse when her little bird heart began to beat erratically, fear overworking it until she worried it would cease to beat entirely. A grackle whistled a warning from the orchard, and Emerald returned the whistle in acknowledgement.

There you are.

The words startled the small grackle. It shot from the safety of the sagebrush in a flurry of feathers. Emerald was safely back at the jeep before she realized there was no evil intent in the voice she heard, only smug satisfaction.

Idiot. Not only did you not conceal your presence you ran like a scared rabbit. Emerald berated herself while she scanned her immediate surroundings for the presence of danger. The ominous cloud still hung in the air, and seemed to be gathering around the farmhouse, but it didn't look like anyone, or anything, had tracked her back to her family.

Emerald shifted as she landed, and stood in front of the jeep dressed in a snug black tank top and dark blue jeans, her breath coming in short gasps while she tried to still the beating of her heart. She shook her long white blonde hair with its streaks of silver and gold so it settled around her shoulders and down her back. Scooping it back with her hands she began to pleat it into a long braid that would hang to just below her shoulder blades. The familiar motion calmed her even further. Jade had wanted Emerald to cut her hair when she was still a child, but Emerald loved it long and flowing. After many tears on Emerald's part Jade had conceded and left it long.

"There are two small windows, probably bedrooms," she finally said. She finished the brain and snapped her head to the left, sighing with satisfaction when her braid snapped to the right stopping short of slapping her in the face. A flick in the opposite direction, and then over her head, and Emerald faced her father.

Luke watched his daughter in silence, used to her ways. Gheorgès checked the knife tucked in his black motorcycle boot, and Quinn exchanged his button down shirt for a snug fitting t-shirt that showed off his muscles. Matthew stood beside the jeep, his hands on the roll bar, and watched the Wulfson family get ready to do battle. Although he would not admit it to anyone, he envied them their closeness, and hoped one day to have a large family with Theresa. Unease coursed through him at the thought of his mate all alone tonight. He did not know about the others, but he could feel the evil growing in the air around them with each passing moment

Do not worry my love. I've bolt the doors and retreated to the safe room. Theresa's soft voice was a comfort in the back of his mind. He loved her so much. Too much he sometimes thought, not knowing how he would survive without her.

I feel the same way Matthew. Be safe and do not worry about us.

I love you.

Ditto.

Luke finally broke the silence. "Are you expecting trouble daughter?"

Emerald shrugged. "There are two unidentified males in there."

"Males as in non-humans?" Gheorgès growled.

Emerald knelt down to tie a lace that had come undone in her runners. "Definitely non-human."

Quinn stepped forward and put a hand on Em's shoulder encouraging her to rise, and offering silent support. "Are they a threat to Mom or Alicia?" He asked the question that was on everyone's mind.

Emerald rose and faced her brother. Quinn always seemed to know when she felt inadequate and was always ready to lend his support. Only one of the many reasons she loved him so dearly.

"I don't think they are a threat," she said hesitantly. "For some reason I think they are supposed to help. At least I get the feeling they are here for Alicia."

Luke faced the farmhouse anxious to reunite with his mate. He wanted to reach out to her but knew it would not be a good idea. She already knew he was here, and by reaching out he might just blow any advantage they had. "If you are ready," he said. "Let's go."

All five climbed back into the jeep, and Matthew turned into the dirt path to the farmhouse at a much slower pace. When they neared the house the door opened and Jade stepped into the yard. Alicia appeared behind her, but hesitated when she saw them.

Emerald had no such hesitancy. She leapt from the jeep and rushed up the steps. "Hi Mom," she said on the way by. When she reached Alicia she wrapped her arms around her big sister, and wouldn't let go until Alicia relaxed and returned the hug. "I missed you so much Alicia. Why would you run away? Don't you know we all love you? Even Gheorgès was frantic."

Quinn reached his sisters in two strides and clasped Alicia close. Then he held her back to satisfy himself she was unharmed. He could see the changes in her. The pale hollow cheeks, the dark shadows under her eyes, the way she smiled without showing her teeth. He kissed her on the cheek. "Happy Birthday, Sis." He winked at her. "If I were as old as you I might not want to celebrate either."

Gheorgès pulled Alicia into a bear hug the second he got the chance, and glared at Emerald. "She's right you know," he said to Alicia. "We have all been very worried about you."

Tears pooled in Alicia's eyes. She missed her family so much, and was both torn and delighted that they were all here. *What will they see when they look at me?*

We will see our sister, the triplets answered together.

Gheorgès still had Alicia clasped in a bear hug and was swinging her around when a tall man clad in black leathers pants, motorcycle boots, and a black leather vest stepped through the doorway. The only visible weapon was the morning star idling swinging from one huge hand.

"Is that a morning star?" Gheorgès dropped Alicia so fast she stumbled and would have fallen if the huge male had not reached out a hand to steady her.

The man's golden orbs shot daggers at Gheorgès despite the forced smile on his otherwise sombre features. To his right, and slightly behind him stood another male. This one was a few inches shorter than the first. He was also clad in black leathers and motorcycle boots, but this male was definitely armed. There were knives tucked in his boots, and Gheorgès could clearly see the hilt of a sword hanging from his back.

Twenty-Nine

Kamenwati stepped through the door to find Alicia in the arms of another male, and saw red. It didn't matter that the male was her brother he still wanted to blast him into another universe. The only thing stopping him was Alicia. Any blast he let go now would be sure to fry her too. He pasted a smile he didn't feel on his lips, all the while shooting daggers at the couple.

Relax he told himself sternly. *This is her family.*

The male holding Alicia saw him and let go of her so suddenly she stumbled and would have fallen if Kamenwati had not reached out to steady her. He could kill the male for risking injury to his ... *his what*? The thought was staggering. He had to assure his place in her life before it was too late.

What had the male said? Something about the morning star swinging at his side. Kamenwati stilled the weapon. Alicia laughed, and Kamenwati's eyes softened, the red veil of rage dissipating.

"If you hurt my sister you will deal with me."

The deep male grumble drew Kamenwati's attention from Alicia, and he actually smiled. The male was just a boy, albeit a very large, very muscular boy, and that he loved Alicia enough to threaten him only earned him Kamenwati's respect.

Kamenwati felt the waves of love coming off this small group, and he suddenly liked them all. These were the people that helped to shape his Alicia after the death of her parents, and for that he would always be grateful. He could also feel their curiosity towards him and Conall, but they said nothing.

Alicia's small hand on his forearm was gently and cool, maybe a little too cool. She would need feeding soon.

Conall glided silently to his side, and then stood as still as a statue, taking in everything around him without giving away a thing. He had a predatory aura that had Kamenwati worried. Did Conall need to feed? How long could a magi stay on earth without the need for blood?

Kamenwati let his eyes follow the path Conall's took, and spotted the young female he had somehow overlooked earlier. The two older wolves, the taller had a proprietary arm slung casually over the *Moarté's* shoulder, and another young one identical to the male standing with Alicia admiring his morning star had created a wall with their bodies, as they tried to keep her from Conall's view. Smart move if they were detecting Conall's aura.

A blast of heat mingled with hunger hung in the air around Conall, and the males growled with low menace.

Conall. The word clipped. Kamenwati felt the hunger and frustration roll off Conall, but the mage did not change position or expression.

In a fluid motion, the *Moarté* shrugged off the large male's arm, and stepped forward. The male was tall and muscular, without an ounce of fat anywhere. Although he was older, it was easy to see the resemblance between him and the two youngest males. This male raised Alicia as his and Kamenwati owed him a debt of gratitude.

Without the *Moarté* and this male, he would never have found the keeper of his heart.

That the male was torn between protecting his mate and his child was evident. When he took a step toward the *Moarté* she waved him back with a slight movement of her hand, and the next moment she stood in front of Conall.

"Back off mage," she hissed. "She is not for you."

Conall raised an eyebrow, but was smart enough not to piss off the *Moarté*.

"Mom," Alicia and the young female cried simultaneously. The young female pushed her way through the blockade of male bodies; her face pink with embarrassment, and an angry fire glittering in her amber eyes.

Moarté. So that is why he had not detected her immediately. The *Moarté* alone had the ability to travel the universe undetected if they desired to do so. Either way, a *Moarté* this young would be easy to overlook in the presence of an elder *Moarté*.

The female wore form fitting blue jeans and a black top with no sleeves that complemented her pale skin, her hair hung in a long braid, and although she held no visible weapons Kamenwati knew she was ready to do battle by the way she moved. By the way she glared at the towering males around her, but it was easy to see she was no pushover. She was young, but Kamenwati could feel her power. He hoped she knew how to use that power; it could be a matter of life or death.

Alicia rushed forward and grabbed the girl's hand, urging her forward. She glared at the males, the youngest of which managed to look at least a little contrite. It was easy to imagine these two women growing up together, siding with each other against the males. The rush of love that came over Kamenwati had his golden orbs glowing, and heat was emanating from him making his own golden aura more pronounced.

Alicia's dark eyes met his, and the tip of her tongue traced the curve of her upper lip as it moved over her aching fangs. Hunger glittered in her dark eyes, and Kamenwati's groin tightened. When she spoke her voice came out light, and breathless.

"This is my sister, Emerald," she swallowed. "Em, this is Kamenwati. I hope you will be great friends."

Kamenwati smiled revealing even white teeth against his deep tan, and nodded slightly. "Little sister," he acknowledged, hiding a grin at the way she bristled at the word little. He would have given her a proper welcoming hug but he was aware of the suspicious looks he was receiving from the males. If this were not Alicia's family he would whisk her away from here, and be damn the consequences. But they were her family, and he knew how much they meant to her so he would play nice.

Emerald stared up at the tall Egyptian with the golden orbs. My god he was gorgeous, and the power. This is what she felt coming from the farmhouse. What was he? Definitely not human. Thank god he was on Alicia's side. Emerald did not want to go against such power, not even with her mother at her side. She knew her mother was powerful, but she had no illusions that she was invincible.

Alicia turned to the dark haired man beside Kamenwati, and hesitated. It was only a slight hesitation but Emerald noticed, and by the way the males dark eyes glittered dangerously, she knew he noticed it as well. Alicia narrowed her eyes slightly, and the male stared back. Kamenwati stiffened at Alicia's side, and the other man shrugged.

"This is Conall," Alicia finally said. "Conall's a friend of," another slight hesitation and she said "Kamenwati's."

What aren't you saying, wondered Emerald, and then forgot all about it when she saw the way Conall was looking at her. Almost like he was hungry, and she was the main course. *No, wait,* that's how she was looking at him. He was absolutely yummy. Not a boy she flirted with to rile her brothers, this was definitely all man.

Conall managed to smile without revealing the fangs that were trying to punch their way out of his mouth. He had forgotten how easily the blood lust could be aroused while on earth, and her blood sang to him like a love song. He stepped forward on stiff legs, and took her hand in his, and lifted it to his lips. He inhaled, savouring the bouquet of her power-enhanced blood racing through her veins before turning her hand over and placing a kiss in her palm.

Emerald was totally mesmerized by the dark sensual look in Conall's eyes as he slowly lifted her hand to his mouth, and then turned it over to place a kiss in her palm. His lips lingered far longer than was necessary, and the heat from his lips scorched her. Her heart skipped a beat, and then started to pound erratically. She wanted to ignore the warning growls behind her, but couldn't quite block them out. *Not now,* she moaned. She nearly cried in disappointment when he finally released her hand, and took a step back.

"Emerald," he said.

It was only her name but he made it sound erotic with his lilting accent. Emerald had to force her attention back to Alicia and the others.

"The mean looking one," Alicia was saying in a soft teasing voice, "is Gheorgès. He is the eldest of the triplets, and therefore thinks he is in charge."

Gheorgès growled low at Alicia before stepping forward to clasp both Kamenwati's forearms, and bending slightly at the waist. "Kamenwati," he acknowledged before turning to Conall and greeting him in the same way.

Conall couldn't help but notice the way he managed to place himself between him and Emerald. *Probably a very good idea,* the thought. *She is much too tempting, and much too young. He did not need the* Moarté's *warning to tell him that.*

"The quiet one is my brother Quinn. Don't let his demeanour fool you. He is every bit as much a warrior as Gheorgès." When Quinn nodded his acknowledgement, she continued. "My father, Luke Wulfson." Her voice echoed her pride and love.

Luke stepped forward and gave his daughter a quick hug and a kiss on the cheek. "Don't think I'm letting you off the hook for worrying your mother, young lady," he scolded her gently, and winked before acknowledging the introductions.

Alicia paused before Matthew, a slight furrow to her brow. "Matthew," she finally said. "Matthew works with my mother. He runs the Mexican branch of O'Connor Search and Rescue. He is the one who brought my mother's body home so we could bury it."

Matthew was startled until he realized that Jade would have told her daughter who he was. "Kamenwati, Conall," he acknowledged but did not move forward. "Nice to see you again, Alicia. You have grown into a fine woman. Your parents would have been proud."

Alicia winced slightly. "Thank you Matthew."

The black clouds were gathering over the farmhouse, and the air felt cooler. Emerald looked into the sky, and shuddered.

"Don't worry." She jumped at the sound of Conall's voice at her ear. "He can't take form until the sun goes down."

How did he get so close without anyone noticing? Gheorgès glared, and Conall shrugged. He was going to move away. Emerald knew it, as well as she knew she did not want him to, and it had nothing to do with the way he made Gheorgès hackles rise. Unlike the boys back home, she found Conall fascinating. Was it because he was more male than anyone she ever met or the power that rolled off him in waves, or the way her blood raced and her heart started doing the tango when he was near? She didn't know but she wanted to find out.

"Wait," she whispered when he started to walk off.

Conall stopped and turned back, his dark eyes glittering. He wasn't smiling; rather he looked like he was in pain. Suddenly unsure of herself, Emerald wished she had just let him walk away.

When she didn't say anything, he lifted his eyes to watch the dark clouds gathering into the large, menacing form of the betrayer. Conall wanted her to say something, anything. Her voice sang to him like a choir of angels, and he could listen to it forever. This was too dangerous. She was too young to realize what she felt, and he was too dangerous in this state.

"The betrayer cannot take corporeal form until the sun goes down." And when it did she would be in danger. "You should not be here," he suddenly said startling Emerald with the anger in his voice. "Your parents were unwise to allow you near this danger."

White- hot anger rushed through Emerald's veins, and her vision blurred red. She was not a helpless infant, and she would show him dangerous. She raised her hand, a ball of molten energy forming in her palm. Conall grabbed her wrist. His black orbs locked with her amber ones. Gheorgès leapt.

Conall waved his free hand, and Gheorgès landed on his ass. Emerald wanted to laugh at the stunned look on Gheorgès face but she was angry. Too angry. The anger clawed at her insides until she thought she would throw up. Her head was pounding like a battle drum.

Fight it. She knew she had to fight the anger. It wasn't real. It wasn't hers. But the desire to blast that stunned look off Conall's face was almost uncontrollable. *Oh god, what is happening to me?*

Do it. Blast him. The disembodied voice was unnaturally seductive. The words beat into Emerald's mind until she wanted to obey them. She forced herself to look into Conall's dark glittering eyes filled with worry and strength, and tried to tell him not to worry. At the same time, she felt the need to blast him with enough power to knock him into the shadows.

The shadows.

Quick as a flash, Emerald ripped her wrist from Conall's iron grip, spun around, and sent a blast of power into the dark form hovering over them. There was a howl of pain and rage, and the cloud ripped apart. Even as she watched the clouds disassemble, they began moving together again.

How dare he try to use own emotions against her? Emerald's fury turned from Conall, to the shadow, to herself in a heartbeat. Maybe Conall was right and she was only a hindrance to her family.

"You were very brave." Conall's soft lilt did nothing to soothe her temper.

Emerald wouldn't look at Conall. She did not want to see the pity in his ebony eyes. *Weak. That's what I am. Weak and useless. A hindrance to my family and a failure as 'Moarté.' I should have let Daniel take me home.*

"I'm sorry," she said in a shaky voice. "Thank you for stopping me." She didn't wait to hear what he had to say. Emerald stalked over to her mother, her amber eyes troubled. "I'm sorry Mother. I couldn't fight it."

Jade shook her head slightly, and grimaced. She wanted to wrap her arms around her daughter and tell her how strong she was, but that would only embarrass Emerald further, and she would not do that.

"You did fight," she told her in a matter of fact, no nonsense voice. "You did not allow him to control your power."

"I could have hurt him. I could have hurt all of you."

"But you didn't. That is the part you must remember. You did not let Theron control your power through your emotions." Jade took both her daughter's hands in hers, and forced her to look her in the eye. "Remember what it felt like so the next time you can fight it sooner."

"You don't understand Mom. I wanted to kill him. I wanted to hit him with a blast strong enough to send him into the shadows."

Jade tugged at her daughter's hands to make sure she was paying attention. "That was Theron not you. You were angry because you think Conall sees you as a helpless child, and Theron used that anger to his own advantage."

Jade smirked at Emerald's startled look, and gave her head a slight shake. "Do you think for one moment that I do not see the way that male looks at you? Your brothers and father are not the only ones with eyes. Stay away from him Emerald."

Emerald glanced at Conall who was deep in conversation with Kamenwati. Suddenly his dusky gaze met hers and she quickly looked away. "It's because he is mage isn't it?"

"That's not the only reason," was all Jade would say on the subject.

Emerald's amber gaze shifted to the dark gathering clouds and her blood ran cold. If Theron held that much control over her what chance would a newly born magi have? She reached out to Alicia.

Be strong.

Thirty

The ground beneath rumbled and rolled as if a massive earthquake shook the very foundation of the world. Chickens squawked and fluttered into the air. Grackles and small Mexican songbirds took to the skies, only to land outside the perimeter of the farm when the dark clouds gathered ominously close. Insects stilled. Fruit trees in the orchard began to wilt; their leaves falling lifelessly to the ground.

The sun was on the downslide. Dusk was coming.

He was coming.

Hurry my children.

The call travelled on silent wings across the universe to every being with a trace of vampire or mage blood. Conall heard the call as clearly as he heard the seductive tones of the betrayer when he attempted to manipulate the *Moarté*. The betrayer was calling the vampire to him, banding them together. He could feel their movement beneath his feet as they travelled through the bowels of the earth to avoid the killing rays of the sun.

Thirty-One

Be strong.

Alicia shivered. Hunger clawed at her insides, and her head ached from all the noise. She was not strong. Conall was strong. She looked at him differently. He was no longer the monster her father sent for her whose only redeeming feature was his friendship with Kamenwati. Now he was a man fighting an evil that was as much a part of her as it was of him, and he had saved her sister while doing it. For that, Alicia owed him a huge debt.

When the seeker had reached out to try to manipulate Emerald, Alicia was too busy fighting her own desire to sink her fangs into Kamenwati's vein that she could not offer her any aid.

Be strong. If only she could. Right now, she felt as weak as a milk-starved kitten.

Prey. The word rang in her mind and her fangs elongated until she had trouble hiding them behind her lips. The scent of blood was so strong it blocked out everything else. Gone was the sweet fragrance of the morning glory, the tangy scent of pine. The beating of hearts grew so loud she thought she would go insane. If she did not get away, she was going to turn into a monster and attack her own family.

She felt Kamenwati's hand at her back, and the sensations that gentle touch invoked made her knees weak.

You need to feed little one. Hot need rushed through her at the guttural tones.

In a less than subtle move, Kamenwati scooped Alicia into his strong tanned arms and strode purposely toward the farmhouse. "We must prepare." His guttural tones allowed no room for argument.

Alicia hid her face against his broad chest so nobody could see the grin on her face. Never before had anyone dared command her father, and the stunned look on his face made her want to laugh aloud. To his credit, Luke simply nodded, and did not try to stop the Egyptian. Alicia felt giddy and blamed it on hunger for the tall, lean male who held her so close to his heart she could feel its steady beat, and smell the rich powerful blood that beckoned her.

Alicia's fangs punched out past her top lip and scraped gently across the bare skin where his vest had opened slightly. Kamenwati's step faltered. Alicia peeked at him from beneath her long silky lashes, her dark eyes glittering with promise, and something dark and compelling.

Stop that, Kamenwati chided softly in her mind. *Unless you want me to take you right now in front of your family.*

Alicia sighed, and snuggled closer. "You smell good," she said her voice husky. Pushing his vest open further, she nipped at the skin against his beating heart. *Good enough to eat.*

It took every ounce of will power Kamenwati possessed to remember to close the door behind them and throw up the protective chimera around the room before falling to the bed with Alicia sprawled on top of him. When she began to crawl slowly up his long body, slinking like a predator stalking its prey, rubbing her body against his and purring like a kitten, he nearly lost control.

Her tongue flicked in and out. He tasted like dark rich caramel, and her nostrils flared at dark erotic spice of his arousal. Alicia's answering lust was so powerful she started to shake. The erratic beating of his heart was a beacon calling to her. The rich scent of blood and lust filled the air. Alicia's fangs punched out.

Kamenwati kept himself as still as possible while Alicia crawled along his long frame. The gentle friction had his blood boiling and his arousal in a painful state. He wanted to claim her as his own. He needed to mark her so no other male would dare answer her siren's call.

He flipped Alicia on her back and nuzzled her neck while he rubbed his encouraged sex against her. He started a crawl of his own kissing and licking her exposed flesh as he removed her clothing.

Kamenwati could spend days just suckling those taut nipples, enjoying the way she squirmed and moaned beneath him, but they were running out of time. She needed to feed before nightfall. She was already weakening and unless she was at full strength, she would not be able to resist the betrayer's influence.

I will.

"What?" Kamenwati lifted his head to gaze into her dark hunger filled eyes.

Alicia took a couple of deep breaths letting them out slowly in an attempt to still the rapid beating of her heart. "Resist," she finally said. "I know what he wants me to do and I will never turn on my family or you."

She grimaced and struggled to a sitting position. Her shirt hung open and the pink tip of her rigid nipple was playing peek-a-boob with Kamenwati. "You don't have to worry about Conall either. He saved my sister and for that I will honour him."

Kamenwati wanted to take that taut teasing nipple back into his own hungry mouth and push Alicia down beneath him, instead he moved to sit beside her, and leaned against the beautiful hand carved headboard. Like everything else in the farmhouse, you could see the love in every stroke of the carving knife.

Alicia's hair was a mass of curls and tangles, and Kamenwati could not resist reaching out and running his fingers through it. The instant his fingers touched her hair the tangles unfurled leaving behind smooth bouncing curls.

Alicia snuggled against his shoulder. "Where were you when I was growing up," she murmured.

"Watching from Chimera."

Alicia playfully thumped his shoulder. "Why didn't you do something? There were times I thought my mother was going to make me bald when she tried to get the tangles out."

"I like your hair. It's wild and free."

Her fingers worried at the bed cover beneath her, and she tried to think of anything except the spicy aroma of Kamenwati's rich powerful blood.

"You need to feed," he said and turned his head to offer his throat.

Tears pooled in Alicia's eyes when she looked at him. "Is it always going to be like this? How does Conall do it?"

"No." When Alicia cocked one eyebrow, he continued. "It's the change. Your body needs fuel to function properly. In the beginning it is always harder. You need to feed or you will become weak and die, or the betrayer will gain control of you and you will be lost forever. He does not care how he gains control of your power as long as he gains it."

"How does he win if I die?" Alicia thought about ending it all so she could never betray her family with her hunger, but she would never do that if it helped Kamenwati's enemy.

"When you die your power is released into the universe. The betrayer ..."

"Theron."

Kamenwati's golden orbs widened in surprise. Nobody spoke the betrayer's birth name since the day he was sent to the Shadows.

"That's his name isn't it? Theron? My uncle?" Her fingers worrying the bed cover suddenly stilled. "That's how he finds me isn't it? We share a blood bond?"

Kamenwati nodded, and Alicia continued. "He sent the vampire that destroyed my mama and papa before my power was even developed because he wanted it for himself." Her hand shot out and a small clay pot sitting on the dresser suddenly flew across the room. It slammed against the far wall disintegrating into a pile of dust. Alicia's fingers wiggled and the pile of powder began to swirl and twirl, taking on the shape of a funnel and starting to dance faster and faster until they became a small cyclone. With a snap of her fingers, the cyclone stilled, and the pile of debris settled.

"Parlour tricks," she said bitterly. "He killed my parents because I can do parlour tricks."

"You are capable of much more than that." Kamenwati barely lifted his index finger to make a circular motion in the direction of the debris. The particles of reddish brown dust gathered until they took on the shape of the small pot, and then they flew across the room to settle on the dresser.

Excitement sparkled in Alicia's dark orbs. "How did you do that?"

"Manipulate the elements. The pot was clay. Made of earth." *You are so beautiful when your eyes glitter like that.*

Alicia snuggled closer, and Kamenwati inhaled her unique fragrance. *You need to feed,* he encouraged silently.

I don't want to. Alicia sounded like a pouty child, but she mentally put her hand up to stall his reply, and added. *I said I didn't want to not that I wouldn't.* She shifted around until her fangs gently scraped the flesh covering his heart, and she hesitated. Peace enveloped her at the gentle voice in her head that drowned out the malicious urgings of Theron.

I offer what is mine to give. My heart, my soul, my life.

I take into my keeping that which is offered. Your heart, your soul, your life, answered Alicia. *I offer my heart, my soul, and my life in return.*

From this moment forward, you shall be the keeper of my heart, my soul, and my life, they said in unison.

There was a blast of brilliant light, and Alicia felt something inside her shift. It felt almost as if something warm and comforting had settled in her chest.

"Drink," Kamenwati urged.

This time Alicia let her fangs pierce the skin protecting his heart. The first pull was a hit of ecstasy. Power surged through her veins making her stronger, more powerful—alive. How had she not wanted this? With every sip came power and knowledge, ancient knowledge she could only dream about. She saw what was in Kamenwati's mind, and felt what was in his heart.

Alicia had finally come home.

"No!" Theron's molecules scattered across the heavens in fury and frustration. Thunder rumbled. Lightning flashed.

How dare he? She was his. His blood. His key to returning to earth. For centuries he had been stuck in the shadows, a part of everything, and yet nothing at all. Each day he plotted and planned his revenge on Ra, and his pansy assed sibling Alaric. Prince of the Magi, ha, he was nothing but a chess piece in this game between Ra and himself.

He spent eons searching for the power he needed to break free of this prison. He crawled like a worm through innocent minds, warping and corroding until they became mindless vessels whose only desire was to do his bidding. Those he couldn't corrupt he had destroyed, thus releasing their power back into the universe where he could absorb it.

He would have her power. He would not let the bastard offspring of that pious Ra cheat him of that. This was going to be fun. By destroying her, he would destroy the heart of his brother.

Come my children, he commanded. *Destroy her. Destroy them all, and together we will rule the world.*

Thirty-Two

Emerald entered the gloom of the old musty barn, and listened to the whisper of wings as the starlings in the rafters shifted position. There was a rustle of hay and a small brown mouse scampered out of the safety of the prickly hay, and stopped to stare up at Emerald with its beady little eyes. Emerald stared back, her eyes narrowing into slits. The mouse suddenly squeaked, and scampered back into the safety of the deep hay.

Emerald laughed.

"So the mean pussy scared the poor little mouse."

Emerald spun around at the soft lilting voice, her face mottled with embarrassment. Conall was standing nearly hidden by a pile of hay in a darkened corner of the barn sharpening the edge of a lethal looking blade. "How? What?" She stammered, took a deep breath, and said. "What are you talking about," in the haughtiest voice she could muster.

Conall ran his thumb along the well-honed edge, and nodded with satisfaction. He tucked the blade into the sheath on the side of one tall black boot, and pulled out a second blade from the other boot. After eyeing it from different angles, he meticulously began sharpening it.

"You made that poor little mouse think you were a large tabby, a very hungry large tabby, and nearly gave it a heart attack." There was no condemnation in his voice. He was simply stating a fact as if he didn't care one way or the other about her or the mouse.

Emerald walked to the back of the barn slowly, letting her eyes adjust to the gloom. "Does the light hurt your eyes?" she asked. "I mean..."

Conall shrugged. "Sometimes. I am not vampire, Emerald. I do not sizzle in the sun, or drain my prey. I am Magi and therefore not subject to the same laws of nature."

Emerald felt her cheeks burning, and shifted uncomfortably. Why did she have to say something so stupid? She knew he was not vampire. "I'm sorry," she began when Conall stalled her.

"I am Magi." He lifted is head to see her more clearly, his glittering ebony eyes almost caressing her pale face. "I'm not vampire, Emerald, but that does not mean I am not dangerous." He thrust the newly honed blade into the pocket of his boot, and suddenly his fangs punched past his lips distorting is handsome features, and revealing his hunger.

Conall moved like lighting. One moment he was standing in the shadows a few feet away, the next he was leaning close enough to kiss her. "Go back to your family, Emerald," he hissed. He turned on his heel and strode deeper into the shadows.

Thirty-Three

The sun dropped behind the horizon like a stone. The ground beneath their feet trembled slightly. Jade shoved Luke away from her and leapt to the sky, shifting and returning to the earth with her claws extended.

The earth where they were standing just a moment before exploded spewing dirt and rocks like shrapnel. A pale figure burst from the hole, its dark eyes glittered with hunger as it dove toward Luke. Luke shifted to wolf and leapt to meet the attack even as the white owl's talons dug into the back of the vampire's neck. The vampire screamed and twisted sideways missing the owl as it fell to the ground, and barely avoiding the large sharp teeth of the two hundred pound grey wolf.

Behind them, the farmhouse door blew open with a blast and Kamenwati hurled a fireball at a second vampire as it tried to escape the earth. Thunder rumbled, and the earth shook as a large black coach came barrelling from the skies pulled by two enormous black bears. Behind Kamenwati Alicia froze in terror as the creatures that haunted her nightmares drove straight for her. In less than a heartbeat, she shook off the terror to shove Kamenwati out of the way of those massive claws and teeth. She leaped in the opposite direction, turning to throw a blast of energy at the bears even as they tried to avoid hitting the farmhouse. The coach behind them was not so lucky. It caught the edge of the wall, and slats of ebony showered down like arrows piercing the earth. Theron's image hovered above the debris, and slowly took corporeal form.

Alicia stared at her uncle's nearly transparent form in awe and hatred. The power glowed around him like a full body halo. He could easily be the most handsome man she had ever seen if it was not for the sneer on his face, and the pure evil that emanated from him like a living breathing entity. Alicia stared, transfixed by that evil, listening to its seductive voice in her head while Theron tried to manipulate her.

My child, his insipid voice whispered. *Join us. We are your true family. These people are not your family. They lie to you. They only want to exploit your meagre power. I do not. I am your family. We are your family. We have no need of your power. We are already powerful. Come to me my child and I will protect you from harm.*

The voice in her head mesmerized Alicia. The seductive, hypnotic tones travelled through her, urging her forward, and her legs acted as if they were no longer her own. First one step, and then another as her traitorous legs carried her closer to the monster that beckoned her. She was not aware of anyone or anything except the voice in her head.

What was only a moment in time felt like an eternity as Alicia slowly moved toward Theron on legs that refused to obey her. With each step closer she took, the figure grew more substantial until she could no longer see Kamenwati and the others through his form.

Several vampires surrounded Kamenwati who swung his morning star with ease, smashing them bloodied and useless to the ground. His foot shot out behind him and he rolled, jamming his heel with its spiked edge into another vampire's throat. The vampire fell to the ground, clasping its emancipated hands against the jagged edges of its torn throat, and tried to hold its life force in even as it sputtered and gurgled, and seeped into the earth.

A ball of energy hit the ground as Kamenwati rolled out of the way and flipped to his feet. His returning blast missed its target and landed mere inches from Theron's feet.

Stop! Alicia ordered her wayward limbs, pleading silently with herself the way she pleaded with her poor papa so many years ago. *See him for what he is. Do not go to him.*

An energy ball twirled above Kamenwati's palm, increasing in size while he searched for an opportunity to dispatch it toward Theron without risking the chance of hitting Alicia. Two vampires chose that moment to attack from opposite directions. Kamenwati released the energy ball at one. The smell of burning flesh filled the air even as Kamenwati spun around slashing his morning star through the air and knocking the other vampire six feet back. It lay on the ground one arm was twisted awkwardly at its side. The other arm rose slowly, its fingers dancing in the air as it tried to call force the energies of the universe.

A lethal blade flew straight as an arrow into the black heart of the vile creature. Conall stepped forward and his sword flashed, easily separating the creatures head from its body. He spun on his heel and began slashing his way to where Emerald and her brothers were fighting.

An energy blast struck Quinn in the forearm. Pain screamed through his arm and his knife fell uselessly to the ground. In a flash of power, he shifted and leapt. All teeth and claws he landed on the nearest vampire and ripped out its throat. Gheorgès appeared instantly with his sword in his hand and Quinn backed off to allow his brother to finish the decapitation with a graceful swipe of his sword.

Gheorgès turned to see Matthew surrounded by vampires. He only took two steps before a large white owl and an even larger grey wolf entered the fray. There was an angry roar overhead. Two gigantic black bears were bearing down on them. Saliva dripped from their long white fangs, and steam blew from their nostrils. They aimed straight for Emerald and Quinn who had their backs turned and were busy with a half dozen vampires.

Alicia was so close to Theron she could smell his putrid odour. He smelled like death and destruction. He smiled in triumph and his glistening fangs dripped yellow. *That's right my child. Come to me.*

Alicia's blood ran icy hot as memories flashed through her mind. Her childhood spent in fear. Papa and Mama destroyed by vampires at her uncle's command. The nearer she got to Theron the angrier she grew, until she was no longer fighting the movement of her legs. Instead, she went with them, letting their momentum carry her to her target.

She was so close now Theron could reach out and take her. He looked into her white-hot eyes and his blood froze, and his step faltered. He wanted to turn and run. He wanted to open a portal and return to the safety of the Shadows. He took a faltering step toward her.

"That's it you bastard," she taunted in a voice that was deadly quiet. "You wanted me. Come and get met." Pure energy streamed from her eyes, her mouth, even her hair stood on end as the energy poured through the strands before escaping into the atmosphere. Alicia focused that white-hot gaze on her uncle.

Theron screamed.

A ribbon of pure white energy hung in the air between them, binding them together. Theron struggled to free himself from its hold. The blood in his veins began to boil. He had underestimated her power, her control, and it could cost him his life. It was not fair. Once again, his pansy-assed brother was going to win without ever having to lift a finger.

There was a small popping sound, less the noise of a kernel of popping corn busting out of its shell, and just before Theron's corporeal form exploded into millions of molecules blowing in the wind, he heard. *Goodbye, brother.*

"No!" His scream echoed through the universe even as he was cast back into the Shadows.

Alicia's legs felt like jelly, and she collapsed into the comforting arms of oblivion.

In the Chimera, Alaric staggered and dropped to his ass with a thump. Ra settled far more gracefully on the stone floor at his side. The Eye of Ra shimmered and rippled, distorting his view of earth before blinking closed the connection.

"You did well my friend." Ra snuck a sideways glance to assure him that his long-time friend would suffer no long-term effects of expending so much power. He did not like the gray pallor of his skin, or the exhaustion he saw in his eyes.

"He should never have gone after my daughter." Alaric let his exhaustion take over, and closed his eyes. He was unconscious before his head hit the floor.

Ra lifted his friend gently as if he were a newborn babe, and carried him home.

Thirty-Four

The gigantic paws pounded the earth like thunder across the hard surface. It sounded like a train wreck waiting to happen as the beast bore down on Emerald and Quinn. Emerald heard the thunderous footsteps coming straight for them. She felt the beast's hot putrid breath on the nape of her neck and turned to face the ursaline monster, trusting Quinn to keep the vampires from her back.

Everything happened in slow motion. Gheorgès was too far away to help, even as he shifted and leaped to intercept the beast she knew he was not going to make it. Jade and Luke were across the yard fighting a half dozen or so vampire who had failed to beat a hasty retreat at their master's defeat. Kamenwati was lifting Alicia's limp form from the ground.

Oh god. What happened to Alicia? Emerald was so intent on her battle with the vampire that she did not have a clue what was happening around her. She reached out to her sister, and let out a sigh of relief when she detected a strong heartbeat. *Exhaustion.* Alicia would live.

Emerald stared into the fanatical eyes of the beast and was not so sure about her own future. The beast intended to tear her apart limb by limb, and devour the remains. The image in her mind was so strong she could feel the bear's claws raking her body, and its teeth tearing into her unprotected flesh.

With a shudder, she shook off the image, and shot a blast of energy at the bear. It shook the blast off as if it was no more than a housefly buzzing around, and snarled. Saliva dripped from its jowls.

The bear's black eyes locked with hers and she watched helplessly as she shifted into owl form only to be swatted to the ground, and her white feathers fluttered in the wind as her crimson blood seeped into the ground.

To her horror, the bear actually seemed to smirk at her, and the scenario changed. Emerald shifted to her wolf form, and instantly the bear's massive paw shot out and raked its claws down her side. The wound was fatal, and she screamed as crimson rivers ran through her white fur. She lay on her side, panting as death slowly and painfully claimed her.

"No." Emerald shouted in order to shake off the hallucinations. What sort of creature was this that could shift into the form of the bear, and possessed such powers?

The bear blinked, pawed the ground, and leaped for her throat. Before Emerald could react to the sudden change in tactics, she felt herself shoved to the side. She hit the ground rolling, and screamed as the bear's massive jaws closed over Conall's head. The sound of crushing bone drowned out all other sounds of battle.

A huge black wolf pounced through the air and locked its jaws in the back of the bear's neck. The bear roared in fury and released its hold on Conall's head. The bear tossed its head back and forth in a futile attempt to dislodge the wolf's hold. Emerald called to the energy surrounding her intending to blast the creature with enough power to incinerate it, when her mother's calm voice whispered in her head. *No magic. He can absorb and use whatever you throw at him.*

Emerald released the energy back into the atmosphere and grabbed Conall's sword where it lay on the ground beside his limp form. With a strength born of fury and despair, she thrust the sword up to the hilt into the side of the massive black beast. Hot blood spurted covering her arms and her face; it ran like a river as it turned the ground crimson. The beast thrashed and howled. Gheorgès clamped tighter on its neck, grinding his jaws as he tried to chew through the large spinal cord. The bear rose on its hind legs in another attempt to dislodge Gheorgès. Quinn's wolf took advantage of the unprotected underside, and attacked. Emerald slashed at the beast with Conall's sword. After what seemed an eternity the beast fell to the ground, shuddered once, and stilled.

Emerald rushed to where Conall lay in a pool of his own blood. She called forth the energy around her and fused the shattered pieces of his skull, squelching the blood flow. His heartbeat was almost imperceptible.

"Don't die," Emerald sobbed. She held Conall's head on her lap, her tears dripping onto his pale, still face. Anger surged through her. This was all her fault. Once again, she let her enemy mesmerize her, and this time Conall was paying with his life. "Don't you dare die, Conall," she ordered her voice desperate with fear. "I am not going to let you die."

The index finger on her left hand grew into a lethal looking talon, and she sliced her right wrist with it. She shoved the gaping wound into Conall's mouth. "Drink damn you," she ordered.

Relief flooded her when he convulsively swallowed the warm liquid as it trickled down the back of his throat.

His lips clamped over the open wound and he began to suck savagely. Emerald began to feel faint, and then grew frightened when he would not release her wrist, but she would not hurt him to save herself. She had hurt him too much already.

There was a flash of light in the sky, and the clouds parted. "Come home my son," a disembodied voice said.

Conall released his hold on Emerald's wrist. His body shimmered for a moment, and then he disappeared.

Thirty-Five

"I can't believe you let that bloodsucker drink from you." Gheorgès wrapped gauze around the jagged tear on Emerald's wrist, and pulled tight enough to make his sister wince.

"That bloodsucker as you call him saved my life."

"I'm sorry, Em," he said his voice contrite.

Emerald wondered if he was sorry for her wound, or for calling Conall a bloodsucker when he immediately loosened the gauze. She winced again when she saw how rapidly the white material turned crimson. She wished she could heal her own wounds as easily as she did those of others. The look on Gheorgès face had her worried. *Why wouldn't the bleeding stop?* Emerald felt dizzy and weak, and was having a hard time keeping her eyes open and her body in a sitting position.

The last couple of vampires escaped into the underground tunnels, sealing the entrance behind them. "Let them go," Jade said when Luke and Matthew began digging.

The large gray wolf began to shimmer, and Luke stood staring at the spot in the earth where the vampires vanished. Over by the orchard a small grackle whistled. Luke swatted an annoying mosquito. "Damn bloodsuckers," he muttered.

The smaller black timber wolf inclined its head slightly in agreement. Neither was sure if they meant the mosquito or the vampires. Their heads turned toward the sound of Gheorgès' voice.

"That fucking bloodsucker is lucky it's gone or I'd rip its throat out." Gheorgès glanced at his sister's extremely pale face, and dull amber eyes, and cursed again. Her utter lack of response to his cursing worried him more than he let on. She looked like she was going to fall over at any moment, and her heartbeat was slowing, and becoming more erratic. Already she had lost too much blood, and he could not get the wound to stop bleeding no matter how tight he held the gauze.

"Let me." Jade put a gentle hand on her eldest son's shoulder. When Gheorgès reluctantly released his hold on Emerald's wrist blood spurted from the wound once again soaking the gauze. Jade carefully unwound the gauze and placed her palm over the wound. Shimmering white light glowed between her palm and her daughter's wrist, and the edges of her skin knit together stanching the blood loss.

Sleep my baby, she sent the compulsion.

Emerald's long lashes fluttered, and then drifted down to cover her pale amber eyes. Luke scooped his daughter into his arms before she toppled over, and carried her to Matthew's jeep. The black timber wolf trotted behind the house, and Matthew emerged dressed in blue jeans and a black t-shirt. He walked over to the jeep and slid into the driver's side.

Prepare the guest rooms Theresa. Company's coming.

Already done my love, came the instant reply.

Kamenwati listened to the jeep as it kicked up stone and dirt in its haste to leave. *Take care of our daughter,*

Godson. The *Moarté*'s voice was both demanding and trusting.

Yes. Kamenwati sat on the bed beside Alicia, and she snuggled against him in her sleep. *Tell little sister Conall lives thanks to her.* The young one would want to know. She blamed herself for something she had no control over, and Conall would not want her to suffer so.

I will. Jade sent Kamenwati an image of her narrowing her eyes fiercely. *Kamenwati, bring her home soon. We miss her.* The brilliant amber eyes sparkled with mischief. *Welcome to the family.*

Welcome to the family. Kamenwati was gazing at Alicia when her dark eyes opened, and she smiled at him.

"You really don't know what you are getting into," she sighed. Her voice was raspy and she coughed slightly.

"Do you need to drink?"

"I need something," she teased. Alicia wriggled her way up Kamenwati's long body, stopping to torture him when she reached his engorged sex, and smiled seductively. Her dark eyes sparkled with lust, and something mysterious. "I'd settle for a glass of water." At Kamenwati's disappointed expression, she hastily added, "for now."

Kamenwati wanted her to stay exactly where she was. He held his palm up and a tall glass of clear cool water appeared.

Alicia lowered her lashes, and chewed on her lower lip. "I wanted water from our well," she said petulantly. When the glass was replaced with another, she quickly added. "In my own cup."

She laughed when her old tin cup appeared in Kamenwati's palm.

Kamenwati bowed his head, his golden eyes gleaming. "Your majesty." He did a perfect imitation of a lady-in-waiting at a palace. "I hope you find my humble offering to your liking."

Alicia smiled revealing the tips of her fangs. The tip of her tongue peeked past her blood red lips as it traced the outline of her teeth. She grinned wickedly when Kamenwati shifted to ease the tightness in his balls, and wiggled her eyebrows in a bad imitation of *Snidley Whiplash,* and twirled an imaginary moustache. "What exactly are you offering?"

"Me."

"Mmmm." Alicia leaned in and slowly licked the side of his neck. "A tasty offering." She took the pitted tin cup that was wobbling precariously on his palm, and drank the sweet fresh water. "Thank you kind sir," she said.

With a nonchalant wave of her hand, the cup began to drift across the room. Alicia didn't wait for it to settle beside the clay pot on the dresser. She leaned forward and captured Kamenwati's mouth, letting her tongue explore its warm cavern. He tasted hot and spicy, like his blood.

Ignoring the hunger clawing at her insides she took her time exploring his sensuous mouth before nibbling her way past his jaw to his throat.

Kamenwati tensed when her fangs scraped over the vein in his neck, anticipating the sharp stinging pain of her fangs piercing his skin before it turned into the most erotic feeling he could imagine.

Her teeth scraped the edge of the vein, and then moved down until she was nibbling at his collarbone, and lower. He jumped when she nipped the tip of his tender nipple, his clothes having vanished with a mere touch of her hand. Kamenwati chuckled. "You're getting good at that."

"That's not all I'm good at," she returned. Her head disappeared down his lean frame. Her tongue licked at his iron hard abs before dipping and twirling around his belly button. His cock, free of its confining clothing reached for the heat of her inner core, but Alicia slid down and caught the tip between her teeth.

Kamenwati moaned and jerked as she slowly sucked in the entire length of him. When she began to let him out, he wanted to knot his fingers into her long silky tangles, and hold her where she was. Instead, he dug his long fingers into the mattress at his sides, and let her play. Lightning wracked his body. He loved what she was doing to him with her mouth and wanted it to last forever, but his balls tightened, his body tensed and jerked, and he ejaculated into those warm depths like a teenager experiencing sex for the first time.

Alicia lifted her head her eyes were drowsy with lust. "My turn," she whispered huskily. He watched her with lowered lashes as she crawled back up his lean length, and impaled herself on his still swollen cock.

Kamenwati couldn't think of anything more beautiful that Alicia riding him, her head thrown back, her eyes half closed, her lips slightly parted, and her long tresses brushing the sensitive skin of his upper thighs. He was on the verge of another orgasm when her head suddenly lifted and she looked at him with wild eyes, her fangs already elongated. He tilted his head slightly, offering the pulsing vein at his throat. When those sharp fangs pierced the skin and she drew in the first taste of his blood, they both fragmented into a thousand pieces.

Much later, lying exhausted side by side, Kamenwati pulled Alicia closer against his lean frame, and playfully nibbled on her ear. "What is your answer?"

Alicia blinked up at him, her dark eyes slumberous and confused. "Answer?"

"Will you have me?"

"I just did, didn't I?" She sighed, and snuggled closer. He smelled like blood, sex, and something very close to home.

"I hope you want a big wedding," Kamenwati said.

Thirty-Six

Alicia paced the long cavernous chamber in her diaphanous pink gown listening to the sound of her heels clicking the cold stone floor. *What is going on in there?* She sent the question through the air for the hundredth time.

They are still negotiating, came Kamenwati's calm voice.

You mean they are still arguing. Alicia tried to hide it but she was worried about Luke. Alaric was very powerful, and she did not trust him. He might be her biological father but Luke was her dad, and she wanted him to walk her down the aisle, no matter what the stranger who seduced and then deserted her mother said. She did not care if he was the Prince of the Magi. He was nothing to her.

Do not fret, little one. I will allow no harm to come to your father.

Which one? Alicia snapped sarcastically. Kamenwati's warm chuckle was almost as good as a hug right now. She could not believe they insisted she stay in this room all alone while that *man* decided whether her own family could attend her wedding. This was her wedding. Her wishes should be the only ones that count.

The lycan of course, he assured.

Alaric had better not lay a finger on Luke, she warned sending an image of teeth and claws floating through Kamenwati's mind. *He will deal with me if he does.*

Kamenwati sighed. *That is what he hopes.*

Alicia growled, and Kamenwati's warm voice wrapped around her like a loving caress. *I love you.*

In another chamber in the palace, Alaric faced Luke with eyes that glittered angrily. He wanted to blast the usurper into the Shadows with his brother, but Kamenwati and Ra had both assured him that was not the way to win his daughter's affections. God she was beautiful. The spitting image of his beautiful Maria with her dark round eyes, pale face, and black curly tresses that refused to be tamed—like her spirit. He understood why she wanted nothing to do with him, but still it hurt, and he would not allow her indifference to continue.

"Look. This is getting us absolutely nowhere." Luke's spoke calmly although all he wanted to do was rip this bloodsucker's throat out. "Alicia specifically made me promise I would walk her down the aisle, and I agreed. Bottom line, I will not break a promise to my daughter." When Alaric's eyes began to glow, Luke hastily added, "You would not break a promise and you cannot expect me to."

"She is my daughter," Alaric spit out through teeth clamped hard together in an attempt to stay calm.

"You donated the sperm, that's all. A father is someone that nurtures, and protects. Where were you when her and her mother needed you?" Luke rolled his eyes, and shook his head in frustration. "Forget I said that. What is past is past. Today is her wedding day, and I am going to walk her down the aisle whether I do it here or in our realm, it makes no difference to me. Here you get to be a part of her big day and I do not have to break my promise. In our realm I still do no break my promise, but you do not get to be a part of it."

Alaric opened his mouth to argue but Kamenwati spoke first. "Enough," he commanded. "The ceremony takes place here and her family will be in attendance." *It is settled, little one. The ceremony is in the hour.*

Jade helped Emerald zip up her pale green silk gown. It clung to her small breasts and then fell loosely to wrap around her lithe form. Her white blonde hair was piled high in a mass of curls that were already loosening to fall in silken wisps down her back. "You look absolutely beautiful, Emmy," she said. "So grown up you make me realize I will soon lose you too."

Emerald forced a smile to her pale pink lips that did not quite reach her amber eyes. "Thanks, mom," she said in a dull voice. "But I'm not going anywhere any time soon."

She glanced at her mother and realized for the first time that Jade was still wearing her bright yellow t-shirt, and brown cargo pants, but at least her feet were bare; nobody wore shoes in the ceremonial chamber. Her eyes widened slightly, and she said in an almost scandalized voice. "Mom! You cannot go to the wedding like that."

Jade looked down at her bare feet, wriggled her toes, and frowned. "There, I painted my toenails."

Emerald was still laughing when Mrs Gray entered the room Alaric had designated for the females. "What's the joke?"

"Mom's toes," Emerald snickered. "She painted them for the wedding."

Charlotte Gray glanced down at Jade's toes and burst out laughing. She was so glad she had agreed to let Randy and Sue watch The Inner Sanctum for the month so she could be here. Each toenail was painted with a different food. There were pork chops, steaks, chicken, and even some fruits and vegetables. "Looks like someone is hungry," she said with a wink at Emerald.

Charlotte pulled a powder blue gown from its hanger, and shook it out. "Come on, Jade. The sooner we get you into this dress, the sooner we can get this show on the road. First the vows and then you eat." She glanced at the toes and her round face broke into a wide grin. "Do something with those toes."

Jade shrugged and her polish turned a pale blue that matched her gown. "Is that better?" When Emerald and Charlotte nodded in agreement, she continued. "How is Alicia?" she asked. She would have loved to be a fly on the wall during the meeting with the Prince of the Magi, but he had refused permission for anyone to enter their realm, only agreeing to the meeting with Luke when Kamenwati pressured him. Jade and Luke knew how Alicia felt about the mage that sired her, she did not even try to hide her feelings. Alicia wanted to be married at The Inner Sanctum in Willow Bend. She only agreed that the ceremony take place in the Chimera when Kamenwati told her his father could not be a part of the wedding if it took place on earth, but she had insisted her own family be granted permission to enter the Chimera for the occasion.

The wedding was going to be huge. Every mage would attend to witness the bonding between the son of Ra and the daughter of their prince. The only 'outsiders' were Alicia's family, and Charlotte who Alicia had insisted was like her grandmother. Alicia had reluctantly agreed that allow Alaric would perform the ceremony, as was the tradition of the Magi.

Jade was glad Luke had convinced Alaric to permit them in the Chimera for the occasion. Whether Alicia liked it or not she was Magi, and Alaric was a part of her life. She would have to learn to deal with him, and Jade did not want her to regret any decisions she might make right now to keep him away.

A gong sounded, and there was a rap at the door. Jade opened the door, her blood heated up, and her bones began to melt. Luke stood in the doorway dressed immaculately in a dark suit; his dark eyes sparkled with desire as he watched his mate's pale blue gown caress her in all the places he would like to be touching. He swallowed, and bowed offering his arm. "May I have the pleasure of escorting you to the chapel?"

Behind him Gheorgès, looking decidedly uncomfortable in his monkey suit, and Quinn who wore his as comfortably as a second skin were waiting to escort Emerald and Charlotte to the wedding.

Magi of every shape and size filled the chapel, but Emerald knew the moment she entered that *he* was not present. He called to her in his pain, screaming in agony and need, and she could not go to him to ease his burden. She was the cause of his pain, and the reason he had to fight this battle alone.

Kamenwati stood at the altar, his golden skin glowing, wearing a simple loincloth that only enhanced his male beauty. He wore thick golden bracelets on each arm with hieroglyphics depicting the history of Ra. The sun tattoo on his chest was glowing so brilliantly it was the only illumination needed in the vast chamber, and yet every two feet a black sconce on the wall held either a blood red or white candle that flickered merrily causing their shadows to dance on the walls and floor.

Ra stood beside his son resplendent in his own simple loincloth his own wristbands discarded during this sacred of ceremonies. He let his eyes roam over the sea of black clad males and white clad females in the chapel, and then across at the pastel coloured gowns worn by the *Moarté*, her daughter, and their friend. *Moarté*. Angel of Death. Death Dealers. Many titles were given their kind, mostly unwarranted. He scrutinized the young female closely, and liked what he saw. She was young, still a babe by their standards, and a young adult by human ones. She had faced the Ursaline as valiantly as any seasoned warrior, and then graciously gave her own life's essence to save one of his children. He owed her a great debt for saving Conall who was a friend of his son's.

A hush fell over the room, and Alicia entered, resplendent in a blood-red gown that fell to the floor completely hiding her bare feet. Her dark curls tumbled down her back in a cascade of wild tangles. Her dark eyes shone brightly against her pale face, and her lips matched the shade of her gown. The tips of her fangs peeked out when she smiled at the tall dark lycan waiting just inside the entrance. The love and respect she felt for the male was evident in those expressive eyes.

Alaric bristled from his place at the altar. Alicia seemed to sense it, and faced it. Her smile was not quite as bright, and did not quite reach her eyes, but it was a start. She accepted the arm the lycan offered, and together they made their way down the aisle to where Kamenwati his own eyes reflecting his love for the petite female who held his heart in the palm of her hand.

Thirty-Seven

It was dark and cold like a coffin. The smell of earth filled his nostrils, and he could hear the scratching of tiny feet as they tunnelled their way through the rock.

They were coming for him.

They were coming for her.

The taste of sour milk filled his mouth as he fought desperately to get back to her. She had tasted so sweet, so powerful. Her blood was ambrosia, a drug that had a stranglehold on him. He wanted more ... needed more.

He could not let them get to her. She was his, and he would save her.

The Angel of Death was near. He could feel her presence in every breath he struggled to take; her presence was both calming and terrifying.

He did not want to die—not yet—not until he tasted her sweet ambrosia one more time. He had to save her from them.

You will taste her, my son, the voice in his head promised. The sound of that voice was almost more terrifying than dying before he saw her again. She would be safe if he died.

You will drain her. That strangely familiar voice insisted. *You will drain them all.*

Blood Obsession

Prelude

"HOLD him down." Madison sneered at the pasty-faced man struggling with the young vampire *volunteer*. It was so hard to find good help amongst humans. They were such a weak race. They were so stupid they didn't realize they were helping a vampire develop the means to destroy them all. They actually believed he was trying to find a cure for cancer ... to save them. What a joke! Madison might have started out searching for a cure, but his experiments trying to mingle animal DNA with human DNA to create a more powerful being soon led him down the road to Theron, and thereby his own destruction. It was his overwhelming desire to become omnipotent that brought him directly into Theron's path. It was almost too easy to corrupt the good doctor with the promise of immortality, thereby offering him the one thing he didn't have enough of on his own—time to finish his experiments. What the poor doctor hadn't realized was that by giving up his mortality the way he had, he also gave up his soul, and was now nothing more than a puppet with Theron pulling the strings. Once he discovered a way for the vampire race to face the sun Theron would be invincible. Nobody could stop him then.

Not even those blasted Magi.

The young vampire, who had so foolishly volunteered for this experiment, began to whimper even while he allowed the pasty-faced human to bind him to the table. The moment he entered the silo on the deserted farm he'd had second thoughts. He didn't like the looks of the silver shackles on the table, or the stench of death that hung in the air. He had learned the hard way shortly after his world changed just a year ago the effect silver now had on him, but he was willing to put up with just about anything to be who he was before this awful transition took place. He had a life to go back to. A beautiful fiancée and a young son were waiting for him to return from overseas.

The volunteer let out a sigh of relief when the pasty-faced human only bound him with leather straps. The mere idea of touching those silver shackles made him whimper again.

"Stop that mewling. You make me sick." Not only was it hard to find a decent human, it was getting harder and harder to find a decent vampire. What had made him think that this puny little gnat would be strong enough to survive a transfusion of werewolf blood? None of the others had survived, but they drank the blood. Maybe the key was not to drink it, but to administer it as an injection. He would find out soon enough.

Madison refused to believe he would not be able to discover the secret of the wolves' ability to face the sun. He had been researching werewolf DNA for decades, and still was no closer to narrowing it down to a specific gene, but that did not mean he was wrong. It had to be in the blood. There was no other plausible explanation. He just had to figure out how to get that blood to work for them. So he began his experiments. After all, he had plenty of guinea pigs at his disposal, thanks to the deal he made with the Dark Lord, Theron.

"What are you going to do?" The vampire's voice trembled and Madison glared at him.

"I'm going to give you a present," he said sarcastically.

The vampire began to sob, the stench of his fear both intoxicating and sickening to Madison. He ignored the whimpering vampire, and adjusted the bag of blood hanging from the pole beside the bed, checking the clamp to make sure they did not lose a single drop of the precious fluid. A red haze blurred his vision. That idiot minion had drained the werewolf completely dry. He was going to have to *find* another donor after this bag was gone. Then he grinned wickedly. What did it matter to him how many werewolves or vampires he destroyed in his quest. He was going to destroy them all anyway.

"Bring me the needles," he ordered his minion. His grey lips twisted into a parody of a grin, and his black eyes glittered in anticipation. "It will work this time," he said. "It had better work," he hissed.

The pasty-faced minion brought a tray holding two silver needles. "Not those ones," snarled Madison. "Bring me the stainless steel." *Didn't the idiot human realize that silver would destroy the vampire?* Once he had the needles, Madison wrapped an elastic band around the vampire's arm between his elbow and his shoulder, tightening it until the vein on the underside of his forearm was more easily visible. He then swabbed the arm with a cotton ball dipped in alcohol, gently tapped the vein until it was more prominent, and carefully slid the needle in. Black goo oozed out the end.

That was the trouble with working on vampires. They were so messy. Madison wiped the putrid liquid away from the needle, attached the clear tubing from the intravenous pole, and turned on the drip.

Madison licked his lips as the vibrant red fluid trickled down the clear, plastic tubing towards the vampire's needle. The blood reached the vampire, and a blood-curdling scream rent the air. Madison watched with clinical eyes as the vampire writhed, pulling at his straps in an attempt to escape the burning liquid. Another scream rent the air, and excitement coursed through Madison's veins. The writhing vampire was stronger than Madison had given him credit. All the others had passed out after the first couple of drops, and died almost instantly. This one continued to fight his bonds, and screech in agony.

Madison adjusted the drip, forcing the liquid faster into the vampire's vein, savouring every scream that came out of the vampire's mouth.

The now familiar prickle along his spine warned Madison that the sun was going to rise soon. He yanked the needle from the vampires arm, and ordered the human to get rid of them. The vampire had stopped writhing, and was now moaning loudly.

"It's almost over," he told the vampire. He unbound the young vampire and lifted him into his arms. "Bring the stakes," he ordered the human, and carried the vampire outside as if it weighed no more than a sack of potatoes.

The sky was beginning to brighten. The terrified vampire sat on the ground sobbing, while the human pounded the stakes into the ground. "Hurry," Madison hissed. "I don't want to be out here when the sun rises."

The young vampire's eyes snapped open. Horror clutched his heart when he saw the nearby trees outlined by the first tendrils of the sun's rays. His first day after the transition he suffered third degree burns when his hand was hit by a ray of sun that found its way between the roof boards of the old barn he was hiding in. There was no way he wanted to repeat that. He tried to dissolve into mist and sink into the ground but his magic wasn't working. He clawed at the hardened earth until his fingers bled. He screamed when Madison and his minion dragged him out into the open field, and bound him to the four stakes.

"Hush," Madison whispered. He touched the younger vampire's lips, and its voice grew silent. Tears streaked its face, and its mouth widened in silent screams. "You have nothing left to fear."

One

GHEORGÈS swung the axe. The muscles in his arms bulged against the tight fabric of his shirt. The blade meeting the wood echoed like a gunshot off the surrounding hills. Chopping wood was his punishment but he didn't mind. He actually liked chopping wood. It was good exercise. Besides it helped to keep his muscles toned, and he liked the scent of the wood.

Even if he hated chopping wood it would have been worth it. The look on Quinn's face when Em dropped the oak mere inches from him was priceless. The fool should have known better than to mention the bloodsucker. For some stupid reason Emerald found it necessary to defend that creature even after it nearly drained her. The mere thought made him want to puke.

Gheorgès wished the monster was standing in front of him right now. He would not hesitate to separate its head from its shoulders. He didn't care what Alicia or Emerald, or anyone else for that matter, said about it. That thing should never have drunk from his sister.

Even after all these years, it turned his blood cold just thinking of that day.

And Emerald was worried about that piece of shit bloodsucker.

It made his blood boil.

Thunder echoed across the sky as the axe came down on another helpless length of log. The gas powered wood splitter stood to the side of the growing pile, untouched. Gheorgès preferred the sensation that travelled through his body with the exertion he put into each swing of the axe to the mind numbing boredom that accompanied placing log after log into the splitter and then simply tossing the pieces on to the pile.

Gheorgès gave up trying to figure out the connection between his normally intelligent sister and the sack of mindless skin that lay useless in the Chimera. It would be better if the creature just gave up and died already. Everyone would be better off.

Well, everyone except the bloodsucker, and Gheorgès didn't give a hoot about him. He couldn't figure out why Em couldn't just forget about him already. It wasn't like she would ever be allowed anywhere near him since he tried to drain her.

Hell, Gheorgès wouldn't even know he was breathing except Em asked Alicia about him every single time Kamenwati came back from visiting his father. It didn't matter how many times Kamenwati told her he was alive and not to worry about him. It wasn't her fault that he got hurt. Nobody blamed Emerald for his condition.

Nobody except Em herself. How could someone as smart as his sister be so stupid as to worry about one of those things? It drove Gheorgès crazy.

The axe came down with an extra vicious clang and four pieces of wood flew from the targeted log. Gheorgès pretended it was the bloodsucker's head, and smiled wickedly.

It was a good thing those so called good bloodsuckers stayed in the Chimera. As far as Gheorgès was concerned any bloodsucker that walked the earth was fair game, and bloodsucker was always in season.

Gheorgès took one more swing with the axe before putting it away. He thought again of the look on Quinn's face when that tree dropped no more than two inches from him, and snickered. At least it hadn't landed on him this time. Emerald's aim was definitely improving.

Two

HE stood in the shadows, a part of them, dark and brooding. When he held out his hand she hesitated, torn between the desire to take all he offered—or run in the other direction as fast as she could.

Desire won out—again.

Emerald Caer Wulfson reached for the offered hand and stepped into the shadows. Strong arms instantly circled her, pulling her closer until she could feel the gentle beat of the heart in his chest, and the not so gentle proof of his own desire for her.

Her bones instantly melted and she had to cling to him to keep from falling.

Conall chuckled deep in his throat and held her closer until it was difficult to tell where one left off and the other began.

"I missed you," she whispered afraid to speak too loudly and spoil the dream.

"Aw my love. It is I who has missed you. It seems a lifetime since I last held you in my arms." He nuzzled the side of her neck, moving up to nibble on her earlobe.

Emerald shivered slightly, and sighed. This was the best part of her days, the nights. It was when she went to sleep that he allowed her into his world; a world of shadows both beautiful and deadly.

Conall's lips moved to claim hers which were trembling slightly in anticipation. Suddenly Conall stiffened and pushed her away. His beautiful black eyes glazed over and he began to speak gibberish.

"They're coming for you." The words he spoke now were clear and edged in fear.

"Who?" Emerald asked but Conall didn't seem aware of her. "Who is coming?"

"You can't have her," Conall growled to someone or something Emerald couldn't see or hear.

An oppressive shadow appeared behind Conall. *Damn! Why couldn't they let them have even this time? Was it too much to ask?* Emerald quickly moved to a defensive position ready to fight by Conall's side against whatever danger stalked them here in this shadowy realm.

It was her fault that he fought these endless battles against the evil that would claim his soul. She was the reason he lay helpless in his own world day after day instead of being able to face his demons like the true Mage he was. But for her stupidity, he would be his dark, deadly, and oh so sexy self.

As she waited for the shadow to take form and attack, she was ready. She was no longer an immature child of seventeen with no control of her emotions. She was grown now, and knew exactly who she was and what she was capable of.

She was *Moarté*.

She was death. And whatever dared threaten them would soon face her wrath.

The shadow drifted forward but didn't attack. It hovered in front of them as if it were waiting for a signal of some sort. Emerald wanted to blast it into a million tiny particles but over the years she learned that here in the Shadow Realm she was impotent until the shadows took on solid form.

The shadow moved with insidious stealth toward Conall, wrapping itself around him like a lover's caress. *It should be me caressing him, not this insidious shadow. This should have been our time.*

Emerald tensed, waiting for it to change, become solid, but it didn't. As Emerald watched helplessly the shadow was absorbed into Conall's body. His eyes flashed red, and his fangs exploded out of his mouth contorting his beautiful features into something hideous and terrifying.

Emerald's amber eyes widened in horror as Conall moved toward her, his features no longer recognizable. Every instinct told her to blast him before it was too late, but how could she? It was her fault he was here. How could she possibly cause him any more pain?

Torn between the need to strike him down and the desire to wrap her arms around him, Emerald did not struggle as Conall wrapped his strong arms around her and pulled her close. His head bent toward her and his fangs scraped the delicate skin on her neck before sinking in.

Too late now she thought as her head grew dizzy and her limbs weakened.

Evil, disembodied laughter filled the shadows around them. *Drain her,* the voice said gleefully. *Drain them all.*

She had lost. The evil had finally beaten them down, and won. "I'm sorry," she whispered weakly as her vision began to dim.

Conall's fangs ripped from her throat and he was staring at her through horror-filled eyes.

"Run," he shouted, shaking her until her vision cleared slightly. "Hide." He thrust Emerald away from him.

Emerald felt herself leaving the shadows and she struggled to stay where she was. Conall needed her. He was going to be okay. It wasn't too late. Together they could beat this.

It was no use. Conall released his hold on her and she was tumbling through the shadows.

Emerald sat up with a snap. Sweat beaded on her forehead and trickled down the nape of her neck. Her limbs felt boneless and her vision was dim. She reached up with one shaky hand to touch the two aching puncture marks on the side of her neck.

What the hell just happened?

The question beat against her brain like a jackhammer. Emerald took a deep breath and tried to calm herself. Reaching out with her mind she probed the universe around her, but all she felt was emptiness.

Conall was gone.

Was he dead? The mere idea of him dying alone in the shadows broke her heart.

Where was he? For the first time in ten years Emerald could not sense Conall's life force and it scared her. Their connection broken, she was completely alone.

Three

CONALL put his hands over his ears to block out the voice but it didn't do much to help. "Shut. Up," he screamed.

The voice continued in its monotonous tone, like a schoolteacher trying to drill a lesson into a particularly obtuse student's brain. *You are starving my son. You must seek nourishment. You MUST feed.*

Conall held his hands over his ears even though it did nothing to keep that insidious voice from tunnelling into his mind, and tossed his head from side to side like a child. "No. No. No." He began a chant of his own trying to drown out that infernal voice.

Was he dead? Is this what happened when a Mage died? Had he been cast into the Shadows with the Betrayer because he failed?

Conall cracked open his eyelids. The world around him was black. There were no shadows. There was no light to cast any shadows. It made no difference if the eyes were open or closed. Everything was the same.

Empty.

Except for that nauseating, persistent, gnat inspired voice. He almost wanted to obey it, just to shut it up.

There was an almost imperceptible movement of air around him. *What was that?*

Voices. They were definitely voices, and not the usual mind numbing voices that kept him company in his isolation. These were the low tones of someone trying not to disturb the ill. That meant he was not dead. There was hope for him yet.

Conall felt a hand touch his forehead. It felt good. Cool against his burning brow. He moved his hands away from his ears so he could better hear what the voices were saying.

"He is still burning up. I worry he will not wake in this world."

Not wake up! What was wrong with these people? "You-hoo. Guys? I'm not asleep here. Will someone turn on the damned lights so I can see you?"

The voices ignored him, much like the voice of the Betrayer.

Wait. His eyes were closed. That's why he can't see anything. Conall tried to open his eyes again but they suddenly felt like they weighed ten tonnes, and his lashes were glued down with cement. He tried to lift his arm, to reach out and shake the body nearest him, but his arm was also dead weight.

Conall began to panic. *What in hell is going on here?* His heart rate spiked in direct proportion to his panic, and he broke out into a cold sweat, but no matter how hard he struggled he could not lift his arms, open his eyes, or apparently even make his lips move.

He was trapped inside his own body.

Helpless.

Alone.

Because he had sent *her* away.

"Something is happening," one of the voices said.

440

Conall knew that voice. It was familiar, and yet he couldn't give it a name. "His heart rate has spiked and he is sweating profusely."

The Mage who spoke lifted Conall's limp arm and let it drop back on the bed. "Still no change. It is like he has lost all will to survive."

Not true guys. Still fighting here. Could use some help.

"Let's just give him his drink and get out of here. Something about this place gives me the creeps."

No! That insidious voice of the Betrayer crawled through Conall's brain, and the panic in it made him want to smile—if only his lips would obey. *Do not drink. They are trying to poison you.*

Shut. Up. Already.

The answering snarl was like a giant bear claw tearing through his already damaged brain. Conall grit his teeth against the onslaught of pain, and fought back the bile that rose in his throat.

You fool, snarled the Betrayer. *They are poisoning you. You are going to die if you stay where you are. Get up. Get up and FEED.*

Drain them. Drain them all.

Conall felt a cool hand on the nape of his neck, followed by warm sweet liquid trickling down the back of his throat. Another set of fingers, warmer than the first, stroked his throat, and he swallowed convulsively surprised his body was capable of even that small thing.

With the warm liquid came peace and Conall relaxed. Soon visions of beauty swam in his mind as his thoughts turned to *her.* Her beauty was the balm needed to ease his shattered mind, and his torn soul.

His angel.

The Angel of Death. She is coming for you and when she does she will destroy you. You can't let that happen. You must find her first, and destroy her.

No. That couldn't be true. Could it? She had saved him. She had fed him. She was exquisite. Her blood was like nothing he had tasted before. He wanted more. He needed more.

She was the key.

She could save him.

Yes. Yes, whispered the Betrayer gleefully. *Find her. Drain her. She will make you strong. She will save you.*

Conall's eyelids flew open revealing eyes that burned red. There was only room for one thought in his mind.

He had to find her.

With barely enough sense to mask his presence, Conall opened a rift in the universe and stepped to earth. Dazed, he looked around wondering where in hell he was now. More to the point, why was he here?

Visions of an angel swam before his eyes and something important tickled the edges of his brain. He had to find this woman. But why? Who was she? She reminded him of someone, but who?

It all came back in a rush. The battle against the Betrayer; His loss to the Ursaline; The *Moarté* feeding him.

That can't be right. Why would the Angel of Death feed him?

In the jumble of thoughts fighting for purchase in his confused mind only two stood out.

The *Moarté* was coming for him.

The Betrayer was coming for *her*. His angel. His saviour.

He had to find *her* before they did, and before the *Moarté* found him.

She was near. He felt her presence. He also felt a presence behind him, but his reflexes were slower than usual, and he couldn't duck the rock that slammed into his temple.

Shit.

That was his last thought as Conall slumped to the ground like an empty suit of clothing.

Four

"WHAT are you going to do? Wait until your own sons and daughters are missing, or dead?" Luke's voice was rough with frustration as he ran his fingers through his long hair.

"Why doesn't the *Moarté* do her job?" The speaker was a wolf from the German pack, unfamiliar with Jade personally, but he knew what she was. *Moarté*. That he held no love for the *Moarté* was clear in his tone of voice.

Gheorgès took a step forward, anger burning in his eyes, but his father waved him back to his position against the wall.

"It is not my wife's job to babysit the packs." Luke's tone was velvet edged in steel.

"Of course it's not. It's her job to destroy us," sneered a wolf from the Russian pack.

This time Luke turned on the speaker and bared his teeth. Gheorgès crossed one ankle over the other and leaned nonchalantly against the wall, arms crossed at his chest belying his readiness to pounce. Things could get exciting after all.

"If my wife wanted to destroy you she would," he spat in clipped syllables.

Several wolves jumped up, in both defence of, and against Jade, but only one dared to place his hand on Luke's sleeve. Luke forced himself to stand down.

Joaquin Pardo was a good man, who still felt the loss of one of his own. The first body found over a decade ago was a young wolf from his pack in New Orleans. He had taken off after an argument with his father. They found him six months later in New York totally drained of blood. There were needle tracks on both his arms, and burns on his ankles and wrists.

"Please," he said. "Let us not forgot the reason we are all here. This is no longer an isolated incident or two. It has been nearly a decade since young Frankie was murdered but we still mourn him greatly. As I am sure the pack in New York mourns their dead."

Five years ago in New York a female had survived the attack on her and her brother. She lived only long enough to tell her father she thought a vampire had been present during the battle. Her brother's body turned up three months later completely drained of blood, needle marks and burns like the first. There was no magical trail to follow.

Last year four wolves went missing in the same month from the same pack. Jade and Daniel had searched every inch of New York, but again there was no magical trail to follow, and the trail had been too old for Daniel to follow. If there was a vampire involved, then it had discovered how to mask its presence from Jade, and that worried her.

Then two months after they went missing the four teenagers were discovered 230 miles northwest in Salem, Massachusetts. This time when Jade and Daniel searched they were accompanied by Luke, but there was no evidence of a vampire ever being in Salem.

"So many of us have lost someone we love. It is time we band together and take care of our own. Every one of us in this room knows the consequences if the humans become aware of our existence. Let us put an end to these attacks before that happens."

Five

HE was helpless, strapped to the stainless steel table; held immobile by silver cuffs burning the skin on his wrists and ankles. The scent of chloroform, disinfectant, and blood—his blood—sickened him. A whisper reached his ears when the door slid open. The smell of rot reached his nose. A smell so strong it masked all the others. It was *his* smell. A smell he would not soon forget.

His tormentor crossed the room without as much as a whisper of sound. With quick, efficient movements, he patted the vein in his arm, drawing it to the surface. The chill of his fingers burned almost as much as the shackles, and he wore the stench of the vampire. A long silver tube was plunged in his pulsating vein. He could not stop his scream of agony, and hated the malicious, triumphant smile it brought to his tormentor's grey lips.

He was suffering the fires of hell, only he was on earth. Or was he in hell? Had he crossed over into the afterlife? Had his tormentor finally drained him of his life force?

He forced himself to concentrate on his tormentor—to ignore the pain, and remember.

He was alive. He was Conall. He was Magi. He could feel his blood slowly seeping from his body. His vision blurred. The room darkened.

The Angel of Death was coming for him. The most beautiful angel he had ever seen. Her platinum hair had streaks of gold and silver. Her amber eyes were shadowed by pain—his pain. She was flying toward him. He could feel her searching for him. He saw her hair streaming out around her feathers, a mist so delicate as to be nearly undetectable.

He would know this angel anywhere, and in any form. She was so close this time. If only he could hold on until she found him.

He had to hold on until he found her.

Six

"DON'T be stupid, Emmy."

Emerald Caer Wulfson swung around to face her brother, amber eyes blazing, and her hands on her small hips. At well over six feet, her brother dwarfed her own five foot plus, but that did not daunt her in the least.

"Did I *hear* you correctly, Quinn?" Her soft, gentle voice was a sharp contrast to her stormy eyes. "Did you just call me *stupid?*"

Quinn's eyes darkened so much they were nearly black, and he growled low in the back of his throat. Emerald was not stupid. Out of the three of them she had graduated with the highest marks, both in high school and college. Nevertheless, she was his little sister, and he was determined to protect her from her own foolishness.

"You are *acting* stupid at the moment."

"Don't you growl at me," Emmy snapped. "I'm not some little wolf you can make cower and bend to your will."

Quinn burst out laughing at the image of his sister cowering before any man, or beast for that matter. She had come out fighting a quarter of a century ago on the night of the long moon, during the worst snowstorm of the century, and she had been fighting ever since.

When Quinn laughed it changed his entire appearance. It made him softer, more approachable. This side of him had women and wolves alike falling all over themselves to please him.

Emerald stood on her tiptoes, threw her arms around her brother's neck, and gave him a quick kiss on his cheek. "You worry too much, Quinn. I'll be perfectly safe. I am just going to take a quick look around. How can there be any danger in that?"

Quinn held his sister close for several heartbeats, and then he set her away from him, keeping his hands on her shoulders. He held her eyes with his, daring her to look away while he read her determination, her strength of will, and her own uneasiness with the situation. She had not slept properly in four days, and her eyes mirrored her fatigue. Nightmares of blood and pain had plagued her since the day they arrived in Willow Bend, leading her to a supposedly deserted farm about ten miles out of town. They had staked out the farm for several days now, and the only thing suspicious about it was the security guard who patrolled the perimeter. Why would someone need to guard an empty farm?

"What if you are right Emmy? What if there really is someone in trouble out at that farm. At least let me come with you." After the first nightmare, they asked around but there were no reports of anyone missing in Willow Bend, or any nearby surrounding towns. According to the Matei brothers, who acted as law enforcement for Willow Bend, nobody had lived out at that farm since a fire had destroyed most of the house nearly fifty years ago. The fields had grown over, and only the old silo was still intact.

"No Quinn." Emerald put her small hands on her brother's chest, and felt his heart beating beneath her

450

palm. It was a strong heart, a good heart. She felt his worry for her. His fears mirrored her own. What if she was right and there was someone out at that farm that needed her help? There was too much of her mother in her to wait another day to find out. Besides, this could be connected with the recent attacks on the Lycans.

There was a sudden burning in her left arm. For a mere heartbeat, Quinn's image blurred before becoming stable again. Someone suffered excruciating pain, and she had to find him.

"At least let me call Daniel and Gregory."

Emerald gently pushed her brother away from her. "I have to do this on my own, Quinn."

"Why? What are you trying to prove?" On a softer note Quinn continued. "You don't have to save everyone by yourself Emmy."

Emerald rolled her eyes. "What makes you think I need to prove anything to you or anyone else? I am a grown woman, and I make my own decisions. You are not the boss of me, and neither is Gheorgès. You think just because you are bigger than me that I can't take care of myself. Well you are wrong." Emerald's eyes were once again ablaze with anger, and she jabbed her small finger into his chest to emphasize her every word. "Bigger is not always better."

Quinn slowly backed up while he tried to put a lid on his own temper. "Stop that!"

"Make me," Emerald taunted.

"You're acting like a little girl."

"And you're acting like an overbearing tyrant."

"Enough!" Quinn took a deep breath, and exhaled slowly. *What would Gheorgès do if he were here?* "I am the eldest and you will listen to me."

Emerald sputtered. Then she burst into laughter. "Eldest! Now that is a hoot. You are only ten minutes older than I am. Therefore, if you think that makes you the boss of me, then Gheorgès must be the boss of you. After all he is two minutes older than you."

"I am ordering you to stay away from that place, Emerald Caer Wulfson. You are not to go anywhere near it until the others get back."

For a mere heartbeat, Emerald actually thought that Quinn might be channelling their eldest brother. They might be triplets but they were nothing alike. Gheorgès was the eldest, and almost as much fun as a heart attack, and that was on his best days. He was also their father's right arm, lieutenant, and body guard all rolled in to one. He had gone with their parents to attend an emergency pack conference in Italy, leaving Quinn in charge. Quinn, although nearly identical in looks to their brother was the complete opposite in personality. He was usually satisfied to let Gheorgès make all the major decisions, preferring to spend his time painting, and taking pictures. It was a great way to meet girls, he said. Not that he needed an excuse to meet girls. There were always plenty hanging around, just hoping to draw his attention.

Then there was Emerald. Jade had gone into labour during one of the most severe storms of the century, under the Long Night Moon in January. Emerald had fought to be born, exhausting both her mother and herself. When she had finally emerged from her mother's womb she had been tiny, and bore the mark of the *Moarté*. Where her brothers' hair had been dark, hers was white with streaks of silver and gold. Where their eyes were dark like their father's, she had her mother's distinct amber eyes. While Quinn and Gheorgès were identical, she was her mother's twin. She almost did not make it through the first year, but then she began to grow stronger, if not larger. What she lacked in stature, Emerald more than made up for in skill, power, and sheer determination. At least once she learned to control her emotions.

Her brothers were both very powerful. Their father had been Alpha of the Willow Bend Pack until he had mated with their mother. He had given up the position of Alpha to make his life with her. The keeper of his heart. Then almost two decades ago the packs decided to band together and form a Pack Council, to try to bring the packs closer. The other Alpha's knew and trusted Lykos, and so they banded together to ask him to lead the Pack Council. Luke said it was because not one of them was willing to step down as Alpha of their own pack to take the position, but she knew he was secretly pleased with the honour.

Their mother was a powerful *Moarté*. Her children had all inherited some of her powers, but only women could be *Moarté*. Emerald believed that it infuriated her brothers knowing she was more powerful even if they would never admit it. They all went out of their way to keep her safe. Her father said it was the wolf in them, that they could not help but protect their females.

"Maybe you're right Quinn. Maybe I should wait until the others get back."

Quinn's sigh of relief was audible in the small room. He eyed his sister warily. *Had she given in too easily?* He was about to reiterate his order when her eyes glassed over and she swayed on her feet. He reached out to steady her.

The fire in her arm was almost unbearable. Her heart was beating erratically. Her breathing matched his. She could barely suck in enough air.

She had to get to him. Now, before it was too late.

Emerald shook her brother's hand off her arm. "I'm sorry Quinn," she whispered. In less than a heartbeat, a small white owl flew out the open window.

Seven

CONALL watched as his tormenter threw papers into a garbage can and set fire to them. Black smoke rose from the can to mingle with other distinguishable odours in the room. A younger man with skin the color of paste shuffled around after his master gathering more papers to thrust into the can. Conall never took his eyes from the tormentor, not even when the vassal turned to glare at him, a malicious grin twisting the corners of its grey lips. "Make sure you burn every last scrap of paper," he ordered his minion before approaching the table where his prey lay helplessly shackled.

His black eyes glittered with hatred, and his foul breath burned Conall's eyes. "It's been fun." His voice alone could freeze the blood in your veins. "Too bad play time is over. I would have liked to stay longer, but we are no longer safe here."

He did not bother searching for a vein. He just jabbed the silver needle into Conall's arm, and hit the plunger. The burn began at the point of insertion, and left a trail of fire along the pulsating vein as it streaked towards his heart. Every inch of its journey was agony. He thought his elbow would shatter when the fiery liquid pulsed through, and continued its race towards his shoulder. His heart began to beat erratically, and each breath he managed to suck in brought more agony with it. He was no longer aware of his surroundings. He did not see the door open, or notice his tormentor's departure.

He used every ounce of energy he had left to concentrate on the path the poison was taking. He needed to slow his heartbeat, to slow the poison, and give his body a chance to fight it. Pain tore through his skull. He screeched like a wild animal pleading for help.

The air around Conall crackled as the power built. The vampire's minion turned just as the heavy sliding door exploded into the room, showering pieces of metal and wood around them. Most humans believed the Angel of Death came to lead them to their reward, but Conall knew better. The Angel of Death brought retribution.

She stood in the doorway, power crackling around her, enfolding her in its golden glow. Her long pale hair danced around her head, shooting sparks of gold and silver. He would know her face anywhere. He saw her face every night in his dreams. He held her lithe body in his arms. He kissed her lush lips.

Moarté. The Angel of Death. His angel.

She aimed a blast of white flame towards him and his shackles exploded. The pasty man shuffled towards her and she threw out a hand tossing him back without once taking her eyes off the man on the table. Without the torture of the silver cuffs Conall was able to concentrate. He forced his heartbeat to a slow, steady rhythm, and focused his energies on stopping the poison from reaching his heart. Slowly he swung his legs off the table and stood. Holding the edge of the table to keep from landing on his face, he closed his eyes and took several strengthening breaths. He did not dare take the time he needed to finish the healing until they were out of here.

He heard the shuffle of feet, and his eyes snapped open. The pasty looking man was coming towards him with a large canister held over his head. The Angel of Death did not look towards the man. "Why don't you just go lay down somewhere?"

Both men froze at the soft, melodic tone. Then the pasty man shook his head as if to clear cobwebs, and began to shuffle toward him again. Black smoke filled Conall's nostrils.

Unable to ignore him anymore the Angel of Death turned towards the pasty man, and with a well-placed kick knocked him backwards. He dropped the canister, and came back at her snarling, teeth snapping, and arms flailing.

Someone was coming. Conall could smell his fear through the open doorway. He pushed himself away from the table, and grabbed the snarling minion, snapping his neck. He took two steps toward the Angel of Death when he saw the glint of steel. The flash of flame and the smell of gunpowder were simultaneous.

"No!" The word wrenched from his parched throat. Conall flew at the gunman, his incisors lengthened and he sunk them into his jugular. The warm, salty liquid quickly rejuvenated him, destroying the remainder of the poison in his system. A heartbeat later the guard's body, almost totally drained of blood although his heart was still beating, burst into flame.

The Angel of Death lay on the dirt floor, her breathing barely discernible, and her heartbeat almost non-existent. The fire from the can spread quickly. Conall gently picked up his broken angel and cradled her limp body close to his chest. Energy gathered around them, a small tornado of power, and a doorway appeared. Conall stepped through the doorway just as the building behind them exploded.

Eight

QUINN stared at the open window. How he hated it when she did that. He sent his senses out into the night and found her exactly where he thought he would, flying straight towards the deserted farm outside town. He used their private mind link to see with her eyes as the treetops blurred with the speed of her flight.

Emerald Caer Wulfson you come back here immediately.

I can't, Quinn. Her voice broke. *He needs me. I can't ignore his pain.*

Quinn quickly left their room, shifted to wolf form, and headed out of town at full speed. He kept the path between their minds open the entire time. Times like this he would rather be bodyguard to their father. At least he showed some sense. He kept her connected with a small portion of his mind, while he ran as quickly as possible to join her.

Emerald flew straight to the burned out farm outside of town. She quickly scanned the perimeter, tracking the guard's movements as he circled first the remains of the old farmhouse, then the silo, and then began the trail again. He walked the exact same route so often there was a distinct trail in the hard earth. She shifted into human form behind some bushes, and closed her eyes, opening her senses to even the slightest disturbance in the atmosphere. The guard was on the other side of the farmhouse, too far away to notice her. A small rabbit hopped into the bushes to her left. A bat flit by on the night breeze. Then she felt it. His pain became her pain. He was in the silo.

Emerald moved silently, just another shadow in the night, until she reached the silo door. It was reinforced with steel. Gathering energy around her, she directed it at the heavy door blasting it into shards of metal that showered the room.

The inside of the silo was furnished the same as a hospital room, or a small lab. There was a desk in one corner, a filing cabinet, a shelf with several medical instruments, a can with flames coming out of it, now that wasn't typical of a hospital room, *and a hospital operating table. A man lay on the table tracking her every move with eyes so full of pain it tore at her soul. He was covered with blood—his blood. There was dried blood on the floor beside the table. Silver shackles bound his ankles and wrists. The skin burned away leaving raw flesh exposed. Blood trickled onto the table from the open wounds. The smell of death made her dizzy. There was pain here—too much pain.*

The only other occupant of the room shuffled towards her—A vampire's minion. Emerald gathered a small energy ball and aimed it at the prisoner's cuffs turning them to powder, and then she tossed the pasty man aside. Relief flooded her when the man climbed off the table of his own accord. Ignoring him, she turned and kicked the pasty man. He dropped the canister he was carrying, and came at her snarling and snapping. Another man was suddenly behind her. She kicked out and knocked him to the ground. She was focussed on the second man when everything went black.

Quinn froze mid-step. *Emmy?* He reached out but she was not there. What the hell happened to his sister? *Emerald Caer Wulfson answer me immediately.* He was already running again. The silo was just ahead, a big gaping hole where the door had been. The limp body of his sister dangled from a stranger's arms.

Snarling, Quinn leapt through the doorway. A blast of heat blew him back across the yard. He struggled to stand, but was knocked down again by another blast. Heat and flames were everywhere.

Quinn struggled to stand. It felt like a rock had blasted a large hole in his heart. *Emmy,* he sobbed across the private path he shared with his sister. There was no answer, only blackness.

Oh God, Emmy. Where are you?

Nine

CONALL stepped through the doorway into a large garden filled with a multitude of blooms. In the center of the garden was an old well, on one side a willow tree waved gently in the breeze, and on the other side stood a majestic Rowan. He inhaled the familiar, healing scents, and vanquished all traces of the doorway.

Ignoring the beauty of the garden, he strode past the well to a tiny, vine-covered cottage nestled in the side of a mountain. Unless you knew the cottage was there you would not detect it until you were almost on top of it. The front door swung open at his approach and Conall entered.

The cottage was merely the entrance to a palatial home built completely inside the mountain. Conall carried the Angel of Death straight to his own private bedchamber, and placed her gently on a bed that nearly filled the entire room. Several candles ignited around the bedside and their healing fragrance quickly filled the air.

Conall gently brushed aside her long pale tendrils and tiny sparks flew from his fingers. His heartbeat quickened as he gently probed the wound in her head.

Emerald moaned softly. Her eyelids fluttered but did not open. She was so beautiful she took his breath away—his angel. This was his fault. He should have been more aware of his surroundings when he sojourned to her world. Hell, he should never have invited her into his to begin with.

It was his fault she was hurt. They used him to get to her. How could he be so stupid as to forget about their enemies? Ra's enemies. He would not forget again. He would track down and punish the monster that was responsible for hurting her.

Then he was going to hunt down and tear Theron's heart out just for kicks and giggles.

Emerald moaned again, and Conall winced. He felt each stab of pain that ripped through her skull. *How could he have been so careless?* He had walked straight into the vampire's trap. He was not some babe in the woods that didn't know any better. He was Magi and he knew better. Now an innocent was suffering because of his stupidity.

If she died it would be his fault, and he would expire right alongside of her. She held the key to his life, his reason for living. He didn't want to live without her. Without her, he was no more than an empty shell.

If he were a better man, he would heal her and let her go. Erase her memories of him and return her to her family. But he wasn't a better man. He was Magi and without her he was nothing.

No. He would keep her here with him where she would be safe until he found a way to stop Theron. Then he would return her to her family.

At least that is the lie he told himself.

"You won't die," he whispered fiercely, his voice husky with unshed tears. "I will not allow it."

A chair appeared next to the bed, and Conall lowered himself on to it. A heartbeat later his body slumped back and a pale green mist left his body to enter Emerald's.

Her brain was swelling rapidly. Conall worked to reduce the swelling and repair the damage the bullet had rent. The bullet was lodged behind her left eye. Conall spent several precious moments to make sure that he removed the bullet without causing any more damage, and then repaired her optical cords so she would not lose her sight. When he was finally satisfied with the repairs he returned to his own body, and let exhaustion claim him.

Ten

JADE left the conference room exhausted and full of pride for the man at her side. Luke managed to convince the others to forget their differences, and their hatred for the *Moarté,* and accept there was a problem they needed to deal with. Too many of the young Lycans had gone missing, only to turn up dead, either drained of blood or pumped full of silver nitrate.

It took nearly a week of arguments, but they had finally agreed there was a threat to their existence, and it wasn't Jade.

If vampires were not draining the blood of the Lycans, then who or what was? Why were they being pumped full of silver nitrate? Was it possible that it was not vampires, but rather humans? How many humans actually knew about the existence of Lycans? The ones Jade knew about she could count on one hand.

Years ago, she had rescued a young wolf from the Institute of Psychic Research. Dr Madison had been doing illegal experiments on him in a bid to create the next indestructible soldier. Once it came out he was performing illegal experiments on humans, the official story, he had retired in disgrace. In reality, he spent the next ten years in a psychiatric ward babbling about werewolves. She wasn't sure where he was now.

Several Lycans were part of an elite military group, choosing to use their special talents to protect the safety of the country, but only their handlers knew what they really were. Had someone else discovered the Lycans? She had to find out what was going on before the Lycans became a household topic, and an endangered species.

The Lycan council agreed to form a task force of their own to help investigate these deaths, on the condition that Lykos' son, and beta, Gheorgès, head it up. It had been nearly as difficult to convince Gheorgès to accept the job as it had been to convince the packs of the necessity of taking action. He was Luke's second, his lieutenant, his personal bodyguard, and he was not happy with the idea of leaving his father unprotected. He had agreed to take the job only after Luke had agreed to accept whomever Gheorgès handpicked to cover for him, and the council had agreed to let Gheorgès personally select the members of the force. He had insisted on Quinn and Emerald, as well as at least one member from every pack. Jade knew most of the members of the council personally, and as a woman and mate to Lykos, they accepted her—they did not trust her. Luke said it was because they did not trust anyone more powerful than themselves, but she knew that was not entirely true. They trusted both Gheorgès and Quinn, and they were more powerful in their youth than most of these men at their full potential. They did not trust her because she was *Moarté*. At least they accepted Emerald as lycan, and trusted her. Jade really did not care whether they liked her, trusted her, or wished she would just disappear, not as long as they did what was necessary to help protect their species.

In the meantime, they had a couple of hours before catching their early morning flight, and she had better ways of passing the time than worrying about things that would never change.

"What are you smiling at?" Luke leaned down and whispered in his wife's ear, sending shivers down her spine. Even after all this time, all it took was a look, or a word, and her knees turned to jelly. Molten liquid pooled low in her abdomen.

Jade glanced seductively at her husband. "Oh, I was just thinking of ways to spend the next couple of hours."

Luke's dark eyes smouldered with passion, and he swatted his wife's round bottom. "Hurry then wife," his whisper a low growl. "We don't want to waste a single precious moment."

They were almost to their room when Jade stopped mid stride. Her face paled, and she clutched at her heart. "No," she whispered. "Not Emmy."

~~~

IN Făgăruş, Romania in a small cottage nestled in the foothills of the Carpathian Mountains, Alicia Martinez Wulfson Horakhty woke in a cold sweat. Her heart was pounding, and she could not stop shaking. Acrid black smoke burned her nostrils, and the heat from the flames made her skin red. Quinn's sobs wracked her body as he knelt in the grass.

Alicia reached out across continents and oceans until she found her brother. He was just outside Willow Bend. *What is it, Quinn? What is happening?* She forced calm to her spirit voice that she did not feel.

Emmy's gone.

Alicia turned to her husband who had held her tightly in his arms from the moment she woke.

We are coming.

Eleven

IT felt like someone was using a jackhammer inside her head. She took several slow deep breaths and tried to shove the pain away, anywhere but where it was. The air shifted and she felt a gentle touch and little electric sparks caressed her skin. It felt safe. Felt like home. She tried to open her eyes to see the face she knew belonged with that touch; the face that haunted her dreams, but her eyelids would not cooperate, and she slid back into oblivion.

~~~

THE birds were singing, the sun was shining, and all was right with the world. Then why did she feel such sadness? Where was it coming from? It surrounded her like a dark, heavy blanket.

She peeked out from beneath one long, pale lash. She was not surprised to find herself surrounded by black and gold opulence. She fingered the smooth, black sheet that covered her, enjoying the feeling of floating on a cloud. Several candles flickered around the room and she followed their flames as they danced along the gold brocade drapes that completely covered one wall. A whisper of breath caught her attention and she turned to the man slumped in the chair beside her. His blue-black lashes fanned the milky quartz cheeks of an angel—or was he the devil? Her heart sped up at the wicked thoughts the sight of him provoked.

His head tilted at an awkward angle, and his mouth was slightly open, showing a glimpse of white teeth. She would not mind exploring that mouth. *Wait a minute. Was that a fang?* She banished the thought as quickly as it came, and continued her perusal of the man. He felt familiar—like coming home.

Who are you?

His dark brows furled and sadness rolled off him in waves. "Poor baby." Compassion brought tears to her voice. She reached out with shaky fingers to smooth the lines from his handsome face. Her fingers touched his alabaster skin—and sparks flew.

"Oh!" Amber eyes widened in surprise and she pulled her hand back. His eyes snapped open and she found herself staring into matching obsidian pools. Her breath caught in her throat. How easily she could drown in those pools.

"How do you feel?" His deep, husky voice sent shivers down her spine.

She nearly choked on a ragged breath when he reached his hand toward her, and she scampered back until she hit the headboard. A flame flickered in his eyes, or was it just a trick of the candle light. His hand stopped midway between them, and the flames were dosed by overwhelming sadness.

Emerald was unable to stop herself. She reached out to entwine her tremulous fingers with his much firmer ones. Sparks flew, only this time she did not pull back. She tightened her grip, and offered him a watery smile. His returning smile brightened the room making her glad she had reached out.

"How's your head?" He asked again.

An accident. That explains why I don't' know this devastatingly handsome man standing so close I can barely breathe? Funny, but at this moment it was not her head that hurt.

"Fine," she squeaked. She cleared her throat. "Fine," she said more forcibly.

His obsidian eyes sparked wickedly, and she almost believed he could read her wayward thoughts. Liquid heat pooled between her legs at that thought, and her breath came in short, rapid spurts. She willed herself to sit perfectly still and not betray her tension when he reached out with his free hand and gently explored the back of her head.

"It feels okay to me. No lumps or bumps."

His gentle fingers sent trails of fire dancing along her arms and down her spine. She sighed with mixed relief and disappointment when he finally stopped caressing her head. The corners of his lips turned up slightly, and he leaned forward, eyes glittering.

Mesmerized by the sight of that delicious mouth moving slowly towards her, she licked her own dry lips. For the life of her she could not remember this man's name, but she wanted those lips on hers. Hot on the trail of that thought was the idea of those very strong, very capable hands, caressing every inch of her.

Knowledge glowed in those obsidian pools, and her blood began to boil. *My god! What is wrong with me? I don't even know his name—Or do I?* She cleared her throat, and he took a step back.

"Conall."

"What?"

His laughter was warm, and resonated throughout the bedchamber. "It's me, Conall."

Is he reading my mind? Her cheeks burned with embarrassment. She had almost allowed a virtual stranger to kiss her. Face it, she would have allowed him to do whatever he wanted, and if he was reading her mind he already knew it. Apparently, she had no more morals than an alley cat.

"So, are you?" She asked to change the subject.

He looked taken aback. "Am I what?"

"A strong wolf. Conall means strong wolf in Gaelic." How did she know that?

He growled low in his throat, sending chills down her spine. "Maybe I'll let you decide that." Conall was watching her with predatory eyes, and she could almost believe that he was a wolf in disguise. *And she was a lost little lamb.* She nearly jumped when he spoke again. "So angel, want to tell me your name?"

"Don't you know it?" she asked suspiciously.

"Sure. I just want to make sure you know it. That was a pretty nasty bump you got."

"Of course I know my name, it's..." Emerald trailed off. *What is my name?* It was right there, on the tip of her tongue. It was ... damned if she knew. She had to think. *How does he expect me to think when he is staring at me with those smouldering eyes?* Eyes that held the mysteries of the universe. *It is not fair for a man to be so hot he can make you forget your own name.*

On the heels of that thought came the knowledge that she really did not know her own name, and that was not a good place to be. Emerald saw herself mirrored in those two obsidian mirrors, and panicked. She didn't recognize the person staring back at her.

Stark, vivid fear flickered in those seductive amber eyes. Conall reached out to comfort her but she pulled farther into the security of the headboard, and tucking her knees into her chest she began to rock. Once again, his hand froze in the air between them only this time she did not reach out to him. This time she stared at him with wide, confused eyes.

"What is it?" For the life of him, he could not raise his voice above a whisper. "What is wrong?"

"Who did you say you are?" He had to strain to hear her anxious words.

"I told you," he spoke with as much calm as he could muster given the giant knot in his gut. "It's me, Conall." She continued to watch him warily, and he forced himself to step back and give her space.

"Who exactly is Conall? And more importantly, who am I?" Her eyes glittered with unshed tears.

Now he understood. The bullet must have damaged something he missed. She literally did not know who she was. For a mere heartbeat, he considered telling her the truth, but he had crossed dimensions to find her, and he was going to keep her. *You are the key to my life. I cannot let you go.* He swallowed the lump in his throat. "You are my mate," he said instead.

"Your what?" Emerald's eyes were two huge saucers.

"My mate," he said again, feeling a nervousness that he did not like. Conall had always considered himself an honourable man, and what he was doing now went against everything he believed in, but he would not risk returning her to her home until he knew it was safe. *She is Moarté. She will always be in danger.*

Shut up, he told himself. *I am keeping her.*

Her eyes hardened with suspicion. In one lithe movement, she went from her rocking position on the bed, to stand in front of him, her small hands on her hips. "If I am your mate, then why can't I remember you?" she demanded.

Humour glinted in his dark eyes, and he struggled not to laugh. "Maybe as a mate I am not that memorable."

Her eyes glowed with an inner light, as she slowly and seductively moved her gaze over his body. "Oh, I don't know. You look pretty memorable to me."

As his lower body jerked painfully to attention, Conall could not help himself. He took a predatory step towards the woman who enticed him with her innocence, even while her blood called to his. There was nothing wrong with his memory. He knew every inch of that luscious form from his dreams, and he couldn't wait to see how reality compared.

"Maybe I'll remind you now," he said with quiet emphasis.

His nearness made Emerald's body tremble with need. She stepped back out of his reach. The back of her knees hit the edge of the bed, and she fell across it.

Conall looked down at the woman looking up at him, her wide eyes filled with a mixture of desire, and fear. He took a deep calming breath, and tamped down his own desire. He did not have the time it would take to fully explore this woman now. He had to cover his tracks. The last thing he wanted was Kamenwati to find them before he was ready. Before he could do something stupid—like claim his woman and taste the hot salty blood coursing through her veins—he turned on his heel and strode towards the door that slid open at his approach.

"Why don't you rest awhile," he said over his shoulder. "I'll be back later."

Twelve

"JADE." Lykos could not hide the frantic note in his voice. He didn't even try. This was his mate. He felt what she felt and she felt what he felt. They were one and the same. Right now Jade was devastated, and Luke was frantic. He was not sure if it was his pain, or his wife's he was feeling, but he could hardly breathe.

Something bad had happened. Gheorgès let out a roar of pain that shook the walls, at the same time Jade stumbled and clutched her heart.

The pounding of running feet heralded Gheorgès arrival. "I can't get through to Quinn. There is too much pain." Gheorgès own voice edged in panic. "Em is gone. I can't feel her. What the hell is happening?"

The panic in Gheorgès voice broke through Jade's own search for her daughter. Her amber eyes, so much like their Emmy's, sparkled with unshed tears. "Gheorgès Wulfson you watch your mouth."

Luke and Gheorgès sighed simultaneously. Jade's tone may lack conviction, but it proved she was once again in control. Several members of the council arrived only to step back in shock when a doorway appeared in midair and a tall Egyptian male, and a much shorter Mexican woman stepped through.

"Witches!" A voice shouted out, only to have the speaker back off when Gheorgès snarled and bared his teeth.

The small, dark haired woman ignored the gaping men, and stepped toward Jade. "Mama?"

Jade blinked at the young woman standing before her. "Alicia. How did you? Oh, never mind." Jade wrapped her arms around her eldest daughter. "Thank you for coming so quickly." Her smile included the tall bronze-skinned Adonis standing like a stone pillar behind his mate.

"We could do no other," the man said without emotion. "Alicia's family is in need and that will always take priority." His voice softened slightly when he spoke his wife's name, the only emotion he ever showed. The doorway behind them dissolved into nothingness, drawing another gasp from the growing crowd of Lycans.

Members of the council were whispering amongst themselves—torn between the fear and grief pouring off their Elder and his family, and anger at the newcomers for bringing their magic to their hotel. Luke could easily hear every word they spoke. He knew that his wife could not only hear them, but she would be feeling their anger, their curiosity, and their fear at least tenfold.

Luke shook his son-in-law's hand, and pulled him into an embrace, clapping him on the back. He hid a smile at the look on Kamenwati's face, and gave his daughter a quick hug and a kiss on the cheek. "Do you know anything?" he asked.

"No more than you, Sir." Kam answered in his usual stoic tone.

"Which is absolutely nothing," Luke growled in frustration. *With our combined psychic abilities, you would think that someone would know something.* He felt like a human who just found out his child was in danger, and there was not a thing he could do.

Jade slid her hand into her husband's, and gave it a gentle squeeze. "We need to go to Quinn immediately. He is in great pain."

Luke returned the squeeze, and used the private spirit path he and his wife shared. *Do you need anything from the room?*

No. Leave it.

"Kam," Luke addressed the tall lanky Egyptian. "If you don't mind?"

Kamenwati began chanting in a low, melodic tone that completely defied his appearance, and weaved a pattern in the air. He did not need the theatrics, but did not want to shock the Lycans anymore than he had already. A doorway opened.

Quinn was on his hands and knees, tears and snot streaming down his grief torn face, as he stared at what remained of a burning building. His mouth twisted in agony, and black smoke surrounded him. Sirens screamed in the background.

Five figures stepped through the doorway before it vanished, along with Kamenwati's invisibility spell. In all the confusion, nobody noticed the appearance of the newcomers. Jade dropped to her knees, and gathered her son in her arms. Luke strode toward the man shouting orders, obviously the one in charge.

"Get back sir," the man barked out the command. "We don't have time for reporters."

"My daughter is in that building." There was no visible emotion in Luke's voice.

The genuine sadness in the firefighter's voice was reflected in his eyes. "I am sorry, sir. There is no way anybody could have survived a blast like that."

She is not dead. There was determination in Jade's spirit voice, as if saying it made it true. *I don't care what anyone says. I would know if my baby was dead.*

Luke agreed with his wife. He could feel nothing of Emerald here. Dead or alive. If Quinn had not seen her with his own eyes, Luke would not believe she had been anywhere near the farm.

Hours later the firefighters were still sifting through the ashes, as were Luke, Gheorgès, and Kam. 'There has to be something here. Why can't I find it?" Gheorgès voice was harsh with frustration.

Luke put a hand on his son's shoulder, and squeezed. "If it is here, we'll find it Gheorgès."

"Luke, Gheorgès." Kam was standing in the center of the rubbish, in the spot Quinn had not taken his eyes off since they arrived. Already Quinn's burns were healing, but they all felt the pain he was feeling. There was a big hole in their hearts where Emerald should be.

Gheorgès and Luke worked their way carefully over to where Kamenwati waited. The closer they got, the stronger the prickle of residual magic.

What is it? Jade chose their private link to communicate with her husband, and he answered the same way. It was safer to use the spirit voice when discussing anything they did not want the humans to overhear, or anyone else that shared the common path.

I don't know. Magic. Not Emerald's.

Put your hand closer to the source, and close your mind to everything else. Let me feel it through you.

Luke reached his hand toward the area where the prickling was strongest and almost snarled when Kam pulled it back. He was not used to his son-in-law precipitating any physical contact with anyone.

"I would not do that."

You know what this is? Gheorgès asked using the common link the family shared. *If you do, we would appreciate you sharing.*

It is the remnant of a door. Kamenwati's spirit voice used the same bland tone as his physical voice, which did not surprise Luke. Kamenwati was a solitary man, who before he found Alicia did not have much use for his voice. Even now, Luke didn't think he spoke much.

A door? Like the one you opened for us?

Yes. This one has a ward on it.

Kam, someone is here? Alicia used the private link she shared with her mate so the others would not hear.

Where?

The trees by the rubble of the main house.

In a blur of movement, Kam moved from his place between his father- and brother-in-law, and appeared near the rubble of the main building. He was too late. "Damn!"

Stay out of it, Kamenwati. This does not concern you.

Thirteen

EMERALD sat on the edge of the bed and stared at the closed door. She was so angry she wanted to scream. *How dare he walk away?* She paced the room for several minutes, fuming under her breath. "'You are my mate,' he says, and then just walks away. Some mate he is. Leaving me alone here. When I don't even know where *here* is." She was looking around for something to throw at the closed door when it hit her. She was all alone in the bedroom of a man who claimed to be her mate, when she could not remember the simplest thing about him, and the only thing that bothered her was the fact he left her alone. *Alone!* She should be thanking her lucky stars that he did not try to jog her memory. Although, if she admitted it to herself, that is exactly what she wanted him to do.

Better still, she wanted to throw him on the bed, and devour every buff inch of him with her eyes, her hands, and her mouth. *How could anyone forget a body like that?* Emerald's natural sense of humour bubbled to the surface and she began to laugh. *That must have been some bonk on the head, it rattled me senseless.*

"Pull yourself together," she chided herself. "You obviously live here, so let's go see where *here* is." She strode over to the curtained wall. "First thing I need to do is let some light in this room." She pulled the curtain back to stare out at ... a rock!

What is this, some kind of a joke? Emerald took a closer look around the room and realized that what she had assumed was stone veneer, or wall covering of some sort, was actually stone. The only normal wall in the entire room was the one with the door. She reached out to turn the handle, and was surprised to find it opened easily. "Well, at least I'm not confined to my room."

Emerald stepped from the opulent bedchamber into the interior of a quaint country cottage. Several large windows opened to a sunbathed garden. There was no other visible means of illumination, but the sunlight brightened the room more than enough. There was a wicker couch piled high with large cushions, two overly large stuffed chairs, and the largest fireplace she had ever seen, complete with a bearskin rug on the floor.

It would be nice if the fire were going. The instant the thought crossed her mind a fire roared to life. "Whoa!" Emerald took an involuntary step back. "Now this is getting way to weird for me. Who are you really Conall?"

There was no television, no radio, nor even a bookshelf in the room. "I wonder what the man does to pass the time," she mumbled. A vision of the man's sinfully sexy body against hers soon had her blushing. *Uh, never mind, I think I can imagine what he does to pass the time.* Her stomach rumbled and she went in search of the kitchen. It was not hard to find, the place wasn't that large. One door led to the room she had vacated, one to the garden outside, and the third to the kitchen.

Emerald looked in dismay around the small kitchen. A cast iron cook stove took up most of the room, and there was a small table with a single chair positioned for the best view of the garden. The garden beckoned her, but her stomach chose that moment to remind her she was hungry. She tore her eyes from the view outside the window and began opening cupboards.

One after another, she opened doors to discover nothing but empty shelves. There was no food, no dishes, and the strangest thing—there was no dust. *Well we don't eat in much, but we sure are tidy.* When she had opened the last door, Emerald glanced around at all the doors hanging open. She no sooner thought about closing them, when they all slammed shut at the same time. "What is this place," she said aloud. "First the fire. Now the cupboards. Hmm, if I ask nicely can I have some food?"

Nothing.

Emerald put her hands on her hips, and tapped her foot impatiently. "I'm waiting here." Suddenly the incongruity of the situation hit her, and she burst into laughter. "That must have been some whack on the head I got. I'm acting like *Alice in Wonderland*. Before you know it, I'll be chasing a rabbit down a hole. Hmm. Actually, if a rabbit hopped by at this moment I'd probably follow it no questions asked." She was a little surprised that a rabbit did not hop by.

Shaking her head at her own nonsense, she went back into the living room. The man did not even have a bathroom. Honestly, he could not for one-minute think she would actually believe she lived here. Leaving the cottage, Emerald stepped out into the garden. She inhaled the myriad fragrances of a dozen blooms, and felt at peace. The garden was breathtakingly beautiful, with its blooms all the colors of the rainbow. The long sweeping branches of a willow danced beside an old well. A majestic Caorthann stood at the other side of the well.

Even as she watched in astonishment, the Caorthann dropped its beautiful creamy white blossoms on the garden floor, and small berries sprouted in clusters everywhere. The willow's branches danced faster as it swept away the fallen blossoms.

Emerald blinked. The Caorthann was there, covered with tiny berries, and the Willow was weaving gently in the breeze. *It's true*, she thought. *I have lost my mind.*

Not lost. Misplaced, perhaps. The wind whispered the words.

Startled, Emerald quickly glanced around the garden. "Who's there?" She could not stop the trembling in her voice.

A bird chirped from its perch near the cottage. Emerald smiled at the sweet sound. "Hey there, little fellow. You didn't just talk to me, did you?"

The bird chirped merrily, and flew away.

Emerald wandered around the garden. She smelled the lilacs, touched the soft petals of a rose, and watched a spider spin a web amongst the English lavender. She rubbed the leaves of some thyme, and inhaled its fragrance. She forgot the impossibility of all these plants flowering at once—she just accepted it.

A sweeping noise drew her attention back to the well. The Caorthann wore resplendent leaves of gold, and the willow was busily sweeping away the fallen berries. The well beckoned, and Emerald took a cautious step closer, careful not to step on any of the fallen berries. She leaned over the side and peered down into the well.

"Hello," she called softly.

Hello, the well echoed.

The water below was clear, and as still as a scrying pool. *How do I know what a scrying pool looks like*, she wondered.

You know more than you think, came the already familiar voice of the wind, or was the Caorthann talking to her.

Emerald did not bother to look around. There was nobody else here. She was alone in this magical garden with only a Caorthann and one of Cerridwen's willows for company. So, what did she have to lose?

Emerald leaned way over the edge until she could see her reflection in the standing water. *Now what do I do?*

Ask your question.

Flashes of fairy tales she had heard as a child ran through her head. "Mirror mirror that I see. Can you show the real me?" She felt foolish, but the water began to ripple and the image of an owl replaced her own, followed rapidly by the image of a wolf.

"Great. I know I am starving. I didn't need a magic well to tell me that."

~~~

HE stood in the shadows, a part of them, and watched with amusement while his broken angel talked to the well. He must have moved or made some other sound because she suddenly stopped talking and looked straight at him.

Conall did not move a muscle. He did not breathe. She knew he was there. He could tell by the look in her eyes. With a squeal of delight, she ran toward him, and flung herself at him. He wrapped his arms around her to keep them both from falling over.

"Conall. You're back."

Conall could not help himself. His fingers moved up to cup the back of her head and his lips descended on her luscious red ones. His kisses began gentle, but quickly escalated to a heated passion. He stole her breath, and instead of fighting him she matched his ardour. Her young lithe body felt incredible in his arms, the reality so much better than the dreams they shared in the Shadows.

"I knew it was magic," she breathed against his lips.

Emerald stepped out of the circle of Conall's arms and chewed thoughtfully on her lower lip. Her eyes narrowed slightly. His heart skipped a beat, and his hands got clammy. *Does she know where I went? Does she remember who she is? Is she going to insist I take her home?* Conall forced the fears away and waited for her to speak. He did not like this feeling of terror that clutched his heart at the thought of her leaving. He would much rather be back in the lair of the vampire.

"You lied to me." She spoke the words he feared the most, but instead of scorn they were accompanied by twinkling eyes and an impish grin.

"Excuse me?" Conall was at a complete loss. She actually sounded happy that he lied. What he did not know about women could fill the bottomless well.

Emerald stepped closer and traced the outline of his lips with the tip of one slender finger. "You do know me," she said dreamily. "That kiss proves it. Nobody kisses a stranger like that. But still you *lied* to me."

Now Conall was beyond confused. *Did she believe they were mated or not?* "You kissed me," he interjected cautiously. "And how exactly did I lie to you?"

Emerald rolled her eyes and let out a heavy sigh. "Let's get this straight caveman." He lifted one eyebrow at the name, and she burst into merry laughter. "Oh, get off it. Do not try to deny you live in a cave. Although, I must admit it is a beautiful cave, I know for a fact that I *do not live* in a cave." Emerald spun around to encompass the entire garden with outstretched arms. "This whole place is out of a fairy tale. Magical trees and scrying wells. Oh, by the way your well is broken."

Conall's head was beginning to ache with the effort it took to try to follow this conversation. *Is she always like this?* he wondered. *Or was it the effect of my garden?* Her sparkling eyes, full lips, and nubile body as she danced around the garden like a faerie did nothing to make it any easier for him to concentrate on what she was saying. He latched onto the last thing she said. "My well is broken?"

Emerald sighed. "Were you not listening to me?"

Conall coughed to hide his laughter, and Emerald glared at him. She was so adorable when she tried to look fierce. If he had not seen her fight with his own eyes, he might make the mistake of thinking her fragile. "I'm listening," he finally said. "What exactly is wrong with my well?"

"Obviously it does not understand English. I asked it, politely I might add, to show me the real me ... and get this. It showed me an owl and a wolf." Emerald was too intent on her story to notice the scowl Conall directed at the well. "I know I'm hungry, but sheesh, I'm not about to eat an owl or a wolf. I'm sure on some level that would just be wrong."

What in the hell was I thinking? Of course she is starved. It takes a lot of fuel to nourish a power like hers. Shifting alone would drain her energy, and not only had she shifted but she had done battle, for him. He did not deserve a woman like her. He did not know how to care for a woman. He had an awful lot to learn if he wanted to keep her.

Conall placed his arm around her shoulder, and tried to steer her toward the cottage. "I should have realized you would be hungry. I will remedy that now."

They were just about to pass the well when Emerald suddenly pulled away again, and glared at him.

"Now what?" Conall did not even try to hide his exasperation. The woman was wearing him out, all he could think about was her hot pulsating blood, and how her lips had made his own blood boil.

"You lied to me."

This again. "I did not lie to you." It took every ounce of strength he had to keep the anxiety he was feeling out of his voice.

Liar. Liar. Liar. The wind carried the chanting to their ears. Conall glared at the Rowan, and the whispering stopped.

"Why make the tree stop talking, if you aren't lying to me?" Even as the words escaped her mouth Emerald burst into peals of laughter. "This is too much. Just bop me on the head again, and this time when I wake up this will all be gone. I'll wake up in my own little bed, in my own little house ..." her words trailed off and her eyes clouded over. "Tell me Conall. Where do I really live?"

"You live with me." Conall steered her toward the small cottage again. "Let's go find you something to eat."

Emerald's stomach chose that moment to make itself heard so she shrugged off her misgivings and let Conall lead her back to the cottage. The cottage, and the garden might not be familiar, but Conall felt like home.

Fourteen

DAMN!

Now what was he supposed to do? What was a Magi path doing here, and what did it have to do with Little Sister's disappearance?

Kamenwati dare not breathe a word of his suspicions without proof. If she suspected the Magi were involved the Moarté would not hesitate to take them all on. Hell, Alicia could barely control herself when she was in the same room as her father as it was. If she even suspected he or his people had anything to do with her sister's disappearance she would tear the entire fabric of the Chimera apart. Kamenwati needed to get to the bottom of this, and quick.

Kam? Alicia's spirit voice carried all the love she held for him. How could he possibly lie to her? *Kamenwati is there a problem?*

No, my heart. There is no problem. There is nothing here. Kamenwati hated himself for lying to her. If anything happened to her sister she would never forgive him, and it would be his own fault.

There is nothing more we can do here. My folks want to take Quinn to Sanctuary. Charlotte is expecting us. All of us. The Inner Sanctum in Willow Bend, was a replica of an ancient Romanian Castle, and was both a sanctuary for all supernatural beings and a popular spot for tourists.

Kamenwati could not face his mate right now. If he did she would know exactly what he was hiding. *I will meet you at Sanctuary.*

Before Alicia could protest, or ask any questions, Kamenwati opened a doorway and stepped through.

Fifteen

AT their approach the door to the cottage swung open silently. Conall stepped back and motioned for Emerald to precede him.

"You just want to look at my ass," Emerald teased swaying said object provocatively as she passed.

Conall groaned. *That is cruel woman.* "What would you like to eat?" he asked.

You. Emerald's cheeks grew hot at the sudden thought.

Stop that girl. You don't even know the man.

Of course I do. He's my mate. She argued with herself.

How do you know? Because he said so? Maybe he kidnapped you and lied about being your mate. Do you see a ring on your finger?

Emerald glanced down at her ring less finger and mentally shrugged. *Doesn't mean anything,*" she argued. *Maybe I lost it in the accident.*

What accident?

I don't know. But there must have been an accident. Why else can't I remember anything?

My point exactly, her inner voice crowed. *You can't remember.*

Emerald watched the way Conall's muscles rippled while he moved, sleek and smooth like a predator. *Shut up,* she told herself. *Did you* see *the man?*

Conall cocked his head to one side and studied the expressions flickering across her pale face. "Well?"

Startled, Emerald snapped her eyes to his. "Excuse me?"

Conall almost grinned but caught himself just in time. "Is there anything you prefer to eat?"

"Food," Emerald said a little too quickly.

Conall rolled his eyes. "Can you be a little more specific?"

"Let's see." Emerald mentally categorized the contents of his kitchen. "I would love a big juicy venison steak, rare, a baked potato with sour cream, and a side of glazed carrots." *Let's see you pull that out of an empty cupboard.*

"How about a beef t-bone and fried potatoes?"

"Still an awesome feat from what I saw of the kitchen." Emerald hesitated and eyed Conall suspiciously. "What's with the empty cupboards anyway? Don't we eat?"

Conall shrugged. "We haven't been home much lately." He moved silently to the end of the counter and placed his hand against the stone wall. To Emerald's astonishment a section of the wall swung in and Conall stepped through the opening.

Curious Emerald followed Conall into a stone chamber nearly the same size as the kitchen. The air in here was a lot cooler and surprisingly fresh. Shelves lined two walls, and a huge freezer stood against the third.

Conall opened the freezer and took out two t-bones. Then he moved to one of the shelves and grabbed a can of sliced potatoes. He glanced around the dark room and his face lit up. "We don't have any glazed carrots but we do have a can of diced carrots."

Emerald wrinkled her nose in distaste. "I think I'll pass on the mushy carrots, thanks."

Conall shrugged and motioned her to lead the way out of the room. He placed his burden on the pristine countertop and opened the oven door where he pulled out an oven tray. He turned on the oven and Emerald realized that the old cook stove was electric, not wood.

"Powered by the sun," Conall said as if he read her mind.

That made sense. Emerald hadn't seen a single power line near the place.

Conall placed the steaks on the oven tray and slid them into the warmed oven. He opened a drawer where Emerald was almost surprised to see knives, forks, and a can opener. After opening the can of potatoes and draining them, Conall opened the door beside the oven and pulled out an old-fashioned cast-iron fry pan, dumped the potatoes in and set it on a burner. Then he opened one of the two upper cupboards that were a part of the stove and took out two stone plates. These he set on the burner above the oven door where the heat from the oven could warm them.

Impressive. A man who knows his way around the kitchen. Emerald turned her attention to the single chair at the small table, and frowned.

"What's wrong?" asked Conall.

"Why is there only one chair? Shouldn't there be two?"

Conall sighed. "The chairs are out in the garden where you prefer to be."

Emerald's face brightened and Conall sighed, this time with relief. He flipped the steaks and stirred the potatoes. Moments later he divided the potatoes onto the plates, placed one very rare steak on each along with a knife and fork, and headed toward the garden.

Emerald was watching Conall as he moved around the kitchen when the room suddenly grew dark and she could barely make him out in the shadows. *Something was moving toward him. Emerald squinted and tried to focus but she couldn't make out what was moving toward Conall. Fear clutched her throat and her heart beat frantically. She had to warn him but she couldn't force a sound pass her lips.*

When Emerald didn't follow immediately Conall glanced over his shoulder with a puzzled look. "I thought you were hungry?"

At the sound of his voice the shadows dispersed allowing the sun to shine into the kitchen. Emerald's stomach growled and she giggled. "Definitely hungry," she said with a slight laugh. She let her eyes travel the lean length of his body and slowly moistened her lips with the tip of her tongue.

Definitely hungry.

Conall groaned and shoved the door open. He walked stiffly to a small table with two chairs in a secluded part of the garden.

~~~

KAMENWATI stepped through the doorway, and found himself in a field of wild flowers. He knew it was a false trail. If this was the home of a mage even he could not enter uninvited. He heard the sound of whispering and water to his left. Kamenwati followed the sound to the Rowan, and a small bubbling well of water.

Why are you here? The words whispered on a warm breeze.

I seek another like myself.

There is no other like you. There is only we.

Kamenwati sighed. Power caressed him like the hands of a lover, and made him think of Alicia. She would be worried by now. He hated making her worry but he could not give up now. If he returned to earth, there was no guarantee that he would be able to pick up the trail again. If a mage was responsible for the recent deaths of the Lycans he had to be stopped, before he brought the wrath of the *Moarté* down on them all.

The bubbling brook beckoned. Like all the waters in this dimension its root was in the Well of Ankh. Kamenwati bowed before the majestic Rowan and inhaled its fragrance even as it dropped its blossoms to scatter in the breeze.

With your permission I would drink from your waters. The Rowan guarded the Well of Ankh, and although it was Kamenwati's right as the son of Rah to drink from any of its waters, it was polite to ask.

The Rowan tipped its branches. *Please. Drink of life.*

Kamenwati dipped his hands into the warm bubbling water and let its power caress him. Then he cupped his hands to drink the sweet ambrosia. The water was cool, the perfect temperature. Power surged through his veins. It had been too long since he had felt power like this. Since finding his mate, he did not have the need to use the well as his nourishment. He would have to start imbibing more often.

As he drank of the life giving liquid, his senses focused, and he could hear the crickets chirping a mile in the distance. He *knew* where the willow swayed in the breeze just beyond the vast field. He felt every heartbeat, heard every breath taken, and other than the crickets, the birds, and the family of rabbits living in a briar patch a half mile away, Kamenwati was the only living mammal.

Every living entity held power, and Kamenwati was a part of all that power. He *knew* every blade of grass, every leaf on every tree. Kamenwati bowed before the Rowan. *I thank you for your hospitality.*

You are welcomed any time my child. Will you stay a while? It gets lonely here.

Nothing would honour me more, but I must decline your most gracious invitation. I must continue my search for my brother.

Once again the Rowan tipped its branches, this time dropping its bright red berries. *I wish you well on your journey.*

It was Kamenwati's turn to bow, and then he vanished.

Sixteen

JADE sifted through the cold ashes of the burned out farm. Luke slid his strong arms around his wife, and pulled her lithe body against his chest. His voice was huskier than usual, and there was a barely concealed growl.

"It's been over two weeks, love. What do you think you will find now that you didn't find before?"

Power shimmered in the air, and Jade began to glow. The wind picked up scattering the ashes and other small debris.

"Easy, love." Luke spoke calmly, and tightened his hold on his mate. This was not the first time she had nearly lost her grip on herself since the disappearance of their youngest daughter. It didn't help that the one person who might have been able to help track her had vanished just as suddenly.

Damn you, Kamenwati. Where are you?

Alicia was back at The Inner Sanctum scrying for both her sister, and her husband, but so far she had come up with nothing. Quinn and Gheorgès had thrown themselves into investigating the murders of the Lycans.

They didn't want to go but Luke commanded them to fulfill their duties with the committee, and no wolf could ignore a command from their Alpha. Besides, there could be a connection between their disappearances and that of their sister. They prayed they would find her before it was too late, and her lifeless body was discovered miles from where it disappeared.

The wind started to spin the debris into a small tornado that quickly grew, picking up larger branches and small stones that were in its path. "It's my fault," Jade spat the words. "I wanted more for Emmy." Tears ran in rivulets streaking her cheeks. "Every single death eats at your soul until it feels like you are empty inside. You and our family help fill that void for me. That's all I wanted for Em. A normal life. Is that too much to ask?" She shouted into the heavens. "I should have spent more time training her, helping her discover her full potential. She is *Moarté*. It doesn't matter what I wanted for her."

"You taught her well my love. She is not helpless." Luke adjusted his hold. "She is stronger than we give her credit for."

The tunnel cloud of debris grew larger with each passing moment, and Jade's voice grew harsh with her anger. "When the Fates tried to take her from us the day she was born I refused to allow it. I'll be damned if I'll allow them to have her now. If it's a war they want, it's a war they will get."

The twirling wind stopped as suddenly as it began, and the debris fell noiselessly to the ground. Jade leaned into the warm circle of Luke's arms. "I won't let them have her," she said, her voice calmer. She twisted around and kissed Luke's chin. Sparks flew, and small delicate shivers slid down her spine. She still could not believe her luck in finding him. Jade loved this man more than she would have thought possible. This is what she wanted for Emerald. What she has with Luke, and what her mother had with her father. They were *Moarté*, but they were also women.

Jade leaned forward, and Luke reluctantly released her. He wanted to hold her and make everything all right, but he knew that was impossible. Jade smiled that crooked smile that always made Luke hard, and her amber eyes glittered. "Let's go find our daughter," she said even as she shifted.

Luke sighed, and watched the white owl wing its way toward The Inner Sanctum, before he shifted into his wolf, and followed.

~~~

"I'M worried, Mama," Alicia admitted. "I have tried everything, and I cannot reach Kam. For some reason he is blocking me out." In her misery Alicia used her pet name for her husband. A name he would not tolerate from anyone else, except maybe his friend Conall, if Conall were *able* to call him anything. "My head hurts. I haven't felt this way since my rebirth."

Alicia chewed on her lower lip and tried to ignore the call of Jade's blood as it pounded through her veins. Hunger clawed at her insides. *What if I get bloodlust and attack my own family? God even my own mother is starting to smell like dinner. I have to get out of here.*

You can't. They need your help.

Alicia's fangs suddenly shot into her bottom lip. She licked the blood droplets away, swallowed convulsively several times and tried to concentrate on what her mother was saying.

"I'm sure Kamenwati is all right," Jade consoled. She really hoped it was true, but it bothered her that Kamenwati had disappeared so suddenly right after Emerald. "Have you tried to reach him today?"

"Today. Yesterday. Last night. Last week. It is always the same. I come up with nothing. He is not answering my call. Like Emmy, he has completely vanished without a trace."

"Tell me again, what you saw at the farmhouse."

"I didn't *see* anything. I felt a presence by the rubble of the main house, and I told Kamenwati." It still bothered her that she had felt the presence when Kamenwati had not. "He said there was nothing there, and then he left."

They had gone over and over this, and they still came up with the same thing. Absolutely nothing. Jade had gone over every inch of the rubble as soon as the authorities had left, but other than very slight traces of residual power, there was nothing there. Two males, or rather the ashes of two males, were all that remained. The official report read:

> The unidentified bodies of two males were almost completely disintegrated during the explosion that destroyed the remainder of the old farmhouse outside Willow Bend. Authorities are unable to determine the cause of the explosion, but suspect the old silo was being used as a drug lab.

It was better they suspect drugs rather than the truth.

~~~

JADE couldn't stay away from the farm. There had to be a clue somewhere. She stood in the cool ashes and let the hot, powerful magic embrace her. She felt every strand, until she knew without a doubt that she would recognize its creator the moment they crossed paths. Every being that used magic left an imprint behind, like a fingerprint left at the scene of a crime. Whoever had created this doorway was powerful, of that there was no doubt. Then again, so was whoever had used their magic only a few feet from this spot. Jade had stood in both spots taking in the very essence of these beings; much like a bloodhound would take in the scent of its prey. She could kick herself for allowing her personal feelings to affect her duty. Instead of letting her emotions weaken her, she should have been standing here when the ashes were still smouldering, and the trail was still hot. Instead, she had allowed Luke, Gheorgès, and Kamenwati to do the initial investigation, and her daughter could be suffering for her weaknesses.

Becoming one with the power, Jade made her decision. There was no longer any doubt in her mind that the Magi were up to their mystical ears in these disappearances. That would explain the lack of a scent trail, and why Kamenwati had disappeared without a word. If he suspected the Magi were involved, he would want to handle things himself.

Fair enough.

The *Moarté* had always left the Magi alone. That was until they had begun using earth as their playground. Earth was *her* responsibility. It was *her* home. And Emerald was not only *Moarté*, she was *her* daughter.

Jade summoned the elements to her. Thunder rumbled and lightning streaked across a clear blue sky.

"Hear me, Alaric, Prince of the Magi. I, Jade Caer, *Moarté*, request an audience."

A streak of lightning flew like an arrow straight into the heavens. In less than a heartbeat a doorway appeared before her and a tall, muscular blonde stepped through, immediately bending into a deep bow. "I regret to inform the *Moarté* that our Prince is not granting audiences at this time."

Anger, hot and powerful coursed through Jade's veins. A crack of thunder startled a rabbit from its hiding place beneath some nearby shrubs. Drawing in a deep, calming breath, she let the air out slowly through pursed lips. She wanted to blast this stranger and anyone else who dared deter her from her path.

Breathe girl. The well known comforting voice whispered inside her head. *Em is alive. I know it as surely as you know it. Let your anger and fear go. Concentrate on getting her back. You are Moarté. You protect the innocent. You do not annihilate them. Don't make me come for you child.*

The tension left Jade's body, and her lips lifted at the corners. Immediately the thunder and lightning ceased, and the birds and crickets once more chirped and sang merrily. Jade curtsied to the messenger. "It would please this *Moarté* immensely if you would return to your prince with my request. Ask may I speak with him parent to parent."

The blonde messenger bowed, and stepped back through the doorway.

Twelve hours passed. Jade looked up when Luke squatted down beside her in the grass. "I brought you something to eat." His rich, seductive tones caressed her as he handed her a warm plate covered with foil.

The mouth-watering aroma of venison and potatoes drifted toward her. Jade threw her arms around Luke's neck and kissed him before settling back and taking the offered plate. "Thank Charlotte for me," she said as she rolled the foil into a small silver ball and shoved it into the back pocket of her jeans. "Have you heard from Gheorgès and Quinn?"

"They called about an hour ago." Another lycan went missing a week ago in New Orleans and the special task force headed by Gheorgès had been sent to investigate. Emerald's brothers did not want to leave, but after a lot of arguing they finally agreed. They would follow every single lead they got, no matter how small. Whoever was responsible for the deaths of the Lycans had to be stopped, and if they were lucky they would find out what happened to Emerald.

Jade's amber eyes glanced at her husband over her steak as she bit into it. It was the evidence of her emotional state that she barely registered the hot salty blood as it hit the back of her throat, or the way the tender meat melted in her mouth. "What have they found?"

"Nothing," Luke said. "The young man was on his way home from a club. He and his friends were celebrating after winning their baseball championship. At two a.m. his friends dropped him off a quarter mile from his home. He never made it. There was no body." Luke hesitated, and then continued. "This time there were signs of a struggle."

"Any bodies turn up in the weeks just prior to his disappearance?"

When Luke shook his head, Jade shoved the last piece of venison in her mouth. She couldn't help the relief she felt. At least Em hadn't turned up as a Jane Doe.

"That's what makes this so strange. Other than Em, there have been no reports. Daniel Matei has been in contact with police departments all over the world, and has checked every missing person's report. No Lycans have been on those lists."

Jade cringed with guilt. How many of those missing persons could she have helped? Althea and Daniel were in Costa Rica searching for a missing family. The call had come in two days before they were scheduled to go to Italy. Should She have gone to Costa Rica instead? It was her job to protect the humans. Was she being punished?

Do not be an idiot, Jade. You cannot personally save everyone. Besides, Daniel and I are here. We will find these people for you. The spirit voice softened slightly on Daniel's name, and Jade smiled. Althea had been leading Daniel on a merry chase for more than a quarter of a century; maybe she was finally ready to let him catch her.

"Who was here, Luke? There had to be someone. There is no way Emerald would have disobeyed and come here herself if someone was not in serious trouble."

Jade wanted to be angry that Emerald had disobeyed her brother but she knew firsthand how powerful the *Moarté* drive was when triggered. Emerald could no more deny her destiny than she could breathe. The Fates meant her to be at this farmhouse at that time, and it was up to Jade to figure out why.

Luke cocked one eyebrow and looked askance at his wife, smiling when she burst into laughter. "Okay," she admitted. "Emmy would have disobeyed Quinn on principle. She never could stand it when her brother's were in charge."

Jade chewed on the last potato thoughtfully before setting the plate on the ground. "There was someone here. Maybe several someones. I can feel their agony hanging like a shadow over the entire area." She stood up and walked to a small clearing, stopping to point to a spot on the ground. "See this. The grass is singed. It is too far from the fire to have been caused by that, and look here." Jade pointed to small holes in the ground. "Something was here, there, and over there." She pointed to three other similar holes. It looks like someone was staked here, and by the singed grass, I'd say it was a vampire. But that would mean that it isn't only the Lycans being targeted."

Luke knelt on the ground and touched the singed area. He closed his eyes, and sniffed. Nothing. He was not surprised. A little more than two weeks have passed since his daughter's disappearance, and all scent trails would dissipate in just a few hours. There were some Lycans who could still pick up the scent after but he wasn't one of them.

Jade stood behind her husband, and gently massaged his shoulders. "It had to be vampire," she said thoughtfully. "Why would someone stake a vampire to meet the sun? Not many people believed they were real. What had Emmy felt? Someone or something brought her to this place, and then took her from it. The question is, was it a trap to lure her here, or was she just in the wrong place at the wrong time."

Someone cleared their throat, and they both turned to see the blonde messenger from earlier. He bowed low, and said, "as one parent to another the Prince has agreed to a meeting. He will send someone for you and his daughter." He held out his hand, palm up, and displayed a small cornflower blue marble. "Take this stone, and when you and the Princess are ready, blow on it. A door to the palace will then open. It will only stay open for a moment, so do not blow until you are both ready."

Jade took the stone from the Magi's palm. "Thank you," she said, but he was already gone.

Seventeen

IT was all Emerald could do to keep from licking her plate clean. She glanced over to where Conall was watching her with a predatory gleam in his eyes, and felt the heat rush to her center. She licked her lips again— slowly.

Conall watched Emerald lick her lips and his cock jumped painfully to attention. *Woman you are killing me.* She wet her lips with the tip of her pink tongue seductively, and he almost squirmed in pain with the thought of her licking something else with that tongue.

Emerald caught her breath drawing his attention to her slender neck and the vein that pulsed there. Hunger tore through him and his fangs punched inside his mouth trying to get free. *Just one little taste.*

Why stop there? Conall froze at the sound of the voice in his head. *One sip is not enough my son.*

I am NOT your son. Conall hissed the words in his mind.

Ah. That may be. But you can't deny you crave the female.

Conall wanted to deny it. He wanted to scream the words at his tormentor, but he couldn't. As much as he wanted to deny it, he did crave her. He craved her lips, her body, and more than anything, he craved another taste of her precious blood.

One moment Conall was watching her with a predatory gleam that had her wet, the next he was staring at her with a look of horror contorting his handsome face. Suddenly Conall shoved his chair back and stumbled away from her.

"I have to go," he mumbled. His voice sounded like he had a mouth full of marbles.

Before Emerald could react he rounded the corner of the cottage and disappeared. *What was that all about?* This time there was no answer.

Emerald rose slowly from her own chair and gathered the dishes. Conall obviously needed a few moments so she would clean the dishes and give him those moments. It didn't take long to clean the dishes and straighten the kitchen, and then Emerald went in search of Conall. He hadn't returned to the garden, and there was no trace of him in the side yards, so Emerald went back into the cottage. A moment of panic had her heart beating frantically.

Get a grip girl. Of course! The woods! Emerald went quickly to the woods by the well where she found him the last time, but he was nowhere to be seen. She had taken one step amongst the trees when she heard his voice behind her.

"Going somewhere, Angel?"

Emerald spun around ready to give him a blast for startling her, but the look of torment on his usually handsome face stopped her. She quickly went to him and lifted her hand to soothe his troubled brow. He looked so fierce as he stepped away to avoid her touch.

Run.

Emerald stumbled as the word echoed in her mind followed by a vision of Conall pushing her away while fangs exploded from his mouth.

She blinked, rubbed at a dull ache beginning just behind her left eye, and the image was lost.

Emerald frowned at Conall. "Did I do something wrong?"

"No."

Rage spread like wildfire. "No," she snapped. "Then why did you push me away. Am I that ugly?"

Conall's jaw dropped then snapped as he closed his mouth. Need burned his soul making it difficult to retain control. The spicy scent of her anger was intoxicating. His vision blurred as the red haze of hunger blanketed him.

This isn't right. He wasn't supposed to feel hunger while in the Chimera.

You belong to me now, the voice of the Dark Prince taunted.

Conall's eyes changed from black to red and Emerald's anger turned to fear. A shadow crept like a stain across the lush green grass toward Conall. A flicker of recognition, and then it was gone, and Conall was once again watching her with eyes that burned with more than mere hunger.

Trying to distract him, Emerald bent down to pet a small brown bunny. "Oh, aren't you adorable," she cooed. "Conall isn't she the cutest thing you ever saw?"

When there was no answer she turned around, and her brow creased. *Now where did he go?* This was the fifth time in less than an hour he had simply vanished. Enough was enough. She wasn't going to hang around here until he decided that he wanted to make another appearance. Besides, she was getting more than just a little annoyed with his rudeness. What kind of man brought you to his home, and then left you without even a goodbye. As much as she wanted to be his mate, there was something that didn't quite fit.

Emerald headed across the garden, paused for a moment, and then changed direction. Her host may be rude, but that didn't mean she had to be. She reached the old well and curtsied first to the Caorthann, and then to the Willow. "I have enjoyed my stay in your beautiful garden," she said. "I must take my leave now. My destiny is out there somewhere." She waved her arm to encompass the world somewhere beyond the garden. "Please thank Conall for me when he returns."

It still seemed a little crazy to be talking to the plants and animals, but when in Rome.

Don't go. Stay. The words carried on the breeze. *He will be angry if you leave.*

Emerald found herself thinking the words, and it did not feel nearly as strange as speaking aloud to a tree, even one as magnificent as the Caorthann. *I must go. I need to find my family. I need to find me.* Emerald knew she was being childish, but she couldn't resist adding. *Besides, if Conall wanted me to stay he should have asked me.*

Emerald turned, and once again started walking to the other side of the garden towards the forest. Ten minutes later she did not appear to be any closer to the trees. She began to run. She ran faster, and faster but didn't get any closer to the trees. She began to feel weird. Not nauseous or dizzy, just not quite herself.

The colors in the garden began to fade until they were merely shades of grey instead of their brilliant reds, yellows, and purples. She started to fall forward, and stuck her hands out to break her fall, only to continue running on her hands and feet. She stopped so suddenly that she tumbled to the ground in an undignified heap.

Okay. That's it. I am not going to stand for any more of your shenanigans Conall, whoever you are. There was fur on her arms. *Fur!* And they were not her arms anymore. He had turned them into legs. And her legs wouldn't work anymore. Every time she tried to stand she fell back onto all fours like some kind of beast. When she tried to speak it came out a growl. She could just imagine what she would look like if she could see her reflection.

A red haze was blurring her vision, and sparks started to fly around her. Thunder boomed overhead, and lightning flashed in the sky. She growled low in her throat and the thunder echoed her mood in the distance. One thought remained constant. She had to reach the safety of the forest. If she reached the woods the spell would be broken. It amazed her how easy it was to lope in this form, but when she looked up she was no closer to the woods than she had been at the beginning. Emerald's howls of frustration joined with the clapping thunder.

There was a whisper of sound behind her. Emerald spun around and glared at Conall with glowing eyes. "Turn me back now!" It came out a vicious snarl. Conall took a hesitant step forward.

Turn me back now!

Black clouds burst apart and Emerald was suddenly drenched. *Terrific!* She turned her great head and sniffed at her wet fur. *Eww! I smell like wet dog.* She turned beseechingly to Conall. *Please turn me back.*

No sooner had she thought the words when she found herself sitting unceremoniously on her naked butt in the wet grass. Conall's eyes flared with lust, and just as quickly went blank. He took a step toward her, and offered his hand, only to find himself flat on his back.

"Do not touch me!" Emerald's voice quivered with fury, and the lightning flashed brighter.

"Calm down," Conall said quietly.

"Calm down!" Emerald sputtered. "You have got to be kidding me. First you turn me into a wolf. But that isn't bad enough. Oh no. Out of some perverse sense of humour you make it rain on me." At his honestly confused look, she relented. "Okay. So maybe you didn't make it rain. But you turned me into a wolf, and when I asked you nicely to turn me back you leave me sitting naked in a wet field. Look at me!" Emerald felt the heat rise in her cheeks. "No. Don't look at me. Do *not* look at me. Do *not* touch me. Do *not* talk to me."

Emerald rose from the ground with as much dignity as she could muster; with her back ramrod straight, she walked toward the house.

Conall watched her glorious backside as she walked away from him. Heat coursed through his veins, and he shifted slightly to relieve the pressure of his erection from pressing against his pants. With a reluctant thought he clothed her as she had been clothed before her transformation. She did not break stride, or acknowledge his gift in any way.

A small fawn made its way from the edge of the woods to the slim woman walking through the garden. Emerald paused to scratch behind the fawn's ears. When she smiled, the clouds dispersed and the sun came shining through.

~~~

KAMENWATI stepped through the doorway and found himself in a field of wild flowers. The sound of running water, and the whispering of the Rowan came from his left. Kamenwati traced the sound to a tall Rowan beside a small bubbling well of water.

Why are you here? The words carried to him on a warm breeze, the voice neither male nor female.

Kamenwati replied, as was the custom when speaking to the spirit of the Rowan, with his own spirit voice. *I regret the intrusion on your home, but I seek another like myself.*

There is no other like you. There is only we.

Kamenwati sighed. Power caressed him like the fingers of a lover. The bubbling brook beckoned. Like all the waters in this dimension, its root came from the Well of Ankh. Kamenwati bowed before the majestic Rowan, inhaling its fragrance even as it dropped its blossoms to scatter in the breeze.

With your permission, I would drink of your waters.

It was the Rowan's duty to guard the Well of Ankh. The Rowan tipped its branches. *Forgive me my inhospitality. Please. Drink of life.*

Kamenwati dipped his hands into the warm bubbling water and let its power caress him. He cupped his hands, and drank the cool, sweet ambrosia. Power surged through his veins. His senses increased tenfold with a single sip. He heard the crickets chirping a mile in the distance. He saw a daisy bend in the wind on the other side of the vast meadow. He *knew* where the willow swayed in the breeze just beyond the edges of the field. He felt every heartbeat, every breath taken, and other than the crickets, the birds, and the family of rabbits living in a nearby briar patch, Kamenwati was the only breathing creature.

Every living entity held power, and Kamenwati was a part of that power. He *knew* every blade of grass, every leaf on every tree, and every pebble of sand. Kamenwati bowed before the Rowan. *I thank you for your hospitality.*

You are welcomed any time my child. Will you stay a while?

Nothing would honour me more, but I must decline your gracious invitation. I must continue my search for my brother.

Once again, the Rowan tipped its branches, dropping its bright red berries. *I wish you well on your journey.*

Kamenwati bowed once again, and continued on his journey.

Eighteen

JADE paced the cold white marble floor; her bare feet made no sound as they threatened to wear a hole through the stone. Her white robe blended perfectly with the bare white walls of the waiting chamber. The only color was the gold and silver streaks in her otherwise pale hair. Jade could imagine herself dissolving, becoming one with the bland room. She couldn't suppress a shudder at the thought. How many had been left waiting in these rooms until they lost all sense of who they were?

She had to give Alaric credit. If his plan was to disorient, he was going about it in a very interesting way. A weak mind coupled with the passage of time could prove disastrous.

Jade stopped suddenly and threw her arms out to her sides. Her fingers tingled with the urge to release a bolt of energy. She took a deep breath and forced herself to calm.

"Damn you, Alaric," she cursed. "We are wasting precious time. Let me out. Now!"

She wasn't really surprised when the door didn't open. This was the Magi's turf and he wasn't about to let her forget it.

The moment they crossed into the Chimera, Jade lost her connection to the outside world. She felt alone and isolated. The only mind open to her was Alicia's and she was struggling to keep her guard up, and the rest of the Magi out.

Unlike Jade, the moment they crossed into the Chimera Alicia's mind filled with the thoughts of all the other Magi. Jade held her while she covered her ears and rocked.

"La la la la la la," she crooned.

After several minutes which seemed like an eternity, and might have been if they were still on earth, Alicia dropped her hands and grimaced. "It sounds like I'm in a conference hall and everyone is shouting at once. But at least I'm not starving anymore."

Crap. Why didn't I think? "I'm sorry Alicia. I should have realized you would be getting hungry with Kamenwati gone."

They both knew they weren't talking about food.

"Don't worry, Mom. It's not like I'm going to attack anyone." *Came pretty damned close to dining on Ghéorges a few times though. And that would be wrong on so many levels.*

Jade pulled up the sleeve of her non-descript white robe and offered Alicia her wrist. "I offer what is mine freely so you may share my strength."

Alicia's face drained of color even as her fangs punched out of her mouth. She stepped toward Jade and furiously pulled the sleeve back down to cover the pulsing vein. "No!"

"You need to feed," Jade said sternly.

"I will not feed from my family. I will wait for Kamenwati."

Jade shook her head slowly while she chewed on her bottom lip. Her amber eyes swirled. She didn't belong in this realm and that made her a prisoner to protocol. She could not leave this room until the Prince of the Magi permitted her to. On the other hand, Alicia was Magi. If she found the strength to shut the others out she might be able to search undetected for Emerald; if she was really here.

"Listen to me, Alicia. I can't do anything here without the entire kingdom coming down on me. This world is silent to me so I cannot even scan for Emerald." *How often I prayed for silence. Why now?* Not even the voice of her conscience reached through these sound stealing walls. "You on the other hand belong here. You can search for Emerald."

Alicia grimaced. "Oh yeah. I can hear everyone in this place and I wish they would all just S*hut Up*."

Jade was nodding her head now as her face broke into a crooked grin. "They can." When Alicia looked at her suspiciously, Jade continued quickly. "You can block them out of your head. All you need to do is feed."

"I'm not hungry anymore." Alicia said petulantly.

"You don't feel hungry because you are here. You were hungry before we came across which means your body still needs to fuel. Think about it. When you and Kamenwati come to visit are you overwhelmed by the others?"

"No," Alicia said hesitantly.

"That's because you feed before you come. Once you feed you will be in control again." Jade pulled back her sleeve and again offered her vein. "If it helps, close your eyes and pretend I am someone else."

Alicia shook her head and rolled her eyes. "Never happen," she snapped just before she dipped her head and sank her fangs into her mother's vein.

Hot salty blood filled her mouth, hitting the back of her throat like ambrosia. *Dear God let me stop in time.* Alicia sucked harder allowing the power enhanced liquid to suffuse her organs, making her stronger. As the blood reached her brain the voices grew quieter until they ceased to be more than a whisper in the back of her skull.

Alicia withdrew her fangs and ran her tongue over the tiny pin pricks on her mother's wrist to seal them. She wiped her lips with her hand hoping there were no telltale traces of what she had done. She lifted her sparkling black eyes to Jade who was smiling indulgently.

"Feel better?"

Alicia felt the heat rush to her cheeks. "Yes. Thank you." It was Alicia's turn to chew on her lip and Jade waited until she was ready to speak. "I didn't hurt you, did I?"

Jade looked at her wrist, at the two tiny red spots that were already fading. "Honestly," she said. "It was a rather pleasant feeling; like I was sedated. I felt like I was drifting on a cloud and I didn't want to get off."

Right. More like someone jabbed you with a vacuum and tried to suck your life out. Alicia grimaced. "Thanks, Mom."

"For what?"

"For lying to make me feel better."

Jade shook her head and grinned. "Yeah, well that's what mother's do. Lie."

They both laughed.

"Okay. Now concentrate. Can you sense anything? Can you feel Em out there?"

Alicia closed her eyes and found the darkness much more calming than the white room. She reached along the paths used by her family as well as the private link she shared with her sister.

Nothing.

It was like Emerald did not exist.

"Maybe it's this room," she said.

Jade's amber eyes sparkled mischievously. "Then why don't you go somewhere else and try? Go to Rah's home and see if you have more luck there."

"But ..."

Jade winked. "I was told to wait here until Alaric summoned me, but I'm pretty sure I didn't hear them tell you to stay put."

Alicia laughed. "You are so bad. And you wonder where we get it from."

Jade rolled her eyes and made shooing motions with her hands. "Go now. Before Alaric summons me and realizes you are not here."

Alicia gave her mother a quick peck on the cheek. "I'll be back as soon as I can," she said and vanished.

Yeah right.

Jade paced the small confines of the white room and let her anger slowly come to a boil. There was no way of telling how much time had passed since they left earth. It could have been a day or even a month. Time moved differently here in the Chimera.

"Damn you, Alaric. Let me out of here so I can find my daughter."

This time the door opened and a tall cowboy stepped in, complete with a 10-gallon Stetson hiding most of his brilliant red hair, and a pair of shooters in the holster slung at an angle from his lean hips.

Jade didn't hesitate. She spun around and flipped the cowboy onto his back, and dug her long fingers into his pale throat. "Don't do it cowboy," she hissed.

Tex's hands that had instinctively reached for the handles of his guns stilled and he glared daggers. His lips began to move silently.

"Think about it Mage. Protocol forbids I use my magic first, but if you so much as hint at using yours against me, then you are the one breaking protocol. I will not hesitate to disintegrate you where you lay."

Tex's lips stilled but there was no doubt he was thoroughly pissed. Jade grinned and eased her hold on his neck, slightly. "There, now isn't that better? Now tell that pompous ass boss of yours that I am through waiting while he plays at being a prince."

Tex stared at the *Moarté* and let his mind and body go limp. He was not about to let her anywhere near his Prince.

Jade shook her head and tssked. "Oh come on." She tapped his forehead with the fingers of her free hand. "I know he's in there. Just concentrate. I know you can do it. Now repeat after me. Alaric, oh our beloved Prince of the Magi, our humble guest requests your presence. Now!"

There was a slight movement and Jade released the Mage so she could face Alaric. There was a sudden movement at her back and Tex's hands were on her arms. Jade glanced over her shoulder and gave him a droll look. The Mage released her instantly and moved to stand beside his prince. His eyes were dangerously dark with a tinge of red surrounding the pupils, and Jade had no doubt that he wished they were alone, and anywhere but here with his prince.

Careful what you wish for Mage.

"*Moarté*. Mother of my daughter ..." He looked around the chamber and frowned. "Where is our daughter?" he demanded.

Jade rolled her eyes. "She is not *our* daughter, and Alicia is not here."

"I can see that. I asked where she was. You were told she was to be with you."

Jade's lips turned into a smirk and she shrugged. "Technically I was told that I could not enter the Chimera without Alicia. I didn't."

Alaric turned his frown on Tex. "Is this true?"

"Yes, my lord. Your daughter was with the *Moarté* when they came through."

"Then where is she now?"

Tex looked nervous but Jade had to give him credit. He did not lower his gaze or turn away. "I do not know. I put them in the room like you told me to, and I told them to stay here until you summoned them."

"Nope," Jade interrupted. "Your exact words were `Stay in this room *Moarté* until the Prince summons you.' Looks like you screwed up. Alicia is a lot of things, but *Moarté* is not one of them."

This time Tex visibly cringed.

"It looks like you will need to be more careful with the words you choose," Alaric said. "You may go now. The *Moarté* ..."

Jade rolled her eyes at the implied insult.

"Excuse us, our guest and I have things to discuss," Alaric said when Tex did not leave immediately.

"But," Tex sputtered.

Alaric waved a hand and the door opened. Tex started shuffling backwards toward it. "Leave us," Alaric snapped.

"Fine." Tex spun on his heel and strode the rest of the way out under his own power.

The door closed with a click and Alaric bowed gallantly to Jade, as if he suddenly remembered his manners. "Would you care to join me for something to eat?"

Jade's stomach growled and she grimaced. "No thank you. I would much rather get down to business."

"Ah, the missing child. I was sorry to hear your reason for requesting this audience. We owe the young *Moarté* a great debt for saving our Conall."

"And how is Conall these days?"

"I am sad to say there is still no change. He simply lays there day after day caught in his own mind. We have tried to reach him but are blocked from our goal."

"When was the last time anyone checked on him?"

"Yesterday. When they took him his nourishment. Someone goes every day to ensure he is fed. Each day we hope to find a change, to get a hint that he will recover, but there is none. I fear he is lost to us."

Jade could hear the honesty in Alaric's words, but she couldn't shake the feeling that Conall was somehow connected to Emerald's disappearance; If not directly, then indirectly. "I want to see him."

Alaric's eyes widened at the request. He could not let her near Conall. Not until he discovered for himself the truth of the situation. The Magi who brought Conall his sustenance last reported no change, but shortly after Conall's mind opened with a vision of the young *Moarté* before again snapping shut. *What did it mean?* Alaric was determined to discover the truth before he let anyone near his friend. First Kamenwati showed up this morning asking about Conall, and now the *Moarté*. There had to be a connection.

Jade's eyes narrowed slightly. *What are you hiding, Alaric?*

"I'm sorry I cannot allow Conall to be disturbed. Our healers say he needs peace to heal."

"And what? You think I am going to find a man laying in a coma and try to shake the truth from him." *Not that I won't if I think for one moment the Mage is faking.*

"Of course not," Alaric was quick to assure her.

"Then let me see for myself. I might even be able to help him."

"You never suggested you might be able to help before this."

Jade shrugged. "It wasn't my responsibility." She didn't think she would be able to help the Mage if he was still under the influence of the Ursaline's poison but Alaric didn't need to know that.

Unable to come up with a single plausible reason to keep her away, Alaric reluctantly agreed to the meeting. "You and I will personally bring him his nourishment this evening. I will not allow him to be disturbed before then." His voice quickly switched from fierce to gentle. "While you are waiting perhaps you will change your mind and agree to a meal with me."

Jade's stomach growled loudly. *Looks like I don't have a choice.* "I will gladly accept your offer of a meal."

"Good, good. If you will accompany me it is already laid out in my personal chambers."

Nineteen

THE blood lust was growing stronger. Conall had only taken enough blood from the man on earth to ease the pain, and start the healing process. To drain them would have meant relinquishing his soul to the darkness, and he was not ready for that yet. Not now that he had finally found his true mate. He watched the young *Moarté* with hungry eyes, and fought the urge to drink.

He rarely left his garden, preferring its tranquility to the chaos on earth. The last time he left the Chimera was to find his Prince's daughter, but what he found was a fantasy. He wanted her from the moment he saw her. Her blood called him. He searched for her from the Shadows. She was his lifeline. Her blood connected them. If not for her, he would have relinquished his soul to the Dark Priest years ago. She fought at his side trying to pull him from the shadows. During that time she grew into the most beautiful being he had ever seen, and she was *his*. He felt her in his soul. She held the key to his existence. Her blood carried the power he needed.

He could take her. It was his right. He was Magi.

He took two purposeful strides toward her, hunger clenching his gut. He could feel the bloodlust burning in his eyes, and lowered his lids to mere slits. *Just one little sip. She need never know.*

She'll know, whispered the Rowan. *She'll know.*

"Know what?" Emerald's voice dripped with suspicion. "Are you trying to hide something from me, Conall?"

Conall swallowed, and glared at the Rowan, using the distraction to tamp down the bloodlust glowing in his eyes. "What could I possibly be hiding from you?" He did not sound convincing to himself, so how could he expect her to believe him. *If you do not mind your own business I will cut you down,* he threatened the tree.

"Conall! How could you?" Emerald ran over and leaned against the tree, spreading her arms around it protectively, and jealousy burned in him. She narrowed her eyes at him. "If you are going to cut down this beautiful tree, you will have to come through me."

Someone was knocking. Emerald looked around the garden. She looked up at the sky, she peered down the well, and then she walked over and peeked under a toadstool. "Well," she finally said trying hard not to laugh. "Are you going to answer the door?"

Conall shrugged. He did not have to answer. He knew exactly who was knocking, and he did not wish to speak with Kamenwati. He knew why his brother hunted him, and he was not ready to let Emerald go. He needed more time to convince her they belonged together.

The knocking stopped, and suddenly the air filled with thousands of little floating sheets of paper. Emerald reached out to snatch one as it fluttered by. Her brow furled in consternation, as she stared at the little symbols all over the page. "I can't read this," she complained. "What language is this?"

Conall shrugged, and ignored the papers landing on his head, and piling around his feet.

"Fine. Don't tell me." Anger tinged her soft voice, and Conall winced. This did not bode well. "If you are not going to answer, then I will." Emerald looked up at the sky, shielding her eyes from the falling papers, and she called out. "Hello. Is anybody there? Would you like to..."

Conall grabbed her, and clamped his hand over her mouth before she could invite Kamenwati into the garden. Emerald struggled in his arms. He leaned into her ear. "Be still," he whispered, and unable to resist temptation twirled his tongue around the delicate lobe.

"Ooh," Emerald breathed beneath his hand, as shivers wracked her warm body. Her blood flamed, and she melted back against his chest, turning into his lips.

The knocking on the door started again, accompanied this time by the steady chiming of a doorbell. "Send him away," Emerald murmured with a sigh against his warm lips. "The sooner you get rid of whoever it is, the sooner we can get back to what we are doing."

Conall might be able to ignore Kamenwati for the moment but he knew their time here was limited. Soon the *Moarté* would come, and she would not wait for an invitation.

Conall claimed Emerald's soft, warm lips and lust claimed every part of his body. He was prepared for her to struggle, to pull out of the kiss. He wasn't prepared for the way she leaned into it, savouring every taste of him, claiming him so he didn't have the strength to pull away, the match that started a flame not even the fates could douse.

Without relinquishing her lips, Conall lifted Emerald into his strong arms and strode toward the cottage, everything else lost in the strength of their need for each other.

Conall stared at the vision she made with her hair splayed out on the pillow, a silky white cloud ribboned with gold and silver, her amber eyes still cloudy with passion. The scent of their love making lingered in the air filling his senses.

How will I ever let you go?

The taste of her filled his senses as her blood rushed to recharge his vital organs and his brain. He should have been sated; instead he craved her even more.

"You are the most beautiful woman alive," he whispered in a husky voice.

Emerald's soft pink lips tilted up at the corners and her eyes filled with an emotion Conall couldn't identify, but the look made his chest tight.

"No I'm not," she said quietly. "My mother is."

Conall stiffened. "What did you say?" His voice barely above a whisper as fear tore through his chest.

Emerald sighed. "I said thank you but I am not the most beautiful woman alive. My mother is. My father tells her every day and he doesn't care who hears him."

Emerald's passion filled eyes cleared and she stared at the man who lay beside her. He was leaning on one elbow, his long silky black hair hanging like a curtain covering his arm. His other hand was at her face, his fingers barely touching her skin. Shock froze the features of his face.

Conall couldn't breathe as Emerald's amber eyes changed from passion filled to clear, and then back to confused.

Don't panic. Conall wasn't sure if he meant Emerald or himself.

In a heartbeat Conall found himself sprawled out on the floor in all his naked glory. Emerald was crouched in the corner of the bed, her back against the wall and the black sheet pulled up to her chin. She was glaring daggers and Conall felt every one pierce his skin. He was suddenly glad to find himself on the floor in one piece and not a pile of ash.

Emerald stared in shock at the man sprawled on the floor. *Blessed Cerridwen, what have I done?* At least Conall had enough sense not to move. He lay where he landed, his tall lean body open to her viewing, barely breathing. *And no finer body had she ever seen.*

She wet her suddenly dry lips with the tip of her tongue and almost smiled when there was a telltale twitch in his cock. *Wait. Shouldn't I be pissed? Yes. I really think I should be pissed. But at who? And what the hell was she doing here?*

Emerald decided to take it slow while she tried to figure out where they were and what she was doing in bed with the gloriously naked Mage of her dreams. *Okay I know what we were doing.* From the scent of sex in the air, it would be extremely hard not to know what they'd been doing, and lord help her she wished they were still doing it. The reality was so much more satisfying than her dreams.

Think Em. What is the last thing you remember? Visions of that strong lean body on top of hers flashed in her mind, and her cheeks grew hot.

Conall watched the blush spread over her cheeks and couldn't help thinking how charming she looked. Innocent and knowing all at the same time.

Blessed Cerridwen, how am I supposed to think with all that eye candy laid out before me? With a blink of an eye Conall found himself dressed in extremely tight black leathers and a form fitting muscle shirt. When he looked askance at Emerald she shrugged.

No reason to completely hide the goods.

Emerald let go of the sheet and slid out of bed wearing form fitting black jeans and a thin, powder blue, long-sleeved turtleneck. She stood in front of Conall with her legs splayed slowly began pleating her long tresses.

"Are you going to lay there all day or are you going to get up and clue me in as to where we are and what the hell is going on?"

Conall cautiously rose to his feet keeping one wary eye on her. *At least she hasn't turned me to ash yet.*

While Emerald continued to plait her long tresses she let her memories play out. The last thing she remembered was being in the Shadows with Conall and being attacked—by Conall. She tilted her head and eyed him curiously. *He looks okay now. Hell girl, he looks more than okay. He looks absolutely divine.*

Stop that! Concentrate.

"I'm going to take a stab and say we are not in Kansas anymore, are we?"

At Conall's blank stare Emerald realized the *Wizard of Oz* reference was completely lost on him. "The Shadows. We're not in the Shadows are we?"

"No."

Emerald rolled her eyes. "Gee, could you be a little more forthcoming." She tapped her forehead for emphasis. "I seem to have a few holes in my memory." Before Conall had a chance to answer Emerald gasped. "Blessed Cerridwen how long have I been here? My family is going to be frantic."

"Not even a day." Conall jumped all over the second question.

"Not even a day! Not even a day! What the hell does that mean? Not even a day." Emerald threw her hands up to stall his answer. "Before you go there I need to know how long I have been here in earth days—or years." She tacked the latter on fearfully.

Conall shrugged and a bolt of lightning landed beside his feet scorching his pristine floor.

Emerald made a funny little buzzer noise, and said. "Wrong answer."

Anger flared in Conall's dark eyes as he stared at the scorch marks. "Fine. I-don't'-know."

"Well at least that's honest. Now for the next question."

Conall glared while he waited for the next question. He couldn't blame her for being angry. He should never have lied to her. And he most definitely should never have taken advantage of her.

I've lost her and it's my own fault.

"Do you have any food in this place? I am starving."

Emerald couldn't help it. She burst into peals of laughter at the stunned look on Conall's face. It took several moments before Emerald could bring herself under control. She might not know what was going on but there was one thing she was absolutely sure about.

Conall would never hurt her.

Emerald stepped toward Conall where he stood, still with that stunned look on his face. She tucked her arm through his elbow. "Come on," she urged. "Find me something to eat. I'm starved and I don't think well when I'm hungry. It makes me irritable." She grinned impishly at him and tugged him toward the kitchen.

While she ate pork chops and green beans, Conall filled her in on what happened back in Willow Bend.

Conall watched Emerald gnaw the last bit of meat from the bone, and then slowly lick the juice from her fingers. His cock spasmed as the thought of that tongue on him made his mind mush.

Emerald's amber eyes twinkled and she lifted one brow. "Something else on your mind Mage?" Her voice was soft and husky.

Conall groaned. Emerald's lips turned up seductively in the corners, and she leaned across the table until their lips almost met. When Conall leaned toward her, she said, "Perhaps you want to tell me where you keep disappearing to."

She sat back in her seat, a smug look on her face, and Conall groaned again. "You are cruel, woman," he complained good naturedly.

Emerald's fingernails began a rapid staccato on the table top.

"I've been leaving a false trail for Kamenwati while I have been searching for the trail left by the vampire."

"Any luck?"

They both jumped at the sound of knocking. Emerald's cheeks mottled with heat at the memory of what happened the last time someone knocked.

"Maybe you should just invite him in this time."

Twenty

IN a moment of clarity, Madison looked around the small operating room and horror crawled like a spider leaving sticky little thoughts in his mind. This wasn't a hospital.

Where in hell am I?

There were two cots set up; one raised slightly higher than the other. Both had occupants held down by silver shackles. Neither was human. The one in the higher bed was dark with an almost angelic appearance, especially now with his alabaster face set serenely in death.

The one on the lower cot writhed and screamed in pain revealing long sharp fangs.

A memory fluttered in the back of Madison's mind, but not near enough to recognize clearly. Like a word on the tip of your tongue that your mind is not strong enough to spit out.

Wait! It was a boy. Found in a jungle. Raised by wolves. Something happened to him. What happened? The wolves did something to him. Something to change his DNA and he changed into a wolf. It was here. No, not here. Back at the Institute. He could have figured out the how and why of it, but someone stole the boy. Who? Who broke into his lab and took the boy?

The creature on the lower cot screamed again, dragging Madison from his reverie, and then fell limp.

"Damn." Madison moved toward the creature and felt for a pulse. Nothing. He was about to snap open the silver shackles when another voice shouted.

Stop!

Madison's head snapped around but there was nobody in the room except for him and the two dead bodies. He reached for the shackle again.

I said stop.

The words were inside his head. Madison's hands hovered over the shackles. "Who are you? What are you doing in my head?"

The who is of no consequence. Just know that if you remove those shackles too soon you will be the one who is dead.

Madison's hand jerked back. He didn't want to die. He wanted to live. He wanted to live forever. The voice was right. How could Madison be sure the creature was really dead? He looked around the room and discovered a small table with an assortment of equipment. He chose a sharp scalpel, and returned to the creature on the lower cot. He removed a long needle from its arm, frowning slightly. *Why was that there?*

You were performing an experiment. Remember? You wanted to see if transfusing a nightwalker with a daywalker's blood would change its DNA so it would be able to face the sun.

Right.

Madison's nose crinkled and he sniffed the air. "What is that disgusting odour?" It smelt like something had died and was rotting right there in the room. The stench was so strong he thought he was going to vomit.

Breathe through your mouth and relax. Theron had trouble keeping the disgust from his own voice. Humans were so weak it wasn't even laughable, it was disgusting. They were no more than cattle, fodder for his army. The army he would create with this stupid human's help.

The earth's sun was beginning to rise weakening Theron's hold. He would need to drink from the human again soon, re-establish his hold before he lost complete control of its weak mind. The man might be obsessed and easily manipulated, but Theron had crawled through every corner of the man's mind, and deep down in a place he'd accessed, was what the goody-two-shoes liked to refer to as `an ounce of humanity.'

If the *good* doctor realized he had technically drained the life of another human in his quest for immortality he might revolt. It was only a slight chance, but one that Theron could not afford to take. Not when he was so close. The beautiful boy on the table hadn't lived through his transformation. Theron hadn't given him the chance. He was too good, and too strong. For months he had completely ignored Theron's every attempt to corrupt him; choosing to believe that Theron's voice was that of the devil and spending hours on his knees in that horrible church repenting for sins he didn't have, and praying to his God to cast out the devil.

Fool. No other God mattered but him. The boy would have been a great addition to his army. His ability to heal would have strengthened with his transformation making Theron's army nearly indestructible. By the same token, Theron could not allow him to live to be reborn to Rah's side.

The door opened admitting two humans in their early thirties, bald, muscular, and sporting equally blank eyes. Madison turned on them. "When the sun comes up, take it out and throw it in the field behind the house."

He looked once more on the angelic face of the pre-transformed male, and his gaze softened before he ordered, "cut off his head and toss the body into the swamp. When you are finished I need you to bring me the female."

"Yes, master," they chorused.

Madison's lips curled in the corners contorting his face into something evil and rotting. "I expect my guest to be comfortably constrained when I return."

With those words a doorway opened in the center of the room and Madison stepped through to the Shadows.

Twenty One

I'M telling you something has happened to him." Lily tried once again to make the police officer listen to her.

"I'm sorry, Ma'am," the officer said for the tenth time. "There is nothing we can officially do for at least forty-eight hours. Until then, he is not technically missing."

"He could be dead in forty-eight hours," wailed Lily. She was so frustrated she wanted to make the light fixture over his complacent head come crashing down. Maybe then he would see the light. She almost snickered at the thought, but her brother's predicament kept her sober.

"Is there any reason to suspect foul play? Does your brother have any enemies?"

"Of course not," sneered Lily. "He is Father Zack. *Everyone* loves him."

Everyone in New Orleans knew about Father Zack, including Officer Frank. They knew him as the healing priest. People came for miles around hoping for a chance to have him lay hands on them. Officer Frank thought he was just another scam until he had reason to see him in action when Father Zack healed his own son. The boy barely turned two when diagnosed with an inoperable brain tumour that made him blind. Officer Frank hadn't wanted to take the boy to see him, but his wife insisted. 'I don't care what it costs,' she'd cried. 'He's our baby.'

In the end, Officer Frank relented willing to lose everything they had if there was a chance for their son, but it hadn't cost a thing—not them anyway. Father Zack didn't even ask what was wrong. He simply moved his hands slowly over young Michael's body coming to rest on his forehead. A soft golden light moved from the priest's hands to his son's forehead. When it was over, Father Zack collapsed in a heap on the floor, and Michael was staring at them with clear blue eyes.

Oh yeah, there was no reason to suspect foul play. Father Zack was a true gift from God, and he denied no one despite the cost to himself.

"I am truly sorry Lily, but officially I cannot do a thing. That does not mean I am not going to look for him on my own. Maybe he just had to get away for a few days."

Lily's smile was wobbly when she thanked the officer.

"Don't worry, Lily. He will turn up." *Please God don't let him turn up dead.*

Lily walked down the steps from the police station and over to the café where Katriana waited. "I'm sorry Lily," Katriana said.

Lily didn't question how Kat knew without her saying a word; a blind man could tell it was bad news by the look on her face.

Katriana had something that drew Lily from the beginning. She couldn't move objects with her mind like Lily, she couldn't heal people like Zack, she couldn't manipulate space like Sangria—then again, nobody could do most of the things Sangria could—yet there was definitely something compelling about Katriana.

"They said they can't do anything for forty eight hours."

Katriana pushed her chair back and rose to her feet. "They might have to wait for forty eight hours, but we don't. Let's go."

Lily followed Katriana. It wasn't like she had any definite plans of her own. "Where are we going?"

Katriana winked, "To find your brother of course."

"And how do you propose we do that?"

Katriana shook her head and rolled her eyes. "Duh," she said drolly. "The dynamic duo had nothing on us. We will start at Zack's. I'll try tracking him from there."

"And what can I do?" asked Lily.

"You can drop a tree on his head when we find him for making us all crazy."

Laughing together arm in arm, the girls headed to Zack's apartment on Chartres just down from Ursuline Convent. When they got there Zack wasn't home. They knew he wouldn't be. Katriana paced off every inch of the small bachelor apartment without finding any scent other than Zack's and their own.

"Nothing," she reluctantly admitted. Kat looked out the window at the quickly setting sun. "Call Sangria," she told Lily.

Sangria was there almost instantly. She stood in the center of Zack's small living room/bedroom, her dark hair a riot of curls falling over the high collar of her long black coat. Her leather-encased legs were splayed, her hands at her sides, fingers extended to allow the air with all its secrets to caress them.

The last two hours had been spent in hell, wearing a hole in the floor of her room on the supposedly closed off top floor of the convent. Lily's fear had called to her, and for the first time in centuries Sangria felt trapped by her inability to face the sun. The moment the sun began to fade she transported herself to Zack's front room.

Sangria closed her eyes, and sighed. She couldn't tell Lily that she'd already been here, in the wee hours of the morning, long before Lily would realize that her brother was missing. She'd felt the Dark Priest's influence and had immediately checked on both Zack and Lily. They were so close to their transformation, thus putting them on his radar.

Lily had been asleep quietly dreaming.

When she arrived at Zack's apartment there was no sign of a disturbance. His apartment was the same as always, sparsely furnished, a hot plate, a nearly empty bar fridge, and a wardrobe in the corner were the only signs of human occupancy. Sangria didn't have to open the wardrobe to know the drawer held a man's socks, underwear, and a half dozen white shirts, while the closet part held two black suits with collar; all exactly the same as what he was probably wearing right now.

From the moment Sangria met him, she thought he was going to make a devastatingly handsome vampire. It was her goal to ensure he lived his new life by the same high standards he lived this life—protect human life at all costs.

The man was of the purest heart and so far none of the Dark Priest's promises or hints of power had swayed him. Even now he was bent on one knee outside his apartment, soothing a frightened child whose mother had fallen ill. She watched from the shadows while Zack stood and followed the child through the darkened streets.

Sangria walked the dark streets herself after that, forever guarding the humans from the Dark Priest's army.

Now, standing in Zack's cramped apartment she wished she had followed Zack to his destination. Maybe then he would be home safe where he belonged. Instead she was trying futilely to find some evidence that he had returned here last night.

They spent most of the evening wandering the streets searching for either Zack or the boy who urged him away. When the music began to throb from Bourbon Street they turned their search in that direction. Someone had to have seen him.

Twenty Two

GHEORGÈS glanced toward the door as the most mix-matched trio he was ever likely to encounter walked in. One was tall, sleek, and walked with the lazy stealth of a cat; one was slightly shorter with a bob of yellow curls circling her pale face; the last had long black curly hair tucked into the collar of her jacket, and despite her olive complexion looked like she hadn't seen sunlight in the last twenty years, and considering she was a blood sucker she probably hadn't.

Just the sight of them slammed home the fact he hadn't had sex in over a month. His groin tightened at the sight of the females. *What I wouldn't give for a piece of that group—even the damned bloodsucker is looking good.*

All three of the females were scanning the crowded room, searching for someone in particular. When a set of those searching eyes met his, his breath caught in his throat. Her eyes were two different colors beneath the brown contacts she wore, one jade and the other amber, and they were the most compelling things he had ever clapped eyes on. *Why would she hide those gorgeous eyes?* He could stare into those orbs forever, lose himself and the world around him, but after barely a glance which sent Gheorgès reeling, her eyes moved on.

"Didn't need the damn complication anyway," he muttered under his breath before snarling. "We're wasting our time here, let's go." He was only a few feet from the door before he realized Quinn wasn't right behind him.

Gheorgès turned back to see Quinn staring at the female vampire like she was an angel. He was already sizing her up for his easel, Gheorgès could tell just by the vacant look in his eyes. *Damn. We don't need this right now.*

A set of obsidian orbs impaled him with their fierceness and it felt like somebody was prodding at his brain with a dull knife. Gheorgès threw up blockers and glared at the bloodsucker.

Who in hell are you? He demanded. Alert now, he tried to pick up something from the trio that would explain their presence at this particular time. He was getting nothing from the bloodsucker shooting daggers, nothing from the tall dark Madonna. *Russian maybe.* The pale blonde was worried about someone named Zack. He hadn't shown for their lunch date and nobody had seen him all day.

This could be interesting. He took a step away from the door when he suddenly stopped. He tried to take another step but his feet felt caught in quicksand. Anger coursed through his veins with the speed of a freight train, and he turned eyes red with rage on the female bloodsucker. *Let. Me. Go. You. Bitch.*

The female cocked one eyebrow inquisitively, and shrugged.

Now! Gheorgès demanded throwing every ounce of command he could summon into the words.

The female staggered, and lost her grip. The other two females instinctively reached out to steady her, but

Quinn was already there. The tall slinky brunette pegged him with her gaze as if she knew he was the cause of her friend's lost balance. Gheorgès tried to read her mind but it was closed tighter than Fort Knox.

Katriana felt Sangria stumble and immediately reached out to steady her but a tall, extremely large male was already steadying her. She felt the tremor of power in the air and turned towards the source.

Oh … my … god! He was breathtaking, an almost exact duplicate to the man now talking quietly to Sangria. The power flowing from this other male was awe inspiring, and terrifying. *Who are you?*

Katriana wasn't surprised when there was no answer as much as she was relieved. At least he wasn't here for her—at least she hoped not. Okay, maybe she would like it if he were here for her. The sexual vibes flowing from him nearly overpowered those of magic. But if they were going to start sending other species after her she would never survive on her own. Maybe it was time for her to actively seek out this Jade Caer that Dom was always on about and ask for asylum.

She tore her gaze from that of the magnetizing male and quickly scanned the rest of the room. It was crowded with people not so much dancing as simply milling around. The place reminded Katriana of a market place, only it wasn't livestock on the market here—not exactly.

Quinn looked at the face of an angel and instantly saw her on his sketchpad, and from there in his bed. Her curly black hair framed an oval face like a dark halo. Her dark passion filled eyes raked his skin as she slowly ran her pink tongue over her blood red lips swollen with his kisses. When she staggered he took it as the perfect opportunity to touch that smooth olive skin. With fluid graceful movement that belied his large size he moved to her side instantly, steadying her with a gentle grip.

Electric sparks pricked his fingertips but he refused to move his hand. "Are you okay," he asked.

Sangria blinked up at the image of the man she had just stopped in his tracks. "How did ..." she began and then realized this was not the same man. This man's eyes were soft and filled with concern. She risked a quick peak toward the door. *Yep. Still there.* Only now he was trying to burn a hole in the back of his brother's head.

Sangria risked another peak from under her long lashes at the man holding her arm, and for the first time she could remember her tongue felt like it was tied in knots. "I'm ... I'm ..."

"She's fine," snapped Katriana, and instantly softened her voice. "We are looking for our friend. Maybe you have seen him. He is tall, dark hair," *and can move things with a mere thought.*

Sangria frowned at Katriana. She gently removed her elbow from the stranger's grip. "What my friend is trying to say," she said. "If you saw Zack you would know it. He stands out in a crowd. He is a priest and always wears his collar and crucifix."

Katriana grimaced and shrugged. "Yeah. That's what I meant to say." She scowled at Sangria.

Quinn's smile transformed his already handsome face into one of absolute beauty. "Sorry girls," he said. "I can safely say we have run into no priests since arriving in New Orleans."

Quinn. Quit your gabbing and let's go.

"I will keep my eyes open for him though," promised Quinn. "If I do happen to see him how do I get in touch?"

QUINN.

"I'll find you," he said before turning abruptly and following Gheorgès out the door.

Twenty Three

GHEORGÈS wasn't paying any attention when he pushed his way out the door; his mind was wrapped around the bloodsucker and Quinn's reaction to her, while his libido was all tied up with the tall brunette. God, what was wrong with him. When she spoke to Quinn he was actually jealous. Her sultry accent had his cock standing at attention, and god forbid she had looked at him with scorn even while sex rolled off her in waves. Women. He'd never understand them.

Gheorgès barely glanced up to check he wasn't going to trample anyone in his haste to get out, only to plow into something solid that had not been there a second before. The man staggered and Gheorgès automatically reached out to steady him when shock nearly knocked him on his ass. Directly in front of the stranger was his sister.

The male dropped into a protective crouch throwing his arm out as he spun on his heel, his palm straight up.

"You." Gheorgès spat the word. He stared into the face of the bloodsucker that almost drained his sister so long ago, and lost all reason. White hot rage was his guide as he leapt for the bloodsucker's throat.

Quinn was almost to the open doorway when he suddenly felt lighter than he had in the weeks since his sister's disappearance. Unsure what was causing this sudden inner peace he stepped out the door to see Gheorgès with his hands clenched around a vaguely familiar male's throat. His sister, whom he feared dead, was trying to pull Gheorgès off the guy.

It was one of those moments that seemed like they moved in slow motion while at the same time everything was moving way too fast. So this was the reason he suddenly felt so peaceful. His sister was alive. The male on the ground must have rescued her. This brought him to realize that Gheorgès, being a wolf of action rather than plan, was trying to throttle the male when he should be thanking him.

"Gheorgès." Quinn growled the command low in the back of his throat at the same time he roared it in his mind. *"Get off him."*

"Yeah, Gheorgès you ass. Get off him," seconded Emerald's soft growl.

Although Quinn's compulsion was not enough to force Gheorgès' compliance, it was enough to break through his rage and allow him to realize the mage was not fighting back, nor had he been attacking his sister. In fact, if Gheorgès had taken the time to notice he would have seen the mage readying a blast to protect her. He had only reigned in his own power when he recognized Gheorgès.

Gheorgès loosened his hold on the mage's neck and slowly rose from the ground only now realizing that Emerald was still tugging on his arm. Ignoring the mage gasping on the ground, Gheorgès pulled his sister into his arms and hugged her tight enough to break the bones of a human.

Emerald returned the bone crushing hug with one of her own before pushing him away and giving him a staggering blow. "You ass," she snarled. "I see you still leap before you look. You could have killed him."

Gheorgès shrugged indifference. Quinn reached down and offered a hand to the mage, who stared at it as if he expected it to turn into a serpent and strike, before hesitantly accepting it. Quinn tugged the mage to his feet, his brow furled. "Conall, isn't it?"

Conall nodded and stepped closer to Emerald, keeping a wary eye on the wolves.

"Are you okay?" Emerald's voice softened at least two octaves when she spoke to him.

"Yeah," Conall returned Gheorgès glare with one of his own. "Does your family always attack first and ask questions later?" Conall was referring to an episode when he first met Emerald's mother, only then it was Emerald's sister he was protecting.

"You're lucky I didn't kill you," Gheorgès snarled.

If you knew I kept your sister from you, you still might. "I'll take that as a yes, then." Conall turned back to face Quinn who was watching the scene with troubled eyes, and still hadn't said a word. "Do you want to hit me too?"

"That depends," Quinn finally answered.

"On?"

"Why you took my sister."

"Don't worry about that right now," Emerald interrupted. "We need to get off the street. Is there somewhere safe we can go? I need to talk to Mom, but she seems to be off my radar." Emerald's amber eyes were darting up and down the street, and her face was unusually pale.

Are you all right?

Emerald turned pain filled eyes on Conall. *It's too loud.*

Quinn watched the exchange between his sister and the mage, and his brow furrowed even more.

"Wipe that look off your face, Quinn," Emerald teased. "Or you'll end up looking like Gheorgès."

Gheorgès scowled at her teasing, even while he let it ease the ache in his heart he'd had since she left. Emerald's sudden grin lit up her face.

There was a sudden tingle in the air around them, the kind that signalled magic. Without a word the three men fell into formation surrounding their female, blocking her from anyone's sights. Emerald sighed, making sure it was loud enough for all three to hear, and grinned. It didn't matter how old she was, or how powerful she grew, the men in her life would always be there to protect her. For once she didn't mind at all. *At least they are no longer fighting each other.*

We are staying at the Hotel St. Marie on Toulouse, room 212. Get my sister out of here.

Fat chance fat head, Emerald quipped. *I'm staying right here.*

Please, Em, Quinn's spirit voice pleaded. *Don't make me lose you again.*

Emerald couldn't stand the pain she felt in those simple words. Guilt racked her. She'd been safe and happy in the Chimera, although clueless, while her family had suffered and mourned her. Although barely a day had passed in her reality, she wasn't even sure how much time had passed here.

Conall tensed beside her and Emerald quickly scanned their immediate vicinity. Finding nothing on the street, she searched the building her brother's just vacated. There was something there, but Emerald felt no menace, simply overwhelming grief and fear that she found almost debilitating. Was this how her family felt when she was missing?

Emerald placed her palm on Conall's arm and said quietly. "I need to get off the street." She broke free of the protective circle and headed toward Toulouse. "Are you coming?"

The three males fell into step with her. They were an intimidating group with Conall and Quinn flanking her, and Gheorgès protecting their back.

On the corner of Toulouse and Bourbon they passed a living statue dressed like a Hollywood vampire complete with black cape and dripping red fangs. The statue's eyes followed them as they passed, and had they looked they would have seen a flicker of recognition in them. Two more vampires, these dressed like tourists in dark pants and shirts, were chatting with a couple of teenage girls.

God, the streets are crawling with them. Conall shot the duo a warning when they passed. The two vampires suddenly remembered they had somewhere else they had to be, pronto, and beat feet down the street.

Emerald raised an eyebrow in his direction, and Conall shrugged. There was no sense courting trouble. There was a tingle at his back and Conall quickened the pace. He didn't need to turn around to know the female from the bar was watching them from the corner. Like the one pretending to be a living statue, and the two on the street, she could sense the stain on his soul as easily as he could sense the purity in hers.

It was after midnight when they entered the lobby of the hotel. They were barely in the door when the desk clerk stepped from behind the counter and barred their way. He inclined his head slightly to the brothers and Emerald. "You may pass," he said simply.

When Conall attempted to follow the desk clerk bared his fangs in challenge. "You have not been invited in," he snarled. "This is not your playground."

Gheorgès barked with laughter. Emerald glared at her big brother. Conall bared his own fangs, and snarled. "Step aside," he commanded.

"You are not a guest in this establishment. You have no right to enter." He had no way of knowing that a mage, unlike a vampire, did not need an invitation to enter a human establishment. A human abode had no wards against the Magi because the ward of invitation was a result of Magi magic.

Gheorgès pushed the call button for the elevator, and tried to tug Emerald toward it. "Guess we'll catch you later, bloodsucker." He could barely conceal his contempt when he spat out the word.

Emerald shrugged his hand from her arm and with her hands on her hips and feet slightly apart she glared. Her amber eyes began to swirl with unleashed power.

"Shit." Gheorgès growled. "Everybody duck."

The desk clerk glanced at Emerald. "You hadn't better be planning on using that on me in here," he snapped.

"Let him pass." Emerald snarled.

Conall suddenly relaxed, and the young vampire automatically followed his lead. "Who are you?"

"My name is Kristoff."

"What are you?"

Kristoff gave him a droll look. "I'm a vampire same as you." The young vampire took a closer look at Conall. "Maybe not exactly the same as you," he conceded.

No. Not like me. There is no stain on your soul.

"Don't worry." Kristoff directed his words to the others in the lobby. "Not all of us drink from humans, and not all of us that do are stupid enough to drain you dry."

"We'll isn't that encouraging," sneered Gheorgès.

Emerald punched him. "Oh shut up, Gheorgès," she snapped and turned to the young vampire. "I know you are reluctant to let him pass but it is imperative that we get him off the street."

Kristoff didn't budge. As young as he was by vampire standards he was strong in his convictions, and he had taken a vow to protect human lives. A vow his father and grandfather had taken before him. He was secure in the knowledge that he was protecting the guests under his care, and that knowledge gave him strength.

"I'll vouch for him," Emerald said quietly.

Conall stood perfectly still determined to allow the young vampire to come to his own decision. He was strong with a good soul and Conall knew he would do what he felt was right. In the hundred years since his transformation not once had he waivered toward the dark side. Not like him. No. Conall would not force this male's compliance. If he continued to refuse him access to the elevator he would simply enter through the balcony. He had no intention of causing a scene.

Kristoff glanced toward Gheorgès who inclined his head slightly.

Emerald fumed. *Men. They are the same in any species.*

Without another word Kristoff stepped aside and allowed Conall to pass. As the elevator doors slid silently closed Kristoff returned to his desk duties. He smiled at Lily and Katriana when they walked through to the elevator a couple of hours later.

It won't be long now, he thought as he watched the nearly newborn step onto the elevator from beneath the cloak of his long lashes. For a brief moment he shared her pain before the elevator doors quietly slid shut.

An hour later he didn't even bother lifting his head when the front doors opened and two human males staggered in. He was used to the drunken tourists coming and going at all hours, and his shift was almost over.

Twenty Four

JADE glared at the Prince of the Magi when he finally strolled back through the door. She wasn't one to sit around and cool her heels, and having to wait for Alaric to decide when she would be *allowed* to visit Conall did nothing to improve her sense of humour. She sat through a long drawn out meal with one interruption after another as Alaric conversed with the tall lanky cowboy, and once the meal was over instead of taking her to see Conall, Alaric announced he had one more thing to do—and so Jade waited—again. He was damned lucky she didn't disintegrate him where he stood.

Just because you can doesn't mean you should.

"I know. I know," she muttered.

"Pardon?"

Jade glared at the mage, her amber eyes swirling violently, and she almost, but not quite, smiled when he took an involuntary step back. It was a small victory. *Good. At least you realize how pissed I am.*

"I was just trying to think of a good reason why I should not send you into oblivion," she said syrup dripping from her tongue.

Alaric blanched. "Are you ready to see Conall?" he asked quickly making Jade think he had actually considered trying to stall again.

In a heartbeat, Jade changed out of the despised white gown and bare feet into a tight fitting, long-sleeved, black t-shirt, black cargo pants, and black hiking boots. There was a silver blade with a wolf head on the handle tucked into her right boot. With a snap of her fingers her backpack appeared, and Jade shrugged it onto her shoulders.

"Now I'm ready." She smiled evilly. Let him stew. She was done playing nice.

Alaric looked like he was about to explode, but thought better of it. His face was mottled and his eyes burned.

Jade lifted one eyebrow in question. *Go for it Mage,* she taunted. *Then you will see just how pissed I really am. Mother!*

It was a definite warning, and Jade threw the image of a grin toward the sender. *Good to have you back, baby.*

"Where ..." began Alaric before Jade shut him off.

"Take me to Conall's home," she said curtly. Alaric may think he had her fooled, but she already suspected Conall would not be there, and she wasn't disappointed.

She *was* surprised at the beauty of the mage's home. Where Alaric held court in a castle of obsidian marble and glass, Conall's home was a garden of magical delights.

A small bunny hopped up to her, and Jade bent down to scratch behind its ears. "Hi there," she cooed. "Aren't you the most adorable thing?"

Alaric cleared his throat. Jade ignored him and strode over to the majestic Caorthann whose branches were adorned with delicate pink flowers. She dropped to her knees and bowed her head.

Rise my child. The air tingled with power. *You are needed back on your earth. A place known as New Orleans.*

Will I find her there?

Yours is not to question but to follow. The voice reprimanded gently but firmly. Jade knew anyone who dared question the Goddess risked immediate annihilation.

Forgive me Grandmother. I meant no disrespect.

Go in peace my child.

There was a brilliant flash of light and Alaric was left standing alone in the garden as the Caorthann dropped her petals.

Twenty Five

A BOTTLE of moisturizer flew across the room, hit the wall between the sliding glass door and the window, and then came to a stop with a dull thud on the thickly carpeted floor. Katriana picked up the plastic container and set it on a nearby table.

"Having a tantrum is not going to help find your brother," she said with a calm she didn't feel.

Lily plopped her butt on the nearest bed. Her shoulders trembled as silent tears slid down her cheeks. "I know."

She looked so forlorn that Katriana wanted to hold her and tell her everything would be all right. She wanted to find Zack and kick his ass for scaring his sister the way he was. Deep down Katriana was afraid they would not find Zack alive, and that made her want to commit violence. "I'll make some coffee," she said instead.

Katriana quickly moved to the small dressing room beside the bathroom that doubled as a walk-in closet, and a kitchen counter. She frowned at the empty coffee bag, and then checked the coffee maker to see if it was ready to go. "Damn. The housekeeper didn't bring any more coffee."

There was a sniffle, and then a swallow from the other room. "That's my fault. I told her I didn't need any today." Lily was a long-term guest of the hotel, and hated being a burden, as she called it, on the housekeeping staff.

Finally something I can do. "I'll just run down to my room and grab some from there." Katriana already had her hand on the knob when Lily spoke again.

"Don't bother. I think I'm just going to try and get some sleep."

"Are you sure," Katriana asked. "It will only take me five minutes."

Lily's blonde curls bounced when she shook her head. "I'm just going to lay here and try to sleep."

Katriana moved so she was standing directly in front of Lily who was forced to lift her head to look at her before Kat spoke. "Do you want me to stay tonight?"

It was purely coincidental the girls had rooms at the same hotel, and became great friends. Katriana met Lily the morning after she arrived. She had already drunk the coffee in her room and gone down to the breakfast buffet to grab another cup of the delicious French brew. The aroma of fresh beignets tickling her nose had proven too much to resist, and before she knew it Katriana had a plate piled high with fruit and the tasty French pastries.

Even at such an early hour the restaurant was too busy for Kat's liking, so she took her plate and cup intending to eat in her room. As she reached for the call button for the elevator, she had an urge to sit by the hotel pool in the small, secured courtyard shaded by tall palm trees.

It had to be the Fates. The only person in the courtyard was this petite, pale, blonde who looked like she would bolt the moment she saw Katriana.

Katriana started to back out the door. "I'm sorry," she murmured. "I can find somewhere else to eat."

Lily smiled and her face glowed with an inner light Katriana had never seen in her life, or even thought possible until she met Lily and her brother Zack.

"You're Russian, aren't you?"

Katriana wanted to lie. The less people who knew her the safer she was, but something about Lily compelled her to tell the truth. "Yes."

"You are a long way from home." Lily waved a hand and the chair opposite her moved out from the small, white, wrought-iron table. "Come. Join me," she said. "Tell me all about your Russia."

Katriana didn't blink when the chair moved of its own accord. Magic was an intricate part of her life. She made her decision to sit with Lily that day, and they became friends almost immediately. She would die to protect her friends. She didn't have that many.

"I can stay if you need me," she offered.

Lily grinned. "I know you would. But really, I'll be okay. Sometimes when everything is quiet Zack and I can reach each other across greater distances. Maybe we will get lucky tonight."

Katriana's gaze drifted to the windows and the sound of the revellers heard all the way from Bourbon Street. The party would go on all night. "You call this quiet," she quipped. "I don't know how you can stand it." Katriana's room overlooked the courtyard that was empty after dark, exactly the way she liked it.

Lily shrugged. "That kind of noise doesn't bother me. Zack and I grew up here. I'm going to miss all the excitement when I move into my house next month."

Katriana didn't know how anyone could possibly miss such volume, but to each his own. "In that case I think I'll call it a night myself."

Five minutes later there was a knock on Lily's door. "I told you I'd be fine, Kat," she said as she swung open the door to the hallway. Instead of Kat standing there with a packet of coffee in her hand, two strangers filled the hallway. Built like linebackers, dressed in jeans and t-shirts, with shaved heads, they could have been anyone.

"Are you Lily?" one asked

"Yes." Lily looked at them curiously but could read nothing in their demeanour that was threatening. It was like they were wrapped in cotton balls. "Can I help you?"

"Your brother sent us to get you."

Relief flooded her veins. Zack was alive. Belatedly she remembered Zack cautioning her about being too trusting. "My brother?"

"Zack," the other man said. "He asked us to bring you to him."

"Where is he?" Lily asked, even as she reached for her jacket. "Is he okay? Is he hurt?" She was halfway out the door when she hesitated. "Wait. I better call my friend and tell her where I'm going."

One large hand clamped down on her wrist and tugged her through the open door. "I'm sorry but we can't let you call anyone. Zack said it was too dangerous to tell anyone where you are going. He said your life would be in danger if anyone knew he contacted you. Come, we must hurry."

Lily hesitated. Something was off. Finally, the need to see her brother won, and she left with the strangers.

Twenty Six

"THE *Moarté* did not detect him because the Dark Priest is *hiding him*." Conall clamped his mouth shut and glared at Gheorgès. He had repeated himself for the last time. *Your move, Wolf.*"

GHEORGÈS paced the floor of a room that was suddenly smaller with three grown males and his sister. Emerald and Quinn sat on the twin beds, in identical positions with their backs against the wall and their knees tucked up under their chins. Conall had taken up a position against the wall on Emerald's right, his left knee touching the bed she was on like he had the right, his arms nonchalantly crossed over his chest. He was as relaxed as a viper ready to strike.

You've done well my son. Gain their trust and then strike.

Never going to happen. God help him the power churning in those veins had his fangs aching to strike.

They are nothing to you. They will destroy you given the chance. Destroy them first. Divide and conquer.

Conall's cheek twitched. *Shut. Up.*

Two pairs of black eyes and one amber pair turned toward him. Conall dared not move for fear his almost fully protruded fangs would show. Hunger gnawed at his composure.

The stain on his soul was growing.

"It's not possible," Gheorgès finally growled. "Madison would be an old man by now. Hell, he should be dead by now." They all knew the story of how their mother had rescued Matthew from the crazy doctor trying to proof the existence of weres, but that was more than fifty years ago and Madison was an old man then.

Conall cast him a droll look. Emerald rolled her eyes.

"How is that even possible?" Quinn asked. "He is a human."

"There are ways," Conall finally said.

Gheorgès grunted. "I supposed you could create your own vampire army too."

Conall pushed himself from the wall, his fists balled at his sides, his eyes glowing with a red tinge. "Wake up, moron," he snarled. "What do you think we've been fighting all these centuries?"

With a blur of movement Conall was out the patio door and over the railing. He dropped the three stories to the street below with ease. By the time the three in the room realized he'd moved he was striding up Bourbon, the tails of his long coat flapping behind him.

Emerald watched Conall stride away and swallowed the urge to call him back. He wasn't going too far without her. That isn't what had her worried. The dark shadow following him did. It had almost doubled in size since their arrival back on earth.

"Do you want me to follow him?" asked Quinn. He was already crouched ready to pounce over the rail.

"Don't bother," Emerald said. "He'll be back."

"I hope not," Gheorgès muttered under his breath.

Emerald glared at him and grabbed a blanket off one of the beds. She folded it in four and put it on the floor between the two beds. "That's your bed," she told Gheorgès. "Consider yourself lucky you aren't sleeping on the balcony."

Conall strode down Toulouse toward Bourbon trying to put as much distance as possible between him and the wolf. The scent of blood hung in the air, fresh, salty, beckoning. He considered heading in the opposite direction, away from the crowds, but he didn't trust himself should he meet someone out alone. Without the possibility of being caught, he was terrified he would succumb to the temptation.

You need to feed.

He needed his woman. He needed her arms around him, holding him steady while he emptied himself inside her. He needed her very essence inside him giving him strength, and more importantly, giving him hope.

Twenty Seven

CONALL was waiting for them at the bottom of the stairs of the New Orleans police station. He looked like hell. Ignoring Gheorgès growl he took his time kissing Emerald hello. "I missed you last night," he whispered in her ear, his gruff voice sending goose bumps dancing along her flesh.

"I missed you too," she answered.

Quinn cleared his throat and they broke apart quickly like a couple of teenagers caught in a clinch. Gheorgès was still scowling at them, and Conall returned his dark look with one of his own, his fangs peeking through his slightly parted lips.

Emerald threw her hands in the air. "For crying out loud this is ridiculous. If you two go in there looking like that the cops will probably hold you both on suspicion of every unsolved crime in the country."

Two pairs of obsidian eyes glared. "Forget it," she snapped. She grabbed Gheorgès by the arm. "Conall you wait with Quinn and try not to draw too much attention to yourselves. Gheorgès you come with me."

When Conall started to protest Emerald stalled him. "Honestly, Mage, at this moment you look downright scary. Try to pull yourself together."

~~~

"I am not leaving here until you agree to search for her."

"I'm sorry miss but there is nothing we can do until she has been missing for forty-eight hours unless there is evidence of foul play."

In the blink of an eye Katriana leapt over the desk and grabbed the official drone by the throat holding him against the wall while his legs kicked helplessly and his face mottled with fury, and then fear, as breathing became difficult.

Katriana was so infuriated she didn't even hear the door to the street open, but she did hear the swoosh of air, and the click of the safety, as the only other officer in the building drew his gun, and aimed the barrel at her head.

"Let him go, lady." The voice squeaked with nervousness. Small wonder. Katriana knew the odds of him shooting her without hitting his partner were astronomical.

She ignored him. "Listen you little toad," she hissed. "My friend came in here yesterday to report her brother missing and you blew her off. Now she is missing and you will not, I repeat, you will *NOT* blow me off as easily."

"Please, lady," the younger officer pleaded. He'd never drawn his gun except at the shooting range and wasn't even sure he could pull the trigger with it aimed at a person. He stood there, his hand shaking, when a very large blur shot past him, and a man wrapped his large hand around the throat of the woman who still held his partner up in the air.

"You heard the officer. Ease up, lady," Gheorgès growled in the ear of the dangerously sexy brunette holding the terrified officer. His cock twitched as he breathed in her scent. He moved closer until his cock was pushing into the cheeks of her ass. "With a little more pressure I could snap your neck."

"Back off you jerk," Katriana growled low in her throat and pressed back into his erection.

Gheorgès was shocked he didn't come right then and there. "You first."

They stood there, Katriana with her hand on the throat of the now still officer, Gheorgès with his hand around her neck, his cock shoved against the soft round cheeks of her ass, and his hot breath tickling her ear; neither one willing to give an inch.

Emerald stepped in front of the rookie whose hand was shaking so much she was afraid he would shoot himself by accident. Her amber eyes swirled with power. "You will put the safety back on your weapon, carefully, and place it back in its holster."

The officer who was dangling against the wall gaped. Part of him was pissed the rookie obeyed, and another part, the self preservation part of him was relieved.

"You will go about your business and forget any of this happened." Emerald then turned to the female holding the officer against the wall. The woman was throwing off confusing vibes—anger, worry, arousal.

Emerald glanced at her brother. She couldn't help but see the way he had himself ground against the female. *You are such a dog;* she shot the insult at him.

Gheorgès managed to shrug without changing the pressure on the female's neck, or anywhere else.

"You will release the officer," she commanded the female.

The female turned her odd-coloured gaze on Emerald. "And if I don't'?" Katriana was not used to taking orders from anyone, much less a female.

Emerald's lips tilted up, and her amber eyes twinkled. "Then my brother snaps your neck." Emerald could have used compulsion on the female but she wanted to know how far the other woman was willing to go. The moment Gheorgès touched this female Emerald lost the thread of her existence, which meant she didn't have a future or it was linked to her brother's; The next few seconds would tell her which.

The female released the officer and he dropped to the floor in a slump. Before he gained his feet he was fumbling for his gun.

"You don't want to do that," Emerald told him. "What you want to do is to go about your business and forget any of us were here."

The officer rose, shook his head as if dazed, rubbed absently at his throat, and sat down at his desk completely ignoring the three strangers. Emerald turned to her brother who still held the female immobile.

Gheorgès, she reprimanded.

Gheorgès growled low in the female's ear enjoying the way her body trembled in reaction. "Good choice, female." He let go and stepped out of range as she twirled around and struck out at him.

Gheorgès smirked, and Katriana whirled on Emerald. "Why did you do that?" she demanded. "Now you've ruined everything."

Frustration, anger, and fear rolled off the female in waves. She was worried about her friend and her brother, and now that the police weren't involved she didn't know how she was going to find them.

"Your friend, Lily, how long has she been missing?"

Katriana eyed the other female cautiously. "How do you know my friend's name? I didn't tell you."

Gheorgès snickered. "You'd be surprised at the things my sister knows." When Katriana took a cautious step toward the exit he matched it with one of his own. "Your friend, Lily," he said. "Is she the blonde you were with last night? The one worried about someone named Zack?"

Who in hell are you? "What do you know about Zack?" she countered. Distrust was a rank scent drowning out all others.

"Not much. Only that your friend was worried about him."

Katriana relaxed, *slightly*. She didn't trust the newcomers. She didn't know anything about them, and as long as there was a price on her head every stranger was a potential enemy.

The older officer fidgeted with some papers and looked up at the male and female standing beside his chair. He seemed startled to see them there, and his temple began to throb. Rubbing absently at the pain he said, "Can I help you?"

His head snapped around when Emerald said, "We are looking for Officer Frank. Is he in today?"

The officer was staring at Emerald like she had two heads. Maybe to him she did. His head was throbbing so hard he probably had double vision. Emerald felt as if she were going to vomit any second.

"Frank. He's not here. He took a couple of days off. Personal days."

"Thank you," Emerald said. "Come on you two," she motioned at the others her fingers fluttering in the air for a moment longer than necessary. "Let's go. Close your eyes and count to ten," she told the officer as they were walking out the door. "You'd be amazed what that can do for a headache."

The officer closed his eyes as the door shut. Ten seconds later when he opened them he didn't have a headache, only the oddest feeling that he'd forgotten something important. "What just happened?" he asked his partner.

The young rookie looked at him oddly. "Nothing," he said. "Hasn't much been happening all week."

On the steps outside the police station, Conall's bloodshot eyes were tracking Emerald's every movement. His fangs were aching from the effort it took to keep them concealed. Quinn sensed his hunger and suggested they go into the bushes where Conall could take his vein, but Conall didn't trust himself, and refused the offer.

Take his vein. Drain him.

The need to feed was a living breathing nightmare inside his mind, urging him to break his covenant with Rah, and sate his hunger on the young lycan.

His hunger reached up the steps to her, and Emerald staggered from the impact. *You need to feed.*

Conall groaned. *Not you too*, he complained. *I don't know how long I can hold on.*

Beside her, the female slapped Gheorgès hand and snarled at him. "Keep your hands to yourself male, unless you want to lose them."

Gheorgès smirked and strode down the stairs. "I knew you liked me," he threw over his shoulder. He barely ducked the stick that came flying at his head.

This is going to be good, thought Emerald. *Gheorgès has finally met his match.* "This is Katriana," she introduced her to the other men. "She was at the station to report her missing friend."

"How?" Katriana started to ask how the stranger knew her name then froze. Dark eyes tinged with red focused on the pulse at her throat. *How is he out in the daylight?*

Everything happened in a blink of an eye. The large male they called Gheorgès growled and flew at the day-walker. The beautiful female with the long, pale hair streaked with gold and silver, and those eerie amber eyes, was suddenly between the two and when she would have thought it was impossible to do so, they both froze before either one made contact with the female. There was another male there in a blink of an eye. Katriana couldn't believe there were two of them. Twins, except where the one wore a dark scowl, this one was smiling.

Oh my goddess. He's the guy from the club last night. That's why the other male seemed so familiar. I thought it was him. Except she knew, deep down, that just seeing a male in a bar for a few moments would not make him feel so familiar.

The smiling male wrapped his huge arms around his scowling twin, and attempted to haul him away.

"Back off, Gheorgès," the smaller female barked, and to Katriana's surprise he actually allowed his brother to drag him away.

Ignoring the other two males, Katriana walked up to the day-walker. "I think you better come with me," she said. "My friend will be able to help you."

"Get away from him," snarled Gheorgès. "If you dare touch her," he growled at the day-walker threateningly.

Macho ass. "Listen," she turned her attention to the female. "You're friend is in trouble. My friend can help."

Emerald extended one hand to Katriana, while keeping her other hand on Conall's arm. The day-walker actually appeared to be calmer now that the female was touching him. "Emerald," she said. "This is Conall. And those are my brothers, Quinn and Gheorgès."

Gheorgès shook off Quinn's hold and moved to stand between Conall and Katriana. "I don't want you anywhere near him," growled Gheorgès.

Katriana raised one brow. "What makes you think I give a damn what you want?" She turned backed to Emerald. "Do you want my help?"

"Yes," Conall and Emerald answered simultaneously.

"Good. You will find help at Ursuline Convent," she said. "Just ask for Sangria."

"We are new in town," Emerald said. "Could you show us the way?"

"No problem." Katriana started down the street.

Gheorgès leaned into Conall. "The only thing that will help you, bloodsucker, is a stake through the heart," he growled menacingly.

"If your that worried," taunted Katriana. "Why don't you come along and keep an eye on him."

In two strides, Gheorgès was at her side.

Twenty Eight

THE convent was deserted except for the young nun selling admission tickets. "Five please," said Katriana.

"Oh, you're back Miss Katriana."

"Yes, Sister. I can't seem to get enough of this place."

"Where is Miss Lily today? We haven't seen her or Father Zack for a couple of days now. It's not like them to stay away."

Pain flickered across Katriana's face briefly before she masked it with a forced smile. "Lily and Father Zack have gone out of town for a couple of days."

The nun handed the tickets over, and Katriana led the way into the convent turned museum. There was a set of stairs roped off with a sign declaring "no admittance." Katriana headed toward the roped off stairs. When Emerald made to follow, Conall clamped his fingers around her wrist. "Stay back," he hissed. The red around his irises was spreading, nearly covering them completely. He looked like he had been on a week's drunk, neither eating nor sleeping.

One delicate hand lifted and gently touched his cheek. "It'll be okay, baby. I promise. We just need to get you fixed up."

Conall was clearly agitated, and he was struggling to keep his fangs from protruding. *Take her. She wants you to. She likes it when you feed from her.*

"Concentrate baby. Don't listen to him."

Conall grimaced and the movement had his fangs aching worse. He didn't want her to see him this way, not his angel. He never wanted to see her look at him as if he was tainted.

She is nothing. Take her. Drain her. Drain them all. Conall felt the stain on his soul growing. Fear and desperation drove him toward the stairway.

Katriana was standing on the bottom step, her hands on the red cord partitioning the upstairs from the downstairs. She was leaning over, trying to peer up the steps. "Sangria," she called lowly, her face barely discernible to a human but loud and clear enough to the non-human occupants.

There was a movement on the steps and the night clerk from their hotel appeared. He had no trouble showing his annoyance at their presence.

Ignoring his scowl, Katriana smiled. Behind her Gheorgès growled. Katriana dismissed him with a shake of her head. "Hey Kris. Is Sangria available? We have a problem."

Kristoff glanced at Gheorgès, who was still glaring, and smirked. "You sure do."

Kat rolled her eyes. "Not him." She pointed to Conall who was staring at Emerald with barely concealed hunger. "*Him.*"

Kristoff took a stance that left no doubt he did not intend to let Conall pass. "We can't help him," he sneered. "Put him out in the sun." He didn't seem to realize that he came here in the daylight with no problem.

Emerald stepped away from Conall and faced the young vampire. Her amber eyes roiled with anger. "This is a sanctuary is it not?"

Kristoff was clearly startled. She was not vampire. She should not know where their sanctuaries were. He didn't think the ancient with her was like them because he clearly needed Katriana to lead him here.

"Well?" Emerald snapped.

"I cannot allow you to pass," he whispered, fear suddenly rolling off him in waves.

"Him you can. He is like you. He *needs* help."

"It is not my decision."

Emerald let her senses flow throughout the convent. The top floor housed at least ten vampires but she focused on only one. Seconds later a female completely covered in heavy robes appeared on the steps beside Kristoff, who hovered protectively at her side.

At her sudden appearance, Quinn's head snapped around and he stared at the dark figure. Emerald sensed his interest, but she had more important things on her mind.

The shrouded female spoke first. "Come my brother." She motioned from within the folds of her robe for Conall to come forward. "We can help you but your friends must wait here."

"No way." Emerald headed for the stairs. She knew Conall needed help but she wasn't sure if she wanted him in a nest of vampires, with a female she was getting absolutely nothing from. What if they agreed with Kristoff and tried to destroy him.

"It is for your own safety," insisted the veiled female.

"I'll be all right." Conall placed a shaky hand on her arm. *Please Emerald. Trust me. I can't protect myself if I need to protect you.*

Emerald sent him a mental image of her rolling her eyes. *We'll go back to the hotel. You will feed from me.*

Conall winced as if in pain. *I can't risk hurting you.*

"We will take good care of your friend," the shrouded female said. "Show them around the convent Katriana. We won't be long."

She led the way up the stairs, Conall behind her, and Kristoff bringing up the rear. The top floor of the convent was set up like a huge dormitory. There was a small cot and dresser in each of the rooms. At the end of the hall was a small sitting room with a beer fridge.

Sangria slipped off the heavy robes and tossed them on the nearest chair. "Have a seat," she said and opened the door to the fridge. "You can't let yourself get this far," she scolded. "You must feed regularly if you wish to win your battle. But why am I telling you this. You haven't survived this long by sheer luck." She pulled a plastic bag of blood from the fridge, snipped one corner, and poured the contents into a plastic glass.

"I have a friend at the nearby hospital who sells me blood. It is better warmed but we don't have time." She shoved the glass in Conall's face. "Drink this."

With hands that shook, Conall took the offered glass and gulped the contents spilling some down the front of his shirt.

Kristoff crinkled his nose in distaste. "You drink like an animal," he sneered.

"Kristoff." It was a reprimand, and Kristoff had the good sense to look ashamed.

Blood rushed to Conall's starving organs and cells, giving him back his self control and changing his eyes from red to black. He growled at the young vampire. "Next time you try to interfere with me I *will* take it personally."

Kristoff blanched and stumbled back. The power twirling in the older vampires eyes promised vengeance.

"Boys." Sangria spoke calmly. "We do not fight amongst ourselves here. If you cannot abide by the rules of Sanctuary you will be asked to leave."

Conall rose from the chair, and bowed deeply. "I offer my humblest apologies for acting so disrespectfully after you so kindly aided me in my time of need. If I can ever return the favour please feel free to ask."

Sangria waved her hand dismissively. "You are already doing it," she said. "Please bring my friend Lily home safely."

Conall glanced around the small sitting room. There were ten vampires living here, all of them day-walkers, except the female who so graciously offered them sanctuary, although none of them seemed to realize it. He had a feeling that the female was the reason for their continued existence.

Sangria offered a sad little smile. "I have much to atone for. This life was not my choice, as it was not the choice of any of us. Some of us struggle more than others to retain our humanity. Some of us fall from grace, but that does not mean we give up the fight."

Conall placed his hand on the young female's head and allowed her memories to flow through him. He staggered under the weight of her suffering. When he removed his hand he bowed before her. "There is no need to carry all this guilt. You have a truly courageous soul."

"You do flatter me," Sangria said. "Your friends are becoming impatient. You should rejoin them. I cannot allow them to come up here, especially the *Moarté*. I cannot risk my family."

As Conall descended the stairs he heard her say. "There is a well known vampire bar here in New Orleans. Anyone can tell you where it is. If you find yourself in need go there and ask for the Sangria special. It's not on the menu but it'll fix you right up."

Conall was smiling when he reached the bottom step. This was some town. The place was crawling with vampires pretending to be humans, and humans pretending to be vampires.

Twenty Nine

A CAR whizzed by and Jade jumped out of the way as the driver stuck his head out the window and cursed her. *Thank you Goddess. At least you didn't drop me in the river.*

Silence.

Then Jade's mind was bombarded with a million thoughts from a million different minds. She was dizzy from the overload and she spent the next few moments shifting through them until she found the ones she searched for. Her knees sagged with relief when she heard her daughter.

Hey Mom. The cheeky brat acted like she hadn't been gone at all. *Meet us at the Hotel St. Marie, room two twelve.*

We have a lot to discuss young lady. Jade tried to sound stern but her happiness bubbled through. Emerald was safe with her brothers and all was right with the world. At least they were as safe as they could be in a den full of vampires. Jade felt malice surrounding her, but right now the malice was kept in check with a fine thread.

There were so many vampires Jade couldn't pinpoint the source of the malice. *Get out*, she ordered.

Emerald sent a mental shrug. *Relax. We have it under control.*

Jade's temper snapped. *Did you have it under control at that farmhouse?* Remorse hit immediately. *I'm sorry baby.* She had to get her emotions under control. Her children were safe. She needed to take them home.

Emerald sent a mental hug. *No. I'm sorry. I should have been more careful. Dad's on his way,* she said on a lighter note. *He should be here any moment. We're on our way back now.*

Twenty minutes later Jade was sitting on a balcony overlooking Toulouse Street munching on a fully loaded hot dog she purchased from a vender on the corner. There were two more hotdogs sitting on a wrought iron table beside her, and the wrappings from the one she already ate.

The street was quiet at this time of day. The blues club at the corner of Toulouse and Bourbon was closed for the day. Further up the road she could hear the sound of tourists checking out the small shops for treasures, and the local fortune tellers to see what life held in store for them. She listened to snippets of a few idle conversations before passing on. She closed her eyes and let her senses drift past Bourbon, down Royal, past a small curio shop with a secret room at the back where the owner kept some very strange weaponry.

Jade unwrapped the next hotdog, and breathed a sigh of relief. There they were, coming down the street.

Thirty

KATRIANA prowled the balcony like a caged animal, snarling at anyone who dared stick their heads in her cage. She was edgy, nervous, and it wasn't just Zack and Lily. There was danger nearby. The hairs on the back of her neck bristled, and the change beckoned her. She hadn't shifted in nearly two weeks, hadn't wanted to risk anyone seeing her, but if she didn't shift soon she was going to implode. *Weres* were not meant to stay in one form for long periods of time. It wasn't natural.

The door to the balcony opened and Katriana turned to snarl, expecting Gheorgès or his quieter, calmer twin. It was the female, Emerald. The one they all seemed to follow, until they returned to their room at the hotel to find another woman waiting for them there. She could have been another sister, except they all called her Mom. Jade was her name, and for one brief moment Katriana thought her search might be over.

But it can't be true?

She had been searching for Jade Caer for so long it wasn't surprising she would jump at the chance to have her search over. But this couldn't possibly be the same woman. The woman she sought travelled alone.

Emerald ignored Katriana standing in the corner of the balcony glaring at her, and walked silently over to the wrought iron railing where she peered down onto the street.

Katriana shifted position and caught movement out of the corner of her eye. The vampire travelling with them was standing in the shadows of the curtains watching the female with the intensity of a predator. *Why is it you can walk in daylight and Sangria cannot?* She wondered. There was a darkness in him that was almost tangible; unlike Sangria whose soul shone through her eyes with the intensity of the sun. A female so pure of heart that it was almost blinding, yet she was cursed to darkness while this male faced the sun unscathed.

It wasn't fair.

Then again, when had anything in life been fair? Was it fair that her parents were dead, and she was doomed to search the world alone?

Emerald felt Conall's eyes tracking her every movement and yet she was forced to ignore his interest and focus on the female who was so jittery it was almost contagious. "This isn't your fault." She spoke so low Katriana would not have heard if she were human.

"What do you know about it?" hissed Katriana. Although she spoke in the same low tones her bitterness came out loud and clear. The vampire turned his attention to her, but when he realized she hadn't moved, he again took up his position in the shadows where he could watch over his female.

"I know you would not hurt your friends," insisted Emerald.

"What if I am hurting them just by being here?" Katriana took a step closer to where Emerald still looked out over the street; drawn to the female despite her reluctance. "What if they are dead because they chose to befriend me?"

"Did *you* hurt your friends Katriana Kuznetsov?"

Katriana was about to take another step closer when she realized what Emerald said. She hadn't told anyone her last name. Not even Lily and Sangria knew her real name. She hadn't referred to herself by that name in a very long time. "Who ...?" Katriana tried to swallow past the lump of fear stuck in her throat. "Who sent you?" she finally managed. The scent of sour milk filled the air, and she was suddenly aware of the attention she was drawing from inside the room.

Emerald didn't turn or acknowledge Katriana directly, choosing to give the female time to compose herself. "Nobody sent me," she said into the gentle breeze. "Not for you." The last words were spoken so quietly that even Katriana had a hard time hearing them.

There was a commotion at the patio door and both females turned to see Conall blocking the way, and Gheorgès glaring at him. Jade sat on the edge of the bed a crooked smile tilting the corner of her mouth, amusement sparkling in her amber eyes. Quinn jumped up to join the two, but stopped when Jade placed a gentle hand on his arm.

"Get out of my way bloodsucker," snarled Gheorgès viciously.

"Stay out of it," hissed the strange vampire, his Irish accent sneaking through.

The scent of sour milk hit her nostrils and Katriana realized what had set them off. She took several deep breaths and forced herself to calm down. Just because the female knew her name didn't mean that they were after her. Besides, if they wanted her dead they could have killed her at any time. They outnumbered her four to one, five to one now.

As the scent of fear dissipated into the night Gheorgès calmed down, and Conall finally stepped aside.

"Open the door Quinn and let your father in," Jade said a second before there was a sharp rap at the door.

The door opened to admit a tall man with at least a week's worth of dark bristle on his handsome face. Jade moved from her position on the bed and into his arms so fast she nearly unbalanced him. Luke caught his wife mid-flight and held her close, nuzzling her soft neck.

"Get a room," groaned Quinn, Gheorgès, and Emerald in unison, none of them in the least embarrassed by their parents' public display of affection.

"Already taken care of," Luke said with a wink at his children. He kissed his wife soundly before letting her slowly slide down his body to stand on the floor. He kicked the door shut behind him, hugged Quinn who'd been stuck between the door and his parents, gave Gheorgès a quick hug, and stopped at Conall for about two seconds before extending his hand. "I never got a chance to thank you for saving our daughter's life," he said.

During a battle against the betrayer when Emerald was only fifteen, Conall jumped between Emerald and an Ursaline taking the death blow meant for her, and sending himself into the Shadows. "I can't say it was a pleasure Sir, but I would do it again in a heartbeat."

Luke inclined his head slightly, and turned his attention to his daughter. "I should turn you over my knee young lady." His voice was gruff, and he held out his arms. "Get over here girl," he growled.

One moment Emerald was standing with her back against the railing, the next she was being crushed in a bear hug. "You had your mother worried," he scolded while tightening his hold. "You are grounded for life."

Emerald's merry laughter rang out making strangers on the street below glance toward the balcony. "I missed you too, Dad,' she laughed, and wiped at the tears trailing down her cheeks.

"Why didn't you call?"

"It's a long story, and I think we need to get some rest. It's going to be a long night."

"So your mother has informed me. Are we sure he's still here? There's no chance he's moved on already?"

Jade reached for the pack leaning against the bottom of the bed, and shrugged it onto her shoulders. "He's here. I can feel him. He's started taking pre-trans."

"How do you know she's still alive?"

"I don't. But he's found an almost endless source here. He won't move on until he absolutely has to."

Katriana stirred from her spot on the balcony and suddenly felt all eyes on her. Gheorgès took a protective step toward her and she was torn between being thankful for the gesture in a room full of werewolves, or being pissed off that he thought she needed his protection.

"I need to go," she stammered.

Emerald stepped toward her. "I think you should stay with us."

Katriana was suffocating with so many strangers around her. She was standing outside on a balcony and she was still having difficulty getting air into her lungs. She recognized the feeling for exactly what it was—panic. She had to run.

She eyed the top of the railing. She could make the leap easily but suddenly the street was full of pedestrians, and even in her panic Katriana realized the danger of drawing attention to herself. She shoved Luke out of the way, leapt over the first bed, ran across the second, and flung herself at the door. After fumbling for several long seconds she managed to throw open the door and bolt like a scared rabbit. In her panic she didn't realize that nobody had attempted to stop her.

Gheorgès was at the door before it closed completely, and glanced at his father. He was torn between the need to protect the female, his female, and his duty to his Alpha.

"Go." The word came from everyone at the same time, except Conall who thought it best to mind his own business when it came to that particular wolf.

"Stay with her," commanded Jade and Emerald. Katriana was going to need him more than they did at the moment. "Do not let her out of your sight."

Gheorgès glanced at his father with pleading eyes. "Go Gheorgès," Luke commanded. "I do not need a babysitter. Besides," he said with a wink in Jade's direction, "I have your mother to look after me.'

Gheorgès was gone in a blur.

"I got us a room down the hall," Luke told Jade who moved toward the door with the grace of a dancer.

With one hand on the doorknob she turned toward her mate. "What are you waiting for?" "We will meet in the restaurant downstairs an hour before dusk," she said as the two of them quietly closed the door behind them.

Quinn grabbed his keys from the dresser where he'd tossed them earlier. "You two can use this room," he said. "Try to get some rest."

"What about you?" Emerald asked.

"I need to go for a run. I'll be back in time for the meeting."

Emerald went to her brother, stood on her tiptoes, and placed a kiss on his grizzled cheek. "Thanks, bro." Quinn was just about to close the door behind him when she said, "I'm really sorry I caused you so much pain."

Quinn shrugged. "That's what sisters are for."

He ducked and closed the door as a pillow hit the back of it and slid to the floor.

Thirty One

CONALL stood in the shadows of the balcony curtains watching the exchange between his female and her brother. They had such an easy relationship, finding it easy to love and forgive each other.

God what I wouldn't give to have that.

You can have that boy. You can have it all.

Shut. Up.

It will be so easy. They won't be expecting you. The Moarté *first and then her mate. They are just down the hall. You can slip in and drain them while they sleep. Kill the wolf. Drain the* Moarté. *She is powerful. Her blood will sustain you.*

No. They are my female's family.

With them gone she will turn to you.

The shadows around Conall were growing thicker, his eyes tinged red. Emerald stepped toward Conall a half smile curving her lips. "Alone at last."

Conall took a step toward Emerald and the shadow moved with him. Emerald tensed, and then relaxed when the curtains fluttered in the soft breeze coming through the open patio door.

There is nothing to worry about. It is just the wind. Her gaze swept the floor. She didn't have a shadow. There were no lights on in the room to cause a shadow, and the sun was not shining in through the patio door. "Conall what's wrong?"

Conall stared straight ahead as if she weren't even in the room.

Conall come back to me. She sent the thought to him not knowing if it would get through the block he threw up when she tried to get inside his head.

He took another step away from the curtain, his eyes blank. Emerald went to the edge of the bed and sat down. She patted the spot beside her. "Come join me," she said quietly.

Conall took two steps toward her, shuddered, and bolted for the door. "I'll be right back." He barely choked the words out before he was gone.

Emerald stared at the closed door. Hurt, and then anger burned through her veins. *One of these days you're going to disappear and I won't be waiting for you to come back.* As suddenly as the anger flared it deflated. What if he were in trouble? It had to be hard for him here on earth. In the Chimera he never craved blood. He drank from the Well of Life to keep him strong and healthy. Even Alicia was forced to return to the Chimera periodically, and she had Kamenwati's powerful blood to sustain her.

God I am so stupid. He's starving.

She was determined to find Conall and demand that he at least feed from her if he wouldn't return to the Chimera. She stepped into the hallway and opened her senses so they would lead her to Conall. His dark spicy scent hung in the air outside the door, and then travelled—away from the elevator. *He must have taken the stairs.*

Emerald came to the doorway leading to a set of stairs and started to push it open when she realized two things. Conall didn't use the stairs, but instead continued down the hall, and her parents scent indicated they went down the same hallway.

I'm losing it, thought Emerald. *Why didn't I see it before now?*

Worried more than she cared to admit, Emerald stepped up the pace as she followed Conall's scent that was definitely following the path her parents had taken. Conall's scent was stronger outside the door to Room 201 because he had paused outside the door. Emerald could hear her parents inside the room, and she quickly tuned them out to leave them their privacy.

Em. What's wrong? Jade's voice was tinged with panic. She'd just got her child back, and was still afraid she might lose her again. As *Moarté* Jade could read what was happening, or about to happen, to everyone within her vicinity, except those closest to her. Family and close friends would always remain a mystery, hidden from her unique talents. It bothered her immensely that she could no longer read the mage, Conall. She could see the stain on his soul, but she could not see what choices he would make, and she could come to only one conclusion—his fate was connected to Emerald's, and Jade didn't like it one little bit.

It's nothing, Mother. Get some rest.

She continued to follow Conall's scent to the next stairwell and down to the underground parking lot. She exited through the underground parking onto Toulouse, and turned toward Bourbon. There were many scents lingering from the night before making it hard to isolate just one in this form. If Emerald took wolf form she would be able to separate them easier, but a wolf would be too visible out on the street. She considered owl form, or perhaps a hawk. People seldom looked up, and if they did most would not even recognize which bird she was. But a bird wouldn't be able to see him if he slipped into a building.

The convent!

Emerald headed toward Chartres but before she reached the street she caught his scent, and followed it down several turns and twists to a small, dimly lit bar on one of the quieter streets. Even at this time of day the sun barely penetrated the interior.

Conall was sitting on a barstool, and although the bar was crowded even at this time of day, the stool on each side of him remained empty. Emerald couldn't blame the patrons for giving him a wide berth. He was lethal looking, dark and menacing, and the sexiest male on the premises.

Emerald slid onto the stool beside him. "If you needed a drink so badly you could have said so."

Conall turned bloodshot eyes her way, and tipped a glass half full of Type-O human blood to his lips without saying a word.

The bartender was a young girl with short mousy brown hair, and a freckle on the left side of her nose. She was definitely nervous and was keeping her distance from Conall. *Wise choice.*

She approached Emerald keeping an eye on Conall as if she expected him to leap over the bar and attack her. By the look of him, she wasn't too far off the mark.

"Can you get him out of here?" asked the bartender in a low whisper. "He's making the customers nervous."

They're not the only ones.

Conall glared at them. "Fill 'er up," he ordered slamming his empty glass on the bar.

The blood was obviously not helping. "You've had enough," Emerald said.

I can't leave.

Emerald scanned the small crowded bar, spying a set of stairs at the back. "Are the rooms back there for rent," she asked.

The bartender fidgeted. *Only so the 'vampires' can make out and pretend they are feeding from humans,* she thought scornfully.

Emerald was only slightly amused that she didn't know that she actually served blood to vampires, and not some high priced wine to vampire wanna-bees. *Tell the truth,* she prompted.

"Yes," blurted the bartender looking surprised by the admission.

"We'll take one."

The bartender reluctantly handed a key to Emerald after quoting a price three times the normal, and receiving it without a flinch. Emerald picked up the fresh glass of blood and beckoned. "Follow me."

Conall trailed after Emerald through the crowd which parted easily at his approach to let them pass. He wanted to bare his fangs and hiss at them, but was too afraid of his own reaction to the enhanced scent of their fear laced blood. Already hunger burned at his gut and he was actually beginning to shake from the effort it took to keep himself from pouncing. If not for the female whose round bouncy ass was leading him across the room he might not have had the strength to rein his hunger in.

While Emerald drifted across the crowded floor she continually scanned the area around them. There were two pre-conversion males sitting quietly in a corner watching the occupants of the room. She knew the moment they sensed what Conall was; their heartbeats quickened and they began looking for a quick escape route. There were a couple of tourists who'd come to check out the well-known "Vampire Bar," but most of the patrons today were local Goths playing at being vampires for the tourists. The real vampires would come in after dark, and not all of them would be satisfied drinking from a glass.

Emerald wondered just how many really believed in the vampires they pretended to be, or how many actually knew the number of vampires that actually frequented this place as a means of controlling their bloodlust.

The moment the door clicked shut behind them Conall turned on her. "Give it to me," he hissed.

The dark stain was spreading. Emerald could see it in the shadows behind his bloodshot eyes, and the darkness encroaching on his aura.

You don't need that weak excuse for a dinner, Theron's voice was stronger, more compelling than before. *The female is powerful. Drain her. Take her strength. She wants you to. She dares you to. She mocks you. Standing there treating you like an errant child, teasing you.*

Conall fought the darkness that beckoned with such temptations. He was weak here on Earth. He needed substance and the weak blood the bar offered wasn't making a dent in his hunger. The *Moarté's* blood was powerful enough to sustain him for several days. It was sweet. Powerful. Ambrosia.

And he craved it.

You need to feed.

"You need to feed, Conall."

Conall covered his face with his hands and groaned. *Go away,* he urged them both.

"Am I that repulsive?" Emerald refused to budge, her amber eyes trusting as she stepped closer to Conall.

When he look up his eyes were red flames. "You are that enticing."

"Then drink from me baby," she urged.

"I cannot."

Emerald took another step closer so that their bodies were nearly touching and the heat he was generating warmed her skin through her clothing. "Don't you want me anymore?"

"Hell yes," snapped Conall. "More than life itself."

"Then take me. We are mated. You said it yourself. And in my family mated is for life."

"I'm no good for you." His fangs ached with the effort to keep them from protruding. The scent of the blood in the glass was completely overpowered by her scent, the scent of hot spicy blood rushing through her veins. She was so close now the sound of her heart beating was like a symphony of drums.

Emerald dropped the glass of blood spilling the contents over the worn carpet.

Conall watched the stain spread, felt it spreading in direct proportion to the spreading stain on his soul.

Emerald lifted her left wrist and sliced the vein open with a swipe of a fingernail. Conall's fangs exploded in his mouth. His mind became no more than a red haze of hunger. He pounced dragging them both to the floor to lay in the growing stain of spilt blood, and began to suck greedily.

With the first draw of the powerful liquid he was lost. Bloodlust took over as power infused his veins, his organs, and his soul.

That's right my son. Take it. It is your divine right. Take it all.

Conall could no more stop his feeding frenzy than he could stop the world spinning. And then he heard it. Above the roar of bloodlust, above the sound of Theron's encouraging voice, above the sound of his own slurping, he heard it. The voice of an angel. His Angel. The Angel of Death, only it was offering life.

"I offer my life for yours," the gentle voice whispered, "freely and without reservation." The whispering voice grew quieter with each word spoken, until it was merely a whisper in his mind.

I offer you my heart and my soul. I offer you my life so you may live.

Warmth, unlike anything he could remember, seeped through his veins, and like a spider wove a web around his heart and soul. The drinking slowed. Conall's spirit merged with Emerald's.

You are the Keeper of My Heart, for now and forever. With each word spoken the web tightened, grew stronger, and the shadows retreated until there was nothing in the room except the two of them. Theron was once again a dim echo in his mind, one he could turn off at will.

Conall licked the ragged wound on Emerald's pale wrist, his saliva acting as a suture. He tenderly kissed the thin scar. "I offer you my heart." He trailed kisses along the inside of her arm, leaving flickers of flame in his path. "I offer you my soul." He nuzzled her collarbone. "I offer you my life." He flicked his rough tongue over the strong pulse at her throat. "You are the Keeper of my Heart, now and forever." He claimed her sigh with his lips.

Thirty Two

HER bones melted and her heartbeat quickened with the deepening of the kiss. She parted her lips to try and draw in a breath and Conall's tongue slipped between them searching, seeking. Emerald opened her senses to his exploration, not thinking, just feeling, revelling in the sensation as her own tongue played with his.

When he finally broke the kiss she felt abandoned even as her lungs gasped for much needed air. His lips touched hers again briefly, gently, before trailing kisses down the vein throbbing in her neck. Emerald tensed as his fangs scraped the vein gently, tensing for the sharp stab of penetration only to have him gently kiss the vein and continue his slow exploration with his lips and tongue to the neckline of her shirt.

With barely a thought, the shirt was no longer an obstacle and his hot tongue and bold lips were teasing her taut nipple through the tiny wisp of silk, that was all that kept them separated. Emerald's hands moved to caress Conall's shoulders and back only to have Conall capture them. He held her hands gently but firmly, lifting them above her head. The new position made her nipples jut higher and he renewed his assault on them; lavishing them equally until her bra was completely soaked.

When Emerald wasn't sure she could stand any more of his tongue and lips they resumed their journey trailing kisses down her rib cage, his tongue playfully searching her belly button. He released her hands so he could slowly undo the buttons on her jeans and slide them down her long slender legs, trailing kisses along each newly bared section of luscious skin.

Squirming beneath the onslaught of his tongue and lips, moaning whenever his fangs scraped teasingly along her highly sensitive skin, Emerald tried to run her fingers through his luxuriously long silky hair that was trailing tickles, and froze. She couldn't move her hands.

Conall lifted his head and grinned wickedly, his sharp fangs openly visible. "You're my prisoner now," he said with an evil chuckle. "Subject to my every whim."

Emerald cocked a brow and fell back with an exaggerated sigh. "Oh, please, sir, what do you intend to do with me," she said in her best imitation of a damsel in distress.

"Well," Conall drew out the word. "First I am going to lick and kiss and suck until your panties are as wet as that silky bit of fluff trying to hold your nipples in place."

At his words, Emerald's nipples tightened even harder until they ached with need of his hot mouth on them, and her panties grew decidedly damper.

Conall's nostrils flared at the physical evidence of her desire and his fangs glistened. "Then I am going to pull them off with my teeth and start all over again, only this time I am going to drink your sweet nectar."

Emerald moaned helplessly and her body arched offering him what he desired. "Don't torture me." Her own voice was raw with desire.

Conall tugged off his shirt and tossed it on the floor, and then he undid the buttons on his own jeans and slowly slid them down his muscled legs to release his huge erection. When his pants hit the floor he kicked them away and stood tall and gloriously naked, towering over Emerald who was bound by his magic to an invisible post. His balls in one hand lifting them, Conall ran the other hand along the long length of his cock.

Emerald stared in fascination at the tiny drop of liquid that beaded at its tip. She licked her lips and groaned.

His cock jumped.

"Then I am going to crawl along that luscious body," Conall continued as he struggled to remain where he was, "and taste and explore every beautiful inch until I have burned it into my memory."

"Conall." Emerald was beginning to pant.

"And then I am going to," he slid his hand along his extended cock again. "Move this inside you until you beg for release."

"Please ..." Emerald begged.

"While I am filling you with my seed I am going to sink my fangs," he grinned to show off those beautiful, lethal, weapons. "Into that pulsing vein at your throat."

Emerald squirmed and moaned.

"And take you into me."

Panting hard Emerald spread her legs in supplication. "Enough talking already," she groaned. "Let's have some action."

Obligingly Conall fell on her like a starving man.

Thirty Three

JADE, Luke, and Quinn were already seated at a table when they arrived at the hotel restaurant. The waitress set a steaming plate in front of Quinn, and Emerald's stomach grumbled.

"Could you please bring us two of the same," Conall asked indicating the nearly raw steak and steaming baked potato on Quinn's plate.

"Would you like something to drink with that?" she asked setting Jade's quarter chicken and Luke's equally raw steak in front of them.

There was a large pitcher of ice water at the center of the table. "Water is good," Emerald and Conall said at the same time. Emerald laughed and her eyes glowed. "Could you bring an extra sour cream?" she asked.

"No problem." The waitress couldn't help smiling at the newly arrived couple.

"And an extra potato?"

"You can have mine." Quinn jabbed the potato with his fork and placed it on a saucer.

"Is there something wrong with your potato, sir?" The young waitress looked decidedly worried.

"Ignore him." Emerald dismissed her brother with a small wave of her hand. "He is a barbarian and can't appreciate the finer things in life." Wherein she was teasing Quinn, she would have probably meant it of Gheorgès.

"Hey," Quinn protested. "Just 'cause I don't eat veggies."

"It's a potato, Bro. A staple. Like steak."

Quinn wrapped his large hands around his plate protectively pulling it closer to his chest, a look of abject horror on his handsome face. "Not like steak." He winked at the stunned waitress. "A potato could never be like a steak. A steak is thick, rich, juicy," he drew out the last word. "A potato could never be like a steak." He made little kissy sounds at his plate. "I love steak."

The waitress laughed and shook her head at his antics. *What I wouldn't give to have him describe me like that.* "I'll be right back with your order," she told the newcomers and headed back toward the kitchen.

"Don't forget my extra potato," Emerald called after her. Emerald felt Jade's worried inspection. "What? Can't a person be hungry?"

"We are just worried about you."

Emerald was instantly contrite. "I'm sorry, Mom. I'm fine. Really. Just hungry. I feel like I haven't eaten in weeks."

Conall shifted in the chair beside her. "I'm afraid that's my fault," he said.

Two sets of male eyes riveted him to his chair.

"You did feed me." Emerald spoke quickly, afraid her family would guess what they were up to all day, and not quite ready to spring their relationship on them yet. "He made me a wonderful meal of steak and potatoes."

Conall took her cue. "I should have insisted you eat more often. I forgot what the effects of the Chimera would have on your system."

Emerald shrugged. "Not to worry. I'm more than making up for it now."

"You should have more steak and less potato," pointed out Quinn as he popped a huge chunk of the tender meat in his mouth.

Emerald carefully cut the potato Quinn gave her in six equal pieces. "I had two hamburgers a little earlier," she confessed.

"Don't forget that piece of flattened chicken," interjected Conall. "If you can call that chicken."

Emerald gave him an evil look. "Keep it up Mage," she threatened. "And you'll find out how cranky I can get when I'm hungry. You thought you were scary."

There was laughter all around the table. Everyone present had felt the brunt of her hunger at one time or another. "Yeah." Quinn put his hands up in mock defence and cringed. "She's an absolute horror when she's hungry."

Emerald balled up her napkin and threw it at her incorrigible brother.

"Children," Jade admonished.

Emerald shrugged and spread sour cream equally over the six pieces of potato, and then proceeded to pop them into her mouth one by one. She rolled each piece around inside her mouth and moaned in mock pleasure.

Beside her Conall's cock hardened and he fought hard not to betray his reaction to the rest of her family. *You are killing me woman*, he complained silently.

Across the table Quinn shook his head and grimaced in disgust. "That is just so wrong. Nobody should react to a veggie that way. Now a steak on the other hand is something worth worshipping."

"I guess it would depend on the *stake*," interjected Conall emphasising stake so Quinn would get the pun. Even Luke laughed.

The waitress chose that moment to return and set their plates down. No sooner had her hand left Emerald's plate when Quinn's fork snagged her steak.

"Hey," Emerald scolded stabbing his hand with her fork.

"Tit for tat," Quinn said plopping down the steak and watching the blood spread out on his plate. "You ate my potato."

"You didn't want it."

Quinn shrugged. "Doesn't matter. You still ate it."

You are so dead brother.

Quinn shrugged off the idle threat and proceeded to cut the pilfered steak.

"Would you like me to bring another steak," offered the waitress. "It will only take the cook a moment."

"No thank you," Emerald replied. "But if you have a bottle of arsenic back there perhaps you could sprinkle a little over *that* steak." She smiled sweetly at her brother.

The waitress hesitated for a second. "Well, if there is anything else you require, please call." She hurried over to lead another customer to an empty table.

Luke turned to his wife and spoke in a very serious tone. "Remember? This is why we never take them anywhere." Everybody laughed.

Conall insisted Emerald eat his steak as he wasn't hungry. "If you don't want it," Quinn looked at the steak longingly. *Honestly, the boy is a bottomless pit.* "If you touch that steak I'll cut your hand off wolf," Conall said in a normal tone.

"I was just asking," Quinn sat back and cut another hunk off his stolen steak.

"I'll eat half if you do." Emerald cut the steak in half her mouth already watering at the delicious aroma. "Where's Gheorgès?"

"Haven't seen him today." Jade spoke normally but Emerald heard the unspoken worry. Gheorgès and Katriana were supposed to meet them for dinner.

Why didn't I notice it earlier? Emerald opened her mind and sifted through the thoughts and conversations in the room and from there spread along every room and floor of the hotel. She was picking up turmoil in a few rooms but nothing concrete, and no hint of Gheorgès. She did pick up a disturbance in the atmosphere in the stairway between the third and fourth floors. *Hey, Sis. We're in the dining room on the first floor.* "Quinn grab another chair." He was already moving.

Beside her Conall was looking a little paler than usual. *Do you need to feed?* She loved that they had their own little private link now so the others couldn't overhear.

Don't worry so much. I have my hunger under control.

He didn't look under control. He looked like a man staring into the face of death. *Shit. Kamenwati. Kamenwati you leave him alone,* she ordered.

Kamenwati's warm chuckle reached her mind. *I do not think my brother will appreciate your attempt to protect him.*

Do not interfere female. Conall's voice was stern, making Emerald wince.

Fine. Get yourself killed for all I care. She could have cried but for the impression of warmth he sent with the command. Warm air caressed the back of her neck and she sighed.

I will never willingly leave you.

Alicia?

Don't worry, Em. We won't let anything happen to him.

Conall raised a questioning brow. Emerald shrugged. Nobody, not even her mate, could listen on her private links with her family.

Do not be so sure female, his voice was amused.

Shit!

The door opened admitting Alicia and Kamenwati to the dining area. Several women stared at the tall Egyptian while automatically dismissing the shorter, dark haired beauty at his side as of no consequence. Kamenwati scanned the room ignoring their blatant stares and courteously urged Alicia in the proper direction.

The waitress approached them cautiously. Kamenwati lowered his head until he was more her own level and indicated their table. He said something else. The waitress bobbed her head, offered them both a friendly smile, and trotted toward the kitchen.

The three males at the table rose at their approach. Luke grasped Kamenwati's forearm in the way of warriors. "It's good to have you back, Son."

Kamenwati released Luke's arm and wrapped his arm around Alicia's waist pulling her closer. "It's good to be home."

He greeted Quinn in the same way. "Brother," they said in unison and then Kamenwati faced Conall.

Conall inclined his head. "My liege."

"I should kill you on the spot for worrying my female," said Kamenwati sternly and with a hint of humour.

"Kam! Kamenwati!" gasped Alicia and Emerald respectively.

Kamenwati shot a glare at Emerald and Conall bristled. "Apparently my female is over it." He extended his arm in the warrior greeting and they clasped forearms. *We will discuss your earlier rudeness toward me at a later date.*

Conall raised a brow slightly at the realization that Kamenwati had not divulged his attempted contact with them.

Oh, he told me Mage. I thought it best my parents never find out you purposely kept Kamenwati from bringing my sister home.

Thank you, Princess.

Alicia's dark eyes flashed. *Call me Princess one more time Mage and you won't need to worry about my parents.*

Conall's lips lifted at the corners. Apparently some things hadn't changed while he was lost in the Shadows. "It is good to see your new life has brought you no harm, Alicia."

"It is good to see you awake, Conall. You had us all worried."

Kamenwati searched Conall's eyes. "It seems that the effects of the Ursaline are wearing off."

"So it would seem."

Kamenwati held out a chair for Alicia and once she was seated the men returned to their seats. The waitress chose that moment to bring out dishes of crusty bread and a bottle of red wine. "Can I get you anything else?" she asked eyeing the two remaining empty chairs.

"I think we are good," said Luke. When everyone nodded their agreement the waitress moved on to another table.

Emerald rubbed at a sudden pain in her temple and tried to concentrate on the people at the table. They were suddenly fading in and out, being replaced by swampland. "I've got to go," she said. "Someone needs me." She knocked her chair over in her haste to stand.

Conall was beside her in a heartbeat. Jade coached her from across the table, her voice all but lost in time and space. "Concentrate, Emerald. What do you see?"

Thirty Four

LILY paced the confines of the small room her fear growing in leaps and bounds with each passing moment. What had she been thinking to blindly leave with strangers just because they *said* her brother sent them?

Where are you, Zack? She cried out for the umpteenth time. She hadn't been surprised or necessarily worried when they arrived at the old abandoned clinic at the edge of the swamp. The creoles that lived in and around the swamp still used the building as a clinic, and Lily had often accompanied Zack when he was called here to help with the ill.

Like a fool, Lily had run into the building calling her brother's name only to find an empty room that was filled with the scent of spilled blood no more than two days old. The smell caused her gums to ache and her stomach to clench in agony.

"Where is my brother?" she managed to choke out noticing for the first time the blank look in her escorts eyes. Fear made her limbs tremble as she tried to back away from their approach only to be grabbed roughly and shoved into this small cubicle that at one time held medical supplies. Now it held a few empty shelves and an increasingly frightened Lily.

Stupid. Stupid. Stupid. She berated herself uselessly. *I should have insisted on calling Kat.*

Should have. Could have. Would have. It was all water under the bridge now. What was done was done and no amount of whining was going to change a thing. What she needed was a plan. *Think girl.*

Maybe they hadn't so much locked her in as locked her away from the supposed threat. *Yeah right. Even you aren't that stupid.*

The room was no more than a closet with a row of shelves against the back wall. She moved to the shelves and started at the floor, feeling carefully around with her hands making sure she checked every inch for anything she might use as a weapon. She repeated the procedure for each of the six shelves.

Nothing. Unless she wanted to pummel her captors with dust bunnies. Lily sat as far away from the door as possible, which was about six inches, and waited.

The sun was setting. Although there was no window in her small prison, her body registered the passing of time. The sound of footsteps outside the door brought her fully alert.

She tensed, readied herself. The instant the door opened she ducked and the shelves behind her flew at the two startled guards knocking them to the floor. Lily was up and running before they realized what had attacked them. She would have made it if the old man hadn't materialized between her and the outside door.

She skidded to a stop and the two burly guards caught her by the arms, and dragged her kicking and twisting to one of the two gurneys she hadn't realized were in the main room. They threw her on the gurney and held her down while they snapped one silver shackle around her wrist. The small tray of needles and other paraphernalia flew at their heads. One guard balled up his fist and punched her up the side of the head so hard she saw stars. They took advantage of her dozy state to snap another shackle around her free wrist.

Lily managed two good kicks before they managed to shackle her ankles the same way. She was concentrating so hard on the men at her feet that she didn't notice the old man move closer until she felt the sharp sting in her arm.

Everything around her grew still until it felt like she was drifting on a cloud. She could hear and see everything but her body wouldn't respond. Just for kicks and giggles she imagined the sinister looking needle in the old man's hand flying across the room into the eye of the creep that slugged her.

It remained where it was. *This is so not good.*

"Welcome, Lily," the old man said. His voice thundered in her head, not at all like one would imagine from such a frail looking old man. "I am so glad you could join us."

Like I had a choice you bastard. But she had a choice didn't she? She could have refused to go with the two strangers in the first place.

The old man's brows furrowed. "Our other guest should be arriving at any moment." He picked up the tray from the floor and set it on the small table beside the gurney. "Get the other gurney ready," he ordered the two burly men who docilely followed his every command. He picked up the needles and other items scattered on the floor, careful not to touch the tips, and placed them gently on the tray, totally ignoring the dust stuck to the tip of one needle. "I do hope that you prove to be more helpful than your brother."

Lily's heart began to beat triple time. *What have you done with my brother?* Her mind screamed the question but no sound came out of her throat.

"We had such high hopes for Zacharia."

Lily cringed at the use of a name most people didn't know and nobody used. *Who are you?*

"He could have been our race's saviour." The old man rolled up the sleeve on Lily's left arm and gently patted while he continued to ramble.

Lily could have been at a real doctor's office for a regular check-up except for the shackles, the guards, and the definitely unsanitary state of the needles.

"Looks like we'll need a little help finding the vein. Probably because of the poison. I didn't want to use it but you gave me no choice. I couldn't let you hurt my attendants could I?" He bent down searching the floor. "Now where is that rubber band," he muttered.

Zack. Where are you Zack? Please answer me.

"Ah, here you are." The old man stood up with the elusive rubber strap dangling from his fingers. "Zacharia was to be our saviour. Instead he chose the enemy. Fool." The old man's voice grew angrier with each spoken word. "He made us destroy him."

Pain wracked Lily's paralyzed body while her mind screamed in denial.

The old man wrapped his rubber band around Lily's arm, pulled it tight, and tied it off. He patted the area between the band and her inner elbow. "Good," he said when the vein swelled. "Much better. Zack was strong but you are strong too. You would make a wonderful addition to our family."

Lily's heart raced. *No way old man. I would rather die.*

The old man's face loomed so close Lily could detect the scent of rotting flesh and her stomach protested. Bile rose in her throat threatening to drown her. "You will die," the old man hissed with foul breath. "Like your brother you will be reduced to no more than food for the 'gators."

Lily's silent screams rent the air. Her mind screamed over and over until she thought she would go crazy. Maybe she already had. Maybe this was only a nightmare brought on by insanity caused by the changes her body was going through. The loss of appetite, the craving for bloody meat, the sensitivity to light, and the insomnia had finally taken their toll and she was caught in the worse kind of nightmare.

Lily's mind didn't register the old man's gentle pat on her shoulder. "It's okay child. Even the 'gators need to eat."

Thirty Five

"THE swamp." Emerald took several deep breaths trying desperately to keep the bile from rising. Her amber eyes swirled with emotion and her face drained of blood as the vision flashed.

They dragged the heavy burlap sack soaked crimson to the edge of the swamp leaving a smooth trail in their wake. The alligators began to gather at the edge of the water, dragging their huge bodies out of the swamp to investigate what the humans had dropped. The human reached into the sack and pulled out—a head. Holding it by its long black hair tangled and soaked in blood the human swung the head several times before releasing it to land with a loud splash in the swamp where some smaller alligators converged on it. The larger alligators waited until the humans dragged the rest of the body from the sack and rolled it into the swamp. The water roiled and frothed red as the alligators fought for their hunk of flesh.

Less than a heartbeat passed and the vision ended. Emerald shook her head to banish the remnants from her mind. "He's dead," she said in a flat voice. "They will never find his body. The 'gators made sure of that. The girl is near the swamp." Emerald shrugged. "I can feel her but I can't tell where exactly she is. Why?" She looked at her mother.

"That's the way it works, Em. You will know when you find the right place."

"Well that bites."

Conall revealed the tips of his fangs in a half grin. "No. I bite," he whispered so none of the other customers could overhear.

Emerald laughed. "You better not let me catch you," she teased back. "I might have to *stake* you."

"Speaking of catching me, how did you know I was being held at that old farm?" Conall shuddered at the thought of the young humans suffering as he had at the hands of the betrayer.

"You told me." Emerald's brows furrowed in concentration.

"I didn't know where I was."

"But you called to me." Emerald listened with her mind and reached out with her soul. She rubbed at the ache in her temple. The murmur of a million voices tore at her open mind. *`you know you want it ...' `I want ice-cream ...' `Please ...' `Don't go ...' `Eat your peas ...' `Well what do we have here ...'* Emerald tried to ignore the overload of information and push farther outside the city toward the swamp.

"Is she all right?" The concern in the waitress's voice snapped her back into the restaurant.

"She will be." Emerald listened to her mother's voice and wondered how she was going to explain this.

Alicia grimaced. "I'm afraid it's my fault. I shouldn't have pushed her to taste the wine but it was so good, and I didn't know she would have such a reaction to it."

"Is there anything I can do?"

"Thanks." Jade smiled at the young girl who had been so helpful. "We'll just take her back to the room and let her sleep it off."

Luke handed the waitress three fifties. "Will this cover the bill?"

The girl did a quick tally in her head and handed back a fifty which Luke refused to take. "Sir, this is way too much. We owe change without it."

"That's okay." Luke spoke with a soft growl. "Split the difference with the kitchen. You all deserve it."

"Thank you." The waitress beamed and headed for the kitchen to grab a tray for their dishes.

Luke pushed the call button for the elevator and two seconds later the doors slid quietly open. The group split apart to allow the occupants to get off and head toward the restaurant.

Kamenwati eyed the interior of the small room. "I'll take the stairs," he murmured.

Conall stared at his best friend in shock. He wouldn't go so far as to suggest that the son of Rah was afraid of the elevator, but he was definitely nervous. If they were alone he might have ribbed his friend, but Conall had more sense than to do such a thing with an audience.

Alicia slipped her hand into her husband's and smiled when he tightened his grip. "I'll take the stairs too."

Emerald took a step toward the open door of the elevator. *That's the wrong way.* She hesitated and stepped forward. *Stop.* The voice was louder, more persistent. Emerald stumbled toward the elevator and her left foot moved toward the lobby.

Alicia glanced at her mother. *We'll find Gheorgès and catch up.*

The voice changed. *Come to me my son. I can give you what you want.*

And what do I want?

603

The light. You want to walk in the daylight like you did before your rebirth.

Emerald rubbed at the knot in the back of her neck and strode into the lobby where Kristoff was sitting at the computer, his fingers idle, staring at his image on the blank screen. The lobby door slammed open to admit a young female dressed in a long black Samuel Dong coat with a high collar. Soft black leather boots encased her calves like a second skin, their four inch heels giving the female added height. Thick black hair crowned her head, the length hidden beneath the collar of the coat. Quinn stopped so suddenly that his father nearly plowed into him.

Sangria shot Conall a challenging look, ignored the remainder of the group, and leapt over the counter with an easy grace. She knelt beside Kristoff and took his idle hands in hers. "Do not listen to him Kristoff. He is a liar. He will destroy you."

Kristoff blinked, and looked into Sangria's anxious face. Sangria who always seemed to be there when he needed her the most; Sangria who fed him so he would survive to his new life; Sangria who taught him how to control his monstrous cravings and live a life of decency.

Come to me my son insisted the dark voice.

You have nothing I want old man.

Sangria searched Kristoff's eyes and sighed with relief. "We do not need his empty promises. We are stronger than that."

Theron was losing his hold on the young vampire and it infuriated him. He could feel the presence of another blood feeder, but he could not pinpoint it. *Who are you?* He demanded. What was the world coming to when a newborn was so hard to manipulate? The world was continuously changing and he didn't like it. Not one little bit.

There was a time when the humans who believed in vampires feared for their lives. Those were the days Theron missed. He fed from their fear; grew stronger. These days there were so many cults of pretenders they wouldn't know the true danger until it rose up to bite them.

Literally.

With so many vampires learning to control their appetites and blend with the humans, to hide their crimes so as not to cause mass panic, their fear was minimal; not enough to feed him. And to make matters worse, it made his enemies stronger while he grew weaker. He would not tolerate it any longer. He would create a new army of day walkers and then the war would really begin.

I can give you the sun. You will once again walk in the day. You will be invincible.

"Do not listen to him, Kristoff. He is a liar."

"Listen to him," interrupted Emerald resting her hands on the counter and leaning toward him.

Sangria shot Emerald a look that clearly said 'Back off Bitch.' She turned her attention back to Kristoff. "Do not listen to him. I don't know who *she* is." She shot another sideways glare at Emerald for emphasis, "but you cannot listen to the Dark Priest."

Conall staggered as shock ran through his system. *How does she know Theron was a priest? Who the hell is she?* He wanted to demand answers but now was not the time. He could hear Theron calling the young vampire to him, and as much as he agreed with the female that Theron could not be trusted, the vampire was their only hope right now.

"He has Lily."

Both Sangria and Kristoff turned toward her. "What did you say?" demanded Sangria. Kristoff looked like he had been kicked in the stomach.

"He has Lily. He has already destroyed her brother Zacharia and he plans to use Lily in his experiment. She will not survive."

Kristoff stood so fast his chair fell back with a clatter onto the floor. "We have to find her."

"How?" Sangria's hand shot out and clamped around Kristoff's wrist, successfully preventing him from dematerializing.

Emerald ignored the female of power and spoke directly to the young vampire. "Theron has chosen you for this experiment that is why he is calling to you. He will lead you to Lily and we will be right behind you."

"I will do this on one condition."

Power sizzled in the air around them as everyone struggled to contain themselves and stay under Theron's radar. Emerald lifted one eyebrow.

"If he manages to corrupt me I want you to chop off my head." He ignored Sangria's nails drawing blood on his arm. "I do not want Sangria to have to do it. I love her too much for that."

"Agreed."

Sangria dematerialized without a word. She didn't dare get that close to the Dark Priest again.

And what do you get old man?

Theron cackled with glee. He had won again. *Was there ever any doubt?*

Kristoff followed the directions to the old clinic on the edge of the swamp. Evil rolled off the place with the force of a steam roller. Beneath the dense, suffocating blanket he felt the presence of pure light.

Lily was still alive.

Behind him two wolves were slinking through the twists of trees silently, while overhead two ghostly white owls kept watch from a safe distance. The ancient vampire was the mist travelling along the ground— Kristoff couldn't wait to learn that trick. The barely contained power that rolled off his escorts made him feel weak. He didn't know if he should trust them, but Sangria must or she would never have left him with them, and that was enough for him.

He knocked on the door.

Thirty Six

KAMENWATI and Alicia materialized outside the open door to Katriana's room. The door hung crookedly on its hinges; the lock broken. Kamenwati pushed the door in cautiously. Although there was no living creature on the other side he couldn't be sure exactly what they would find.

The room was in shambles. The bed was on its side shoved against the far wall. The contents of the dresser were spilled all over the floor. Alicia's nostrils flared at the scent of blood. She knelt beside a small brown stain her heart racing. "Gheorgès," she whispered almost imperceptibly.

There was a large crimson patch on the carpet close to the balcony door. Moving toward it Alicia closed her eyes and let the visions flow over her. She plopped her ass on the floor as relief washed over her. "It's not theirs," she whispered. "Three males were waiting for her when the female returned to her room. They jumped her but she fought them off. Gheorgès broke the door when he heard the struggle. They escaped with barely a scratch but the three males weren't so lucky." She chuckled. "They left limping. They called for reinforcements to help track her."

She allowed Kamenwati to help her to her feet. "Fools." She shook her head. "They actually think they have a chance." She grinned at her husband, her fangs peeking past her lips. "I say we are probably going to be more useful getting Lily back. Gheorgès is more than a match for a bunch of cats."

Kamenwati frowned. "Why would the cats risk coming here to grab a female?"

Alicia shrugged. "I don't know. But they aren't going to give up." She wiggled her fingers straightening the room as she spoke. "Let's go. Gheorgès will call when he needs us."

They fixed the door on the way out.

Thirty Seven

INSIDE the small clinic Lily lay in silence, her mind numb with the loss of her brother. She moved her eyes toward the sound of someone knocking on the door. When Kristoff walked into the room she wanted to shout a warning but no sound came out. *Run,* her mind screamed.

Kristoff's dark eyes looked straight into her pale blue ones and she would have wept if she could. *I'll never leave you,* they said.

They were doomed.

"I'm glad you could join us."

Kristoff spun around and came face to face with a frail old man. Evil permeated his skin—his human skin that was rotting on his bones. The smell nearly gagged Kristoff and he took an involuntary step back coming to rest against the gurney where Lily lay in shackles. "Who are you?" he demanded. "What is wrong with Lily?"

"Lily is just fine," Madison said. "She is going to help me help you."

Kristoff kept his eyes on the old man. "How?"

"There is something in her blood that allows her to walk in daylight."

"She is a human," Kristoff said scornfully. "Of course she can walk in daylight."

The old man smoothed the cover sheet on the other gurney. "We are going to use her blood," he continued ignoring Kristoff's outburst, "to allow you to walk in the sun." Madison moved to a small table on wheels and methodically checked every piece of medical paraphernalia lying there. He seemed unaware that he was in a deserted building and not in a real clinic. "I have spent years trying to isolate the proper gene without success. At first I thought the wolves had the answer but that wasn't to be. But I will not give up. I know the answer is in the blood and I will find it."

Kristoff silently moved to the shackle holding Lily's wrist. If he could get it undone, free her hand, she could escape. His eyes on Madison he reached for the shackle— and screamed. The skin on his fingertips instantly turned red and blistered.

Madison spun around. "What are you doing?" he hissed, his voice no longer that of the frail human.

Kristoff cradled his burnt hand in his other and glared at the human host. "Let her go now old man before I kill you."

Laughter rumbled through the small room rattling the windows and echoing off the walls until Kristoff wanted to cover his ears with his hands. "You ... kill me? Think again parasite. I am your Lord."

"You're not *my* lord," spat Kristoff.

"You cannot kill me," Theron's voice boomed.

"Maybe not," Kristoff conceded. "But I can kill him." A flash of lighting flew from his burnt fingers and hit Madison square in the chest.

Madison staggered. Theron howled. If the old man died he would lose his foothold into this realm. The two guards in the doorway stood like zombies staring into space and awaiting instructions. "Help him" roared Theron and the guards finally moved.

The outer door split open and a ball of light slammed into one guard's chest just as he lunged for Kristoff. Screams rent the air as he clawed at the gaping hole in his chest and fell face down on the floor. His body twitched for another ten seconds before finally laying still.

The other guard ignored the newcomers and tried to drag Madison's stinking, rotting, twitching body out the door. Kristoff ignored them all and turned to face Lily. He tore off his shirt, wrapped it around his hands, and tried to force her shackles apart.

A hand landed on his shoulder and a soft voice said, "let me." All four shackles flew apart releasing Lily and still she laid there, her pale blue eyes pleading.

Kristoff took one limp hand in his and rubbed furiously trying to restore circulation. "What has he done to you?" He looked toward the female whose aura glowed with power. "What is wrong with her?"

"She's been poisoned," Emerald said. Emerald was standing beside the gurney one moment and the next she was at Conall's side.

Conall stood over the rotting flesh that was once Madison but was now no more than a walking corpse— well a breathing corpse. Conall's eyes glowed red with hatred. His nostrils flared, and his fangs contorted his handsome face turning him into a monster. There was no mistaking the stench of the creature that gleefully stabbed him with his silver needles while keeping him helplessly shackled with silver cuffs. This was the creature responsible for Emerald getting a bullet in the head. This was the monster that had no qualms about destroying innocent lives be it lycan, vampire, or human. Conall was going to enjoy tearing him limb from limb before he ripped his head off.

"Don't do it." Emerald wanted to obliterate the creature twitching on the floor for the atrocities he committed, the innocent lives he'd destroyed, but he was no more than a pawn of the dark priest, and still a human. Did he deserve to die for his crimes? *Yes.*

Madison's eyes opened and he looked at Conall with clear cunning eyes. "Surprise!" he crowed in Theron's voice.

A sword suddenly appeared in Conall's hands and he neatly sliced through Madison's neck. Conall ignored the severed head rolling on the floor, spun around on his heel and neatly decapitated the vampire approaching from behind. The room was suddenly filled with creatures carrying Theron's evil scent.

Kristoff cradled Lily's limp body and kicked at the bloodsucker blocking his path. Another fell on him from behind forcing Kristoff to his knees. His hold on Lily tightened and he curled into a ball around her, trying to protect her from the onslaught of fangs. She was helpless against the creatures that craved her sweet human blood.

Growling and snarling, Quinn leapt on the nearest vampire, his canines ripping into the creature's neck as he tore him off the helpless young vampire.

"Allow me." Quinn released his hold on the vampire as a sword blade swung down to separate its head from the rest of the body. The severed head was still rolling when they turned to dispatch the next one.

It was all over in a few moments. Kamenwati crinkled his nose in distaste; the stench of rotting corpse permeated the small room. "My turn." He snapped his fingers and Madison's rank corpse disintegrated.

"Show off," teased Alicia.

* * *

Lily's mind screamed as the fire spread up her leg. Her body twitched in Kristoff's arms but he managed to get her to the gurney without dropping her. He could feel her pain and his heart bled.

She was changing.

Jade and Emerald felt her scream at the same time they heard it, and turned to see Kristoff trying to keep Lily's twitching body from flinging itself to the floor.

"It's begun." Alicia was at the young female's side gently smoothing the blonde hair back from her brow.

"Make it stop," begged Kristoff the agony in his voice almost unbearable. "It's too soon. She's not ready."

"We can't stop it." Alicia's worried voice floated to him barely penetrating through a fog of panic. The wound on Lily's ankle was quickly turning the dirty linen crimson. She was losing way too much blood for such a small wound. Something was wrong.

Conall felt the child's pain and fear, trapped in a body that would not obey her simplest command, her life passing before her eyes. It brought home to him the pain and fear of being trapped in his own body, fighting the shadows, unable to convince anyone that he was not asleep, but trapped. He didn't stop to take a minute to think about what he was doing. He moved to the gurney and leaned over the child. One moment he was staring into the palest blue eyes, the next he was on the floor trying to avoid a set of sharp fangs.

Get off me boy, he hissed the warning while trying to hold the enraged young vampire off without hurting him in the process. *Idiot*, he snarled. *I was trying to save her life.*

An invisible hand hauled the young vampire off Conall and set him down on the opposite side of the gurney where he automatically checked his female for damage. Conall didn't blame the young fool. He would have acted just as stupidly if he thought Emerald was in danger.

Kamenwati offered a hand and hauled Conall to his feet. "Glad to see the Ursaline didn't fry every brain cell my brother."

Conall scowled. More than a decade passed while Conall lay trapped in his own body; a result of jumping between the giant bear and its intended target, Emerald. Yeah. A bonded male had only one goal in life. *Protect his female.*

Kamenwati chuckled. "How close do you have to be to heal her?"

"Close enough to touch her. The drug is poisoning her system and stopping her ability to fight."

Their whispered conversation was interrupted by an argument across the room. "No way. If he so much as breathes on her I'll kill him with my bare hands."

"Don't be stupid. If you don't get control of yourself she will die. Is that what you want?"

Kristoff blanched. Lily's body spasmed. Her mind was already beginning to shut down. "You do it," he begged.

"I'm sorry," Emerald smoothed the damp hair on Lily's forehead. "I can't do it. He is the only one here who can. He has dealt with this poison."

"Fine," Kristoff spat the word with almost as much venom as was coursing through Lily's veins. "But if he tries anything."

Conall didn't wait for a second invitation. *Hold him* he directed Kamenwati. *I don't want a repeat performance.* He rubbed at his neck for emphasis before placing his hand over the wound on Lily's ankle. It healed instantly. This was the reason for the early transition. The vampire's venom kick started her change. Conall moved so he could see into Lily's eyes.

I can help you, he told her. *But you cannot fight me. I know you are scared, but trust is essential. Besides,* he winked conspiratorially. *Your friend there will kick my ass if I hurt you.*

There was a second of soft laughter before it changed to a pain filled scream. A soft light started to glow in Conall's dark eyes and then a ribbon shot out into Lily's pale orbs connecting the two of them. Several heartbeats later, moments that felt like an eternity, the ribbon broke. Conall's knees buckled. Kamenwati caught him before he could hit the floor and the two dematerialized.

"Where did they go? Where's Sangria?" Lily asked before pain wracked her body turning her words into a long scream.

Luke and Quinn stood by the broken door their faces pale. Jade and Emerald winced as her pain swept through them. Kristoff held Lily's hand and murmured words of encouragement, everyone else in the room forgotten.

Lily's fangs exploded from her mouth contorting her face into something unrecognizable. She escaped Kristoff's hold and her fangs flashed mere inches from Emerald's hand.

"You should go," urged Alicia. "Let us deal with this. She can smell your blood and it is not helping." Alicia could clearly remember her own transformation and the blood cravings that accompanied it. "She is going to crave blood and yours smells better than anything else in the room. We can't risk her getting to any of you. Kristoff is what she needs right now." Alicia successfully steered her mother and sister to the door where her father and brother waited, and without much effort she managed to get all four of them outside. "Go back to the hotel and check on Conall." *He needs you, Em.*

Alicia was right. They couldn't help Lily with what was happening to her. Their presence was only making it worse. A heartbeat later four adult wolves sped toward the city. Behind them painful screams rent the air.

Thirty Eight

EMERALD lay across his chest and listened to the fading beat of his heart.

Conall stood alone in the Shadows, a part of them, watching his female. She was playing with a dark-haired boy; their laughter was music to his ears. His body throbbed with need but it was better this way. There was a stain on his soul and he couldn't risk infecting her.

No. It was better this way. She would find a male worthy of her and have his children. He took a step further into the Shadows.

Emerald stopped their play to stare into the shadows. The sadness in her beautiful amber eyes shredded his heart.

The boy tugged at her hand and frowned up at her. "What's wrong, Mommy?"

Emerald bent to lift the boy into her arms, her lips turned up in a smile that didn't reach her eyes, and she kissed his furrowed brow. "Nothing, baby. We have to go now. Daddy's waiting."

The boy turned toward the Shadows then, and his face broke into a wide grin revealing small white fangs. "Daddy," he squealed happily, pointing straight at Conall.

Conall staggered. *This isn't possible.* He took another step into the Shadows and Emerald matched it with one of her own.

"What's it like, Mommy, where Daddy is? Are there birds? I like birds. Are there bunnies? Will I have a sister or brother to play with?"

Emerald held the child tighter. "You will have Mommy and Daddy to play with."

Stop Conall commanded as Emerald took another step toward the swirling shadows.

We can't stay here. Her soft voice was filled with love. Love for him. *Where you go I go. We are mated.*

Pain fisted his heart until he thought it would break in two. *What have I done?* He couldn't let her die. *You deserve a life, a family, love.*

I have all that. With you. You are the keeper of my heart and soul. Where you go I go. She stepped into the twirling shadows carrying their son.

Conall forgot about the stain on his soul and his unholy connection to the Shadows. Only one thought ran through his mind. *Keep your family safe.*

With a roar Conall wrapped his arms around Emerald and the boy and leapt from the shadows to land with a thud on the floor beside the bed. Emerald was sprawled on the floor beneath him, dazed. There was no sign of the boy. "Where is he?"

Emerald blinked and her face lit up as she grinned. "You're awake." Then she frowned. "Where's who? And why are you laying on me?"

"The boy." Conall's eyes scanned the room. "Where is our son?"

Emerald shifted and Conall adjusted his weight so he wasn't leaning on her so completely, but he kept her close.

Her lips tilted at the corners and her amber eyes darkened with emotion. Emerald took Conall's hand and placed it over her abdomen, where Conall felt little electrical shocks as his fingertips skimmed her bare smooth skin. His eyes widened. "I don't think he is going to make an appearance any time soon," she whispered.

Conall kissed her abdomen jumping back when he got a small shock. "Hey kiddo," he scolded. "Be nice to Daddy."

Emerald laughed and Conall captured the sound with a kiss. The outer door opened. "Get a room," Quinn said.

Keeping their lips locked Conall waved his hand, and Quinn suddenly found himself outside in the hall with the door closed in his face. His warm chuckle could be heard clearly. "Glad to see you awake bloodsucker."

"Me too," sighed Emerald beneath his lips.

Thirty Nine

WIND howled past the window swaying the cedar until its branches brushed the pane. Thunder crashed and lightening flashed. The storm matched Emerald's mood—dark and angry. "I look like a house," she complained as she waddled from the couch to the kitchen to grab another bag of AB positive.

"You are beautiful," Conall said shadowing her movements. "You are glowing."

"Yeah," Emerald snapped back. "Like a house on fire."

Conall's warm chuckle was rewarded with a cushion from the couch whacking him in the back of the head. He sent the cushion back where it belonged, and quickly grabbed a glass from the cupboard beside the fridge.

Emerald poured herself a glass of the AB positive and grimaced. "I want a steak and a baked potato," she complained. "And lots and lots of sour cream. Instead I get this." She glared at the offending glass.

The baby kicked and her stomach bounced and rolled with his movements. With a gentle pat she cooed lovingly. "It's okay, baby. Mommy doesn't blame you." She glared at Conall leaving him in no doubt as to who she *did* blame, and Conall grimaced.

At the look on his face Emerald's mood switched and she started to laugh. The storm outside quickly ceased and sunshine brightened the room. She looked at the offending glass. "Bottoms up," she said and gulped back the liquid.

Something was wrong.

Instead of relaxing the baby started kicking and clawing. Emerald screamed and doubled over. Warm liquid gushed between her legs and blood pooled on the floor.

Conall lifted Emerald as if she weighed no more than a baby and carried her to their bed where he carefully set her down. He smoothed the hair from her brow and winced when he felt another spasm wrack her body.

It's time. He silently sent the message and Alicia materialized beside the bed.

"Get out," screeched Emerald.

Conall bolted for the door and nearly knocked Jade on her ass in his haste. "Sorry," he murmured slipping out the open door.

Quinn was already in the hallway with his father and brother pacing a hole in the carpet. He stopped short when he saw Conall's pale face. "Do you need something my brother?" They all knew he stopped feeding from Emerald when the baby began demanding blood of his own.

Conall stared in the direction of Quinn's voice but all he could see was Emerald's pale face contorted in pain. "It's too soon," he stammered. "I'm not ready."

"You've had a year to get ready my brother," Quinn snapped. "Man up. Get back in there."

"She sent me away." Conall's voice was an agonized whisper.

All three men in the room held the identical lift to their brows. They didn't have to say it. Conall took a deep breath, turned, and entered the room. He moved silently to the side of the bed and took Emerald's delicate hand in his much larger one. *I'm here, baby.*

I know. She sent him a smile that turned into a grimace of pain. *We both know.*

Several excruciating hours later it was finally over. Conall sat on the side of the bed. Emerald was sitting up leaning on a propped up pillow. Her pale hair was pasted to her pale skin with sweat.

She glowed with happiness.

Their son was nestled against her breast, his dark hair tousled and damp. Emerald's eyes met Conall's over their son's head. *He's beautiful.*

Conall wanted to argue, to tell her that boys were not beautiful; Strong, handsome, good looking—but never beautiful. *Like his mother*, he said.

The baby squirmed and his small, perfect mouth sought Emerald's swollen breast. Emerald shifted to help him find the nipple. He opened his mouth and sank his two, small, perfectly formed fangs into the nearest vein.

"Ow!"

"What's wrong?" Conall asked fearfully.

Emerald shifted so Conall could see his son. "He takes after his daddy," she said. "Looks like you'll get your turn at feeding the little imp after all."

www.ingramcontent.com/pod-product-compliance
Lightning Source LLC
Chambersburg PA
CBHW050837030726
47503CB00007BA/2213